OUTSIDE CHANCE

LYNDON STACEY

KU-521-856

arrow books

Published by Arrow Books in 2006

3 5 7 9 10 8 6 4

Copyright © Lyndon Stacey 2005

The right of Lyndon Stacey to be identified as the author of this work
has been asserted by her in accordance with the
Copyright, Designs and Patents Act, 1988

This book is sold subject to the condition that it shall not, by way
of trade or otherwise, be lent, resold, hired out, or otherwise
circulated without the publisher's prior consent in any form of
binding or cover other than that in which it is published and
without a similar condition including this condition being
imposed on the subsequent purchaser

First published by Hutchinson in 2005

Arrow Books
The Random House Group Limited
20 Vauxhall Bridge Road, London SW1V 2SA

Random House Australia (Pty) Limited
20 Alfred Street, Milsons Point, Sydney
New South Wales 2061, Australia

Random House New Zealand Limited
18 Poland Road, Glenfield
Auckland 10, New Zealand

Random House (Pty) Limited
Isle of Houghton
Corner of Boundary Road & Carse O'Gowrie,
Houghton 2198, South Africa

The Random House Group Limited Reg. No. 954009

www.randomhouse.co.uk

A CIP catalogue record for this book is available from the British Library

Typeset in Plantin by Palimpsest Book Production Limited,
Polmont, Stirlingshire

ISBN 978 0 09 946344 3 (from January 2007)
ISBN 0 09 946344 X

The Random House Group Limited supports The Forest Stewardship
Council® (FSC®), the leading international forest-certification organisation.
Our books carrying the FSC label are printed on FSC®-certified paper.
FSC is the only forest-certification scheme supported by the leading
environmental organisations, including Greenpeace. Our
paper procurement policy can be found at
www.randomhouse.co.uk/environment

Printed and bound in Great Britain by Clays Ltd, St Ives plc

OUTSIDE CHANCE

Lyndon Stacey is the bestselling author of *Cut Throat*, *Blindfold*, *Deadfall* and *Outside Chance*. She lives in the Blackmore Vale.

Praise for Lyndon Stacey's previous novels:

'The closest to taking Dick Francis' crown . . . terrific, pacy stuff' *The Bookseller*

'This highly adroit piece has a more sophisticated level of characterisation than even Dick Francis himself ever attempted . . . stirring and entertaining' *Crime Time*

'Few thrillers have such an arresting opening section as this one' *Amazon.co.uk Editorial Review*

'Splendidly exciting . . . the whole book moves at a cracking pace . . . A sparkling debut' *Publishing News*

'Entertaining . . . fast paced . . . absorbing, enlivened by witty dialogue' *Publishers Weekly*

'Great characters both human and equine. The climax of the story makes it a real page-turner and offers the reader plenty of surprises' *Horse Magazine*

524 827 89 5

By the same author

Cut Throat
Blindfold
Deadfall

This one is for Sue, James and all at Hutch and Arrow, for their continued support and enthusiasm. Thanks, guys.

Acknowledgements

Many thanks are due to Peter Maughn, retired travelling head lad to David Elsworth; the staff of Edward and Jose Veterinary Practice in Gillingham, Dorset; Gill Thompson (and the Gals) for racing contacts and advice; Jill Todd for a brilliant job of test-reading; and Inca, my dog, for the countless patient hours of company while I write.

Prologue

The smart, maroon and gold liveried horse-transporter negotiated the roundabout at the bottom of the hill with obvious care and moved out on to the dual carriageway, attacking the gradient with carefully controlled power. In the cab the wiry, weather-beaten, fifty-something driver settled back in his seat and prepared for the long haul, listening tolerantly to his two younger companions arguing in the seating area behind the cab about the outcome of a private bet.

In a lay-by at the top of the hill, three men with peaked caps and fluorescent green tabards over their uniforms lounged against a white Transit van. A row of cones stood waiting, presumably to funnel reluctant motorists into the checkpoint, but at present the men appeared more interested in the contents of the mugs they cradled in their hands. It was February, late afternoon and bitterly cold; the clouds low, grey, and inclined to drizzle. A stream of vehicles swished by on the wet road, their lights reflecting off the surface and their occupants noting the disinterest of the officials with relief.

A phone trilled and one of the men reached into the cab of the van and withdrew a handset. He spoke briefly, nodded, replaced the phone and turned to say something to the others. Their relaxed attitude disappeared in an instant. Mugs were emptied, caps straightened and soon all three were moving to take up new positions: one at the roadside near the end of the lay-by, the other two nearer to the van. One of these picked up a clipboard and his companion held what could have been a torch. They were, it seemed, ready for business.

As the horsebox reached the top of the rise, the driver spotted the waiting men and groaned.

'Not me, *please*,' he begged as he drew closer. 'Not me. Not me . . . Ahh, shite!'

The unsmiling official stood back and waved him through the cones, pointing towards his waiting colleagues, and the driver nodded, 'Yeah, yeah. I know.'

'What's happening?' The two lads in the back, barely more than teenagers, had broken off their argument and one of them appeared between the seats.

'Checkpoint. Probably Department of friggin' Transport,' the driver growled. 'If we've got a light out, I'll kill that bloody Nigel!'

The lorry rolled to a halt just inches from the man with the clipboard, who had planted himself directly in front of it. He didn't so much as twitch a muscle.

'Cold-blooded as a fish!' the driver muttered,

robbed of even that satisfaction. He pressed a button and the window dropped smoothly. 'Yes, officer?'

'Immigration,' the man with the clipboard announced, briefly flashing some documentation. 'Turn the engine off, please.'

Resignedly he complied, and as the sound of the engine died away, the man with the torch moved to the passenger side where he kept his head averted, apparently inspecting the tyre.

'What are you carrying?' The clipboard man had glasses and a dark moustache, which, in combination with the peaked cap, seemed to hide a good deal of his face.

'Er . . . *Racehorses*, maybe?' the driver suggested, shaking his head in disbelief and indicating the panel of the cab door. It displayed – as did the body of the lorry – the words *Castle Ridge Racing* in large gold letters.

It seemed that they were the last unlucky travellers of the day. In the mirror the third uniformed man could be seen already gathering up the cones.

'Come on, mate. We don't particularly want to be here either. Let's keep this civilised, shall we?' The man stepped up on to the footplate and peered inside the cab, where the second lad had now joined his colleagues. 'Can I have your names?' His hand, on the framework, was encased in a thin plastic glove.

The driver sighed. 'Ian Rice; Davy Jackson; Les Curtis,' he said, indicating himself and the other two in turn. 'Look, you don't want to open the back, do you? Only, the horses get upset and . . .'

He never finished the sentence.

In one fluid movement, the clipboard man dropped down to the ground, opened the door, and stepped up again.

'Move across,' he ordered, and suddenly he had a gun in his hand, the muzzle applying pressure to Rice's neck, just up under his jaw.

For a moment he appeared uncomprehending and then he gulped and a sheen of sweat formed on his brow.

'Please . . . Don't . . .'

On the other side of the cab, the second man had moved with perfect synchronicity and now held a similar weapon to one of the lads' heads.

'Just move,' the first man repeated and, as Rice did so, slipped into the seat beside him and pulled the door shut.

'Now, into the back. All of you. Slowly; no sudden moves.'

'All right, lads. Do as he says.' White-faced and trembling, Rice had nevertheless pulled himself together now.

The lads scrambled across the seat and back through the central doorway, the younger of the two whimpering faintly with fear. Rice followed and the two bogus officials brought up the rear; the one who'd held the clipboard kept his gun on the three, while the other produced lengths of fine nylon cord from his pocket and swiftly and efficiently tied them hand and foot. He then tied their ankles to their wrists, behind them, leaving them as helpless as calves at a branding. A strip of silver duct tape across their mouths ensured silence and, stripping off their

4

tabards and caps, the two men returned to the cab.

Wasting no time, the clipboard man slid into Rice's vacated seat. Starting the engine he checked the mirror, indicated right, and the lorry moved ponderously forward and out into the traffic, its new driver waving a hand in thanks to a helpful motorist.

The whole incident had taken less than five minutes. Behind them, the remaining man bundled the cones into the back of the white Transit and set off after the horsebox.

In the deserted lay-by, an empty crisp packet tumbled end over end in the wake of the van and then lay still.

1

The white horse was galloping wildly, mane and tail flying and hooves throwing up chunks of peaty earth. The saddle had slipped right over to one side and it didn't seem possible that the man who clung desperately to the underside of the animal's outstretched neck could retain his grip for many moments more.

Those watching held their collective breath. He *had* to hang on. The pounding, steel-shod hooves made the alternative too horrific. But a further disaster loomed: the horse was running out of space. Ahead, two concrete walls converged to form a corner from which there was no escape, but the horse's breakneck pace didn't slacken. Just strides away now, it appeared oblivious to the danger.

Somewhere someone screamed and, almost in the same instant, tragedy was averted. The man, so apparently helpless until now, pulled himself up and over the horse's withers in one fluid movement, gathered his flapping reins and guided the animal into a perfectly controlled turn.

To the accompaniment of relieved cheers and applause from the thousand or more onlookers, he then proceeded to unstrap the useless saddle and hold it aloft, whilst bringing the beautiful white horse to a flamboyant, plunging halt. The clapping turned into an ovation as the crowd rose to its feet almost as one, and the rider responded with a wide grin, his teeth flashing impossibly white in the spotlight as he acknowledged the admiration.

'Ladies and gentlemen; Nicolae Bardu!' the announcer cried with a flourish.

From his position six rows up, near the entrance to the indoor arena, Ben Copperfield relaxed and joined in the general appreciation. No matter that he'd watched all the rehearsals for the show; he still couldn't help holding his breath and gripping his seat. He could have sworn that Nico left his recovery until later and later every time.

The music struck up once more, signalling the beginning of the finale. The horse and rider made their jaunty exit and Ben slipped out of his seat and found his way up the tiers to the doorway at the back. The strains of Tchaikovsky's *Marche Slave* faded as he pulled the door to behind him, and he descended the steps to the warm-up area where the performers were gathering to make their final triumphant entrance.

Nico was there, still full of the arrogant confidence he exhibited throughout his performances. Ben knew that some people found such rampant egotism objectionable, but he had observed it before in other high achievers: dancers, sportsmen, and athletes. They seemed to feed off their audience. They worked ceaselessly behind the scenes to hone their skills but somehow it was as if the very presence of those watching inspired them to reach the peak of their abilities. He had witnessed just a few of the countless hours of practice that went into producing those brief moments of glory and, personally, he felt that a little arrogance was perfectly excusable.

Someone Ben knew only by sight was replacing the saddle on the magnificent white stallion, which stood like a rock, only its proudly arched neck and frothily champing jaws telling of the hyped-up eagerness within. Nico was standing to one side, brushing real or imaginary specks of dust from the short, gold-braided black jacket he had just put on.

'That was a bit close to the knuckle, you mad bugger!' Ben approached to within a few feet, taking care not to get in anybody's way. The horse swung its head to look at him, its big dark eye rimmed with white, and the rich warm smell of it filled Ben's nostrils. Almost involuntarily, he took a step back.

Nico turned, his fine, arching brows drawn down momentarily, then he broke into a smile as he recognised the speaker.

'Tomorrow I go closer!' he promised extravagantly. He seemed in particularly high spirits this evening.

'Well, I hope you're insured against causing heart attacks in the audience,' Ben observed. 'Mine was going like the clappers, and *I* knew it was all part of the act! You ought to put a health warning on the tickets!'

Nico laughed delightedly. 'You ain't seen nothing yet!' he declared, the Americanism sounding strange in his slightly stilted English. He was, as were all of the troupe, of Hungarian Gypsy origin – which no doubt accounted for his smouldering good looks – and Ben suspected that his grasp of the English language was attributable to a combination of questionable sources, including contact with European tourists and a few too many of American films.

'Ladies and gentlemen, I give you . . . The Hungarian Csikós!'

The trio of riders immediately before him in the parade moved forward and, with a wave of his hand, Nico vaulted on to his horse.

'Later, my friend,' he called and turned towards the arena, his back straightening and his expression settling once more into one of macho hauteur as he faced the bright lights.

Ben stepped back and watched him go. He'd been following the troupe on and off ever since they had docked, en masse, at Dover three days ago. His job, as a freelance journalist specialising in all things equine, had brought him into the sphere of a number of fascinating people, but he couldn't remember any who had so instantly captivated him in the way these Gypsy horsemen had done. He had never been a fan of circuses and had accepted the assignment with a measure of reserve. His prejudice, however, melted away within minutes of seeing their first performance, and he was now happily devoting a large proportion of his time to the in-depth article he'd been commissioned to write.

In his pocket, his mobile began ringing with the particular call-tone reserved for family members. He dug it out. The display told him it was his half-brother, Mikey, and he pressed a button to accept the call.

'Mikey. How ya doin'? Sorry I couldn't get over to see you this afternoon.' Just seventeen, Mikey was a conditional jockey – jump racing's equivalent of an apprentice – and Ben knew he'd been due to ride in a novice hurdle at Sandown Park.

'I'm at the hospital.' Never relaxed on the phone, Mikey cut straight to the chase.

The shock jolted Ben.

'What happened? Did you fall off? Are you all right?'

'No, I didn't fall off. It was on the way home, but I'm not supposed to talk about it.'

'What do you mean? Were you in a road accident or what? Why can't you talk about it?'

'The Guvnor said not to. But I just wanted to let you know I'm all right.'

'But Mikey . . .' Ben paused in amused frustration. 'If you hadn't rung, I wouldn't have known anything was wrong anyway.'

'No . . . I know . . .'

Ben was picking up a strong thread of anxiety in Mikey's voice. Something had clearly upset him. Fifteen years separated them and sometimes he felt more like Mikey's father than his half-brother; the more so because Mikey had grown up with certain learning difficulties, resulting in an overall lack of confidence and a childish need for reassurance. It was nearly always to Ben that

10

he turned rather than to their mutual father, bloodstock agent John Copperfield, who, although he had many virtues, could not count patience as one of them.

'Why did Mr Truman tell you not to ring?'

'He said not to tell anyone, but I shouldn't think he meant you, did he?'

Ben's lips twitched. He most assuredly *did* mean him. If Eddie Truman had something to hide, the very last person he'd want Mikey to tell was his journalist brother.

'Which hospital are you in? Would you like me to come over?' he asked, avoiding the question.

'We're going home in a minute. They just checked us over. But we've got to wait for Les. He has asthma and the shock made him bad.'

'So you *did* have an accident.'

'No. It was these men . . . Look, I can't tell you. I'll get into trouble.'

Intrigued, Ben made an instant decision. 'Listen, Mikey; I'll come to the cottage, okay? But I'm in Kent so I'll be a couple of hours at least. And perhaps it would be best if you didn't tell Mr Truman you've spoken to me. Just to be on the safe side. All right?'

'Yeah. Maybe. See you later, then.'

Ben switched off, feeling thoughtful, and in due course he excused himself from the post-performance get-together and set off for the Castle Ridge Racing Stables on the Wiltshire–Dorset border. The Csikós were touring and due to move on. When he caught up with them again, it would be in Sussex.

*

11

Eddie Truman's yard stood in an enviable position on the edge of a stretch of chalk downland, which formed beautiful natural gallops for racehorses. Because of the large number of horses he had in training – ninety-five, the last Ben had heard – Truman had a fair number of staff. These included two PAs, a farrier, an odd-job man, an assistant trainer, two head lads, a travelling head lad, a box driver and a fluctuating total of somewhere between twenty-five and thirty stable-lads and lasses. Some of these had digs in the nearby village of Lower Castleton but a number of the lads occupied two former farm-workers' cottages. Mikey and four others, one of whom was the head lad, shared a cottage just a stone's throw from the yard itself.

It was in front of this that Ben parked his four-wheel-drive Mitsubishi, just before midnight. He had hesitated outside the high wooden gates at the end of the back drive, wondering if perhaps he was too late and Mikey might have given up on him and gone to bed. Something in his voice, though, had suggested a crisis that would not be solved merely by getting a good night's rest, so he'd carried on; now the well-lit cottage windows showed that nobody seemed to have sleep on their minds just at the moment. Across the intervening field, a blaze of light at the main house seemed to tell the same story. Ben began to be very interested indeed.

The Mitsubishi's wheels had barely stopped turning when the door of the lads' cottage opened and he could see Mikey looking out.

'You were watching for me.' Ben crunched across the frosty gravel to meet him. The afternoon's clouds had disappeared and it was a clear, starlit night.

'Actually there's a buzzer that goes off when the gate's opened at night. Ricey says it's better than having it locked because people will always find a way in if they're determined, and this way we know they're coming.'

'That makes sense,' Ben agreed. 'Where do you want to talk, in or out?'

'You can come in. There's only me and Davy here. They kept Les in for the night 'cos he was still wheezing. Ricey and Bess are over at the house and Caterpillar's on holiday.'

'Caterpillar?' Ben queried, momentarily distracted. He followed Mikey into the kitchen; a blue-and-white-tiled room with pine units, a large pine table, and a state of tolerable tidiness that Ben suspected was entirely due to Bess's presence in the cottage.

'Yeah, he's new. You haven't met him yet. We call him Caterpillar 'cos he's got this huge moustache. Ricey says it's a relic from the seventies.'

'Oh, I see. You're not making coffee are you? I could murder a cup. It was a long drive. Talking of which . . . ?'

'Yeah . . . look, I'm really not supposed to say anything.' Mikey busied himself with filling the kettle and finding mugs, his golden blond fringe flopping into his eyes as it habitually did. At five foot seven he was fully six inches shorter than Ben, taking after his mother rather than the Copperfield side of the family. He had inherited his colouring from her, too, and had dark-lashed, brilliant-blue eyes that had the girls in raptures;

13

the shame of it was that he was far too shy to appreciate his luck. Ben was a true Copperfield, tall and fairly lean, with mid-brown hair – at present short and a little spiky – that curled if it was allowed to grow, and eyes that couldn't make up their mind if they were green or grey.

'But you already *have* said something. You can't just expect me to forget it,' Ben pointed out reasonably. 'Come on, you know you can trust me. I won't tell anyone if it would get you into trouble.'

'I know, but . . .'

'Mikey. I've just driven over a hundred miles to get here because I was worried about you. I'm not about to turn round and go away without finding out what's going on. Why all the lights everywhere? I could see the main house was all lit up as I came over the hill. And why are Ian and Bess over there now? You can't tell me *that's* normal at midnight. *You've* been to hospital; Les is still there. So who were these men you were talking about? Come on. You're not being very fair. Something happened on the way home, didn't it? Was there an accident? Has one of the horses been hurt? What?'

'Not *hurt*, exactly,' Mikey responded reluctantly.

'Then what?' Ben was trying very hard to keep his frustration under control.

Mikey was stirring the coffee, his lower lip caught between his teeth and his brow creased with the agony of his indecision.

Ben tried again. 'Okay, if not hurt, then . . . did you lose one somehow?' He read Mikey's stricken expression. 'That's it, isn't it? No! My

14

God, you've had one stolen! Which one? Not Cajun King?'

Mikey didn't try to deny it. 'Yes. But you mustn't tell anyone. The Guvnor would kill me.'

'No, of course I won't.' Ben's mind was buzzing with this new development. Cajun King: strong ante-post favourite for the Cheltenham Gold Cup. Castle Ridge's great hope for National Hunt glory. Stolen. Or kidnapped, perhaps? He instantly thought of Shergar. 'Where and how did they do it?' he asked.

'It was a checkpoint. They pretended to be immigration officials.'

'And then what?'

'They had guns. They threatened Ricey and the others, then tied them up.' Mikey handed Ben a mug of exceedingly milky coffee and they both sat down at the table.

'So where were you? In the back?'

'Yeah, I was in the luton, asleep. Nigel – our other driver – has got a bed up there, over the cab. I went up there after racing and I'd been there ever since. I didn't even wake up when we set off for home.'

That didn't surprise Ben. Mikey had a remarkable propensity for taking catnaps as and when he felt like it, regardless of where he was or what was going on.

'So where was this?'

'About twenty minutes after we'd left the race-course, in a lay-by on the side of a dual carriageway, Ricey says.'

'But . . . you'd have thought someone would've seen what was going on and called the police.'

15

'Ricey says it was all over in a minute or two, and then they drove the box away. They took it to some private land where they could transfer the horse to another lorry.'

'And you slept through it all.'

'Yes. I didn't know anything about it until they drove down this bumpy track and I woke up.' Now he'd started, Mikey seemed eager to tell the whole story. 'We stopped, and then I could hear these men's voices calling to one another, and someone opened the back. I knew it wasn't Ricey 'cos he always thumps on the roof of the cab first, when we stop, to wake me up – and anyway, their voices sounded . . . different. Not from round here.'

'Well, you weren't "round here" when it happened,' Ben reminded him. 'But you mean they had some kind of accent?' He knew it wasn't any earthly good asking Mikey what kind of accent it had been. The boy was hopeless in that department. He could recognise an accent again once he'd heard it, but he couldn't tell South African from Geordie, or Indian from Scots, and if he didn't know he had a tendency to guess, to try and please you.

'Yeah. Could have been Welsh, maybe.'

'So what happened next?'

'Well, I could hear these men in with the horses, so I stayed hidden.' Mikey looked down at his coffee, shamefaced.

'I don't blame you,' Ben said, adding without irony, 'Best thing to do.'

Mikey looked unhappy. 'Davy says I should have done something.'

16

'Well, Davy's a moron,' Ben observed. 'What the hell could you have done on your own? Nothing; and there was no point at all in getting yourself hurt, or tied up like the others. You did the right thing.'

'Is that what you'd have done?'

'Oh, absolutely.'

'Yeah, well, I thought it was the best thing,' Mikey stated, growing in confidence now that Ben had approved his actions.

'So what happened then? Could you hear what they were saying?'

'Not really. There were two of them in the back of the lorry but they didn't say a lot, really. Just talking to the horses as they got them out. And then the other lorry turned up.'

'They got *all* the horses out?'

'Yes. They took them all out of the box and let them go. I heard them chasing the others away.'

'Playing for time, I suppose,' Ben said. 'So they transferred Cajun King to the other lorry and drove off. What then? Did you call the police?'

'Well, I was going to, but as soon as I got down from the luton I found Ricey and the others all tied up, so I got some scissors from the grooming kit and cut them free. Then we found a note stuck to the dashboard. It said that nobody was to call the police or King would be killed.'

'And what did Ian – er, Ricey do then?'

'He said he was going to call the Guvnor but we were in a valley and he couldn't get a signal on his mobile, so we decided to try and catch the horses first.'

17

'And you found them all right?'

Mikey nodded. 'One of them was hanging round the lorry and the other two weren't far away.'

'And then you came home.'

'Well, we were going to, but on the way Les started to have an asthma attack, so we had to take him to hospital.'

'So when did you ring Truman?'

'When we got back to the main road. Ricey told him . . .' Hearing the sound of the outside door opening, Mikey broke off and looked anxiously at Ben.

Before Ben could say anything voices were heard, one of which announced, 'They're in here,' and then the kitchen door swung inwards to reveal a thin-faced, mousey-haired youngster, full of self-importance. 'Mikey and his journalist brother. I told you.'

'Yes, thank you, Davy. You can go now. We'll call you if we need you.' The second speaker was a diminutive man in his late fifties, with thinning grey hair and pronounced crow's feet at the corners of his shrewd grey eyes.

Ian Rice – Ricey – was Castle Ridge's travelling head lad, responsible for the well-being of the horses when they left the yard to go racing. Ben had met him a couple of times before, on visits to see Mikey, and liked him a lot. He was quiet – both with animals and people – efficient, and very patient with Mikey.

'Hello, Ian.' Ben could see two much bulkier figures looming behind him, and it only took a glance to recognise them as policemen, even though they wore plain clothes. His work had brought him into contact with the police on numerous occasions and he had developed an unerring eye for members of the constabulary, in whatever guise they chose to appear.

'Ben; the Guvnor – that is, Mr Truman – would like to see you over at the house, if you've got a minute,' Rice told him.

'Is it in the nature of a summons?'

'It is, rather,' he said apologetically. 'As I'm sure Mikey's told you, we've got a bit of a crisis on our hands.'

'Yeah, Mikey's told me, but don't be too hard on him,' Ben said, getting to his feet. 'He didn't want to tell me. I'm afraid I prised it out of him.'

'I'm not in trouble, am I?' Mikey glanced from Ben to Rice, and back.

'No, no, you're not in trouble, Mikey.' One of the police officers stepped into the room. 'We just need to ask you a few questions, that's all.'

'I'll stay with him,' Rice told Ben quietly, as he moved towards the door.

In the narrow hall, the second policeman blocked his way. 'You wouldn't be thinking of using your mobile phone between here and the house, would you?' he enquired.

Ben looked down at the hand that was preventing his forward movement and after a moment it was removed.

'I hadn't been,' he said.

'All the same, perhaps I'll just come with you.'

Ben sighed. 'I've got a better idea.' He reached into his inside pocket and withdrew the tiny, metal-cased phone. 'You look after this for me, and I'll find my own way over. I think I can manage.'

Following the cinder path that led from the cottage to the main house, Ben thought over what he'd learned, and reflected wryly that it was typical that when the scoop of a lifetime fell into his lap, he should be honour-bound to keep it to himself.

Castle Ridge House – home of racehorse owner, trainer and self-made millionaire Eddie Truman – was an imposing edifice, built less than five years previously in red brick, with concrete pillars flanking its glossy, white double doors. It sat on a natural plateau, on the site of the far smaller manor house it had replaced, and had everything a rags-to-riches businessman could have wished for; including an indoor swimming pool, garaging for eight cars, an adjoining tennis court, and a conservatory that could have housed a modest bungalow.

Ben had seen it several times in the daylight and, privately, he thought it vulgar.

Crossing the pea-shingle drive, he counted six cars drawn up in front of the mock-Georgian façade. None of them were obviously police vehicles but, under the blaze of the halogen lights, Ben could see only one that bore the personalised number-plates with which all Eddie Truman's cars were fitted.

A door at the side of the house stood ajar, a thin sliver of light escaping to lay a line down the path; at his approach it opened fully and a feminine figure stood silhouetted in the aperture.

'Ben?'

'That's right.'

'Good. Come on in. Mr Truman's waiting for you in the study.'

Ben stepped into the hall where the speaker was revealed as a pretty female in her late twenties, with big, dark eyes and glossy, shoulder-length, brown hair. Bess Wainwright, one of the two PAs at Castle Ridge, and the one who shared Mikey's cottage. Ben followed her through the quarry-tiled back hall, along a corridor and across an inner hall to a white panelled door with brass fittings. There, after knocking briefly, she leaned in to announce Ben's presence before ushering him through.

There were three men in the room that Ben entered: two who were unknown to him but almost certainly policemen, and one seated at the desk, whom he recognised from newspaper photographs and TV racing coverage as Eddie Truman.

Even when he was seated you could tell he was a big man, and Ben knew, from the way he dwarfed interviewers, that he must be well over six foot tall. Square shoulders and a square-jawed freckled face added to the impression of bulk, and the fingers that tapped impatiently on the desk were short and spatulate. Hair that had once been bright ginger was fading now that he was in his fifties, greying at the temples and decidedly thin on top, but it was still easy to see why the trainer had picked up the nickname of 'Red' Truman.

'Ah, come in, Mr Copperfield. Take a seat.'

21

Truman's voice held a rich Yorkshire burr, apparently the one part of his background that he had not tried to hide. 'Gentlemen, this is Ben Copperfield – Michael's brother; Ben, this is DI Ford and DS Hancock. Doubtless you already know why they're here.'

Ben inclined his head, sat in a buttoned leather wing-chair, and waited, taking in the overstated opulence of his surroundings with an interested glance. Chairs, desk, footstool and window seat were all finished in red leather; all fittings were of burnished bronze, including the fireplace surround; and several art deco maidens held glass lampshades aloft at strategic points in the room. One wall supported shelves of expensive, leather-bound books from floor to ceiling, but none of the spines bore any signs of use. Tassels were very much in favour on cushions, gold velvet curtains and a bell pull, and there was enough mahogany in evidence to have laid waste to a small rainforest. Ben had no doubt that it was real. For someone who had spent a sizeable number of his student days protesting against various environmental crimes, it was a sad sight.

'I'm not going to mince my words, Ben – may I call you that?' Truman began. 'I was deeply disturbed to find that you were here and talking to Mikey. I suppose he contacted you and asked you to come – it would be too much to suppose your appearance was a coincidence.'

'Yes, he called me. He was, understandably, very upset, but he didn't tell me why. It was my decision to come and see him. I was worried.'

DS Hancock cleared his throat. 'Mr

Copperfield, we understand you're a journalist. Is that correct?'

'Yes, that's right.'

'What paper do you work for?'

'I'm freelance.'

'May I ask you what you're working on at the moment?'

'You can *ask* . . .' Hancock's attitude was putting Ben's back up.

'Obviously your brother has already told you what's going on.'

'Obviously.'

'And I suppose you're thinking this is the scoop of the century . . .'

Hancock had two millimetres of dark hair and the eyes of a cynic. Plain clothes for him were black jeans, a black turtleneck and a tailored black leather jacket. Ben felt that, had he not been a police officer, he would have worn an earring.

'I could more or less name my price,' he agreed.

Hancock glared at him, plainly squaring up for a confrontation, but his superior stepped into the breach.

'But you won't, will you, Mr Copperfield? You're intelligent enough to understand that this is a delicate situation in which inappropriate publicity could be disastrous, and you have conscience enough to put moral duty before monetary gain.'

'Do I indeed?' Ben regarded the DI through narrowed eyes. 'That's pretty analytical. Are you always that quick to form an opinion, or have we met before?'

'Neither. I just remembered a certain journalist called Ben Copperfield who was instrumental in exposing the Goodwood betting scandal a couple of years ago.' He smiled. 'That was good work.'

Somewhere in his forties, Ford could not have been many years older than his colleague, but nature had taken the controlling hand in his hair loss, leaving him with a thick brown fringe circling a completely bald pate. Slightly over-weight, he presented an avuncular air, but his rank alone would suggest that there was a sharp mind behind the genial appearance.

Ben acknowledged the praise with a slight inclination of his head. The Goodwood affair had started out as a simple reporting assignment, but he had caught the whiff of corruption and, antic-ipating a diversion from what was becoming a fairly monotonous string of jobs, he'd jumped into the investigation with what, in hindsight, could be described as rather foolhardy zeal.

'A journo is a journo, as far as I'm concerned,' Hancock persisted.

'Oh, I think Ben will toe the line,' Truman interjected confidently. 'After all, he wouldn't want to do anything that might jeopardise Mikey's career.'

Ben frowned at the trainer. 'I'm sure you didn't *intend* that to sound like a threat,' he remarked softly.

'Of course he didn't,' Ford cut in. 'Look, let me propose a deal. For better or worse, Ben already has part of the picture, so I suggest we fill him in on what we know so far. Ben will undertake not to breathe a word of it to any outside party, in return for which we grant him exclusive rights to the story, as and when it's safe to print it. What do you say?' He looked hopefully from Ben to Truman.

Ben nodded, keeping his eagerness hidden. 'That seems fair.'

'Truman?'

'Well, if you say he's to be trusted, I'll go along with that. But if the whole story is splashed over the morning papers tomorrow, I'll hold you personally accountable,' Truman promised, the expression on his heavy featured face giving weight to the warning.

Ford was not noticeably intimidated. 'Good. Now, gentlemen, given that we've established that we're all on the same side, can we shelve the attitude and move on? Ben, you know that this afternoon, at approximately five-fifteen, the horsebox bringing four of Mr Truman's horses back from Sandown racecourse was hijacked, near Guildford, by three men, driven to an out-of-the-way location, and one horse, er . . .' He consulted his pocketbook. 'Cajun King, was then removed while the others were set free.'

Ben nodded.

'It would seem to have been a well-planned and executed operation,' Ford continued. 'Mr Rice says they came through Guildford and over the Hog's Back to avoid the M25, but the hijackers obviously knew which route the horsebox would be taking and had posted a lookout to call ahead to the men who were waiting to pull the vehicle over.'

'Mikey says they posed as immigration officials,' Ben commented.

'Yes, after a manner of speaking. According to the driver they had a white van with an orange flashing light on top, a quantity of cones, fluorescent green jackets, a clipboard and some kind of laminated ID card. All fairly easily sourced. Nothing to challenge the ingenuity of anyone with reasonable intelligence. Rice is kicking himself for being so easily taken in, but the fact is that almost anyone would have been. People see what they expect to see, to a great extent. If you set the scene well enough, people will fill in the gaps for you, it's been proven time and time again. He's not to blame.'

'Mikey says the men had some kind of accent but he couldn't say which.'

'That's interesting. Rice only heard one of them speak but he remembers the man as being quite well spoken. He describes him as of average height with a moustache and glasses, and a rather sallow complexion.'

'So, what did he say?' Ben asked.

'Not a great deal.' Ford consulted his notes again. 'Asked him to turn the engine off; said he was an immigration officer and wanted to know what they were carrying, and all their names. Then, before Rice had even finished talking, the hijackers jumped them.'

'Mikey said they had guns.'

'Yes, they did,' Ford said grimly. 'Of course, we can't be sure that they'd have used them, but we have to assume they would. It makes the whole business extremely serious.'

'Lucky that Mikey wasn't found,' Ben commented. 'Or rather, that they didn't look for

26

anyone else. He wouldn't have been hard to find if they'd bothered to look. Presumably Rice didn't tell them he was there.'

'No. He said, in the heat of the moment, he completely forgot the lad was there, which was lucky, because then Mikey was able to set them free when the hijackers had gone.'

'So, are you treating it as kidnap?'

'Well, there's been no ransom demand, as yet, but it seems most likely. There's not a lot you can do with a stolen racehorse, and especially not one who's as well known as Cajun King. You certainly can't race it.'

'And I suppose he's gelded – being a steeple-chaser?'

'Yes, and microchipped,' Truman interposed. 'Easily identifiable if we do find him. I just wish – if they do want money – that they'd get on with it.'

'They'll leave you to stew for a bit,' Hancock told him. 'Softens you up. Makes you more ready to part with your money.'

'Is the horse actually yours?' Ben asked.

The trainer nodded.

'So . . . will you pay, if that's what this is all about?'

'Oh, yes. DI Ford says we more or less have to, and I agree. I want that horse back where he belongs as soon as possible. Cheltenham's only three weeks away, and every hour he spends away from here screws his chances even more.'

'Paying's the only real option,' Ford explained to Ben. 'We can stall for time and try to set up a dialogue, because of course the more contact

27

we have with them, the greater the chance that they'll give something away. But realistically, the best chance we have of catching them is at the handover. That's potentially the weak point in any kidnapper's plan.'

'But if they do manage the pick-up, what then?'

Ford shrugged. 'We have to hope that they keep their word. After all a horse can't give us any information about where he's been – except forensically, I suppose. And setting him free somewhere has got to be a whole lot easier than digging.'

Truman groaned. 'It never occurred to me that there'd be any security risk with King. One of the colts, maybe. I mean, two years ago when Pod Pea won the Guineas, I was quite paranoid about security. That horse was worth millions in potential stud fees, but King? Sure he's worth a few grand, and quite a few more if he does win the Gold Cup, but nothing in comparison with a dozen or so others I've got here.'

'But Mikey says it would be your first Cheltenham Gold Cup,' Ben pointed out. 'It's the prestige at stake here. It comes down to how much you're willing to pay for the chance of running the favourite in one of the biggest steeplechases in the world.'

'Damn them to hell!' Truman slammed his fist on the desktop and stood up, pushing his chair back so violently that it rocked and nearly fell over. He stepped round it and went to the window, pulling the edge of the curtain aside so he could look out into the darkness. 'I've worked so damn hard to get that horse fit for the race, and now he's spot on. Or was. God knows what state he'll be in when we get him back.'

'*If* you get him back.' Hancock voiced the fear that was in each of their minds. 'The precedent isn't good. Think of Shergar.'

'I don't want to think of bloody Shergar!' Truman responded, with what Ben thought an entirely pardonable flash of temper.

'Hancock. Can you go and get an update from forensics?' Ford asked quietly. 'They're working on the lorry and the note,' he told Ben as his colleague left the room. 'We're not expecting fingerprints, because Rice told us the one he spoke to was wearing plastic gloves, but there may be something else – a hair, perhaps, or clothing fibres. It's unfortunate that the cab has been occupied by upwards of two dozen different people in the last fortnight alone, but all we can do is look for something unusual, something that doesn't fit.'

'What about the hijack site? Nothing there, I suppose.'

'It's a popular overnight stop. Rice says it was empty when he drove up – the bogus checkpoint saw to that – but by the time we got someone there the burger van had arrived and half a dozen lorries and commercial travellers had gathered. It was hopeless.'

'Weren't they taking a bit of a chance? I mean, what if one of your lot had driven by?'

Ford shook his head. 'They'd probably just have raised a hand. We don't get involved unless we're asked to.'

Ben digested this. 'And the note?'

29

'The usual format: "We will contact you. Do not call the police or you will never see your horse alive again."'

'Damn them!' Truman said again. 'If this is those bloody animal liberation people, I'll see every one of them strung up!'

'I'll pretend I didn't hear that,' the DI stated quietly.

'Is there any reason to think it is animal lib?' Ben enquired.

'Mr Truman has been having a bit of trouble from a local splinter group calling themselves ALSA, which, I'm reliably informed, stands for Action for the Liberation of Sport Animals. They're a fairly small group but well organised. They spend their time protesting about race-horses, greyhounds, animals in circuses, dog shows – you name it. If they had their way, all animals would be returned to the wild. They make a lot of noise but so far that's pretty much all they have done. I have my doubts as to whether they would take on something like this.'

'They stole those greyhounds a couple of months ago.' Truman was pacing the room now.

'Yes, but that was a publicity stunt. They handed them in to the RSPCA two days later. There were no threats.'

'They've sent *me* threatening letters,' the trainer persisted. 'I lost a horse in the King George on Boxing Day and had a flood of abusive letters. They sent a load more to the owner. It was the last straw for him; said he'd had enough, sold his other horse and quit racing altogether. They wrote to all the papers, even organised a petition. They can't seem to understand that losing a horse upsets us just as much as it does them – more, really, because they're personal friends to us. Some of the lads are depressed for days, for God's sake. It's not just about the money.'

'Didn't you lose another one a week or two ago?' Ben remembered. 'Mikey said something about it.'

'Yeah, on the gallops. Stress fracture. Just suddenly went, mid-stride. Promising two-year-old, too. Bloody tragedy.'

Taken at face value the words were almost casual, and Ben could see how the man's attitude could be misconstrued by someone on the watch for evidence of brutality.

'I suppose they picked up on that too?'

'Oh yes. They don't miss a bloody thing. And Sod's Law made it happen on the gallops nearest the road. I think they're up there most days; they seem to be on a personal crusade against me at the moment. Thing is, even if you could chase them away, you can't tell them from the bloody journalists.'

'It's a public highway,' Ford reminded him.

'Yeah. Don't I bloody know it? If it wasn't such a perfect slope I'd shift the gallops somewhere else. It doesn't seem right that you lot can't do something about them.'

'Well, in future we should be able to do a bit more. New proposals are being put forward to deal with animals' rights activists but I can't promise the problem will go away entirely. It's still got to be policed, and staffing numbers aren't

– as you well know – as high as they might be.'

'Bloody ridiculous, if you ask me! Don't know what we pay our taxes for.'

There was a tentative knock at the door; at Truman's terse invitation it opened and Bess came in. She was carrying a tray holding a kettle, teabags, a jar of instant coffee, sugar, milk, mugs and spoons, and – especially welcome from Ben's point of view – a large packet of digestive biscuits. Aside from a bag of crisps bought at a petrol station, he hadn't eaten since six o'clock that evening.

'Thought you could probably do with a drink but I wasn't sure how many were in here, so I brought the makings,' she announced, putting the tray down on the end of Truman's desk. 'Any news?'

Truman shook his head, coming to sit down. 'Not yet.'

Bess started to dispense coffee and tea according to preference. Ben eyed her thoughtfully before saying to Truman, 'You've got, what, forty-odd staff? How do you propose to keep this thing a secret, with countless journalists eager for any snippet of news about the horses?'

'I don't suppose we shall be able to in the long run, but for now we're going to tell the lads that King's picked up a slight muscle strain and has been sent straight from the racecourse to have some intensive physio. If Mikey and Davy Jackson can hold their tongues for a few days we might just carry it off.'

'Mikey's pretty good with secrets,' Ben commented, accepting coffee and biscuits from Bess with a grateful smile. She twinkled back at him in a mildly flirtatious manner, which he knew from previous encounters to be standard issue in her case. It was, however, common knowledge that she was seeing a lot of Rollo Gallagher, Castle Ridge's highly successful stable jockey.

As if drawn by the lure of a hot drink, Hancock reappeared.

Ford raised his eyebrows hopefully but was rewarded by a shake of the head.

'No. Nothing yet,' he reported. Then to Bess, 'Tea, please love.'

'Where did they take the horsebox to unload the horse?' Ben asked. 'Mikey said it was private land. Do we know who the land belonged to?'

'Yes, it's up for sale at the moment. Disused brickworks just outside Guildford. Big, locked-up factory building with a huge concrete apron where they used to stack the bricks. Tucked away in the woods it is, down a private back-road. Not much chance that they were seen, especially on a wet day like today. It seems like everything went their way.'

'Except for Mikey being there to let the others go,' Ben suggested.

'Yes, but even so, I should think they were well away by the time Ian Rice telephoned Mr Truman to let him know what had happened.'

'And he immediately phoned you.'

'Yes, but unfortunately by that time the horsebox was on its way home. If we'd known sooner we'd have stipulated that it should remain at the transfer point until CSI could get there. Still, it couldn't be helped. Rice says he couldn't get a signal.'

'They seem to have thought of everything,' Ben observed.

'Mm. As I said, we've located the brickworks but as yet that's yielded no clues, and we found no trace of them *or* the lorry they transferred the horse into: no cigarette butts, no soft ground for tyre tracks; the place looks clean. But if there *is* anything, forensics will find it. It was rather late in the day for roadblocks, but we did cover the major routes for an hour or two. Meantime, we've got people watching ports and airports but, to be honest, without much hope. If that's their game, I should imagine they'll have organised a flight from a private airfield. So there you have it, Mr Copperfield. You know as much as us. Possibly even more, as I haven't had a chance to speak to Mikey myself yet. Talking of which . . .' He drained his coffee mug and slid forward on his seat, preparing to stand up.

'Thought you were going to put a tracer on my phone,' Truman said.

'We are.' He looked at his watch. 'It should be on by now.'

'Oh. I thought . . .'

Ford smiled and shook his head. 'No, there's nothing to see. No gadget with dials and tape spools. It's all arranged through the telephone company. All it takes is the proper authorisation.' Ford got to his feet. 'Come on, Hancock.'

'But I've only just got my tea,' Hancock protested, pausing in the act of taking a biscuit.

'Well, swallow it down or bring it with you. I don't mind which, just as long as you come.' He turned to Ben. 'Here's my number. If you have any further thoughts on any of this, I'd be glad to hear them.' At the door, with a surly Hancock on his heels, he turned again. 'I've taken a chance, trusting you. Please don't let me down.' With a wave of the hand he was gone.

In the silence that followed, Ben finished his coffee, studying the card in his hand and wishing all of a sudden that he didn't have to move. The leather chair was comfortable, the room warmed by a top-of-the-range, coal-effect gas fire, and he'd had the sort of day that made the morning seem like a distant memory.

Bess took his empty mug from him, adding it to those already on the tray.

'Anything else I can do for you, Mr Truman?'

'No, Bess; thanks. I should get to bed.' Truman had been sat at his desk, chin on hands, staring into space, but as the door closed behind her he straightened and looked directly at Ben.

'DI Ford seems pretty impressed with you,' he stated. 'Is he right to be, I wonder?'

It wasn't really a question to which he could give an answer, even if Truman expected one, and Ben wasn't sure he did.

'I wonder,' the trainer repeated, almost to himself, 'just how straight *are* you, Ben Copperfield?'

2

Ben looked steadily at Eddie Truman, his mind racing. He didn't want to compromise himself in any way, but he dearly wanted to know what was behind the trainer's question.

'I can bend if I have to,' he said slowly. 'But I have my principles.'

'Hmm. What would you say if I asked you to work for me?'

'I'd say I'm freelance. I don't work for any one person or company. That's the way I like it and that's how I intend to keep it.'

'All right. Let me put it this way. How would it be if I were to commission you to do a little job for me?'

'What sort of job?' Ben's journalistic instincts were up and running. 'Why don't you just ask me and find out?'

'It's . . . ah, a little delicate,' Truman hesitated.

'Well, when you've made up your mind whether or not to share it with me, you can let me know. Here's my number.' Ben got to his feet

36

and fished a dog-eared business card out of his jeans pocket. 'Just at the moment I'm too tired to play guessing games.'

'No, wait! Time is important. You see, it might just have something to do with the Cajun King business.'

'And you haven't told Ford?'

'No. As I said, it's a little delicate.'

'Ah, let's see . . .' Ben said slowly. 'There's someone you know who has a grudge against you, and you don't want to tell Ford because whatever you did to upset this person, or persons, wasn't strictly legal. Am I close?'

'You might be.'

'And . . . Let me get this right – you want to tell a *journalist*?' Ben shook his head in disbelief. 'Am I missing the logic here?'

'Ah, but this particular journalist has a vested interest in not upsetting me,' Truman observed.

There was that threat again. Ben's eyes narrowed. He didn't pretend to misunderstand. It had always been Mikey's dream to become a jockey, but in spite of him being a truly gifted rider, Ben knew it was their father's influence that had secured the apprenticeship with Truman. If Mikey lost this job, his lack of social skills and limited academic ability would make it difficult for him to find another.

'There's only so far I'll go, even for Mikey,' he warned.

Truman looked thoughtful for a moment, then he forced a laugh.

'Oh, come, now. I'm not asking you to be a party to some major crime. I just want to know that if you come across something, let us say, irregular, you'll come to me for an explanation, and not just go running straight to the authorities.'

Ben hesitated. He had a strong suspicion that he should turn Truman down without further ado, but his professional curiosity was difficult to override, and things had been getting a little mundane lately on the work front.

'I don't come cheap,' he said eventually. 'And I'll make no promises.'

'I wouldn't expect you to come cheap,' Truman assured him. 'I believe in paying well for good work. But neither will I stand for being double-crossed.' He fixed Ben with a steely eye. 'I'm not threatening you, I'm just stating the facts. I'm a man as won't be messed with. Deal fairly with me and I'll deal fairly with you. Now, on those terms, will you work for me?'

Still Ben hesitated.

'All right,' he said finally. 'But on these terms: I'll take payment in arrears; I won't do anything I consider morally wrong; and if I don't like where my investigations are taking me I'll drop the case and you'll owe me nothing.'

'My my, you are a cautious fellow, aren't you?'

'Just careful.'

Truman smiled and held out a hand. 'Very well. It's a deal.'

Ben ignored the hand.

'You'd better tell me just what this is all about,' he said, sitting back on the chair he'd recently vacated. 'And I want *all* the details.'

Truman leaned sideways and opened one of the drawers in his desk. He withdrew a file and took from it a single sheet of paper, which he pushed towards Ben.

'Read that.'

Ben picked it up. The document was printed on headed notepaper. It had been created by one Cecil Rackham – who resided at Cranleigh Place, Nr Sherborne, Dorset – and recorded the sale, to Edward Truman of Castle Ridge Racing, of a sixteen-hand, eight-year-old bay gelding, registered with Weatherbys as Cajun King, for the sum of £12,000. It had been signed by both parties and witnessed by a third party, and was dated two years previously.

Ben read it through again and looked up.

'Am I missing something?'

'Look again.'

Ben looked.

'Nothing . . . Except perhaps the price? But then, I'm not really au fait with the price of racehorses. Presumably jumpers aren't anywhere near as valuable as flat horses.'

'Not normally. But take into account the fact that Cajun King had won a top novice chase, just the week before,' Truman told him. 'He was actually worth at least three times what I gave Rackham, even then.'

'And now?'

The trainer shrugged. 'Whatever anyone is prepared to give. A hundred grand, two? Who's to say? I wouldn't sell him at any price.'

'So why did *he* sell?'

'Because he found himself embarrassingly short of cash just then, and I had the money to hand. And because his marriage was going through a rocky patch and he was desperate that his wife shouldn't know that he'd spent the money bequeathed to her by her mother.'

'And you threatened to tell her,' Ben guessed, careful not to show his contempt. 'That's a dirty trick but not exactly illegal.'

'Nevertheless, I'm not eager to see it splashed across the sporting pages of the newspapers,' Truman said.

'And you really think this Rackham might have stolen Cajun King back? What on earth would he do with him?'

'Perhaps he thought he might recover something of what he thinks I owe him.'

'But surely he'd guess you might suspect him. Where on earth could he hide the horse?'

'Where could anyone hide him?'

'At a riding stable perhaps?' Ben suggested. 'With a false passport. Or, better still, a racing stable. You know, I can't help thinking that a bit of publicity might be a good idea. It would make it much more difficult to keep him hidden.'

'No, I can't risk it. We've got to do as they say, whoever they are. I can't risk them panicking and just shooting him out of hand.'

Privately, Ben agreed with Hancock that it was highly unlikely that the horse would ever be seen alive again, but he didn't say so.

'So, can you think of any legitimate reason I might use for approaching Rackham directly, or is it to be a case of rooting round behind the scenes?'

Truman pursed his lips thoughtfully, but offered none.

'Well, is he an owner, or a trainer? Does he have any other horses? What does he do for a living?' Ben prompted.

'He's an owner, and yes, he does have other horses. Two more. Belinda Kepple trains them. I believe he actually has a runner in the Gold Cup himself, an outsider. Fifty to one, I think it was, last time I checked.'

'Well, it's a start.' Yawning, Ben got to his feet. 'I'll see what I can do, but, as I said, I'm not making any promises. And that's another thing – I won't make any threats, either. It sounds to me as though this poor bloke's had a rough enough deal as it is, so if that's what you've got in mind, you'd better start looking for someone else.'

'Holier than thou, is that it, Copperfield?' Truman shook his head. 'I don't think so. I know what you journalists are like. As twisty as politicians, and about as truthful, in general.'

Ben raised his eyebrows. 'You approached me, remember?'

'Yes, well, Ford seemed to think you were a cut above the crowd,' he said gruffly, clearly uncomfortable with the concept of climbing down. 'I'm sorry. This business is getting to me. I love my horses, you know.'

'And you'd love to get your hands on that Gold Cup, too.'

'Of course I would. I'm not going to pretend otherwise. We're all in it for the glory, you know; it's the name of the game. You don't compete if you don't care about winning.'

'Granted. Look, it's occured to me . . . I know Cajun King's a household name but I'm not at

41

all sure I'd recognise him if I were standing next to him. Have you got a photo I could have? And does he have any distinguishing marks – you know, scars, unusual whorls in his coat, or ridges in his hooves? Anything that might identify him amongst all the thousands of other bay thorough-breds?'

'I got Bess to print these off earlier. Ford has a couple too,' Truman said, taking a computer-generated colour image from a file on his desk. 'He has a star on his forehead, slightly to the right, as you face him. No scars I can think of.'

'Is his tail always this short?' Ben queried, studying the print. The dark bay horse in the picture had a tail like a yearling, bushy but not even reaching his hocks.

'Yeah. It was damaged when he was younger – got it slammed in the horsebox door, appar-ently – and it's never grown properly since.'

'Well, that's something, I suppose.' Ben folded the picture into his pocket and headed for the door. 'I'll be in touch, then.'

On a final, fleeting visit to the cottage Ben collected his phone and found Mikey enjoying a cup of hot chocolate with Bess and Ian Rice. Ford and Hancock were nowhere to be seen, and Mikey seemed fairly relaxed now.

Wishing them all a good night, Ben went out to the Mitsubishi. As he opened the door of the vehicle a small whiskery face appeared, blinking as the interior light came on, and Mouse, Ben's whippet-sized grey lurcher, sat up, stretched and yawned.

'Hello, sausage. Need to go pennies?'

Her big, dark eyes regarded him for a moment from under her brows and then she got up, turned round, and lay down again with a small sigh.

'Suit yourself.' Ben climbed in, started the engine and set off on the twenty-minute journey home.

On waking the following morning, his first thought was that it was nice to be in his own bed after a couple of weeks on the move. His second, accompanied by a vague sense of unease, was to wonder what he'd let himself in for. He'd turned freelance to avoid having to work for people he didn't like, and there was no denying that his first experience of the Castle Ridge trainer had placed the man firmly in that category.

As always when returning home after a few days away, Ben had slept deeply and long, and his thoughts were soon interrupted by Mouse's appearance beside his bed, resting her chin on the quilt and plainly suggesting that it was time he got up to let her out.

With a groan he slid out of bed and made his way through the single-storey building to the French doors, stepping carefully from rug to rug to avoid the chill of the stone floor on his bare feet. Dairy Cottage was part of a small development of rented-out converted farm buildings around a central courtyard. Low walls partitioned off a parking space for each residence on the inside of the square and they all had a walled garden on the outside, backing on to fields. Inside, the rooms retained many of their original features, but the lofty beamed ceilings and stone floors that kept them beautifully cool in summer also meant that they required a fair amount of heating in winter.

Mouse followed, head and tail low, patiently listening to Ben's mutterings about troublesome females who wouldn't allow a bloke the luxury of a few minutes' lie-in. Opening the arched French windows in the dining room, Ben let her out into the pocket-handkerchief-sized garden. Surrounded by five-foot-high stone and flint walls and well-stocked borders, the frosted lawn sparkled in the morning sunlight and ice coated the water in the central birdbath. Mouse picked her way delicately over the grass to attend to business and Ben turned back into the house to answer his own call of nature, put the kettle on, and fire up the wood-burner.

Some three-quarters of an hour later, having showered, dressed, fed Mouse, and satisfied his inner man with a plate of bacon sandwiches and a cup of coffee, he wistfully put aside the Sunday paper and tried to apply his mind to the matter of the missing racehorse.

Although he'd agreed to go and see the horse's former owner, he didn't really hold out much hope of discovering anything useful. With Cajun King's disappearance a secret, there was a limit to the amount of probing he could do without giving the game away. Personally, he thought it incredible that anyone should have taken the horse at all; the logistics were horrendous. And if the motive was revenge for some past grievance, then surely it would have been easier, and just as effective, to destroy the horse where it had stood, in the horsebox.

He thought back to his encounter with Truman and reflected that rumours he'd heard – of the man having clawed his way to the top, in business and racing, over the bodies of several less ambitious men – were probably all too true. Such a man could have made any number of enemies in the course of his career.

Waking up his PC to download the professional scribblings of the past few days from his laptop, Ben checked his email, deleted the spam, read and replied to a couple of others and then stayed online to call up his favourite search engine. He entered the words 'Cajun King'.

The resulting list was impossibly long so he tried again, adding the keyword 'Rackham', which produced something a little more manageable.

Scrolling through, he found that the majority of listed sites were connected to the artist, Arthur Rackham, but there were a few besides. The most promising was an excerpt from a newspaper article which, when Ben went to the website, proved to be an account of the surprise sale of the horse, just days after his first major success. The sale price was not recorded, but it was speculated that a 'pretty penny' was likely to have changed hands between the eminent surgeon, Dr Cecil Rackham, and an up-and-coming owner and trainer, Eddie Truman. Better known as a flat trainer, it was the columnist's opinion that 'bluff Yorkshireman, Eddie,' would be just as successful over the sticks. Ben wondered who had notified the press. In view of what he'd learned, it was unlikely to have been Rackham.

As he severed the internet connection the telephone immediately began to ring.

'Ben?' It was Truman and, from the sound of it, he was on a mobile and in a vehicle.

'Speaking.'

'Just to let you know we've heard from the kidnappers.'

'Oh, right. And?'

'Bess found an email first thing this morning. They say they have Cajun King; he's unharmed but if we talk to the police they'll shoot him. They say they want half a million in used notes and they'll be in touch with the details.'

'That's a hell of a lot!' Ben exclaimed. 'Realistically, that's more than he's worth, isn't it?'

'Ford reckons they're trying it on. He thinks they'll take less, if we can only set up some form of two-way communication.'

'If it was email, isn't it traceable?'

'Yes, but he reckons they'll probably have used an internet café and opened an account under a false name. Ford thinks it's unlikely they'll use that connection again.' Truman sounded depressed. 'All this technology, and it's still impossible to pin people down.'

'Mmm. And you can't even be one hundred per cent sure the horse is still alive. Can you organise that much money in a hurry?'

'I'll need a few days to sell off some stock, but it shouldn't be a problem. Anyway, I must go. Third lot is just going out and I'm on my way up to watch. Will you be able to do anything about Rackham today?'

'Yeah, I'll call on him this morning.'

Ben rang off and sat staring thoughtfully at the phone; then, on an impulse, he picked up the receiver and tapped in a mobile number.

It was answered after only a few rings.

'Yeah, Ben. How are you?' Mark Logan was a friend of some three or four years' standing, and a useful one, being a member of the Dorset Constabulary. Initially their work had thrown them together but now, although their paths rarely crossed, Ben considered the policeman one of his few real friends.

'Not so bad,' he replied. 'And you?'

'Knackered,' came the succinct response. 'Half my bloody shift has taken a sickie this week. Anyway, what can I do for you?'

'Well, actually, I wanted to ask a little favour.'

'Hmm.'

'Why "Hmm . . ."?'

'Because – as I recall – the last time you wanted to ask me a "little favour" it involved three weeks' work and two broken fingers on my part!'

'Ah, but I only asked for info – it was your decision to get involved.'

'Well, I couldn't leave an amateur bumbling around on his own, could I?' Logan observed provocatively. 'Anyway, what is it this time?'

'A little matter of a missing racehorse; do you know about it?'

'Er . . . Be more specific,' he hedged.

'Eddie Truman; Cajun King; a lay-by outside Guildford?'

'Yeah, all right. Just checking. Can't be too careful with you reporters.'

47

'I wouldn't do that to you,' Ben protested.

'So, how did you get on to it so quickly? It's not even common knowledge at the nick.'

Ben explained about Mikey. 'DI Ford bought my silence with the promise of an exclusive,' he added. 'And Truman tried to do the same with threats. But then he decided I might be useful to him. If I were to give you a name, would you be honour-bound to pass it on to Ford?'

'Well, I *should* do . . .'

'I didn't say *should*, I said *would*,' Ben pointed out.

'If it were told to me in complete confidence, I'd respect that, unless someone's life depended on it.'

'OK. Truman put me on to a guy called Cecil Rackham, who used to own the horse. He's a surgeon, I think. Anyway, there's some bad blood between them. I wondered if you could run a check on him. And also on Truman himself, while you're about it.'

'Oh, you don't want much then?' Logan enquired sarcastically. 'Actually, I've already run a quick check on Truman.'

'For Ford?'

'No. For myself. I was curious. You know, self-made millionaire; rags to riches. They don't usually get there without treading on somebody's toes.'

'And?'

'A few well-greased palms here and there. The odd spot of muscling in. Nothing actionable, that I could find. Lately, many good works – including quite large sums of money for underprivileged

48

and abused youngsters, and a sizeable contribution to the hospital scanner appeal. A veritable pillar of the community. Rumour has it, he's up for a knighthood.'

'Are you serious?'

'Strings are being industriously tugged.'

'Well, well,' said Ben, his mind busy.

'Look, I'll see what I can do, and be in touch soonest. Must go now, I'm on "obbo" and things are moving.'

'Thanks, Mark. Speak to you soon.'

A knighthood? That was interesting. No wonder Mikey's boss was keen to avoid any breath of scandal.

The morning was wearing on and, after stoking up the wood-burner, shutting down the dampers and coaxing the reluctant Mouse from her position on the rug in front of it, Ben set off to find Cecil Rackham, blithely putting out of his mind the pile of mail that had wedged under the front door when he let himself in last night, and that now sat on the coffer in the hall.

Cranleigh Place was found without difficulty, after enquiring at the local post office and convenience store, and Dr Rackham answered the gleaming white door in person and in his dressing gown, looking tousled and bleary-eyed. He was carrying a Sunday paper under his arm and, on the hall table behind him, Ben could just see a tray laden with teapot, cups, saucers, toast in a rack and marmalade.

He just managed to avoid glancing at his watch. A late breakfast in bed; very nice. And not quite the behaviour – one would imagine – of a man involved in the risky business of kidnapping a world-class steeplechaser and holding it to ransom.

'Dr Rackham? Cecil Rackham?' Ben enquired, with his best apologetic smile. 'I'm sorry to have called so early on a Sunday, but I wasn't sure when else I'd find you in . . .'

'Yes, well, what do you want?' Rackham was short and rather plump, with thin, greying hair and moist-looking pale skin. He was quite possibly a very pleasant man but at that moment he looked less than encouraging.

'I'm a journalist,' Ben announced, showing his press card and noticing Rackham's slight withdrawal. That meant nothing. Almost everyone, except perhaps the most desperate minor celebrities, showed that reaction. 'Ben Copperfield. I'm doing a feature on the Cheltenham hopefuls, and I wondered if you'd mind saying a few words about Tuppenny Tim's chances in the Gold Cup.'

'If you were a journalist worth his salt, you'd know that the horse is thought to have little or no chance in the Gold Cup. He's a fifty-to-one outsider.' The door closed a few inches.

'Ah, but everybody reports on the favourites. I wanted to do an article about the others. After all, there can only be one winner, but there wouldn't be a race at all if it wasn't for the also-rans. People who keep horses for the sheer love of the sport are the real backbone of the industry.' Ben laid it on thickly, mentally gagging on the syrupy words.

'Well, of course, everybody likes a winner; we

50

wouldn't do it otherwise,' Rackham said, unbending a little. 'But, as you say, it's the horses themselves that are important when all's said and done.'

A voice hailed him from the top of the broad sweep of stairs and Rackham pulled the door a little closer, his body blocking Ben's view of the interior almost completely. 'Look, it's really not the best moment . . .'

'Of course, I'm sorry. Some other time, maybe? The thing is, I'm on a bit of a deadline here.'

'This evening, perhaps? I could meet you at the yard. The horses are with Belinda Kepple at Wincanton – but then of course you'd know that. I usually look in at evening stables; six o'clockish. Can you make that?'

'Certainly. I'll be there. Thank you.'

The voice called again and Ben caught sight of an unmistakably feminine pair of legs descending the stairs before Rackham nodded his dismissal and withdrew, pulling the door smartly shut in his visitor's face.

Ben turned away, smiling to himself. Whoever that had been on the stairs, he was prepared to lay odds it wasn't Mrs Rackham. Those legs and that slightly husky voice had belonged to a female far younger than the doctor, and his demeanour had smacked of someone with a guilty conscience. He wondered if Rackham's wife was away temporarily or for good. Perhaps his sins had finally caught up with him. Either way, Ben reflected, the good doctor wasn't letting her absence get him down.

Deprived of the chance to interview Rackham

immediately, Ben found himself with no excuse not to return to the cottage and make a stab at clearing his daunting backlog of mail. And there was always the bookkeeping to do.

If they were positioned tidily, it was just possible to fit two cars on the small rectangle of gravel in front of Dairy Cottage. However, the cream, 1972 VW Beetle that was occupying this space when Ben got back, was parked diagonally across it. Leaving the Mitsubishi on communal ground, he went across to open his front door and, raising his voice to compete with the strains of *Madame Butterfly*, called out, 'Lisa?'

'Ben! I'm in the bath.'

'You've parked the stegosaurus across both spaces. Where are the keys?'

'On the hall table,' came the response, to the accompaniment of watery sounds. 'Sorry.'

Having repositioned the vehicles, Ben returned to the cottage, turned the radio down, made two mugs of coffee and took them into the bathroom. 'Coffee?'

The large, white-tiled bathroom was foggy with fragrant steam, and Ben crossed to open a window.

'I'll catch my death!' said a voice from the huge, corner bath, with a theatrical shudder.

'Nonsense. Fresh air is good for you.' Ben turned to survey the bather fondly.

Up to her chin in bubbles, Lisa Nelson, his girlfriend of eighteen months or so, reached out a frothy hand to accept the mug. On the rounded side of slim, she had shoulder-length, dark blonde hair, blue eyes and good – if unexceptional –

features that were lifted to beauty by her dazzlingly sweet smile.

'Join me,' she invited.

Ben shook his head. 'Too cold with the window open,' he said, and then stepped back smartly as she threw her wet sponge at him. 'What are you doing here, anyway? I thought you had a tour this weekend.'

Lisa worked for a company that organised select holidays in the south-west of England, taking in sites of cultural and historical interest. Small groups of wealthy tourists were put up for two or three nights at a time in country house hotels, from where they were collected by guides like her, who showed them the best that the area had to offer. This meant that she was, like Ben, away for days at a time, sometimes returning to the cottage and sometimes to her parental home in Hampshire – whichever was the closer.

'Yes, I have. I worked all day yesterday and did a garden visit this morning, but this afternoon's trip was scuppered by some protest group making a nuisance of themselves. Management decided to implement Plan B, so my lot joined up with Natasha's group and did Stonehenge instead.' She took a sip of coffee. 'Actually, I think most of them were quite pleased, but it means finding somewhere else for them later in the week when they should have been going to Stonehenge. Oh, well.'

'So who was protesting, and where?' Ben asked, only mildly interested.

'Some animal rights group. We were taking our lot to the open day at Belinda Kepple's stables – you know, the racehorse trainer, just outside

Wincanton. Unfortunately these animal liberation people got to hear about it and apparently they were marching up and down outside the gates, chanting slogans and waving banners. The open day was going ahead but management thought it was an unnecessary risk, besides spoiling the experience somewhat.'

'You wouldn't happen to know which group it was, would you?'

'No. Not the foggiest. I was told, but it wasn't one I'd ever heard of.'

'It wasn't ALSA, by any chance, was it?'

Lisa frowned. 'It could have been. Something about animals and sport, I think, if that helps. Why? Is it important?'

'It might be.' Ben finished his coffee. 'I think I might just go over there and have a look-see.'

'Good Lord! You must be hard up for news,' Lisa exclaimed. 'Do you have to go? I've got to go back this evening for the theatre, but I thought we might spend some quality time together this afternoon – if you know what I mean . . .'

'Sorry. Hold that thought though, I shouldn't be long,' he said, leaning over the edge of the bath to kiss her.

Lisa lifted her face to accommodate him, but at the last moment substituted a large handful of foam, and then squealed as he threatened to duck her.

'I might not be in the mood later,' she called as he went on his way, wiping soap bubbles from his chin. 'Especially after you stole my bacon from the fridge!'

*

By the time Ben got to Wincanton the road outside Belinda Kepple's stables was empty of any protesters. A couple of bright orange, printed leaflets had blown against the hedge, and he picked one up. It was indeed from ALSA, and the content held no great surprises. Full of righteous zeal, it urged the good people of England to lobby their local MPs to ban all forms of sport and entertainment that involved the exploitation of animals. It listed several incidents in which racehorses had had to be destroyed, and preached at length about the cruelty of forcing any creature to work or perform: from circus animals through to greyhounds and riding horses, even sheepdogs. The message ended by calling on all compassionate people to join the crusade and bring some hope to the lives of thousands of helpless creatures.

At the bottom of the leaflet there was also a website address where, it was suggested, monetary donations could be made to help further the cause.

Ben pocketed the note thoughtfully and then looked up to find that he was being watched fairly closely by a burly policeman and his equally burly German Shepherd dog.

'The fun's over, mate. You might as well go home,' the policeman told him.

'And the open day?'

'Cancelled.'

Ben looked back down the road to where the Mitsubishi was parked, at a discreet distance, then back at the dog handler. The German Shepherd licked its lips, eyeing him intently.

'Bet you were flavour of the month, exploiting one of God's creatures as you do,' he said with amusement, nodding towards the dog.

The policeman had obviously been born without a sense of humour. 'If you'd just move along please, sir.'

'You don't happen to know where the group were going when they left here?'

Man and dog took a step forward, the dog looking a little too eager for Ben's liking. He held up a hand. 'OK, I'm going.'

Back in his car, he drummed his fingers on the steering wheel for a moment or two. Where would the protesters go after so resounding a victory? Somewhere to celebrate, perhaps? It was just possible, he supposed, that that somewhere might be Wincanton. It was worth a try. Reversing the vehicle into a convenient gateway, he set off back the way he had come.

Ben had only visited Wincanton once before but he struck lucky straight away. He pulled into the car park of the first of its half-dozen or so pubs, backed into one of the few remaining parking spaces, and the first thing he saw was a young lad of not much more than thirteen or fourteen, with a handful of familiar orange leaflets and a collecting box. Ben switched the engine off and sat back in his seat.

On the face of it, it didn't seem likely that he would learn a lot from someone as young as this lad, but there had been times in his journalistic career when a youthful contact had provided a wealth of useful information. People tended not to notice when kids were around. They were easily overlooked. Many a frank discussion had been overheard by a youngster and repeated, almost verbatim, to Ben's receptive ears.

It was worth a try. But where were the others? In the warmth of the pub having lunch, or around the town, spreading the word?

With a mental shrug, Ben stepped out on to the tarmac. The lad had given up his position by the door and now sat on one of the deserted picnic tables, looking cold and fed up. He was a lightly built child, and Ben wondered whether he had overestimated his age.

Ben looked away to get his jacket and lock the vehicle and, when he turned back, trouble had arrived in the shape of four older and far bigger boys who had surrounded the lad with the flyers. Ben guessed the collecting box was probably the object of the newcomers' interest, but they had plainly decided to have a little sport with the youngster first.

He started to walk over.

Still too far away to catch what was being said, he could nevertheless see that the boy was very frightened. He'd scrambled over the table to get away from the bullies, but this had left him trapped between them and the wall of the pub. The boys approached, swaggering, and the gaps between them decreased until they were virtually shoulder to shoulder.

Drawing closer, still unseen by any of the players in the drama, Ben judged that the older boys were in their late teens, and two of them were quite sizeable. He seethed, inwardly. Mikey had been bullied at one of his schools, due no doubt to his academic difficulties, and the experience had blighted his life for several long months. Ben had been furious when he found out, and that same fury rose in him now.

Where were the other ALSA members? They should never have left a young lad on his own with a collecting box; it was asking for trouble.

'Everything all right, Kenny?' Ben had no idea what the lad's name was, but tried it on the premise that the bullies might be deterred if they thought he was connected to the boy in some way.

All five youngsters turned to look at him; the ALSA boy with a dawning hope, the others with varying degrees of insolence.

'Fuck off,' one of them said, dismissively, before returning his attention to his victim.

'Sorry. No can do,' Ben said lightly, but beneath his turtleneck sweater his heart-rate was climbing rapidly.

The one who had spoken swung round.

'*What?*' he asked incredulously.

'I said, no.'

The other three turned to face Ben as well, sensing new sport. The smallest of them, a lad with a thin, spotty face, grinned nastily and said, 'You can take him, Mal.'

Ben stopped, not six feet from the group, and tried to catch the eye of the one he'd temporarily christened Kenny, to urge him to make a run for it while the bullies' backs were turned. But he seemed rooted to the spot.

The ringleader, presumably Mal, took a couple of steps forward and leered unpleasantly at Ben, showing teeth already stained by tobacco.

'Well?' he said.

Ben stared back at him, silently. He couldn't think of any response that wouldn't further inflame the situation.

His very stillness seemed to unnerve Mal a little. His confident snarl faltered and he glanced to his side, as if to reassure himself that the gang were still there. They were, and one of them advanced a step or two, stabbing a finger in Ben's direction.

'Why don't you fuck off before you get hurt?'

'I expect you know you're on CCTV,' Ben said quietly. 'How long d'you think you've got before the cops get here?'

Two of the gang looked round uncertainly but the one called Mal shook his head crossly. 'He's bluffing.'

He was right. Ben had no idea if CCTV was operational in the vicinity, but the thought of it was clearly unsettling them.

'C'mon, Mal. Let's get the money and go,' the spotty one said, and at that moment the ALSA lad made a break for it, dodging round the tables and heading away towards the car park.

He wasn't quite quick enough.

Mal threw an arm out sideways as he passed and fastened on to the lad's bomber jacket, swinging him round and gathering him in like a spider with a fly.

The others abandoned Ben in favour of easier prey, and the youngster squealed in fear as the collecting box was torn from his grasp and he was pushed backwards to the point where the fixed bench of the picnic table caught him behind the knees, forcing him to sit down. The thugs gathered round, Mal leaning over the lad and resting one hand on the table either side of him, his face not six inches from the boy's own.

The youngster whimpered, petrified, and Ben saw red.

With clenched jaw he strode forward, caught hold of Mal's shoulder and pulled him roughly away.

The ringleader staggered back, a look of incredulous surprise on his face, and Ben shoved him backwards, hard, before he could regain his balance. He stumbled back a few more strides, then lowered his head and charged like an enraged bull.

Ben sidestepped neatly, casually hooking his toe round Mal's ankle as he passed, and his would-be assailant measured his length on the tarmac amongst the table legs.

That was all very well as far as it went but, unfortunately, the idea that by taking out the leader, you take out the gang, didn't hold true. Ben turned his head to see what, if anything, the rest of them were going to do about this manhandling of their comrade, just as the spotty one launched himself, with a kind of primeval scream, at his back.

3

Even though Spotty was the smallest of the four, the combination of his weight and momentum, catching Ben off balance, was enough to send him crashing sideways into another of the wooden tables, and from there to the ground. The fall shook the two of them apart but, even as Ben rolled and came to his feet, the others, emboldened by Spotty's success, joined the attack.

Ben managed a couple of wild swings with his fists before he was overpowered and pulled backwards. The hard edge of the closest bench caught him behind the knees and, with one of the lads holding each arm, his upper body was bent back over the tabletop and held there, the planking digging painfully into his ribs.

He couldn't move.

For a moment sheer, blind panic took over. Reason went out of the window and, with no regard for the discomfort of his unnatural position and the fact that struggling would make it worse, he fought against them, writhing and kicking out blindly with both feet.

'Christ! Hold him! The bastard nearly took my knee out!' From somewhere in front of Ben, Mal's voice cut through the haze, bringing him to his senses. He stopped kicking, took deep breaths and forced himself to calm down. He found though, to his dismay, that whilst he could to some extent control his breathing, he couldn't control the muscle tremor that had set in.

At Mal's bidding, the two holding Ben transferred their grip to pin both his wrists and his shoulders flat to the table, and he had to bite his lip in an effort to stay silent under the increased strain. It occurred to him, dismally, that it wasn't the first time they'd done this; their moves were way too efficient and well-synchronised for that. He managed to get his feet flat on the tarmac and lift some of the weight off his body, but his back was arched and his stomach felt horrendously vulnerable. He tried not to think about what Mal might intend doing next.

He found out soon enough.

His feet were swept forward and, robbed of even that tenuous support, Ben's bodyweight dropped, wholesale, on to the right angles of the table and bench. Wincing, he fought another surge of terror.

'Ahh. He's shaking. The tough guy isn't so tough after all, is he boys?'

Mal came round to Ben's right side and leaned over him, grinning and affording him a less than enviable view of the stained teeth, pale skin and eyebrow stud. He opened his mouth and put out his tongue to display another stud then laughed and, with his forearm, bounced on Ben's midriff.

That was more than enough. This time he couldn't prevent a grunt of pain. His back was killing him. Much more of that kind of abuse and he was afraid something would rupture. His knowledge of anatomy was sketchy at best, but something plainly had to be done, and fast.

Mal moved his forearm up to rest across Ben's throat.

Oh God, no!

Mal must have seen the fear in his eyes because he chuckled again. 'You don't like that, do you? Well, now you know why no one fuckin' messes with me!'

He began to lean and Ben felt panic rising as his breathing was restricted. He couldn't think that Mal really intended to kill him in broad daylight, in so public a place, but neither was he sure the youngster knew his own strength, and how easily fatal damage could be caused in just such a way.

'Credit card – back pocket,' he gasped.

The pressure continued to mount.

'I can take those anyway,' Mal pointed out.

Ben shook his head slightly.

'Pin . . . number,' he managed, hoarsely. His vision was dissolving into a mass of black patches.

The thug leaned closer.

'Tell me now.'

Ben shook his head again. At first he thought it wasn't going to work, that Mal was enjoying himself too much. But then greed took over, the pressure on his windpipe eased and blessedly sweet air flooded back into his lungs.

'OK. Let him up,' Mal told his cohorts. 'But hold him.'

Somewhere nearby Ben heard a door open and the sound of it obviously registered with Mal, too, because he snapped, 'Stand him up. Quickly!'

As they hauled him to his feet, Ben purposely let his weight drag on his two captors, causing them to move closer together as they tried to support him. Using the leeway he'd gained, he suddenly straightened his legs and turned his head to butt the one on his right side with all the force he could muster which – it had to be said – wasn't nearly as much as he would have liked.

It was, however, enough.

The youngster hanging on to his right arm immediately let go with one hand and clutched at his face, allowing Ben to pull his arm free and swing it at the second one. This lad, unwilling to take on Ben without a substantial advantage, released his hold instantly and tried, unsuccessfully, to dodge the punch.

'You cretins!' Mal screamed, but a shout from behind him signalled that help was on its way for Ben. 'All right, go! Go on. Go – go!'

Finding himself abruptly unsupported, Ben staggered slightly, tripped over the table leg, and would have fallen if he hadn't managed to catch hold of a neighbouring table at the critical moment.

'You all right, mate?' Someone had arrived to help, slipping his hand under Ben's arm to steady him. 'I should sit down for a minute, if I were you.'

Ben thought that was an excellent idea, and did so.

'You all right?' the man repeated.

Ben nodded. Broadly speaking, he was. He'd have a few bruises and his throat felt sore but it could have been a lot worse. If his escape bid had failed and Mal had discovered that the wallet containing his money and credit cards wasn't in his back pocket, after all, but in the inside pocket of his jacket, he might well have been in real trouble.

Rubbing his bruised back, he straightened up and found that several more people had emerged from the pub and a small crowd had gathered, one of whom was the young lad he'd rescued.

'That was pretty impressive,' someone said approvingly, and there was a general murmur of agreement. 'For once those Jones boys didn't get it all their own way.'

Ben shook his head. 'I don't think I'd have had much chance if you lot hadn't appeared,' he said, his voice husky. 'But you know them, do you?'

'Yeah. Three of them are brothers: Mal, Kevin and Leroy Jones. I don't know the skinny one but they're always together, and always causing trouble. They get away with it most of the time, too, 'cos no one wants to report it. Things happen to people that get on the wrong side of that lot, if you know what I mean.'

'That's Billy Larkin,' someone called out. 'The skinny one with the spots. He lives down our road.'

'Well, *I'll* damn well report it!' Ben said without hesitation.

A couple of people cheered and someone said, 'Good on yer!'

The man who'd spoken first carried a dish-cloth over his shoulder and Ben assumed he was the barman or pub landlord. His next words confirmed this.

'Come on in and I'll get you a drink. On the house, of course. You can phone the police from there.'

Ben fell in readily with this plan and, waving away offers of help, rose to his feet, a little shakily, to join the general movement back into the pub.

'Um, I just wanted to say thanks.'

Ben turned and found by his side the young lad with the ALSA leaflets, still clutching both those and the collecting box. Incredibly, he'd almost forgotten the boy whose plight had been the start of it all.

'*I* should thank *you* for fetching help,' he said. 'Are you OK?'

'A bit shaky,' the lad admitted.

'That makes two of us. But how come you were out here on your own? Where are the others?'

'We're here.' A voice spoke up from behind Ben as he ducked to enter the low doorway. 'We only popped in for a minute . . . It was just unfortunate . . .'

The speaker was one of two hippyish individuals; the sort that make protesting a way of life, whether it be *against* road building or *for* the rights of obscure minorities. Ben thought one was probably male and the other female, but he couldn't be sure. He favoured them both with a withering look. 'Yeah. It was *very* unfortunate.'

Inside the pub a seat was found for him, and coffee and a cordless phone were produced. Ben

66

availed himself of all three, suggesting to the police that if they cared to come out to the pub they might find any number of witnesses to the Jones brothers' latest offence, and, after some hesitation, they agreed. It appeared that some of these potential witnesses had had their ears carefully tuned in to his conversation because within a few moments of the end of the call, the population of the public bar had thinned out quite dramatically.

The barman caught Ben's wry look at the departing backs and nodded.

'What did I tell you? Another coffee? Are you sure you wouldn't like something stronger?'

'Coffee's fine.'

'Bit odd with steak and chips.'

'With steak and chips I'd probably have a beer,' he agreed.

'Comin' right up.'

The food beat the police to Ben's table by a good twenty minutes and he was, in fact, just wiping the juices from his plate with his last chip when a diminutive WPC came in, followed by a stout and ponderous colleague who looked to be pushing retirement age.

'Ben Copperfield?' she enquired of the room in general.

Ben put up a hand and spent the next quarter of an hour answering her questions. Finally, closing her pocketbook, she got up to go.

'Aren't you going to take a statement?' he asked.

'Well, that depends . . . .Would you be prepared to give evidence?'

'I thought that's what I'd just been doing.'

67

'I mean, in court,' she said. 'You see, we've been through all this before. People start off full of anger and good intentions but somehow by the time the court case comes around, they aren't interested any more. It's just a waste of everyone's time and effort.'

Her portly sidekick, who had been enjoying a cup of coffee over by the bar, nodded his agreement. 'Bloody waste of time.'

'Well, if you can get *them* there, *I'll* be there,' Ben promised, and the landlord announced his willingness to back him up.

Shortly after the officers left, Ben also took his leave, pausing in the porch to scan the car park area for undesirables.

'Come on, I'll see you to your car,' a voice offered and, looking to his right, Ben saw a pleasant-faced, fair-haired young man sitting at one of the outside tables with the collecting-box boy. 'I wanted an opportunity to thank you for what you did for Seb,' the man added. 'Henry Allerton, by the way. Seb's my nephew.'

'Well then, it's a pity you don't take a bit better care of him,' Ben observed sardonically. 'He should never have been left on his own with a box of cash. It was asking for trouble.'

'And he wouldn't have been if I'd had anything to do with it,' Allerton assured him. 'I wasn't here at the time, but I've had words with those concerned.'

'So, you're one of the animal lib protesters too,' Ben observed, starting towards his car. 'I hear you pulled off quite a coup, up at Belinda Kepple's stable earlier.'

68

'We did what we set out to do.' He sounded smug.

'And you think stopping a couple of thousand people looking round a racing stable is going to make a real difference?'

'If we cause even one of those people to think again about what they are helping to support, we will have achieved at least part of our aim.'

Ben stopped and turned to face him. 'You really believe in all that stuff, don't you?'

Allerton frowned. 'Of course I do, or I wouldn't be doing this. I believe that it's gross arrogance on the part of humanity to think we're justified in using animals for whatever purpose we please. And even more so when it is solely for amusement.'

'No need to ask if you're a veggie,' Ben murmured. Then, before Allerton could respond, 'Listen, I'm a journalist. I specialise in horse-related topics and I've had stuff published in some of the big national dailies as well as many of the top horse publications. What would you say to some real countrywide coverage?'

Allerton's eyes narrowed. 'That would depend what slant you put on it. We don't need the kind of publicity that makes us out to be New Age troublemakers. We're dealing with serious issues here, that we're passionate about.'

'Try me. If you can convince me, I'll do my best to convince the readers. If you can't, I'll put your case forward and leave it to people to decide for themselves, with no personal opinions included. Come on, you can't say fairer than that.'

Ben was subjected to a long, hard look.

'All right. But it's not entirely up to me. I'll have to get back to you.'

On cue, Ben took out a business card and handed it over. 'Call me, then. But don't leave it too long, I've got other commissions coming up.'

Allerton half saluted and peeled off, taking the lad with him and leaving Ben on his own. Luckily, no one was lurking in the car park with mischief in mind, and within moments he was safely in the driver's seat and pulling the door shut behind him. For a moment he leaned back against the headrest and closed his eyes. His ribs felt sore and he guessed it would be several days before he would be able to swallow comfortably, but, all in all, he supposed he'd got off relatively lightly. It wasn't the first time he'd been roughed up in the course of his career; before he started specialising in equine matters he'd reported on a couple of controversial issues where the parties involved had made it very clear that his interest wasn't welcome. He did feel a bit peeved, though, that this time the violence had been almost incidental.

'Well, Mouse,' he said over his shoulder. 'Next time I go charging in like some Hollywood vigilante, just remind me of how I feel now, would you?'

Mouse lifted her whiskery muzzle enquiringly for a moment, flattened her ears in pleasure, and then settled down again with a sigh.

'Yeah, you're right; I probably wouldn't listen,' he said, starting the engine. 'Always engage my muscle before my brain . . .'

*

70

By the time Ben got back to the cottage, Lisa was just leaving.

'Too late mate, you missed your chance. I've got to pick up my Americans at six-thirty.' They had met in the doorway, she dressed for the evening in a navy trouser suit and smelling rather strongly of some expensive perfume.

She spoke lightly, but Ben caught an undertone of hurt disappointment.

'I'm sorry, Lisa. I really am. I ran into a spot of bother and had to give a statement to the police. It all took time.'

'What happened?'

'Oh, just some louts picking on a kid outside a pub. He was one of your protesters, as a matter of fact, collecting money, and the others thought they'd help themselves.'

'Hang on,' Lisa caught hold of his jaw and turned it this way and that, peering closely. 'No black eyes . . . Don't tell me you broke the habit of a lifetime and kept out of it?'

'Well, not exactly, but there were a few others who came out of the pub to help. Anyway, I'm only telling you because that's why I didn't get back in time to help you enjoy your "quality time".'

'Well, it's your loss.'

'It is, indeed,' he said, pulling her into his arms as she tried to edge past. At close range the scent was almost overpowering. 'Is this a new perfume?'

Lisa made a rueful face. 'No. I knocked the bottle over and some of it soaked into my sleeve. I would have changed into my other jacket but I know it isn't ironed. Is it too awful?'

'Not *too* awful. It's probably making a statement. Of sorts.'

'Yeah, and the statement is probably that I've got terminal BO,' she grimaced, pulling away from him. 'I'll have to change, ironed or not. The trouble is, after a few minutes you get desensitised and can't tell how bad it is.'

At this point Mouse, who'd grown tired of the doorstep conversation, slipped between their legs and into the hall, where she began to sneeze violently.

Lisa scowled at her.

'All right, all right. No need to rub it in; point made!'

A couple of minutes later, having unearthed the replacement jacket, she had another crisis.

'Oh God, it's all hairy! That wretched dog! I'll turn her over to Mike the Masher one of these days!'

'You wouldn't!' Mike was Ben's landlord, an ex-army man who was rumoured to have been in the Special Forces, and looked as though he had certainly represented the army in the boxing ring. A mountain of a man with a deep rumbling voice, he lived just a few yards from the farmyard development, in the tall stone building that had been the original farmhouse. Nobody knew how he'd come by his money, and no one was about to ask. He was an undemanding landlord who kept to himself and imposed few rules on his tenants, but one of those few was that no pets of any kind were allowed in the cottages.

'I would so!' she declared. 'Look at this. How can I put that on? It looks like she slept on it!'

72

Ben, who had indeed found Mouse curled up in the washing basket one afternoon, wisely held his tongue. Instead, he fetched a clothes brush and set about remedying the situation.

'I don't know how you've got away with sneaking her in and out all this time,' Lisa said, as Ben brushed vigorously. 'He must know.'

'Of course he knows. And what's more, he knows that I know he knows. But as long as nothing is actually said, we can all pretend we know nothing. There, that looks okay; it'll be dark, anyway.'

'Thanks.' She picked up her handbag and keys and headed for the door once again, pausing to say, with a glint in her eye, 'You know, I reckon he's a bit sweet on you. You want to be careful.'

'Mike the Masher? Yeah, right! You're just jealous. Now go find your rich Americans. When will I see you again?'

'Well, this lot move on on Tuesday morning but I've got another lot on Wednesday, so I'll probably stop over at Mum's. It might be the end of the week.'

'OK. Well, give me a ring, then. And sorry about the bacon.'

'That's all right.' Lisa leaned towards him and they kissed briefly. 'I was going to chuck it away, anyway. It was out of date.'

Ben was laughing as he closed the door behind her. They had a good relationship: steady but not intense; mutually noncommittal, as they'd agreed it should be when Lisa had first started to stay for the occasional night over a year ago. With both of them working irregular hours and sometimes being away for several days, there were times when they were like the proverbial ships in the night, but, in a way, Ben felt this kept the relationship fresh. When they did get together, it was like discovering one another all over again. The arrangement was loose and it suited them both that way; there were no promises to be broken, no tears and tantrums, in fact, very few arguments at all. The gentle reproach, imperfectly hidden, with which she'd greeted him that afternoon was about as heavy as it got. He counted himself very lucky.

With only an hour or so to spare before his arranged meeting with Rackham, Ben decided that his time would be most usefully spent soaking in a hot bath. His back felt tender and exhibited the beginnings of some quite promising bruises, but these bothered him far less than the shame he felt at the memory of his rapid descent into panic when he'd found himself trapped. It had been a long time since he'd gone to pieces like that and he'd thought he was past it. It was disturbing to find that he wasn't.

Belinda Kepple's yard was, like its owner, neat and competent, with no frills. Whitewashed walls, black painted doors and a well-swept concrete apron indicated an efficient regime and a certain pride in appearances. On the gate the name – Laurel Farm – was spelt out in simple black letters on a cream background. In spite of the modesty of its appearance, Ben knew that this was one of the most progressive establishments in the racing business, and Belinda herself was the most successful female trainer of the current season.

Five minutes late, he found Rackham already in conversation with the trainer, who bent a look of slightly frowning enquiry towards Ben as he approached.

'It's all right, he's with me,' Rackham told her, looking – in corduroy and sheepskin – far more in command of himself than he had done earlier that day. 'He's a journalist, doing a feature about the Gold Cup horses. You don't mind, do you?'

'Well, no,' she said, not sounding exactly overjoyed. 'If you're OK with it, that's fine.' Fiftyish, of medium height and wiry build, she wore her grey-speckled dark hair short. In jeans, a Guernsey and a thick fleece jacket the whole effect was somewhat androgynous but she was, nevertheless, quite an attractive woman.

'Ms Kepple?' Ben asked, turning on the smile. He wasn't sure of her marital status and didn't want to offend. 'Ben Copperfield.'

'Belinda,' she responded, accepting the handshake. 'Ben Copperfield . . . Are you Johnnie's boy?'

Ben was a little taken aback. It was a long time since he'd been described as a boy and, even when his parents were together, he could never remember hearing his mother use that form of his father's name.

'I might be. Which particular Johnnie are we talking about?'

'John Copperfield the bloodstock agent. Son called Michael who's a jockey, and another who's a journalist; you, I presume, unless I've got entirely the wrong family.'

Ben shook his head. 'No, you haven't.'

'I thought not. You've a look of Johnnie about you. You didn't follow him into horses, then?'

'No, I didn't.'

'Should've thought it was in your blood, with your mother, as well.'

She paused, eyebrows raised as though expecting an answer, so Ben provided one.

'A lot of hard work for little return,' he said. It was his stock answer; brief and to the point, it usually put a stop to further questioning. Never mind that, in his case, it was also completely untrue.

'Oh, it has its own special kind of rewards,' Belinda said, her expression showing that Ben had fallen a degree or two in her estimation. 'Well, Cecil, do you want to come and look at this horse of yours, or shall I leave you to your interview?'

'Oh, I expect Mr Copperfield can wait ten minutes or so,' Rackham said. 'Besides, this is as much about the horses as their owners, surely.'

'Absolutely,' Ben agreed, as they started towards the stables.

Tuppenny Tim, apparently known as Tuppy around the yard, was a huge, steel-grey horse with a long head and an honest eye. He would never have made a show horse but, then again, everything was in the right place and Ben didn't think he'd ever seen such a deep chest and sloping shoulder. The horse had an impressive back end, too, with well-sprung loins and powerful quarters. Tuppy turned his head with casual interest as the trainer opened his half-door, then returned his attention to his hay net.

Belinda went in and patted the horse on his

neck and shoulder, which produced a glance of slight irritation from her charge, and then ran her hands down his legs, feeling the cannon bones and fetlocks for signs of heat or puffiness.

'Cool as a cucumber,' she announced with satisfaction. 'Gave him quite a hard workout this morning, too. Got legs like iron. I wish all my horses were this easy to train. What do you think of him, Ben?'

'Well, he certainly *looks* like a Gold Cup horse. Can he jump?'

'Like a stag.'

Ben looked at her. The undercurrent of excitement he thought he'd detected in her voice was echoed in her face.

'You think he's got a chance, don't you? But surely his form is mediocre, at best.' He'd done his homework before setting out.

'Last year it was. But if you'd seen him last year you wouldn't have recognised him. He's been a late developer. Last year he still looked like an overgrown gawky youngster whose legs didn't belong to him. We ran him a few times but he was so backward, we decided to give him some more time to mature. He came back into work at the beginning of the season, and now look at him! It took an outing or two to get him back into the way of things but he's won his last three.'

'Easily,' Rackham put in, and Ben could see that his eyes, too, were shining.

'You really think he could do it, don't you? So, if he's been winning, why haven't the bookies picked up on him?'

'The first two were fairly modest races. He didn't beat anything of note but he beat them well. His last time out was a different kettle of fish altogether. He took on some quite nice opposition and won easing down. The thing is, the going was heavy – which was said to have put paid to some of them – and the favourite fell at the last. But what everybody seems to have ignored is that the favourite fell because he was tired. Tuppy was still full of running but Fred Flanagan has his head screwed on and knew I wouldn't want him winning by a mile.'

'If you want to keep it quiet, why tell me?'

'It's not that it's been a big secret, I just didn't want too much of a buzz too soon in case it prompted the handicapper to take a second look. But the weights have been allocated now and he's come off rather well. *He* obviously thought his form was a fluke, too.'

'However well he's going, he's still got Cajun King to beat, though.' Ben turned to Rackham as he said this, watching him carefully for any abnormal reaction.

Rackham merely looked sour.

'He's been beaten before.'

'Not lately, though,' Ben persisted. 'The bookies have him three to one on, already. How does it feel, knowing you sold the horse that's hot favourite to win the Cheltenham Gold Cup?'

'How do you think it bloody feels?' Rackham demanded. 'You journalists are all the same, asking the bloody obvious!'

'We have to get our quotes,' Ben said without

apology. 'Quotes can make fantastic headlines. So why did you sell the horse to Truman?'

'For the money, of course. I didn't want to sell him, but . . .' His voice tailed away as he realised he was getting himself into awkward territory.

'But?'

'I was going through a bad time and needed the money,' Rackham said.

'Truman's a shit!' Belinda cut in. 'He uses people.'

'Do you know him well?'

'Rode for him a couple of times when I was starting out – until he laid out his terms.'

'His terms?' Ben probed.

'Oh, no,' she said, shaking her head. 'I'm not going to give you any juicy quotes. Use your imagination. But all I'll say is, when I turned him down I was jocked off, for good, and I'm not the only one he's dumped.'

'Names?'

Belinda wouldn't be drawn.

'Shall we just concentrate on the matter in hand? Tuppy, wasn't it?'

'So, how do you feel about Truman?' Ben asked, turning back to Rackham.

'Look – as Belinda said – is this about the Gold Cup, or are you just here to dig up the past? All that's over and done with now and I've got another horse. How I feel about Truman is irrelevant.'

'So, do you feel you got a good price for Cajun King?'

Rackham's eyes narrowed but it was Belinda Kepple who spoke.

'You don't give up, do you, Mr Copperfield?

You know, I really think we can do without this kind of publicity.' She came across to stand just inside the stable door, her eyes hard and unfriendly. 'I'm not a fan of journalists, but I was prepared to give you the benefit of the doubt for your father's sake. As it is, I think perhaps you should go now. If Cecil wants to speak to you again he's welcome to do so, but not on my property.'

Rackham shook his head. 'I don't want to.'

'So you see, Mr Copperfield. You've outstayed your welcome. Please go.'

Ben held her gaze for a moment then inclined his head and turned away. After a couple of strides he paused, looking back.

'For what it's worth, I'm sorry,' he said. 'There was just something I had to know.'

Rackham frowned slightly but the trainer's expression held no compromise so, with a wave of his hand, Ben walked away. The experience had left a sour taste in his mouth. It wasn't by any means the first time he'd played the hard-nosed reporter, but it didn't come naturally to him, and usually his grilling was reserved for people he didn't particularly like; Belinda Kepple was someone he felt he could have liked a lot.

Back in the Mitsubishi, he drove a little way up the road before stopping in a convenient gateway where he switched off the engine, sank down in his seat and prepared to wait.

About twenty minutes later Rackham appeared, apparently in no particular hurry, and, after he'd passed, Ben started the engine and followed.

It was a wasted effort. Rackham's silver BMW headed for Cranleigh Place, deviating only once to take in a visit to a local convenience store, where he bought cigarettes, a bag of crisps and a magazine. Shortly afterwards, the car disappeared through the pillared gates of Rackham's home and, presumably, to its garage.

Ben considered sitting outside to see if he reappeared but his back was aching and he really wasn't in the mood. On top of that, he very much doubted that it would do any good. Rackham's demeanour wasn't that of a man with a weighty criminal matter on his mind. His reaction to Ben's questioning had been one of annoyance and discomfort but not, as far as he could tell, of guilt. He was as sure as he could be that the man had nothing important to hide.

Having reached this conclusion Ben set off home, reflecting that, on the whole, it hadn't been one of his better days. Quite apart from the fracas at The Pig in the Poke, he'd been summarily shown the door by both the police officer at the scene of the demonstration and Ms Kepple, and in the meantime had missed the opportunity of a couple of very pleasurable hours with his girlfriend.

All in all, a bit of a bummer.

4

The following morning brought three telephone calls in fairly quick succession.

The first was from Logan, Ben's police contact, and came before he was fully awake.

'Christ, don't you ever sleep?' he mumbled, peering somewhat blearily at his alarm clock. Half past seven; he remembered counting the hours from two until five o'clock, having jolted awake from a bad dream, trembling and drenched in sweat.

'Yup. Did the late shift, slept for three hours, got up and been for a run,' Logan announced cheerfully.

'Bastard!' Ben said.

Logan laughed. 'This Rackham guy,' he said, getting down to business. 'Can't find a lot on him. Age fifty-four, married to Maria, with one child – a daughter, currently at Southampton University studying law – lives just outside Sherborne. School; college; medical college; now a respected surgeon working at various hospitals throughout the South-West. Specialises in gynaecology.'

'*And* in his spare time,' Ben muttered. He told Logan about his visit to Rackham's home. 'No sign of Mrs Rackham then. Unless she's the owner of the long legs and husky voice.'

'According to the electoral roll she's fifty-two,' Logan told him. 'So basically, you already know all this?'

'Most of it,' he admitted. 'But I hoped you might turn up something else.'

'And I suppose you're going to tell me you already know that it was Rackham who sold the missing horse to Truman.'

'Er . . . yes, I did.'

'So what's the story?'

'I'm not sure there is one. Truman gave me a tale of some minor blackmail but I had a feeling he wasn't telling me everything. Having met Rackham, though, I don't think he's got anything to hide – except his mistress, perhaps. I'd be very surprised if he had anything to do with kidnapping Cajun King.'

'So is that the end of your interest in the affair?'

'Well, officially, I guess.' Ben hesitated. 'What do you know about ALSA?'

'The animal lib lot? Load of ex-hippy, vegan environmentalists. They're serial protesters; if they're not protesting about that it'll be something else.'

'Nice to know a policy of open-minded tolerance is alive and well in the modern police force.'

'Yeah, well. It's easy to be tolerant and open-minded when you don't have to deal with the

83

buggers,' Logan observed. 'Sorry; I've got a bit of history with these kinds of groups. This ALSA lot are mainly harmless as far as I know, but even so, I wouldn't suggest tangling with them. Fanatics can be a dangerous breed.'

'Actually, I met a couple of them yesterday. Henry Allerton, do you know of him?'

'Ah, Henry. The acceptable face of the organisation. A gentleman, is Henry, and a true believer in the cause. Which is probably more than could be said for the rest of them. If you take my advice you'll stay away from them – but when have you ever taken my advice?'

The second call came just as Ben was emerging from the shower. He grabbed a towel and padded through to his bedroom, leaving a trail of wet footprints.

'Ben?' It was Truman. 'Any news? Did you see Rackham?' The wind noise suggested he was outside; perhaps on the gallops.

'I did.'

'Do you think he's got him?'

'Well, I didn't exactly ask, but I'd say not.'

'How can you be sure?'

'I can't – not one hundred per cent – but I'd be willing to put money on it. I pushed him pretty hard but he seems to have put the whole Cajun King thing behind him.'

'Oh, you can't take any notice of what he says, he's a slippery bastard,' Truman said.

That's rich, coming from you, Ben thought.

'It wasn't just what he said, it was the way he said it; the way he looked. And besides, he's got his own runner in the Gold Cup.'

Truman snorted. 'Tuppenny Tim. That's about what he's worth! I told you, he's fifty to one, a no-hoper.'

'That's not what his trainer thinks. Look, I don't quite know what more I can do other than watch him twenty-four seven and, quite frankly, I'd rather not. If you really think he's behind the kidnap, you should tell the police.'

'You know why I can't do that.' Truman sounded cross. 'So what next?'

A large splash landed on the telephone and Ben used the end of the towel to wipe his face.

'Well, I've done what you asked me to do. I guess that's it. I'll put the bill in the post.'

There was a slight pause. 'What if I asked you to go on working for me? I want that horse found, and two lines of investigation must be better than one.'

'But surely I'll just be covering the same ground the police will.'

'So, between you, you should come up with something,' Truman persevered. 'What do you say?'

Ben shrugged. 'It's your money, I guess. But I'd want a free rein. That means freedom to question your staff and contacts.'

There was another slight pause.

'OK. Where will you start?'

Ben sighed, not really happy about it.

'Well, I've made contact with the animal lib group. I might follow that up. You haven't heard any more from the kidnappers, I suppose?'

'Nothing. Look, got to go now; the second lot have just arrived. I'll wait to hear from you.'

As he put the phone down Ben sat back heavily on his bed, still wrapped in his damp towel. His back and ribs were sore, he was tired and a little depressed and, left to himself, he probably wouldn't have followed up the ALSA connection, in spite of what he'd said to Logan. But now it seemed he was committed.

'Damn!' he said after a moment, and Mouse raised an enquiring eyebrow. 'I've already got a commission. Why don't I just stick to that and stuff Eddie bloody Truman?'

The dog looked uncomfortable, recognising the tone but not understanding the words. Ben put a hand down to rub the top of her head. 'You don't know what I'm talking about, do you, sausage? Don't worry about it; you're a good girl.'

Thinking about his feature on Nico and the Csikós, Ben was within a whisker of ringing Truman back and reversing his decision, but, before he could do so, the phone rang yet again.

Muttering under his breath, he picked up the receiver.

'Hello.'

'Ben Copperfield?'

'Yep.'

'Henry Allerton here.'

Oh, shit.

'Hi. What can I do for you?'

'Your offer, yesterday . . .'

'Yeah, about that—' Ben began.

'I've talked it over with the others, and we'd like to take you up on it. It's high time we had a chance to put forward our point of view.'

Ben looked heavenwards.

'OK,' he heard himself saying. 'Where and when?'

'Could you possibly come over today?'

'I guess so.'

'Meet me at the pub – The Pig in a Poke – at nine-thirty, and I'll take you there.'

Ben looked at his watch. 'Make it ten o'clock and it's a date. But can't you just give me directions?'

'It's better this way,' Allerton said, and rang off.

Putting the receiver down Ben groaned, long and loud.

'Oh God! I've done it again! Why does my mouth say yes, when my brain is shouting no?'

Mouse uncurled herself from her basket, gave herself a shake and silently left the room.

At ten o'clock in the morning The Pig in a Poke was not yet open and the car park was almost empty. It was raining as Ben parked next to a mud-splashed Volvo estate and he had to dodge the puddles as he ran across the tarmac to the paved seating area. He thought enviously of Mouse, whom he'd left curled up on the sofa, close to the wood-burning stove.

Allerton was waiting in corduroys and a waxed jacket, leaning against the wall under the over-hang of the roof. He straightened up as Ben approached.

'I wasn't sure you'd come.'

'*I* wasn't sure I'd come,' Ben replied. 'I'm not keen on these cloak-and-dagger tactics, they make me nervous.'

'Yes, I'm sorry about that. We just wanted to make sure you turned up alone. We had the place trashed once, when we invited someone there in good faith. So you see, we're cautious now, and we don't take kindly to impostors.'

'I could have someone following me, or I could be wired,' Ben suggested.

Allerton looked a bit taken aback.

'Are you?'

'No,' Ben said wearily. 'Lead on.'

'We'll take my car.' Allerton set off back across the car park.

'Or we could take mine.'

'No, it's all right. I'll drive. It's a bit tricky to find. Easier for me to drive than to keep giving you instructions.'

'Look, hang on,' Ben caught hold of the ALSA man's arm and pulled him to a halt. 'I offered to write an unbiased article; I didn't sign up for a magical mystery tour! I'm here, alone. Why can't you tell me where we're going?'

'I told you. We got trashed. The whole place turned over and two of our members injured. We don't take chances any more. Besides, even if I were to tell you, you wouldn't know where it was. It's way out in the sticks.'

Ben scanned Allerton's face for a moment but could only detect an earnest anxiety; nothing sly or underhand. Reluctantly, he gestured to the man to continue and, shaking his head, followed.

The Volvo was almost as muddy inside as out, and it smelled strongly of wet dog. Henry Allerton removed a lead and a rather grubby towel from the passenger seat, giving it a token brush-off with his hand before Ben got in.

'Keeping pets doesn't come under "exploitation", then,' Ben observed wryly.

'My dogs stay with me out of choice, and I hardly have to force them to go for a walk,' Allerton said. 'I do hope you're not going to be confrontational. You promised an open mind, remember?'

'I'll try.'

From Wincanton, Allerton joined the A303 going east, hammering along it at great speed and staying on until just short of Andover, where he headed into the countryside. He then proceeded to work his way through a bewildering maze of single-track lanes, turning left, right and back on himself countless times.

'Wouldn't it have been quicker to blindfold me?' Ben asked eventually, faintly amused.

'I didn't think you'd stand for that,' Allerton said in all seriousness.

'No, you're right. I wouldn't.'

The journey finished at the end of a long gravel track down which the vehicle lurched, wallowing in and out of a series of muddy puddles that stretched from hedge to hedge. They pulled up in a grassy hollow, in front of a green painted Nissen hut that had seen better days, parking beside an old VW camper van that was decorated with a rainbow and various stylised animals.

'Greenpeace meets Disney,' Ben muttered, and Allerton shot him a suspicious look but said nothing.

The hollow was bounded by untidy hedges and

overhung by several large ash trees. Apart from the lane down which they had come, the only other access was by way of a gate in the back left-hand corner, beyond which another track wound off into the distance.

'So who does this belong to? Is it rented, or are you squatting?'

'It was falling down. The farmer who owns the land was grateful to have us do it up, in return for which we get it rent-free for a year.'

'A farmer? Isn't that exploitation of animals on a grand scale? No, don't take offence – it's a fair question.'

'You don't understand the issue here, do you? A.L.S.A. Action for the Liberation of Sport Animals. Making animals perform unnatural tasks in the name of entertainment. Farming doesn't come into it. Granted, a good few of our members are vegetarian – I am, myself – but farming can be seen as a regrettable necessity, provided it's carried out humanely; sport isn't.'

'OK, you've made your point. I'll try not to ask any more stupid questions.'

He followed Allerton across to the door of the Nissen hut, where they were met by a young woman with a shock of frizzy pink hair and more visible body-piercings than Ben had ever seen on one person. The unseen ones, he didn't care to contemplate. Her clothes were eclectic and each article seemed to have been carefully chosen with the intention of not matching anything else.

'Della, this is Ben, the journalist I told you about.'

Ben said 'Hi,' and the pink frizz nodded.

Allerton gestured at the open doorway. 'Shall we go in?'

The inside of the metal hut had been painted cream and at present it housed four people, to whom Ben raised a hand in friendly greeting.

The response was mixed. One smile, two raised hands and an unencouraging stare from a young man with dreadlocks and a nose stud.

Ben turned his attention to the building itself. The end wall nearest the door was lined with free-standing metal shelving and a row of desks ran down each side. Above them cork notice-boards bristled with pins attaching maps, memos, and calendars marked with equine and canine sporting features, details of hunting fixtures and notes such as *John Taylor's Circus arrives – Sherborne*. He moved to look more closely but Allerton blocked his way, shepherding him on.

The other end of the hut had been made more comfortable, with a couple of easy chairs, a sofa, a coffee table and a fridge and microwave. More cartoon animals looked down from the walls, some spouting slogans. They were beautifully painted, and Ben's eye was immediately drawn to them.

'Who's the artist?' he asked, wandering down the hut to get a better look.

'Della is,' Allerton said. 'She's a trained illustrator.'

'She's good.' Ben looked round. 'So this is the nerve centre of the organisation. I must admit, I expected something a little more hi-tech. You have a website, so where are the computers? Where, for that matter, are the telephones?'

'We haven't been here long but we'll have a telephone just as soon as BT get round to it. In the meantime we have mobiles, and I've got a laptop in the car.'

'Where do you send your emails from? Or don't you?'

'Mostly from home or the library.'

'So at the moment you use this for . . . ?'

'We meet here, discuss strategy, organise fundraising, that sort of thing.'

'How many of you are there?'

'It fluctuates. Locally, I'd say somewhere between thirty and fifty. Nationwide, nearly four thousand paid-up members at the last count.'

Ben was surprised. It was far bigger than he had expected. He took a notepad from his pocket and unclipped its pencil.

'So, how long has the group been operating?'

'Five and a half years. Look, would you like a coffee?'

He accepted and settled himself into one of the armchairs. Coffee made, Allerton sank on to the saggy sofa opposite, where Della promptly joined him and the other four drifted closer to listen, ranging themselves on and around another smaller chair. Ben would have preferred to talk to Allerton in private but it was obviously not to be, so he tried to put the others out of his mind.

Over the next half-hour Ben learned far more than he wanted to know about ALSA, their origins, ideals and aims. A staunch supporter of animal welfare himself, he could not entirely condemn the group for their principles, but felt they were pursuing them to a ridiculously radical degree. In his search for quotable material he argued the opposing view, and, although Henry Allerton seemed to understand what he was doing, Ben noticed that Bella and the others were regarding him with increasingly stormy expressions.

Eventually the owner of the dreadlocks could bear it no longer.

'This is fuckin' stupid!' he exclaimed explosively, stepping towards Ben. 'He's not going to give us a fair go. He's like all the fuckin' others and he'll sell us down the fuckin' river, just like they did!'

Ben gave the young man a cool stare, trying not to recoil from his rampant aggression, and Allerton stepped into the breach.

'No, he won't. He's promised to be fair and I believe him. I told you, it was Ben who saved Seb in town yesterday.'

This reminder seemed to appease most of the group but Dreadlocks clearly preferred to see him as the enemy, for he continued to glower.

'I still say it's a mistake. Especially *now*. We don't need some nosey bastard from the press poking round.'

Ben's ears pricked up.

'Why does he say "especially now"?' he asked. 'I should've thought you'd always want publicity.'

For the first time, Ben saw Allerton looking annoyed. He directed a furious glance at Dreadlocks.

'Because he's an idiot,' he said shortly. 'We have a . . . let's call it a project, in the planning stage. A campaign, if you will. It's not something

93

you need to know about, and if he'd kept his big mouth shut you probably never would have.'

'But he didn't keep his mouth shut, did he? So tell me now,' Ben invited.

'I'm sorry. I can't.'

Ben looked from Allerton to Dreadlocks, who had resumed his sullen scowl, and sighed. He was quite plainly going to get no further revelations from either.

'OK. So tell me what you realistically hope to achieve in the long run.'

Happy to be back on safer ground, Allerton became expansive and it was some time before Ben was able to wind the interview up.

Once outside the Nissen hut Ben wandered away from Allerton, climbed a slight bank and stood looking out over the hedge to the adjacent farmland. Most of it was grassland, some fields occupied by cattle, some empty. He could see what he presumed to be the farmhouse on rising ground in the distance and, closer to hand, a cluster of ramshackle buildings including a low shed with a rusty, corrugated tin roof, a barn stacked half-full of hay and a couple of stables. He could just make out a single horse grazing in the field nearest the buildings, but it was wearing a green, New Zealand rug and he couldn't make out the colour of its coat.

Ben stared, his mind racing. It couldn't be that simple, could it? But then again, why not? A horse was a horse; it couldn't be hidden away in a dark corner: it needed to move around, to eat, drink and lie down. Dreadlocks had definitely been jumpy about something, but would they have brought him here if that were indeed Cajun King?

The answer again was, why not? They could have no way of guessing that he knew anything about the kidnap. After all, apart from Eddie Truman himself, no one was supposed to know.

'Are you coming? What are you doing?'

Ben turned to find Allerton approaching. He looked a little impatient but not particularly anxious.

'Who does the horse belong to?' he asked.

'What horse?'

'The one in the field across there.' Ben pointed.

'I've no idea. I didn't even know there was one.'

He sounded a bit testy. Ben had discovered that horses were a bit of a moot point in the ALSA philosophy. Making a beast carry a human for pleasure was definitely against their principles but, on the other hand, it could not be denied that horses seemed to enjoy associating with mankind. The ideal was, apparently, that they might be kept but not used for work, sport or entertainment.

'What's the farmer's name?'

'I don't think you need to know that,' Allerton said. 'If he gets any grief he'll probably throw us out.'

Once again Dreadlocks stepped forward, all fired up.

'I told you he'd be trouble. He's gonna start poking around. Remember what happened last time.'

'Oh *please*. Put a sock in it!' Ben said, stepping off the bank to join Allerton.

Dreadlocks advanced threateningly but a sharp word from his comrade stopped him, and he contented himself with muttering obscenities under his breath as Ben passed.

'I don't suppose you ever considered a career in the diplomatic service,' Allerton observed dryly.

'I did say please,' Ben pointed out as they got into the Volvo.

When, having lurched back down the track, the vehicle reached the blessed smoothness of the tarmac once more, Ben kept his eyes peeled for informative road signs, but there was a distinct lack. In fact, they had travelled a couple of miles before he saw any at all, and then it was a rather confusing four-way job at a remote crossroad.

On the return journey Allerton seemed disinclined to talk and drove, if anything, even faster.

'Is there something wrong?' Ben enquired as they reached the outskirts of Wincanton. 'Was it something I said?'

He shook his head. 'No. Not really. I was just wondering if Baz was right and it *was* a mistake to take you there. I don't blame you for being inquisitive – it's your job, after all. I blame myself for not thinking it through.'

Ben didn't quite know how to respond to this. Allerton's openness was somewhat disarming.

He turned into the car park of The Pig in a Poke, where a few more cars had now gathered. As he pulled the handbrake on he looked across at Ben. 'You won't crucify us, will you? Even if you don't completely agree with our aims, you must see we have the animals' interests at heart.

I'd rather you didn't write anything at all than drag us through the shit.'

'I said I'd be fair and I will. But I can't promise one of the nationals. I'd need something hugely controversial for that, a real exposé, but we should get a slot in one of the locals.'

'Thanks.'

Allerton looked down at the steering wheel, a frown of concentration furrowing his brow. Ben waited, sensing that there was something else on his mind, but when it came it wasn't the breakthrough revelation he had hoped for.

'When you preach, you can't choose your disciples,' he said eventually. 'I'm aware that Baz and Della don't necessarily present an ideal image for the organisation, but they are loyal, and their hearts are in the right place.'

'Even Baz?'

Allerton smiled. 'Yeah, well, he's maybe a bit headstrong,' he conceded.

'That's one word for it,' Ben said as he got out of the car. 'I'd be careful if I were you. Too many like him and you'll have a mob on your hands. Tell me, do you get much bother from the police?'

He shook his head. 'Only when we're actively protesting, but then they just move us on. It's all quite peaceful. Why?'

'Just wondered. It'd be another angle but never mind.'

Allerton leaned across as Ben turned to slam the door. 'And the article?'

'I'll let you know,' he promised.

*

Ben had intended to spend the rest of the day dealing with his mail but somehow he couldn't settle to it. In the end, the discovery that he didn't have any stamps proved to be all the excuse he needed to put it off until another day, and he was able to let his thoughts run in the direction they had been pulling all afternoon.

Could the horse he'd seen that morning really have been Cajun King?

On the face of it, it was extremely unlikely. Given that ALSA had been a thorn in Eddie Truman's side for some time, if they had the horse they must have known that they would be prime suspects, and therefore it would be monumentally stupid to 'hide' the animal within a couple of hundred yards of their HQ. Or were they completely confident that they could keep the location of their Nissen hut secret? If so, they were fools. The police would certainly know the identity of the more prominent members of the group, and it wouldn't take long, however careful they were, before one of them was trailed to their base.

Ben couldn't think that Allerton was anywhere near that stupid.

He made a cup of tea, stoked up the wood-burner and started again.

What had it been that Baz was so desperately afraid he would find out?

Why did he say they didn't want someone poking around *especially now*? Allerton had apparently not considered it a risk. But then again, when pressed, he'd spoken of a project. Could that be significant?

By the time he'd finished his tea, Ben had acknowledged the decision his subconscious had made somewhere on the journey home that morning. He was going to go back to ALSA HQ and take a second, unauthorised, look round. And because time was of the essence, he would have to do it tonight.

It was no longer raining when Ben left the house that evening, just after eleven, but the clearing skies had caused the temperature to drop and, with a lively wind, it felt raw out.

Once again he'd left Mouse behind and she'd made no complaints.

'So much for the idea of Man's Best Friend – faithfully following at his heels through thick and thin!' he said as she regarded him sleepily from under one bushy brow. Clearly unimpressed by his histrionics, she closed her eye and sighed deeply. 'If you wanted a guard dog, you should have bought a Rottweiler,' she seemed to be saying.

Because he didn't have to go to Wincanton Ben could cut a chunk off the journey and join the A303 further east, and it wasn't long before he was into the maze of roads through which he'd been taken that morning. Allerton had sought to confuse him, and had done a very competent job; but for all that they had forgotten to cover up the maps on the walls of the Nissen hut, and the one that Ben had managed to get a good look at had many coloured pins stuck in it and also a star near its centre. Armed with that information, and knowledge of the crossroads and the geography of the immediate area, Ben had been able to consult a map of his own and make a fairly definite estimate of the position of the ALSA HQ.

Pulling up at the entrance to the muddy lane, Ben considered his options. He could, of course, drive straight up the track to the hut and park outside, and he was ninety per cent sure that it would be quite safe to do so. The other ten per cent of his mind, though, pointed out that if he did run into trouble, then the top of a long lane with no turnings wasn't the smartest place to be.

The ten per cent won out. He drove the Mitsubishi slowly on until he reached a convenient gateway, then parked up and disembarked into the cold night wind. Even though there was only the occasional gleam of moonlight, Ben had come prepared in what he jokingly thought of as his cat-burglar's outfit: jeans, roll-neck, leather jacket, woolly hat and gloves, all in black. It had come in useful on similar occasions in the past, but he thought, not for the first time, that if he was ever stopped by the police when wearing it, he would probably be taken in for questioning as a matter of course, whether they could connect him with any crime or not.

Rejecting the lane as a means of approach, on the grounds that it was too exposed, Ben took to the neighbouring field, keeping to the hedge line and finding after only a few steps that the grass was long and unpleasantly wet. By the time he'd covered fifty feet or so, both his leather trekking boots and the lower legs of his jeans were soaked through.

100

His plan was to look out for the tall ash trees that overhung the clearing and, after about two hundred metres, he saw them, silhouetted against the cloud-streaked sky. Locating the clearing was one thing; finding a way through the dense mass of tangled hawthorn and brambles that made up the hedge was another. By the time he did so he'd managed to rip his jeans and his face smarted from a dozen or more scratches. He was very thankful that he was wearing his gloves, although several of the more determined thorns had found their way through the thin leather and embedded themselves in his flesh.

As he'd hoped, he emerged from the undergrowth behind the Nissen hut, in the opposite corner of the grassy hollow from the approach track.

There was no sign of life. No lights burned behind the curtained windows and, as far as he could see, there was no vehicle parked on the grass in front of it. Ben relaxed a degree but clouds were masking the moon now, making visibility poor, so to be completely sure, he set off to patrol the perimeter, keeping as close to the hedge as he could.

It was just as well that he did.

About twenty feet up the track that led away to the farm, and barely discernible in the shadows, a small, dark-coloured car was parked.

Ben shrank deeper into the hawthorn. It was possible that it was just a coincidence – maybe the farmer's car – but he thought not. It was also possible that it was an amorous couple, but the car was a ridiculous distance from the road, even supposing they were quite excruciatingly shy.

All in all, he felt pretty sure that someone had suspected he might return and had planned a little reception for him. The question was: were they waiting in the car, or in or around the hut? It seemed the only way to be certain was to try and get a closer look at the car, but it was obvious that he hadn't a hope of reaching it by way of the lane without being seen; so, reluctantly, he returned to the hollow and began to search the adjacent hedge for thin patches.

A couple of minutes and several more scratches later, Ben was in the field, level with the car. The wind was blowing across the lane towards him and it brought with it the low, monotonous jangle of a music radio station and a trace of smoke that wasn't tobacco.

Ben would have dearly liked to know how many people were in the car but the rampant hawthorn between him and the lane precluded that.

There were two objectives for this night-time visit, one being to have a closer look at the contents of the Nissen hut; the other was to pay a call on the horse in the neighbouring field. Having no wish to traverse the hedge more than was strictly necessary, Ben decided to deal with the horse first.

'Neighbouring' was a loose term, he discovered, after negotiating a barbed wire fence and tramping for a good ten minutes across uneven ground, some of which was definitely on the damp side of marshy. Clouds, whipped along by the wind, intermittently covered the moon, leaving him stumbling in almost complete darkness and able to navigate only by keeping his eye on the small cluster of outbuildings outlined against the sky. When he finally reached them, he found himself on the wrong side of an extremely muddy gateway, which he discovered by plunging his foot ankle-deep into a rain-filled hoofprint. His boot, already soaked, immediately filled up with icy-cold water.

Ben cursed under his breath but it was a little late to turn back, so, grimacing as his other boot filled too, he plodded on, nearly losing one of them altogether as he dragged his feet out of the mud to climb the metal five-bar gate.

Moonlight, which would have been helpful a minute earlier, now flooded the scene, showing him four buildings in various stages of disrepair, the closest of which was recognisable by its half-door as a stable. Ben froze, feeling horribly vulnerable, but either he hadn't been seen or there was nobody there to see, because the dreaded shout didn't come, and a few seconds later the moon went behind a cloud again and blessed darkness returned.

Moving closer to the building Ben made his way to the door and peered inside, almost jumping out of his skin as the horse had the same idea from the other side. It threw up its head and backed away, equally startled.

Unsure how close the farmhouse was, Ben unlatched the top door and pulled it, creaking and protesting, to join its counterpart, then he opened both by eight inches or so, took a deep breath and slipped inside. Somewhere in front of him the horse moved restlessly on its straw bed, and Ben's heart-rate accelerated into the hundreds. With shaking hands, he took a small, rubber-coated torch from his jacket pocket and switched it on.

One glance was enough.

It wasn't Cajun King.

It was the right colour and size but anyone who had been brought up with horses, the way Ben had, could tell at a glance that it wasn't a thoroughbred. It was wearing a dung-stained, navy and red padded stable rug, but its visible parts – head, neck and legs – belonged to something more in the hunter line than to a racehorse. Unnerved by this unexpected late-night intrusion, the horse stood with its head high, showing the whites of its eyes as it watched Ben suspiciously. The stable wasn't by any means large and the animal seemed to fill it as it shifted first forwards, then back, on the verge of panic.

A few soothing words might have helped but Ben couldn't conjure up anything even remotely calming. His priority was to get out and shut the door before the horse did something stupid.

Within seconds he was out and leaning on the closed door, eyes shut, trying to steady his breathing.

So it wasn't Eddie Truman's missing horse. To be honest, he hadn't really expected it to be, but he had to be sure. If he'd had any real expectation, he'd have contacted the police and let them deal with it – scoop or no scoop.

Another ten minutes or so was spent on the return journey and it took him a further five to locate the thin patch in the hedge that he'd forced himself through. Ben could hear the car radio still pulsing out its heavy beat but could no longer see it because by now the moon had deserted him, and he made his way to the door of the Nissen hut by guesswork and a fair amount of luck. Naturally, it was locked, but the whole affair was so flimsy and ill-fitting that a little judicious attention with the blade of his penknife, between door and jamb, soon had it swinging open. Swiftly he stepped inside and pulled the door to behind him. Then, swapping the knife for the torch, and shielding its light with his other hand, he moved towards the nearest desk.

Suddenly, shockingly, the lights came on.

5

'Leave something behind, did yer?' The voice came from near the door and Ben swung round to see the all-too-familiar head of dreadlocks.

Baz.

Damn! Why hadn't he checked the car again?

'What can I say? You made me so welcome,' Ben said, lifting his hands expressively and stepping back so that he was touching the bench.

'I knew you were a bastard! I told him.'

'Clever you!' In one fluid movement, Ben reached behind him, caught up a pot of assorted paperclips and corkboard pins and threw them in Baz's face.

Baz ducked, bringing his arms up to protect his eyes and, not wasting a moment, Ben lunged forward and gave him a powerful shove, sending him reeling back into the corner of the hut. Here, due to the contours of the building, his head connected rather firmly with the ceiling and he sat down, grabbing at the metal shelves to save himself but succeeding only in pulling one of the five-by-three-foot sections over on top of himself.

The air turned blue.

Ben didn't offer to help him up. Taking advantage of the spectacular success of his spur of the moment attack he flicked the light switch off, whisked out the door and pulled it shut behind him.

After the brilliance of hundred-watt bulbs and the cream interior he could see absolutely nothing outside, and he didn't see whatever it was that landed a stinging blow across his shoulder and head, causing him to stumble and drop to his knees. He was, however, ready for it when it came again, throwing out his arm and grasping the weapon even as it cracked across his back a second time. Wrenching it from the hands of his assailant, Ben found himself holding what felt like a short length of partially decayed two-by-two timber.

Robbed of this instrument the attacker laid into him with fists but, as with the timber, the blows were only moderately competent, and Ben was able to discard the wood and catch hold of the flailing arms. He discovered, from the size of bone, that he almost certainly had a female to contend with. It seemed likely that it might be the pink-haired artist, Della.

To someone with ethics this presented a thorny problem, but when, a moment later, she made very efficient use of a set of surprisingly sharp teeth, Ben found his conscience liberated. Turning rapidly on his heel like a hammer thrower, he swung Della round through three-hundred-and-sixty degrees and released her in the general direction of the hedge. The crash of twiggery and muffled screaming that followed seemed to suggest that his efforts had been successful and, recovering his balance, Ben sprinted away.

Unwilling to face the perils of the hawthorn yet again, he hoped he had enough of a head start to make it down the muddy track before Della and Baz could get their act together, get back to their vehicle and come after him.

In the next instant he decided that as Baz had not yet reappeared it might be in his best interests to try and disable the car first, or even – as he was prepared to gamble that they wouldn't have removed the keys – use it himself.

This last idea strongly appealed to him and he altered course accordingly, feeling, as he did, the first few large drops of rain that probably presaged a downpour.

The car was there, unattended, and so too were the keys. Ben slid thankfully into the driver's seat, almost choking on the lingering smoke, and gunned the engine. Old and shabby it might have been, but after turning over a few times, the car started as sweetly as he could have wished. At last, he felt, something was going his way.

Standing on the accelerator Ben tried all the levers and switches, turning on not only the headlights but also the windscreen wipers, the indicators and the heating system in the process. As the lights lanced out through the rain, the first thing they illuminated was Baz's running form. No more than thirty feet away, his stride faltered and stopped as he registered the oncoming car.

Ben wouldn't have run him down but Baz didn't know that, and, though he held his ground for the space of a few heartbeats, his nerve broke, and he dived for the tangle of brambles and hawthorn that comprised the lane boundary. As he drove out into the hollow and skidded round the corner into the muddy track Ben thought, with amusement, that the surrounding hedges had taken quite a battering over the past hour or so.

With the window wound right down to avoid becoming high on the car's residual fug, he took the rough lane at a highly uncomfortable rate, bottoming the vehicle out several times on the ridges between the puddles before lurching, thankfully, on to the tarmac at the end.

Transferring to the Mitsubishi moments later, Ben was about to drop the keys of the borrowed car in a ditch when an idea occurred. Retracing his steps, he tossed them through the open window of the car, on to the driver's seat, before jumping into his own vehicle, backing out of the gateway and accelerating noisily away, leaving a trace of rubber behind him on the road surface.

A couple of minutes later, he was back on foot, having tucked the Mitsubishi out of sight in yet another gateway twenty or thirty yards down the next turning he'd come to. Panting hard from his run, he hid himself behind the hedge and waited.

He needn't have hurried. It was a full five minutes before he heard Baz and Della approaching and *they* certainly weren't hurrying.

Ben could hear them from a long way off, bickering like a pair of children over whose fault it was that he'd managed to get away.

'There's the car. I told you the one we heard was a different one. This old heap of crap never sounded like that!' That was Della.

'I bet he's taken the fucking keys! I'll fucking kill him!'

'Yeah? You and whose army? You haven't exactly been impressive so far.' Her voice was loaded with scorn.

'Well, neither were you.'

'At least I hit him. You just got dumped on your arse!'

'I told you. He threw stuff in my fucking face!'

Ben heard the car door open.

'The keys are here. I'll drive.' Della again.

'You fucking won't!'

'I will. You're stoned out of your mind.'

'So are you.'

'Not as much as you. That's why he made a fool of you. No, come to think of it, you were a fool already!'

'Oh, ha fuckin' ha. At least he didn't have a chance to start poking around. I knew he was trouble but Henry wouldn't listen – oh, no. "We can trust him," he says. Just wait till I tell him!'

A door slammed, the car started up and, over the sound of the engine, Della said 'Come on, get in.'

Presumably he did, because after a moment Ben heard a second door slam and the car pulled away.

In the silence that followed its departure, Ben

stepped cautiously from his hiding place. Unwittingly, Baz had supplied the one bit of information that had been worrying him: whether or not they had already alerted Henry to the attempted break-in. As they hadn't, now was undoubtedly the optimum time to pay a return visit. Throwing caution to the wind, he jogged back to his car and then drove it along the track to the Nissen hut.

This was in darkness once more, and again Ben used his penknife to effect entry, pausing on the threshold this time, to switch the lights on before entering.

The hut was empty, as he'd been pretty sure it would be, and, shutting the door behind him, he pulled a chair across the doorway. At least if anyone did turn up whilst he was there, they wouldn't be able to creep in without him knowing. His search of the ALSA premises was brief and almost completely unrewarding. What little paperwork he found was mainly concerned with protest campaigns, both past and planned, fundraising, and newspaper advertising.

The calendar and maps were dotted with what might have been interesting information, but as this was displayed in some sort of shorthand, it was of little or no use to Ben. On the day of Cajun King's abduction there were no entries on the calendar, and nowhere could he find any reference to Eddie Truman or his stables, until he discovered, on one of the notice-boards, a newspaper cutting about the death of one of Truman's horses on the gallops. Underneath this someone had written, 'Murderer!' in red capital letters. Looking forward through the next month or two was no more informative. At the beginning of March 'Operation Big Top' was announced but, although it sounded most likely to be a circus, Ben could find no further clue as to what the operation entailed.

With growing frustration he turned his attention to the racks of metal shelves near the door. Someone, presumably Baz, had stood these upright again and piled the files, books and pamphlets untidily on them. A cursory glance through one pile wasn't promising, and Ben was ready to admit defeat. In films and on TV he'd watched detectives calmly sorting through the contents of desks and address books, even taking photographs with miniature cameras and rock-steady hands, but Ben wasn't a TV detective: his heart was pounding, he was perspiring freely and he was as jumpy as a cat.

Regarding the remaining jumble of material with weary hopelessness, he gave up. Turning the lights off he removed the chair and cautiously opened the door, waiting silently for a moment or two before venturing across the threshold. If anyone was waiting they were holding their breath, just as he was. Half a minute later he was out of the door, had locked it, and was in the Mitsubishi. Nobody sprang from the shadows; in fact no one moved at all. It looked as though Ben had been completely alone in the clearing this time, but, even so, the thought of returning to continue his search held no allure whatsoever. Feeling suddenly dog-tired, he headed for home.

Ben slept late the following morning and awakened, for the second morning running, to the sound of the telephone ringing.

He put out a hand to locate it, picked it up and said, 'Yeah, hello,' without opening his eyes.

'You lying shit!' a voice greeted him.

Ben's eyes snapped open and he sat up, frowning.

'Who is this?'

'As if you didn't know. I thought you were on the level. I persuaded the others to trust you, and you pay me back like this!'

'Allerton? Henry?'

'Yeah, Henry. Gullible Henry,' came the bitter affirmation. 'Why the hell did I trust a reporter? I must need my bloody head seen to. And now I've got Della and Baz on my case and the office looking like a bombsite. Why did you have to trash the place, Ben? After everything I told you. Christ, I really had you wrong, didn't I?'

'Hold on,' Ben exclaimed, trying to take it all in. 'Trash the place? I didn't.'

'Don't give me that crap, Baz saw you.'

'Oh, and he'd be a reliable witness, wouldn't he? High as a kite half the time, I'd say.'

'Are you denying you went back to the hut last night?'

Ben hesitated. His inherent honesty had got him into trouble a number of times, and had almost certainly held back his career, but he just couldn't seem to shake it. 'I'm not denying that I was there, but whoever trashed the place, it wasn't me,' he said. 'If I were you, I'd look a little closer to home.'

The conversation with Allerton left him feeling a little unsettled. He seemed a decent, if misguided, sort and Ben hadn't liked going behind his back in the first place, but, on top of that, to be blamed for something that he had not and would never have done made it so much worse.

A late breakfast was interrupted by yet another call, this time from the editor who had commissioned the piece on the Hungarian horsemen, checking on his progress. The idea of spending the day in and around Truman's yard held little appeal for Ben in his current state of mind, and so he seized on this alternative with alacrity, promising that he was intending to spend the rest of the day with the troupe, who should by now have arrived and started to set up at their new venue.

Deciding to put Eddie Truman and the whole Cajun King incident out of his mind for the day, Ben set off just before midday for West Sussex and the equestrian centre where the Csikós were to put on their show for the following three nights.

In mainland Europe, the troupe rarely put on such a quantity of small-scale performances, their reputation being for spectacular equestrian *son et lumière* style shows, staged at historic outdoor venues on spring and summer evenings.

The circumstances of their touring England at such a strange time of the year had come about precisely for that reason. When the millionaire promoter who had paved the way for this visit had first approached them they had turned him

114

down, their diary for the year already full. But Ronnie Devlin was determined, finally convincing them that a series of smaller shows at indoor venues in the early part of the year was an ideal way to introduce their special magic to the English public. He planned a tour for them that would culminate in three full-scale spectaculars, shortly before they were due to start their season on the continent. He was, he told them, completely confident that at the end of it their troupe would be a hot property and able to push their performance fees sky-high when they returned the following year.

After much persuasion the Csikós agreed. It had been their intention to extend their tour to England – one of them confided in Ben – just as soon as they had enough financial security to make a trip across the Channel a viable proposition. Devlin had provided that security and so the deal was struck, with all parties very content.

After stopping twice to ask directions, Ben located the Csikós' new camp in a field close to the indoor arena where they were to perform. As before, the four enormous horse-transporters and one big stock lorry were drawn up in a row; beyond those, Ben could see the two articulated lorries that carried the props, sound-and-lighting equipment and feed supplies. Parked in a quiet corner was the farrier's van, the gas-powered forge already in use, and, under trees at the side of the field, business was underway at the large catering wagon.

As he turned through the gateway and saw the hustle and bustle of the camp, Ben experienced a bubbling undercurrent of excitement. It reminded him suddenly, sharply, of the sensation he'd often felt as a child when he and his brother had arrived – in their parents' horsebox – at a particularly important show. The memory wasn't one he welcomed.

He parked and went in search of a familiar face. The entire troupe was well aware of him and knew his business but, having only known them for a relatively short time, he found their collective dark, gypsyish looks rather confusing. The majority of the Csikós were members of two families – the Bardus and the Vargas; some, by marriage, were members of both. As yet, with the exception of Nico and two others, Ben could not, with confidence, put names to the faces.

He found Nico and one of his brothers busy with a mallet, two iron posts and a quantity of orange plastic netting, apparently mending the fence that formed the boundary of a temporary paddock. In the far corner of this, standing together in a big, open-fronted barn, were the ten untrained horses that formed a 'wild' herd for the purposes of the performance.

There were also, Ben knew, fifteen highly-schooled performing horses. Most of these were Hungarian-bred but they also included two Arabs, three Andalusians, one huge grey shire, and Bajnok, the beautiful black, Dutch-bred Friesian, who was Nico's pride and joy. These ridden horses, many of them stallions, were never turned out together for fear of injury.

'Nico. How's it going?' Ben called as he approached.

'Ben! Good, good.' Nico flashed his brilliant smile. 'But where were you when we had all the hard work to do?'

'Oh, you know us Englishers, soft as butter; can't stand the pace,' he replied airily. 'Trouble?' He indicated the fence.

'Oh, no. It is just these horses still think they're at the races. They run round and round and one of them catches his foot and phoom! – the fence is down.'

As if to illustrate his report, one or two of the horses started to move again, snaking their heads at the others to get them moving, and suddenly the whole herd were in motion, streaming across the field to the fence and then turning at the last moment to run round the perimeter. Ben watched them appreciatively.

'There's some quite nice stock there.'

Nico nodded. 'Sadly it's not looks that win races, but something in here.' He put his clenched fist against his chest. 'And none of these horses has it. Each one of these is somebody's broken dream.'

'Why, Nico, you're quite a poet,' Ben teased. 'Do you know where Jakob is?'

'He's at the stables helping Tamás with the shire. The horse – how would you say? – he stepped on himself in the lorry.' Nico made the 's' in Tamás soft, as in sugar. 'It is no problem but a stitch is put in; yes?'

'I understand. I'll go and find him.'

Jakob Varga (pronounced Yackob) was a retired performer, now head trainer and part of the road crew, and he was the troupe member whom Ben

117

knew best. Tamás Istvan, his son-in-law, was a qualified vet as well as being one of the riders. Ben had a great deal of respect for this quiet man, having watched him perform an extremely delicate operation, under local anaesthetic, to extract a splinter from the vicinity of a horse's eye.

He set off in the direction indicated by Nico's carelessly waved hand, passing the towering horse-transporters, each of which provided travelling accommodation for four horses and three or four of the troupe. Static, the horseboxes were roomy enough to comfortably house one or even two of the horses, and they had generous living space for their human occupants.

He found Jakob and Tamás tending the massive grey shire in one of the loose boxes they were renting from the equestrian centre. The yard was a busy place, with what seemed to Ben a surprisingly large number of resident staff in evidence, their faces alight with excited curiosity over their exotic visitors.

'Ben. We thought you had deserted us.' Of wiry build and somewhere between fifty and sixty years old, Jakob was no more than five feet seven inches tall, but it was five-feet seven of whipcord toughness. Shrewd black eyes looked out of a face with leathery brown skin, and his smile had a hole at its top right corner. He was the patriarchal figure among the Csikós, loved and respected by all, and the natural choice as group ambassador in dealings with press and the public. Ben had liked him immediately.

'It's only been three days,' Ben protested. 'How's the horse?'

'He's good. Tamás has performed his miracles, as usual. Melles will be fit to perform tonight. Is that not so?' He addressed this last to his compatriot, who was packing surgical instruments away in his bag.

Tamás looked up and nodded with a slight smile.

'Melles?' Again the soft 's'. Ben rolled the word around his tongue. 'What does it mean?'

'Big-chested. Like me,' Jakob joked, putting a hand on his upper torso. 'Will you be here for the performance tonight?'

Ben said he would, ruthlessly suppressing any stirrings of conscience regarding his agreement to work for Truman.

'Good, good. Come and watch Ferenc ride Duka.' He gave the big grey a friendly slap on the shoulder and came to where Ben waited, by the door. 'This will be for you a big treat.'

'It will be a big treat *for me*,' Ben corrected him, with a smile. Jakob's English was already better than many of the others' but he was keen to improve, and had asked for Ben's help as soon as they were introduced. 'But you're right, it *will* be a big treat. Lead on, my friend.'

Ferenc Kovac – who, with his sister Anna, was the only member of the troupe who was not related to either the Bardus or Vargas – was schooling the white Andalusian stallion, Duka, in a sanded round-pen behind the centre's indoor arena. The area was ringed by several raised tiers of bench seating and covered by a felted roof supported on what looked like sawn-off telegraph poles; the whole effect was something like an auction ring. Ben and Jakob slipped into seats two rows back and watched, for the most part in admiring silence, as horse and rider went through their paces.

The white horse wore only his workaday tack, his mane hanging in loose braids and his tail doubled up and bandaged to keep it clean. Ferenc also, in grubby jeans and a sweatshirt, was a far cry from the glamour of his showtime persona, but to Ben the effect was just as magical. Horse and rider moved in perfect harmony, performing the intricate moves with seemingly effortless ease, never giving a sign of the cues that passed between them. The cold wind whistling around the back of Ben's neck was forgotten and when, at length, they stopped in the centre of the circle and saluted an imaginary audience, he broke into spontaneous applause.

Ferenc looked up, apparently having been unaware of their presence, and repeated the bow.

Jakob and Ben made their way down to open the entrance gate as horse and rider made their way over, and Jakob called out something to Ferenc in his own tongue.

Ben saw a touch of annoyance flash across the rider's swarthy, hawk-like face, and he threw up one hand in a gesture of frustration.

'What did you say to him?' he asked, stepping back slightly as Duka passed on his way out.

'I told him the horse was a little stiff on some of his right turns; he was – what's the word? – pulling away, er . . .'

'Resisting,' Ben supplied. '*I* couldn't see it.'

'No, neither could I,' Jakob confessed,

laughing. 'But Ferenc has the big head. If you praise him he becomes lazy and thinks he does not have to try so hard the next time.'

'Who is the better rider: Ferenc or Nico?' In the few days he had known them, Ben had picked up on a thread of tension between the two and he suspected that Ferenc, who was the senior by some five or six years, envied Nico his position as star of the show.

'Ah, now you could get me into trouble,' Jakob said, shaking his head. 'I have for years refused to answer this question.'

'It's not for the article, and I won't tell anyone,' Ben promised.

'I suspect you already know the answer. Tell me, if I asked you the question, what would you say?'

'I'm no expert and I couldn't really say why, but I think . . . Nico.'

'Hmm. Actually, as riders there is little between them. Indeed, Ferenc is perhaps the more correct . . . er, sharp?'

'Accurate? Precise?'

'Yes, precise. But Nico,' his face softened fractionally. 'Nico is the better horseman. He is a natural. He is not complete until he is on a horse. It is a God-given gift and it shines from him when he performs. It is something that you cannot teach. Nico has it and Ferenc has not; he knows he has not but I will never tell him so and he keeps hoping that one day . . .'

They were making their way back across the field in the general direction of the catering caravan as they talked. Passing the first of the horse-transporters they heard a voice raised in what sounded like an angry growl, and a horse's chestnut rump backed rapidly into view just feet from the two of them. It was one of the Arab horses and it stopped with head and tail high, showing the whites of its eyes and stretching its top lip forward in obvious agitation. Hanging on to the other end of its lead rope was the man who'd been helping Nico earlier. As quickly as the whole thing had started, it was over. The handler had the horse under control and, patting its neck to relieve the tension, gave them a rueful smile.

'Trouble, András?' Jakob enquired mildly.

András rattled off something unintelligible, adding in a tragic voice for Ben's benefit, 'He bites me!'

Ben laughed as they moved on.

'Vadas is a wicked horse,' Jakob said, shaking his head. 'Vadas,' he spelt it out for Ben, 'means "hunter". You turn your back for just a moment and he will stretch out his neck and bite you. It is a big joke to him but it hurts a little.'

Ben, who was well-acquainted with the size of equine teeth, imagined it hurt a lot.

Beside the last lorry Ferenc was washing the sweat off Duka with a sponge. Relaxed, the Andalusian looked a shadow of his showy self. Jakob went across to speak to the horse, finding something in his pocket to feed to him. The damp, whiskery nose snuffled his palm for more.

Jakob looked round to where Ben stood, still some feet away.

'He's handsome, is he not?'

'Beautiful.'

Jakob's gaze lingered thoughtfully on Ben's face for a moment, then he turned his attention back to the horse, giving him another titbit before moving on to the catering wagon with Ben.

'You interest me, Ben Copperfield.'

'I do?' Ben said warily.

They had collected coffee and hot pies and were sitting at one of the plastic tables under the wagon awning. 'Yes. You love horses – I can see it in your eyes – and yet you shrink from them. You seek them out but you don't want to be near them.'

Ben was taken aback.

'It's a job, that's all,' he said dismissively.

'There are other jobs.'

'There are. But you're right; I do love horses. I think they're beautiful creatures but that doesn't necessarily mean I want to ride them.'

'Have you never ridden?'

'As a child. I lost interest.'

'Did you?' Jakob's intense scrutiny was becoming uncomfortable.

'Look, what does it matter? I'm here to do a job; I don't have to get involved with the horses; just write about them. And about you.'

The Hungarian nodded, lowering his eyes at last.

'You are right. I was rude; you will forgive me?'

Immediately Ben felt remorse.

'There's nothing to forgive. But you've reminded me. I do have a job to do and I ought to be getting some notes down.' He took a hand-held cassette recorder from the pocket of his fleece. 'So, tell me about the Csikós.'

123

'Csikós.' He pronounced it Tchikaush, as Ben had learned to. 'It is the name given to the Magyar horse-herders. There is a saying in my country – "Hungarians were created by God to sit on horseback" – and we believe it is true.' Jakob sat back in his chair, successfully diverted and clearly happy to talk at length about his passion.

Ben sighed a secret sigh, placed the quietly whirring recorder on the table and prepared for the long haul.

The show that evening was the best Ben had seen so far. The arena was bigger than the one at their first venue and the facilities better. The troupe made good use of the extra space and had rigged up a dry-ice machine and better lighting. For the first time, Ben began to get a real taste of what it was that had made the Csikós the talk of the town all over Europe.

The show opened with low, greenish lights and all the untrained horses loose in the arena. First they were seen as just so many silhouettes shifting restlessly in the mist, then they were gathered and sent round at a gallop by one of the trained Spanish stallions, himself free and riderless.

Ben knew the herd consisted mainly of ex-racehorses, bought cheaply by Nico and Tamás a couple of weeks in advance of the troupe's arrival in England. They had chosen all geldings so the stallions wouldn't be distracted from their work, but they fulfilled no other criteria except for physical soundness and a basic willingness to mix with one another. Unbridled, though, and with long manes and tails flowing, they gave all the impression of wildness that was necessary.

Two ridden horses joined those in the arena and what followed might have been described as an excerpt from some kind of equestrian ballet: ridden and loose horses whirling and running with supreme grace in the mist; the whole so well-timed it was almost impossible to believe that only three of the thirteen were actually under human control.

As the loose horses were allowed to escape from the arena and the three stallions came forward to make their bows, Ben joined in the rapturous applause with just as much enthusiasm as those around him. He was watching from a seat at the head of the arena, just behind the commentary position, which was manned by an overweight, retired rider called Emilian who had a flair for the dramatic.

The performance continued and, as before, Ben was enchanted by it all: displays by the three Andalusians, sometimes together, sometimes individually or in pairs; appearances by the two chestnut Arabs in the flowing robes and tasselled trappings of the desert; the novelty of Melles, the shire, performing quite intricate high-school moves with surprising grace; and Nico, garbed in black and silver, with a wide-brimmed black hat, aboard the magnificent black Dutch stallion, Bajnok.

András and Miklós – Nico's brothers – first on foot and then mounted, displayed mindboggling skill with the traditional twelve-foot-long bullwhips of the Hungarian herdsman. They then returned later with one of the Andalusians to perform a clowning routine that disguised the difficulty of the vaulting they were doing.

A surprise for Ben was the sight of Nico's sister, Jeta, emerging first as an Eastern siren, veiled and mysterious aboard the mischievous Vadas, then later accompanied by Ferenc's sister, riding Duka and one of the other Andalusians, and exhibiting a skill and daring to rival their male counterparts.

It was clear that Jeta, like her brother, thrived on the charged atmosphere of the theatre. Dressed alike in sparkling costumes of scarlet and black, and riding matching white stallions, the two dark-eyed girls were intended to mirror one another as they performed the same routine in perfect synchronicity. In reality though, Jeta's sparkling presence drew the eye in a way that her co-star failed to. As they left the arena to tumultuous applause, Ben found that he'd been watching Nico's sister almost the whole time.

The part of the performance that followed was one of Ben's favourites. It featured all the six male riders – including Tamás, the vet, and Sulio, his son, who had yet to reach his fourteenth birthday – proudly riding the Magyar horses with their girthless felt saddles, and demonstrating the native horsemanship that had made them famous. In his commentary, Emilian explained the practical origins of the 'tricks' the audience were seeing.

The purpose of the unfastened saddles was, he told the crowd, to enable the Csikós to catch and mount their horses in seconds in the event of a stampede or other emergency.

126

The six, dressed in the Csikós' traditional costume, rode into the arena at a gallop, reined in hard and leapt off the horses, who then dropped to lie flat in the sand at their feet. Within moments their riders were also lying down, and where there had been half a dozen ridden horses, there were now just so many mounds in the dust.

'The *puszta*, or plains, of Hungary are very large and very flat,' Emilian informed the watching crowd. 'In days gone by, if a horseman wanted to hide – whether from bandit or lawman – this was the only way to do it.'

As he finished speaking, the six riders got to their feet then stepped up on to the ribcages of their mounts and began to crack their whips with flamboyant enthusiasm. This exercise, the audience learned, was to accustom the horses to gunfire; privately Ben doubted that many of the plainsmen, past or present, led such exciting lives.

Having demonstrated the horses' courage under fire, the Csikós lay down with them once more, resting their heads in the angle of belly and hind leg, and tipped their hats forward over their eyes.

'Warm, comfortable, and always ready to leap up and make their escape – what better place for a siesta? And when it rained, this . . .' the commentary continued after a pause, '. . . was the driest place on the *puszta*.'

On cue, the horses rolled on to their stomachs and sat up like so many dogs, holding the position while their riders moved to sit between their straightened front legs. Ben's cynicism deepened.

Still, it made good entertainment and the applause was greatly appreciative.

Ten seconds later, the horses were on their feet and the Csikós were once more in their saddles. 'But it's not all work . . .'

One of the riders produced a red bandanna from the pocket of his culotte-like trousers and waved it aloft. With whoops and cries, a madcap game of tag ensued, the nimble horses twisting and turning faster than the eye could follow, as the riders endeavoured to snatch the cloth from each other.

'Try and keep your eye on the handkerchief, ladies and gentlemen,' Emilian urged. 'See if you can guess who has it at the end.'

Ben had tried three times before, and been wrong three times; tonight was no different. As the game wound to a close, the crowd shouted suggestions and each rider showed his hands in turn until finally Miklós owned up; *he* had the bandanna.

After they had taken their bows and galloped out Melles, the shire, returned with András and his brother reprising their clowning routine. Partway through this a commotion was heard in the area beyond the entrance. Heads had just begun to turn that way, momentarily distracted, when there came a warning shout and one of the white stallions burst into the arena, galloping wildly with its saddle half under its belly and its rider clinging precariously to its side.

Even though he knew it was a sham, Ben couldn't prevent the lurch of shock that seized his body in that first instant. It was so well set up. He defied anyone to sit through it with completely unruffled composure. Wrenching his gaze from Nico's play-acting he watched the people around him, seeing in their faces the horror that he'd felt the first time.

As Nico pulled off his miraculous 'recovery' Ben saw the expressions shift through relief to slightly embarrassed amusement, as the audience looked around them and realised that they had all been similarly taken in. Ben clapped with the rest of them. He had to take his hat off to the troupe; it was a wonderful piece of theatre.

The arena cleared, the lights dimmed, and one by one the riders returned to do a lap in the spotlight and assemble for their final bows. Jeta and Anna sat sideways behind Miklós and András on two of the Spanish stallions, with Ferenc on Duka; Tamás rode Melles, and Ben was surprised to see the young Sulio riding Bajnok – normally Nico jealously guarded the privilege of partnering the black.

The rest of the crowd had noticed Nico's absence too, and had just begun to murmur to one another when they were interrupted by a slow drum roll.

'This is a special moment,' Emilian announced dramatically. 'Ladies and gentlemen, you are about to witness a feat of extraordinary skill and daring. Nicolae Bardu will demonstrate – for perhaps the first time in this country – the almost unbelievable Great Plains Five: the *Puszta Otus*!'

The drum roll intensified and Ben joined the rest of the audience in looking towards the entrance expectantly. This was new to him, too.

129

A fanfare of trumpets heralded Nico's triumphant reappearance and, after keeping them waiting for a few more expectant seconds, he erupted into the spotlight riding a tide of galloping horses and whooping at the top of his voice. As they swept around the arena it could be seen that he was actually standing on the rumps of the two rearmost animals and holding the reins of those and three others in his hands, somehow keeping their jostling forms together and also finding time to crack the whip above his head.

He circled the arena twice at great speed, to rapturous applause, before guiding the Magyar horses into the centre where the rest of the troupe were gathered, and jumping down with a flourish. At once, the horses separated a little, and it became obvious that all that had held them together was their own forward motion and Nico's skill with whip and reins.

'Ladies and gentlemen; the *Puszta Otus*!' Emilian cried. 'Thank you for sharing this evening with us. We hope you have enjoyed yourselves. If you wish to meet the Csikós and some of the horses, please make your way to the foyer when the lights come up. No unaccompanied children please, and please to hold on to the hands of children under twelve. Thank you. If you have had a good time, do come again and please, tell your friends about us.'

Outside the arena, five minutes later, Ben waited in the shadows and watched while Nico, Jeta, Ferenc and András supervised the introduction of the crowd to Duka, Melles and Bajnok.

'Not too close – give the horses some room. Now, who has a birthday today?' Ferenc enquired, as the people gathered round.

Several of the children put up their hands.

'And which of you deserves a treat?'

'Me! Me!' Most of them started to jump up and down.

'OK. Make a nice queue and we'll ask the horses if you can sit on their backs.'

Suddenly, at least twenty more children remembered that it was their birthday, too. Smiling, Ben watched as the queue grew and grew. Ferenc didn't seem to mind; in fact he appeared to be enjoying himself. It was a side of his character that Ben hadn't seen before. Then, as the first of the happy children were lifted on to the horses, Ben caught a glimpse of a familiar face on the other side of the crowd. He shifted position to try and get a better view but the man was no longer there. Skirting the throng, he scanned the shadows in vain for another sight of him, trying to remember where he'd seen the man before.

'Ben! What did you think of our show tonight?' Jakob came out of the darkness.

'Amazing! It gets better every time.'

'Ah, this is nothing. When you see the complete performance you will not believe your eyes,' he said proudly. 'Listen, you will stay tonight, yes? We have plenty of room.'

'Well . . . If you're sure.' He didn't particularly relish the idea of the drive home. His business with Truman could surely wait an hour or two in the morning.

'Of course I am sure. I said so didn't I?' Jakob clapped him heartily on the back. 'Now I must find Emil . . .'

Alone again, Ben glanced at the crowd around Nico, Ferenc and the others and decided, as his last cup of coffee was but a distant memory, to head for the catering wagon. He knew that once the horses were settled it was customary for the troupe to gather there after a performance for hot dogs and beer, and he was sure that Gyorgy would have preparations well under way.

The area around the horse-transporters was quiet and dark. There was a light inside the first of them, where he knew Vadas and the other Arab were housed, but the next two were in darkness, the ramps down and waiting for Bajnok and Duka to finish their public relations exercise.

As he drew level with the last of the lorries there were definite sounds of activity from inside. Heavy scraping noises and several dull thuds were punctuated by bursts of excited discussion. The words were unintelligible to Ben, spoken in the Csikós' native tongue, or a mixture of that and Romanes, the language of the Gypsies.

There was another more violent outbreak of banging, and Ben hesitated. Something was obviously wrong. He knew he should go and see but the thought caused a swift stirring of panic deep inside.

While he stood in an agony of indecision, a door opened in the side of the horsebox and a slight figure jumped down into the rectangle of light it shed and ran towards Ben.

Sulio.

Coming from the light into the darkness the boy nearly ran into him but, seeing him at the last moment, he stopped and grabbed Ben's arm, saying his name with a breathless mixture of relief and urgency.

'Ben. Ben! You come now! Please! You help us!'

Resisting the insistent tug on his arm, Ben looked round helplessly but no angel of mercy hove into view.

'What's happened? What's wrong?'

In his agitation Sulio garbled something incomprehensible, lapsing into his own language.

'Slow down – slow down,' Ben told him. 'In English.'

'Ben. You must come. Please!'

There was just enough light to see the beseeching look in the boy's eyes and, in spite of his reluctance, Ben allowed himself to be led, half-running, towards the open door.

As they reached it the banging started again with renewed vigour and Sulio leaped inside, confident that Ben would follow.

It was the first time Ben had been in the back of one of the transporters; in fact, it was the first time he'd been inside a horsebox of any kind since he was about the same age that Sulio was now. As he followed the boy towards the back of the lorry the thudding intensified and he could feel the whole vehicle rocking on its suspension.

The partitions in the main body of the transporter, usually arranged to form several small travelling compartments, had been folded back and arranged so that two larger stalls were

133

formed. In the first of these one of the Magyar horses was shifting nervously, looking back over its shoulder towards the other compartment.

With mounting apprehension, Ben went further.

Sulio stopped in the entrance to the second stall, spoke rapidly to whoever was inside, then turned wide anxious eyes to look at Ben as he caught up.

Ben paused in the doorway, taking in the scene.

The occupant of the stall, another of the Magyar horses, had rolled too close to the partition and got itself cast, its legs trapped in a tangle against the wall and, just to compound matters, its head was wedged in the corner. In an effort to try and stop it panicking, Tamás had thrown his jacket over the animal's head and was kneeling on its neck. The partition bore the evidence of the battering it had taken from the steel-shod hooves and the horse's chestnut coat was drenched with sweat.

Tamás looked up at Ben from his position in the corner.

'Ben . . . We need to get a rope . . . on his legs,' the vet said, breathing hard.

'Where do I find one?' Ben asked, his voice giving no sign that he was fighting a rising tide of terror.

Sulio tugged at his sleeve and lifted a canvas lunge rein from the rubber matting.

'Here. I bring – but . . .'

'It's too dangerous – the boy's not strong enough. We'll have to pull him over and . . .' Tamás rode a determined surge by the horse,

'. . . and out of the corner, or he could break his neck.'

'We should get some more help,' Ben said, trying to function normally while a voice in his head was shrieking, *You can't do this. Get out, now!*

The vet shook his head. 'No time.'

Sulio held the roughly coiled, flat canvas rein out to Ben.

'You do it,' he said imperatively, unaware that he was asking Ben to relive a nightmare.

Somehow Ben found himself advancing into the compartment, the lunge rein clasped in his shaking hands and his eyes fixed on the ungainly bulk of the upturned barrel of the horse.

'Right. Make a loop,' Tamás instructed, 'and see if you can get it over his back legs. Both, if you can.'

When Ben was a couple of feet away from the horse's rear end, it suddenly launched into a fresh attempt to free itself. With a groan of desperate effort it lurched and began to thrash its legs against the partition wall. The noise was deafening and the hot sweaty smell of the animal filled Ben's nostrils. He froze, rooted to the spot, his chest constricting as a cold wave of panic washed over him.

The voice in his head was thunderous. *Get out! Now!*

6

'No, Ben, get back!'

Even as he stood there, transfixed, hands
caught his shoulders and pushed him further
away, sending him staggering into the wall next
to the opening. The shock of the contact seemed
to clear his head and as he spread his arms against
the padded metalwork to regain his balance, he
could see that help had arrived in the capable
shape of Jakob and Emilian.

In the corner by the door the Magyar saddle
was propped against the wall; alongside it was one
of the bullwhips used in the display. In a seam-
less movement Jakob snatched up the whip, with
its twelve-foot thong, turned towards the horse
and, employing a deft flick of the wrist, sent the
plaited leather snaking out to coil itself round the
animal's front legs. The thong only made a turn
or two, but that was all that was needed.

'Now, Tamás!' he barked, Tamás scrambled
clear, and with Emilian's help, Jakob managed to
tip the balance of the chestnut horse away from

the wall and roll it into the centre of the stall. With another flick the whip was loosened and, as Ben slid sideways to the open door, taking Sulio with him, the animal lurched to its feet and stood swaying on spread legs.

All at once the close confines of the lorry were too much for Ben. His heart was pounding like a trip-hammer and he felt as though he would suffocate if he didn't get out to the open air. Leaving Sulio at the stall door he all but ran along the narrow corridor to the side-access door, dropped down on to the grass, and leaned back against the bodywork to drink in deep, reviving gulps of cold night air, the evaporating sweat on his face and body accentuating the chill.

He was still there, albeit a good deal calmer, when Jakob appeared in the doorway a couple of minutes later and jumped down beside him.

'You all right, Ben?'

'Yeah. Bit claustrophobic in there.' Ben brought both fists up towards his chest as he searched for a word that the Hungarian would understand. 'A bit close – not enough space.'

Jakob gave him a long, considered look in the moonlight, then nodded.

'It can be.'

Ben looked down at his toes. 'I, er . . . wasn't much help.'

'It was dangerous. Tamás was wrong to have asked you. I told him so.'

'It's not his fault. He didn't know what else to do. He was afraid Sulio would get hurt.'

'Even so.' Jakob looked along the row of lorries to where a lamp shone strongly under the awning

137

of Gyorgy's wagon. A tempting smell was wafting on the breeze. 'Anyway, Tamás has things under control now. What do you say we go and eat before the vultures arrive?'

Ben didn't feel particularly hungry but, grateful for the change of scene and subject, he fell in readily with this plan.

A spare berth was found for him and Mouse in the lorry shared by Jakob, Emil and Vesh Bardu. Vesh was a contemporary of Jakob and his brothers, and the troupe's resident farrier. He was also some relation to Nico and his brothers, but Ben was too tired to work out this further addition to the complexities of the Bardu–Varga family tree and, at that moment, not sufficiently interested either.

The events of the evening had shaken the very foundations of the barriers he had built up over the years. He'd thought he had it all under control; that aside from the occasional disturbed night when the dreams returned, he had put it all behind him. He'd grown adept at avoiding situations where he'd be challenged, so why the hell had he allowed himself to be drawn so close to this one?

Tossing and turning on the surprisingly comfortable bunk, his eyes wide open, sleep was a million miles away. He was kept awake partly by the buzzing of an overactive brain and later, when weariness threatened to slow the thought process down, by the fear of what sleep would bring.

He wasn't sure whether or not his paralysing fear had been recognised by the others in the heat of the moment, but he was pretty certain

that Jakob had both seen and correctly inter-
preted his panic. The knowledge caused Ben
shame. He had great respect for Jakob.

After an hour or so of wakefulness, listening
to Emil's stentorian snores and feeling increasingly uncomfortable in the narrow confines of
the vehicle, Ben slid off the bunk and put his
shoes on. With Mouse at his heels he gathered
his jacket and let himself out of the lorry, hoping
there was no alarm set.

The site was peaceful; only the odd thud of a
restless hoof inside the transporters disturbed the
silence and, now and again, the call of a tawny
owl. Ben remembered how, as kids, he and his
twin brother had learned to imitate the owls
around their home, becoming so convincing that
more than once they had been swooped on by a
patrolling bird, guarding its patch.

God! Why did he have to think about Alan,
now? He'd come out to clear his mind, not to
drag more memories out of the closet. There was
no point in trying to remember the good times
– sure, there'd been plenty of those, but he knew
from experience the brain's stubborn determin-
ation to dwell on the melancholic in the small
hours of the night. Something to do with brain
chemistry, a GP had once told him, but knowing
that was no bloody help at all.

He began to walk, his feet crunching on the
frosty grass and the full moon illuminating his
way. Mouse, trotting as though on hot coals, kept
close, her back hunched and ears flat on her head.

'Are you cold, sausage? I'm sorry. We'll go back
in a minute.'

Walking along behind the vehicles, Ben wandered across to the area where the untrained geldings were corralled. They were all in the barn now, a collection of shadowy shapes pulling hay from the racks or just dozing sleepily on their feet. Four legs and joints that locked out enabled them to do this, but still Ben found it difficult to imagine. What if humans could do the same? he mused. Hotels could really pack 'em in, then. They could advertise Standing Room Only.

Moving along the line of the fence he wondered what the horses made of their altered circumstances, and hoped they weren't too cold. Most of them were clipped out and had probably come from stables or had, at the very least, been rugged up. Nico said they would soon acclimatise, but Ben would have put rugs on them.

For the first time that day he thought about Cajun King. He was clipped. Was he standing shivering somewhere, or was he in a stable being looked after? Was he even alive? How would you get rid of a creature that size? Dig a hole? Not with a spade, surely? You'd need a JCB. Or what about an existing pit? A quarry perhaps, or a slurry tank. Would they ever know what had happened to him?

Ben sighed. What a waste.

One or two of the horses caught sight of him and came to the front of the barn, looking enquiringly in his direction. Calm, inquisitive, uncomplicated; eager for human company. As always, Ben felt their pull, but the idea of getting close brought the faint flutterings of panic deep inside.

Depression settled on him and he turned away.

Maybe it would be better if he kept his distance from horses completely and concentrated his career in another area. It wasn't the first time he'd considered the idea, though, and, as before, he found he couldn't imagine a life without them.

The chill had penetrated his jacket and, feeling sympathy for Mouse, Ben headed back towards Jakob's lorry. As he reached the first of the transporters a figure detached itself from the shadows and a voice asked quietly, 'Did it help?'

Jakob.

Ben didn't pretend to misunderstand him.

'Not really. It never does.'

'If you want to talk . . .'

'I don't think so. Thanks all the same.' Ben kept walking, but slowly. In a way it was a lie. Part of him longed to talk but suppression had become a habit he was wary of breaking. It was as if to bring it out into the open would be to give his fear substance.

Jakob fell in beside him.

'You *should* talk about it, Ben,' he advised softly. 'Fear is a natural reaction. It is nothing to be ashamed of.'

A picture of his brother as he'd last seen him – eyes closed in a white face – flashed across Ben's mind and a fizz of remembered shock stung him, making his reply sharper than he'd intended.

'What the hell do you know about it? You know nothing about me!'

As soon as he'd uttered the words he wished them unsaid. It was no way to speak to someone who'd shown him nothing but courtesy. He checked his stride, desperately trying to formulate

141

an apology, but it was already too late. Jakob merely inclined his head and turned away without a word.

Damn and hell! Ben thought explosively. But how could he open up to someone he'd only just met – when he'd bottled it all up for almost twenty years? He'd never even told Lisa, for God's sake!

Heartsick and frustrated, he gazed up into the star-filled sky, but the millions of cold pinpricks of light did nothing except ridicule his concerns.

On the edge of his vision, something moved.

Ben's head whipped round and he stared hard into the darkness, his depression forgotten in an instant.

Nothing. Everything appeared calm.

It was tempting to just shrug it off. Movement in itself wasn't alarming. It was probably just the loose horses having a minor disagreement and kicking up their heels. They would settle.

No. There it was again. The moonlight gleamed on something metallic, way over by the horse barn. Surely if it was one of the Csikós they would be carrying a torch, wouldn't they?

'Jakob!' Ben hissed, hoping the Hungarian hadn't gone too far. 'Jakob, there's someone over by the horses.'

'Ben?'

He could hear Jakob's feet crunching towards him over the frosty grass and was just about to repeat himself when there was a dull crack, followed immediately by a flurry of hoofbeats as the ten loose horses burst out of the barn en masse and stampeded across their corral.

'They'll run the fence!' Jakob hurried to Ben's side.

Ben was looking the other way, over towards the field's boundary with the road.

'Shit! The gate's open!' he exclaimed and broke into a run.

'Ben!' Jakob's shout followed him, but he knew there wasn't time to answer. From the sound of it, the horses had broken through the fence and some could well be heading for the gateway. Ben had the angle and distance on his side, but the horses had turn of foot emphatically on theirs.

It appeared to be a lost cause but he had to try. He'd never been any great shakes as a sprinter – his height and build leant themselves more readily to endurance running – but he was fitter than most, and he had desperation spurring him on.

That gate had been closed before the troupe turned in for the night, which meant that someone had opened it, and that could only be because they intended the horses to go through it.

The other side of the hedge was a B-road leading left towards a village, or right, a very short distance to a dual carriageway. If the horses got on to that there could be carnage.

The night was full of noise now. As Ben tore over the crisp, sparkling turf, he could hear, above the drumming hooves, a whip cracking and several people shouting. Moments later an engine started up and then lights came on, sending his shadow racing far ahead of him.

A quick look showed him that the horses had scattered and, thankfully, not all were running towards the gate, but the two or three that were were overhauling him fast. He couldn't beat

143

them. He'd have to try and turn them. Some hope, in a field this size.

As he sensed them drawing near, he swerved towards them, throwing up his arms and whooping as loud as he could in his breathless state.

It worked – for all of a second.

They threw up their heads, as one, and veered away from him, describing a neat semi-circle before swinging back on to their original course, making a beeline for the gateway. Reaching it just yards ahead of Ben, they shot through without hesitation, their hooves slipping and sliding on the tarmac as they took the corner, turning right for the dual carriageway and chaos.

Racing through the opening some ten seconds behind them, Ben's progress was rudely checked as he cannoned, at full speed, into someone waiting just outside. They both went sprawling on the tarmac but, carried on by his momentum, Ben rolled and came to his feet first, glancing down at the figure he'd flattened.

Dreadlocks and a ferocious scowl; even in the half-dark they were unmistakable.

Baz.

'You stupid bastard!' Ben yelled at him. He had intended to close the gate and then continue the chase, but Baz's presence put paid to that plan. He'd almost certainly open it again.

Ben hesitated. Should he stay and guard the gate, or follow the runaways? Visions of broken limbs and twisted metal filled his head but, in reality, on foot, he hadn't much hope of averting a disaster.

'*Damn* you!' Moving to shut the gate, he took

out his frustration on Baz. There must have been venom in his tone because the tousled one scrambled to his feet and backed off, holding his hands in front of him as if to ward Ben off.

Keeping a wary eye on the ALSA man as he fastened the catch, Ben became aware of the sound of running feet and someone, possibly Nico, called breathlessly, 'Ben! Stop him!'

Squinting back down the beam of light he was able to make out the silhouettes of two figures running in pursuit of a third, and braced himself to take whatever action was needed.

In the event physical force wasn't necessary. The foremost runner saw Ben waiting and slowed up of his own accord, turning to face his pursuers and holding his hands in the air resignedly.

Nico was the first to catch up. He caught hold of one of the man's arms, twisting it behind his back with perhaps a little more enthusiasm than was called for.

'There's another one here,' Ben called, but when he turned Baz was nowhere to be seen.

The third man loped up, breathing heavily. It was Gyorgy, the ageing cook. With a word or two in his native tongue, Nico handed the prisoner over to his burly countryman and vaulted the gate to land at Ben's side. He had obviously dressed in haste, and wore black jeans and an unzipped leather jacket over a bare torso that would have been the envy of many a fitness fanatic.

'Where are the horses?'

'They went towards the main road,' Ben told him. 'I couldn't stop them.'

Suddenly, in the shadow of the hedge, just a

few yards from them, a car engine started to turn over. In a flash, Ben was at the driver's door, yanking it open and pulling Baz unceremoniously out on to the tarmac and taking his place.

'Nico!' Ben yelled, but the Hungarian was right there, sliding into the passenger seat even as he turned the key in the ignition. The starter motor did its stuff once more and after a few tense moments the engine hiccupped and started.

'Yes!' Ben breathed, shoving the gear lever forward. With wildly spinning tyres they were away. 'Will Gyorgy be all right?' he asked anxiously as they sped down the road.

'Sure. No worry,' Nico declared airily.

It only took a matter of seconds to reach the slip-road that carried traffic on to the dual carriageway, but the loose horses were nowhere to be seen.

'What now?' Nico asked, peering out in all directions.

'We can only go this way, and hope,' Ben replied, accelerating hard. Baz's dilapidated car rattled and shook as the revs mounted.

They saw the lights first. A mess of rear lights, brake lights and hazard lights gathered up ahead.

'Shit!' With a sinking heart, Ben drove on, slowing up as he reached the assembled vehicles and adding the borrowed car's hazard lights to the collection.

Nico was out of the car almost before it stopped and running between the others to reach the front. Following him, Ben pushed through the ragged line of watching motorists to the centre of the drama. There he found Nico inspecting the knees of one horse, on a verge at the side of the road, while a capable-looking woman in tweed held it by means of what looked like a dog lead looped round its neck. Another horse stood nearby, its head drooping and what looked to be a nasty gash on its shoulder. Nobody had caught hold of it yet, but it didn't look as if it was going anywhere in a hurry.

'Came out of bloody nowhere!' a youngish man in jeans and a sweatshirt was proclaiming to all and sundry. 'I 'ad no chance. No-o chance! Ran smack into the side of me. And who's gonna pay for that, I wanna know? Looks like a bloody write-off to me and I've only had it a week!'

'Don't worry, it'll all be taken care of,' Ben told him soothingly, as Nico showed no signs of even having heard the man. 'The insurance will cover it.'

He hoped to God it would, but this wasn't really the time or place to raise the question with Nico.

'Did anyone see another horse?' he asked then, raising his voice to address all those standing near. 'There were three of them.'

There were a number of negative replies but one man had seen it.

'Took off down there like Old Nick was after it!' he called out, pointing further down the road. 'Probably gone into the copse.'

'Thanks. Is that one all right, Nico?' As far as Ben could see, the horse wasn't badly injured.

Nico straightened. 'I think so.' He moved across to the other horse, which raised its head but offered no further resistance to being caught. 'This one is worse. Tamás will have to look at it.'

'I can hear a police car,' someone announced

147

and, falling silent to listen, several others murmured that they could too. Within moments the sound of the siren was unmistakable, and shortly after that the accompanying blue lights could be seen. The car appeared, racing down the opposite carriageway, braked hard as it approached the hold-up, and bumped on to the central reservation where it came to a stop, disgorging two uniformed officers who instantly took charge of the situation.

All in all, by the time the blockage on the dual carriageway had been sorted out and all the horses rounded up, the best part of two hours had passed. The stock lorry was sent to pick up the two horses caught on the road and the third, which was found grazing on the edge of the nearby copse. Tamás dressed their wounds, stitching the gashed shoulder, and, with the fence mended, they were returned with their companions to the barn area where a watch was mounted.

As far as could be established – given the chaos that had reigned – four people, probably all ALSA supporters, had taken part in the raid. Two of them had got away but Gyorgy had held on to Nico's catch and an unmarked police car had come across Baz trying to thumb a lift and picked him up. Ben would dearly liked to have seen his face when he realised just who he'd caught a ride with.

He did see his face a little later, when the police transferred him to one of the duty cars to take him back to the station. Many of the troupe had already returned to their beds but several, Ben included, had gathered under the canopy of Gyorgy's catering wagon for coffee and hot dogs.

No doubt drawn by the prospect of refreshments, the police had been using the area as a makeshift interview room and, as he got to his feet after making a statement, Ben found himself on a collision course with Baz for the second time that night.

The ALSA man, hands secured firmly behind his back and escorted by a policeman, glared with undisguised loathing for a second or two, then spat at him.

'Oi! That's enough of that.' The officer hurried Baz away but he twisted round to look over his shoulder.

'I won't forget this,' he promised and, a little further on, passing Ferenc and Jeta, Ben saw him say something to them too.

Ferenc half-turned to watch him, then his eyes sought out Ben, his expression very thoughtful.

Ben had no problem getting to sleep for what little remained of the night and he slept dreamlessly until past eight, when he awoke to find himself the sole human occupant of the transporter. Mouse was there, curled up at the foot of his bunk. She'd disappeared during the confusion the night before and later, when Ben had called for her, she'd crept out from beneath one of the lorries, shaken herself and followed him to bed.

He got up and dressed, switching on his mobile phone as he did so, and was surprised to find no less than three messages on it. The first was a chatty one from Lisa, telling him that she couldn't stop over with her mum so she'd be back at the cottage that evening after all.

The second was from Logan, saying he'd ring back another time, and the third was Truman, asking why the hell he hadn't answered the previous messages he'd left on his landline.

Feeling that he couldn't really face Truman before breakfast, Ben turned the mobile off again, shaved and went in search of sustenance.

He arrived at the catering wagon about the same time as Jakob, Nico and the others were starting to appear, the difference being that they had already seen to the horses. Most of the troupe members had seen him around by now, and he came in for a share of good-natured ribbing about his late rising.

'How are the horses, the ones that got out?' Ben asked Tamás.

'They are good. A day or two and they'll be good as new.'

'They were lucky.'

'But I still don't understand. Why did they let them out? It was a stupid thing to do. What did they hope for?'

Ben had tried to explain the liberation group's ideals to some of them the night before, with limited success.

'They say they are worried for the horses and yet they let them out into the road,' Nico said shaking his head in bewilderment. 'It makes no sense to me.'

Ben was about to agree with him but Ferenc got in first.

'Maybe you're talking to the wrong man, Nico. Maybe Ben knows more about last night than he tells us.'

'What do you mean?' Nico asked. He looked from Ferenc to Ben and back again.

Ferenc switched to his native tongue but Ben broke in on him.

'No! If you're going to make accusations against me, I've got a right to hear what you say.'

'He's right.' Jakob spoke up, coming over with a plate of toast and bacon. 'But be careful what you say, Ferenc, Ben is our guest.'

'All right. That man last night – the one with the . . . the hair,' Ferenc made a scornful gesture with his hand to illustrate his description. 'He said he'd met Ben before. He said Ben set us up.'

This time Nico launched briefly into Magyar before remembering and changing to English. 'You're crazy! How can you trust the word of a man who has just done such a thing?'

'*Had* you met him before?' Jakob asked Ben. He didn't look particularly perturbed about it.

'Professionally, yes. I was doing an article. We didn't exactly hit it off.' He didn't feel that relating the circumstances of his last run-in with Baz would help his cause.

'Ben helped us last night, Ferenc. I think you must be forgetting that.' Jakob took a large bite of his bacon sandwich and then spoke through it. 'Does anyone else have anything to say about it?'

Apparently nobody had, but Ben wasn't altogether happy.

'I can defend myself, Jakob. Thank you all the same.'

Jakob shook his head emphatically.

'But as our guest you shouldn't have to. No, it is finished now. We'll hear no more of it.'

For a moment there was an awkward silence and then Emil and Miklós started to discuss plans for the day and the talk became more general. Slanting a surly look at Ben, Ferenc shrugged his shoulders, picked up his bacon roll and walked away.

'Emil and I are going to teach Melles a new trick today,' Jakob told Ben after a while. 'Would you like to watch?'

'Oh, I'd love to, but I don't think I can,' Ben said with genuine regret. 'I think I'm going to have to leave you for a day or two.'

'Not because of Ferenc?'

'No. I have another job, which I've been neglecting. I've had messages on my phone. My client is getting impatient.'

'But you will come back to us?' Jakob seemed anxious that he should.

'Yes, I will. But it may not be until your next stop.'

'You should come and see us move – it's quite impressive.'

'I'd like to. Maybe I will.'

'Hey, Gyorgy! Any breakfast left or are we too late?' A feminine voice called out, and Ben glanced up to see Jeta and Anna coming across the field. It was a crisp, bright morning after the clear night and the two girls wore faded denim jeans, thick jumpers and fleeces. Slim and dark, with long, shiny black hair, they were very easy on the eye, and something of Ben's appreciation must have shown in his face because Jakob said with a wry smile, 'Good to look at but hell to live with!'

'Who?' Ben asked, surprised. 'Jeta? Or Anna?'

'Women in general, and Romani women in particular. But I guess you'll have to find out for yourself.'

Ben shook his head. 'Not me. I've got a girlfriend.'

'Well, don't tell Jeta that. What is the saying? A red rag to the bull. Is your girl pretty?'

'Yes, *I* think so,' Ben said, and hesitated. She was Lisa; familiar and comfortable. Part of his life. But it was difficult even to picture her with Jeta around. 'Yes, she is.'

'You don't sound too sure,' Nico said, laughing. 'My sister has that effect.' Clicking his tongue at Mouse, he put his hand down to offer her a piece of toast, but after sniffing it politely she turned her head away.

Jeta was there now, weaving her way between the tables with sinuous grace. She gave Ben a provocative glance from under her lashes as she passed, her hip lightly brushing his shoulder.

Was it provocative? Or was that just how he'd read it? He decided that for his own peace of mind he would do much better to move.

Leaving the canteen behind, he took a deep breath and rang Eddie Truman as he walked across the field. He answered after three rings, his impatience evident straight away.

'Ben! Where the hell are you? I've been trying to reach you.'

'Calm down, Truman. I'm not one of your stable lads,' Ben reminded him. 'What's happened?'

'I can't tell you over the phone. How soon can you get here – ten minutes? Half an hour?'

'No way. I'm in Sussex – it'll be two hours at the very least. I'm sorry.'

'What the bloody hell are you doing in Sussex?'

'Working.'

'Have you got a lead?' Truman asked eagerly.

Immediately Ben felt sympathy. 'No, sorry. This is another job. Something I was already working on. Look I'll be with you as soon as I can.'

As he put the phone back in his pocket, Jakob came up.

'Duka is working well today.'

'Sorry?' Ben suddenly realised that, while he'd been talking to Truman, he'd stopped by one of the schooling areas, where Ferenc was putting the white Andalusian through his paces. 'Oh. Yes, he is.'

'The curse of the mobile telephone,' Jakob mused, correctly interpreting Ben's confusion. 'You can never be alone. They . . .' he brought his hands together expressively '. . . they shrink the world.'

'Yeah. They have their advantages but they've certainly put paid to a whole heap of excuses. But I'm afraid I really do have to go. What it is to be wanted,' he joked.

'Yes, you must go. And when you come back, you and I will find a horse that you can ride.'

'Me?' Ben was jolted. 'But I don't want to ride, I told you.'

Jakob nodded. 'Yes, I know what you said, but I don't believe you.'

'Well, I meant it.' He started to walk away but, undeterred, Jakob fell in beside him.

'Fear itself isn't weakness, you know,' he said,

154

after a moment. 'The weakness is not admitting it. Every time you turn from it, you give it more power over you. You mustn't let it rule your life, Ben.'

'Has it ever occurred to you that I might be quite happy as I am?'

'No. I've seen your eyes. The way you watch Nico and the others. Whatever you may tell me, your eyes betray you.'

Ben shook his head. 'You're wrong.'

'I'm not!' Jakob caught hold of his arm. 'Ben, let me help you. Please?'

'Why do you want to? What does it matter?'

'Because . . .' the Hungarian paused, rolling his eyes heavenwards. 'Oh God, this sounds like a bad movie, but you remind me of my son, Stefan.'

Ben shook his arm free and continued walking. 'You're right. It does sound like a bad movie. So, where is he now?'

'He died in a car crash, many years ago. He was a jockey, a very good one, but he never had a chance to prove himself.'

'I'm sorry. But I'm not your son, and I have my own life to live, in whatever way I choose!' Jakob's persistence had unsettled Ben and he felt that bringing up the subject of his son's death was akin to emotional blackmail. 'Now, I really have to go.'

'But you will come back?'

'Maybe.' Ben threw the word over his shoulder as Jakob slowed and dropped behind but, after a few steps, he stopped and turned. 'Yes. I'll be back. After all, I've got a job to do.'

Jakob smiled. 'Ah yes. The job.'

7

Ben arrived at Castle Ridge just before midday and found Truman on the drive in front of his house, just about to get into his Range Rover. The trainer was wearing olive corduroys and a hefty sweater, topped off with the obligatory waxed jacket, and carried a pair of expensive-looking binoculars slung round his neck. His skin looked sallow under the freckles and his eyes hooded. Ben thought he looked exhausted.

'Ah, Ben. At last. Come on, get in – I'm just going up to watch the last lot.'

'Right, but can I just let my dog out first to stretch her legs? She's been in the car for a couple of hours and she might need a pee.'

'Bring her along. She can get in the back with mine and have a run when the horses have finished.'

'OK, thanks.'

As Ben let Mouse out, Truman opened the tailgate of the Range Rover and two Jack Russells and a bull terrier spilled out on to the gravel in a kind of yapping, growling whirlwind.

'Get back in!' he ordered, and two of them did. The third, and smallest, was picked up unceremoniously by its scruff and dumped with its fellows.

Mouse approached Truman and sniffed his trouser leg suspiciously before looking up at him with just the faintest wag of her long, whiskery tail. However, Ben's suggestion that she jump into the back of the man's car was greeted with a look that unmistakably said, 'You *cannot* be serious!'

'Go on. It'll do you good to mix with your own kind for a change,' Ben said firmly, lifting her in.

She turned round and sat like a débutante amongst prostitutes, neither looking to the right or the left but instead gazing imploringly at Ben as the hatch was slammed.

Truman drove down the drive and along the road for a quarter of a mile before turning into a narrow lane. The Range Rover climbed steeply and his foot was heavy on the accelerator until the rump of the hindmost horse came into sight. The column of walking thoroughbreds stepped off the tarmac on to the verge as the vehicle slowly coasted past. There were maybe thirty in total, money on the hoof; the representation of the dreams of dozens of people tied up in a fragile bundle of flesh, bones and muscle.

The stable-lads and lasses wore an assortment of navy and brown jodhpurs with windproof jackets, and were muffled up in gloves and scarves against the cold north-easterly. Halfway along the string Ben saw Mikey mounted on a lean chestnut, but he was looking straight ahead and didn't see Ben.

Truman was apparently deep in thought and had said nothing so far – surprising, given his volubility on the telephone – so Ben broke the silence.

'How's my brother coming along? Are you pleased with him?'

'Not too bad.' Passing the lead horse, the Range Rover began to pick up speed once more. 'He's riding at Wincanton tomorrow. He's got a couple of quite decent rides, too, because Rollo's picked up a three-day suspension. You should come and watch. I'm going; I'll give you a lift if you like.'

'Thanks. That'd be good.'

Truman turned off the lane through an open field gate and followed the rising crest of the hill to its highest point, where he swung the vehicle round to face the slope and turned the engine off.

'We had another email early this morning,' Truman said, as soon as the diesel motor stopped turning over. 'I have to have the money by Friday. I'm to put it in a black bin-bag, drive to Fordingbridge car park and wait there with my mobile phone for further instructions.'

'Fordingbridge? Why there, I wonder? Does Ford know where the emails are being sent from yet?'

'Yes, but it's no help. The first was from Tunbridge Wells and this morning's was from a library in Basingstoke. There's no problem finding the terminals they were sent from, but no way of tracing the user unless they were stupid enough to log on under their real name, and there's not much hope of that.'

'So what's the plan? Do you pay up?'

'What else can I do? You haven't come up with anything at all?'

Ben shook his head. 'Not yet.' He gave Truman a summary of his dealings with Rackham and the ALSA group. 'And last night four of them were in Haywards Heath making trouble for a touring horse circus that I'm doing an article on. God! They'd hate me calling them that, but I don't know how else to describe them.'

'You spend your working life around horses, but you don't ride, Mikey says.'

'It's not a necessary qualification.'

'But you used to ride for your father, didn't you?'

Ben sighed inwardly. Questions; always questions. Why did he always have to explain himself?

'Yes, I did, but I haven't ridden for a long time,' he said, hoping that would be sufficient; it was, probably because Eddie Truman wasn't a rider himself and didn't understand what an addictive habit it could be.

'So you're confident that ALSA have nothing to do with it?' he said, switching back to his original topic.

'Well, as sure as I can be. I don't know what else I can do; I think I've worn my welcome a bit thin there, to say the very least. To be honest, if they *had* got Cajun King, I shouldn't think they'd be getting involved in all this other stuff or inviting a journalist to interview them. Anyway, I imagine Ford is on their case, too?'

'Yes, I think so, but he doesn't tell me much – just that they're doing all they can and I'll be the first to know if they come up with anything. So what will you do next?'

'That depends on you. What else can you tell me that you aren't telling the police? Who else have you upset?'

Truman took off his cap and scratched his balding head.

'Anyone who's as successful in business as I've been is bound to have made a few enemies on the way,' he said, replacing the cap and turning his green-eyed gaze on Ben. 'And I suppose there've been a couple of people who've left my employment muttering threats about revenge, but I can't think of anyone who'd go so far as this to get back at me – at least none who'd have the wit and resources to do it. I mean, it's one thing to harbour a grudge, but quite another to organise and carry out something of this scale.'

'Mm. That's the thing, isn't it? And, having pulled it off, where the hell do you keep a race-fit thoroughbred? I suppose the police can't organise much of a search in case they put the wind up the kidnappers.'

'They sent a couple of their young female officers in plain clothes to put posters up in all the tack shops and feed stores within a fifty mile radius of Guildford, saying just that a bay thoroughbred has been stolen from his stable and asking people to report any unexpected new arrivals. They've notified riding schools, too, but of course we might be looking in completely the wrong area. It's a needle in a bloody haystack.'

'And you're not even sure you've got the right haystack.'

Truman grunted. 'That's about it.'

'So how are you coping?'

'It's been bloody awful, but when you've got ninety-six other horses, all with their own individual needs, you have to keep going. One horse – however special – is just one among many, and everything else has to go on as normal. I suppose, in a way, it helps. After all, there doesn't seem to be anything I can do.'

'And what about your staff? What have you told them?'

'Occasionally I send a horse or two to a yard near Petersfield for a few days of TLC. There's a girl there who does acupuncture – incredibly good – and I've told them King pulled up a bit stiff after his race and I've sent him there. That'll satisfy the lads for a few days, and the sad fact is that most of them don't care much. About three quarters of the lads are foreign. Come from all over the place: Brazil, Czech Republic, Poland, Colombia – you name it! It's quite common in the industry. The lads come over on a work permit, work here for a year or so earning three or four times what they would back home, and then take their money and go. You can't blame them, really. For some of them it's the only way to pay for an education, and there's not exactly a queue of English youngsters waiting to get into the profession. But it means that there's often very little interest in the long-term success of the stables; no real loyalty.'

'I didn't realise,' Ben said. 'Why do you think English kids don't want to come into racing any more?'

'Several reasons. For one thing, it's hard work and they can earn so much more sitting on their bums playing with computers. And another thing is their size. Kids in this country are huge these days! No good at all for exercising racehorses. Too many Big Macs and not enough activity.'

'So what about your head lad and your office staff?'

'Well, Bess knows, of course, and I've had to tell my assistant trainer, but then he's my son-in-law, so I think we're safe there. Trent, my head lad in the yard, doesn't know yet, but he'll probably start asking awkward questions if King isn't back in the next couple of days. Even as it is, I think he's picked up on the atmosphere. Who else is there? Oh, Vicki, Bess's assistant in the office; she's only part-time. We haven't told her. Of course I've told my family – Elizabeth, my wife, and my daughters, Helen and Fliss – but none of them knows you're working for me, for obvious reasons.'

'Meaning that you'd rather they didn't know how dirty you play?'

Truman's eyes narrowed. 'You must have led a very blameless life, Mr Copperfield. Ah,' he sat up and lifted his binoculars to his eyes, 'they're coming.'

Starting from a point well below them, the horses set off in pairs to canter steadily for a couple of hundred yards along the floor of the valley and then shift into a gallop as they hit the rising ground. As the first two powered up the incline at what Ben judged to be about three-quarter-speed, he and Truman got out of the Range Rover to get a better view.

The wind cutting across the ridge was bitter, and Ben zipped up his leather flying-jacket and raised the collar, whereupon Truman furnished him with the information that locally, the spot was known as Windwhistle Hill.

'We've got four grass gallops: three longer ones here, and a five-furlong one over the other side of the yard. And there are three all-weather ones, with differing distances and surfaces. One plough, one sand and plastic, and a pig-hair and mushroom-compost one. There's usually something we can use, whatever the weather.'

The approaching horses, one bay and one chestnut, were matching stride for stride, their heads dipping in unison, legs striking forward to cover the ground and breath steaming from their widened nostrils to hang in the frosty air. Muscles rippled under clipped coats burnished with gold by the winter sun. Crouched over their withers, the lads stood in the stirrups, letting their hands move with the rhythm of the gallop and suddenly Ben wished, with a passion that surprised him, that he could be in one of those saddles.

Where had that come from?

'Jewster is being lazy,' Truman murmured to himself. 'Why doesn't he work him with Cokey? How many times have I suggested it?'

He pulled a mobile phone from the pocket of his coat and pressed a button or two. 'Trent? Why didn't you work Jewster with Cokey like I asked you to? . . . Oh, is he? . . . Well, Dibble would have been better than Rocky. Rocky wouldn't inspire anyone to run! . . . OK, next time.'

'Cokey's lost a shoe,' he informed Ben, who,

feeling an answer was required, nodded and said, 'Oh,' adding, 'Do you have your own farrier at the yard?'

'Part-time. He's with us every afternoon.'

'So, tell me about the horses. I'll need a cover story if I'm going to be around the yard for a day or two, so let's make believe I really am doing a story on the Gold Cup horses, as I told Rackham. Actually, I might as well do the bloody story – I'm doing all the research. So, do you have any other runners?'

'Yes.' Truman was looking through his binoculars once more. 'The chestnut with the white face in the next pair. He's entered and he's in with a squeak. He's owned by a syndicate from the pub in the village. They take it all very seriously – I expect some of them are in that group watching over there.'

He swung an arm and Ben looked across to see a bunch of perhaps seven or eight people, with binoculars, standing just inside the boundary hedge.

'Do you always have an audience?'

'Not always, but leading up to a big race like this . . . Ah. Ray's coming up. Ray Finch, my son-in-law; married to Helen, my eldest.'

As the next two horses crested the rise, Ben could see someone out to the side and some fifty yards behind, riding on a general-purpose saddle with longer stirrups. His mount, as it drew closer, was obviously an older horse – probably retired, Ben guessed.

Truman strode over to the newcomer as he dismounted and immediately engaged him in conversation while the horse, held on a loose rein, lost no time in putting his head down to crop the grass.

Seeing them side by side, Ben thought that Truman and his son-in-law could have been cast from the same mould. Finch was, at a guess, in his early forties and not yet carrying quite as much weight as Truman, but he was of a similar height and his sandy hair was already sparse.

He wondered idly if Truman's eldest had seen her husband as a replacement father figure.

Truman didn't bother to introduce them and, beyond giving him a brief, curious glance, Finch took no notice of Ben. The discussion mostly concerned the horses, with a few comments thrown in about one or two of the lads. As it drew to a close Truman said, 'Well, have a word with Davy, would you? If his heart's not in it, he might just as well move on. He's no good to us.'

Finch nodded and made to move away.

'Oh, and by the way, I've just had yet another bill from Farm Fuels. What the hell's going on there? I got Bess to look back through the books and our diesel consumption's just gone up and up over the last few months.'

Finch shrugged and shook his head. 'I suppose we've done a few more of the northern meetings, and of course the new lorries are bigger.'

'Yes, but even taking that into account, it seems excessive.'

'I reckon it's the tractor boys you want to have a word with – they're forever filling up.'

'Oh, I intend to, believe me, but I think we've

been too free and easy with this. I'd like you to think about setting up some kind of record book or chart to keep a track of just who has what. See to it, will you?'

Finch nodded at both of them before mounting and riding back down the valley once more.

Two by two, the rest of the horses came along the valley bottom and up the slope to pass before Truman's critical gaze. Every now and then he would call out words of praise or censure, to which the lads would reply, 'Thanks, Guv,' 'Sorry, Guv,' or just simply, 'Guv'.

Mikey, in his turn, rode his chestnut alongside a powerful bay, keeping it just at the bigger horse's flank. As he pulled up Truman called out, 'Well done, Mikey,' adding for Ben's benefit, 'That's a difficult two-year-old. He did well there.'

Ben saw the undisguised joy on his half-brother's face and was glad for him.

By the time some of the horses had been round again and the exercise session wound to a close, Ben's feet and hands were frozen and his face felt stiff with cold.

Stretching their heads and necks down, the horses started to head back to the yard in single file. Once they were a safe distance away Ben let the dogs out of the back of the Range Rover and Truman produced a flask from a rucksack on the back seat.

'I've only got one cup,' he said unscrewing it from the Thermos. 'Can you manage to drink from the flask?'

Ben nodded eagerly. Just at that moment he'd

166

have drunk from the dog's bowl rather than miss the chance of a hot coffee or tea.

Gradually the feeling of incipient hypothermia began to recede. They sat in the cab of the vehicle and watched the dogs' antics with amusement. At some point during Mouse's enforced incarceration with Truman's pack she had developed a soft spot for the trainer's bull terrier, Bandy, who was so named because of the shape of his front legs, Truman said. Bandy seemed completely unaware of, or maybe indifferent to, Mouse's flirtatious advances and while she followed him adoringly, he continued to snuffle around the roots of the hedge, quite oblivious to the honour she was bestowing upon him.

'You're shameless!' Ben told her severely, as he put her back in the Range Rover, adding for her ears only, 'And I don't think much of your taste, either.'

'If you want to meet the family, you'd better come in for lunch,' Truman said as he parked the Range Rover on the weedless sweep of gravel in front of his house.

Ben raised an eyebrow. 'I've had more gracious invitations.'

The trainer gave him a half-smile.

'It's all these bloody questions. Every time I turn round it's either Ford or Hancock questioning someone; you don't feel like you've got any private life at all. I know they have to cover all the bases but honestly, it's not as if anyone in my family has taken the horse. They're just as devastated as I am. The yard is a family concern.'

'Yes. But Ford doesn't know them as well as you do. He has to make his own judgements; as do I, if you want me to carry on.'

Truman took off his cap and scratched his head in a way that Ben was coming to recognise as characteristic.

'Yes, I know; I know. It's just that this whole damn thing is getting to me. Why can't the bastards get on with it? Tell me where to leave the money, give King back, and let me get on with training him for the Gold Cup. They're being so bloody casual about it! You'd think *they'd* want to get it over with, wouldn't you?'

'Perhaps they're getting cold feet,' Ben suggested. 'As Ford said, the pick-up is always the most risky part of a kidnapping, apart from the initial snatch.'

'Oh God, don't say that. I've been spending hours every night picturing a JCB and a hole, with King at the bottom of it.'

Ben would like to have been able to say something encouraging but the fact was, in all honesty, that it was a picture his mind had also conjured up, more than once.

'Well, I suppose the alternative is that they thought the waiting would soften you up; make you so desperate that you'll be ready to pay up in full, exactly when and where they choose.'

'Well, it's worked,' Truman observed.

'What proof have they offered that King is still alive?'

'None,' the trainer said gloomily. 'And we've no way of asking for it.'

'So you're expected to cough up – what is it?

half a million? – on demand, with no guarantee whatever that they are willing, or even able, to return the horse.' Ben shook his head. 'What does Ford say?'

'He's not happy, of course, but what can we do?'

Ben didn't know, but was saved from the necessity of replying by the front door opening and a slim, auburn-haired girl leaning out to call Truman to lunch.

'Ma says it's ready *now*,' she said, with an interested glance at Ben. 'Are you staying to lunch?'

'Yes, he is,' Truman said.

'If it won't put you out too much.' Ben added.

'No. People are always dropping in,' the girl assured him. 'I'm Fliss, by the way. See you inside.'

She'd gone before Ben could introduce himself, but Truman performed that office as he showed him into a huge kitchen that was a symphony of cream paint, black marble and natural stone; it also incorporated the biggest cooking range Ben had ever seen, resplendent in black and gold. The room covered more square feet than the entire ground floor of some houses Ben had been in, and was occupied at that time by four women and a baby.

He recognised Bess, Truman's PA cum secretary, and Fliss, whom he'd just met, but the others were unknown to him. At a guess he thought the fifty-something lady who wore her long, faded blonde hair in a chignon was probably Truman's wife.

169

'This is Ben Copperfield,' the trainer announced to the room, then, turning to Ben, 'You know Bess, don't you?'

His secretary, who was putting a basket of bread rolls on the table, smiled at Ben and said, 'Hi.'

'This is Felicity, my youngest.'

At second glance, the tallish girl who'd introduced herself as 'Fliss' appeared to be in her late teens or early twenties. Wearing jeans and a cream roll-neck sweater she looked almost boyishly slim, and with an equally boyish, fine-boned face and her copper-coloured hair cut short, the overall effect was one that would have looked at home on the catwalk. Personally, Ben preferred a slightly more rounded figure. An image of Jeta Bardu flashed into his mind and he pushed it away.

'Ben's a journalist. He's doing a feature on the Gold Cup horses,' Truman added, and Fliss shot her father a frowning look.

'Is that wise?'

'It's all right, he knows. He's Mikey's brother.'

'Oh, of course; *Copperfield.*' Fliss gave Ben an appraising look up and down. 'You don't look much like him.'

'He's my half-brother. Takes after his mother.'

'Oh, I see.'

'This is Helen,' Truman said, taking control again and indicating a well-built female of around Ben's age, who was holding a baby against her shoulder and gently patting its back. 'And that's Lizzie, my first grandchild.'

Helen's long, golden-brown hair framed a

rounded face with blue eyes and a full-lipped, if slightly sulky, mouth. She gave Ben a brief smile and a nod, then returned her attention to the infant.

'Elizabeth, my wife,' the trainer said finally, and the lady with the chignon turned away from the stove for a moment to greet Ben, revealing a small-featured, rather anxious face that might once have been quite beautiful.

'Hello, Ben. I hope you don't mind soup and rolls. We normally have a proper meal in the evening.'

'Soup sounds brilliant at the moment,' he assured her. 'It was bitter up on the gallops.'

'Ah, you want more meat on your bones,' Truman told him.

'It's always cold watching. It's not so bad when you're riding,' Fliss said.

'Do you ride out?' Ben enquired.

'Yes, most days. I went out with the first two lots this morning.'

'That reminds me,' her father remarked. 'How did Cokey feel to you, yesterday? Trent says he walked out a bit sore this morning, and he's lost a shoe so he didn't work him.'

'Yeah. He was a bit pottery on the way home,' Fliss replied, and they became immersed in a discussion about the state of fitness of several of the yard's inmates, in which Ben, as an outsider, could take no useful part.

Elizabeth had returned her attention to dishing up the soup, suggesting, over her shoulder, that those assembled washed their hands and sat down. Helen seemed totally occupied with her child, so Ben drifted across to Bess.

171

'So, how long have you worked for Eddie?' he asked.

'Eight years,' she said promptly. 'I started here straight from college.'

'Not much point in me asking if he's a good employer, because you'd say yes, whatever, wouldn't you?'

She laughed. 'I suppose I would. But as a matter of fact, we get on very well. Of course he can be difficult at times, but then it's a very demanding job and it can be bloody frustrating. But when things aren't going right we all just tread carefully until it blows over. After all, that's what we're paid for. In general it's pretty good here. Certainly beats a city office job.'

'You live over at the cottage, don't you?'

'Yeah, but I spend all day here. They treat me like one of the family.'

'So, you're all treading carefully at the moment, then?'

'Sorry?' She frowned.

'The kidnap? Cajun King?'

'Oh, I see. Yes, it's been awful. And one of the worst things has been keeping it quiet. Remembering who knows and who doesn't. When it's on your mind all the time, it would be so easy to blurt it out in conversation, especially to Rollo, my boyfriend.'

'The jockey?'

'Yes. It's not that Eddie doesn't trust him, it's just that the more people that know, the more likely it is that someone will let it slip.'

Ben would have liked to continue the conversation, but at that moment the door opened and

172

Ray Finch, Helen's husband, came in, followed closely by DS Hancock.

'Just turned up as I came over from the yard,' Finch told his father-in-law.

'Any news?' Truman asked in the tone of one who wasn't really expecting any. Hancock shook his head.

'No. I was just passing.' He caught sight of Ben. 'What's he doing here?'

'And hello to you, too,' Ben commented.

Hancock glared at him.

'He's working on a feature about the Gold Cup,' Truman said.

'Is he? How convenient.'

'Oh, come on. We've had this conversation,' Ben observed wearily. 'Can't we move on?'

'Now we're all here, let's eat,' Truman suggested. 'Hancock?'

'Thanks. Don't mind if I do.'

Hancock and Truman tended to dominate the conversation at the table, the detective regaling the party with colourful tales of a life spent upholding the law and consequently, by the time coffee was served, Ben had had a chance to observe the other diners at his leisure. In doing so he found a certain amount of food for thought.

It seemed to him that, within his family, Truman was regarded with affection mixed with varying degrees of admiration, bordering – in Fliss's case – on reverence. Introduced almost as an afterthought, Elizabeth was clearly the last person in the group whose feelings would be consulted on any matter, but she was just as clearly inured to it, although her air of anxiety suggested that possibly she lived in dread of her husband's brusque tongue.

Somebody who was not nearly so content, he thought, was Truman's eldest daughter, Helen. Having laid her sleeping baby down in its buggy, she came to the table wearing a distinctly sullen expression which didn't alter for the duration of the meal. If there was any one person who appeared to be the focus of her displeasure, it was her father, although her husband was also given short shrift on the one occasion he addressed her directly. Ben wondered if she was suffering from post-natal depression, although he wasn't sure whether the baby was too old for it to be that.

Ray Finch seemed, at first sight, to be an uncomplicated person. Sitting between his wife and mother-in-law, he applied himself to his large bowl of soup as if it was the first food he'd seen in days, but his air of ruddy-cheeked and robust health suggested otherwise. The talk at the table didn't extend to include him very often but that didn't appear to worry him. He gave off an impression of placidness which, given a moody spouse and a forceful father-in-law who doubled up as his employer, was probably no bad thing. Ben wondered if the arrangement suited Finch; it certainly wouldn't be for everyone.

Sitting next to Ben, with Hancock on her other side, was Fliss, who took an active interest in the conversation, watched indulgently by her father. From the sound of it, she seemed to have a greater input into the running of the yard than Finch did. As he was Truman's paid assistant, this must have been galling, even to someone as phlegmatic as him. And indeed, watching carefully, Ben did intercept a rather surly glance at one point. It was quite possible that Fliss was aware of this though, for – pausing in the middle of an observation she was making about one of the horses – she looked across at Finch and said, 'What do you think, Ray? Should we try Jewster in blinkers tomorrow or do we give him one last chance without?'

'I think he's had all the chances I feel inclined to give him. I say put the blinkers on and see if that does the trick.'

Hancock, who had temporarily lost his position as centre of the attention, now spoke up. 'Where are you racing tomorrow? Any tips?'

'Wincanton,' Finch said. 'Best tip I can give you is keep your money in your pocket – at least where our runners are concerned. Our regular jockey is suspended.'

'Oh, I don't know. Axesmith has got a chance,' Fliss responded.

'Got the halfwit on him,' Finch grunted, and the following silence was deafening.

'I was telling Ben how well his brother's coming on,' Truman remarked casually.

A swift reddening of his cheeks showed that Finch hadn't made the connection.

'His brother . . . Yeah, he is. I didn't mean . . . The thing is, he lacks experience.'

'There's only one way to gain experience,' Ben pointed out with deceptive mildness. 'And you don't need GCSEs to ride well.'

'Of course, I know that, but –'

'Actually, he's really lucky,' Fliss put in. 'He's a natural. The horses all seem to go well for him. I wish I could ride like that.'

A natural horseman. That's what Jakob had said of Nico. A God-given gift that couldn't be taught. It seemed that what Mikey had missed out on in the academic department he had made up for elsewhere. Ben hadn't seen him ride for ages. Suddenly he was looking forward to his trip to Wincanton the next day.

'Do you ride, Ben?' Elizabeth's innocent query came out of the blue, and Ben's heart sank as everyone's eyes focused on him.

'Used to, but not any more,' he said lightly, praying they would leave it at that.

'Don't you miss it?' Fliss asked earnestly. 'I can't imagine not riding.'

'Not really. I guess I'm just too busy.' That was a lie, but it was his only defence against the inevitable follow-on. *I've got a horse you can ride. Dobbin could do with the exercise – you'd be doing me a favour, etc, etc.*

Fliss was still looking thoughtfully at him so he smiled and, after smiling in return, she looked away and the conversation moved on.

8

Ben spent the afternoon at Castle Ridge looking round the yard and talking to any of the senior staff that he came across. His first port of call was the cottage adjacent to the yard, to see Mikey. Technically the lads' working hours were seven until midday and then four till six, but Ben was aware that – as with all animal-related jobs – they didn't stop until the work was done. He knew from Mikey that unpaid overtime was a fact of life for all of them.

On this occasion Ben found his brother watching a video in the cottage's small living room, with Ian Rice, Davy Jackson, the lad he'd met the day Cajun King was taken, and five other lads, one of whom sported a huge, seventies-style moustache. That, he decided with amusement, must be Caterpillar, back from his holidays.

Accepting Rice's offer of a guided tour, Ben walked with him to the stables, leaving Mikey and the others to their film.

An eight-foot high, flint-topped perimeter wall

enclosed the stable complex, leaving Truman's house, the cottage and the lads' hostels on the outside. At this time the double gates were open, leading on to a gravel parking area where three maroon and gold horseboxes stood – two large and one smaller – all emblazoned with *Castle Ridge Racing* across the doors and body.

'I'll show you those later, if you like. But I'll have to get the keys from the office.' Rice shivered theatrically and pulled his fleece closer around his wiry frame. The sun had disappeared completely since lunchtime and the wind was bitter as they walked up the cinder path between two stable blocks.

'Brr! Brass monkeys, isn't it? Days like this you almost envy the guys with desk jobs.'

'Really?'

Rice pursed his lips. 'No, not really. Not for long anyway.' They had entered the yard and turned into the end of the first, American-barn-style stable block, where the horses occupied loose boxes that looked in on a wide central corridor. Hearing their footsteps, several of the horses came to look over their doors. 'As soon as I see those heads I know I'm in the right job. Aren't they wonderful?'

Ben agreed that they were.

'So you're writing an article on the Gold Cup runners. That's a bit difficult, isn't it? With King not being here, I mean.' Rice was a good eight inches shorter than Ben and had to look up when he spoke to him.

'It might be, if they don't get him back. But then, I guess, I'd be able to name my own price on the story. It's an ill wind, as they say . . .'

'Do you think we will get him back?'

'I really don't know,' Ben said frankly. 'And I don't think the police know either. I shouldn't imagine there's much precedent for horse-napping, except for the notorious Shergar case, of course, and that doesn't inspire much hope. But, on the other hand, if they'd intended killing him, you think they'd have done it straight away.'

'I suppose so,' Rice said gloomily. 'The bastards really picked their time well, didn't they? Having a fancied runner in a big race like that makes such a difference to yard morale. Some of the older lads were talking about it the other day; it's going to be a real blow if the old boy doesn't come back. But quite apart from that, I'll miss him. He can be an awkward old sod sometimes, but I'm very fond of him.'

One of the horses stretched out its neck towards them and Rice stopped to rub its forehead.

'In what way is he awkward?'

'Oh, he's not bad, really. They all have their habits. It's just that he can't bear to have his ears touched, so we have to kind of buckle his bridle on round him. And he's a devil for treading on your foot, too. If you let your attention wander even for a moment while you're grooming, he'll have you!'

'Is he really such a hot chance for Cheltenham? Or is it hype?'

'On past form, there's nothing that can touch him, as long as the going doesn't get too heavy.'

'So, can you think of anyone who might be involved? Anyone with a grudge? Truman mentioned one or two ex-employees who weren't exactly happy when they left, but he didn't seem to think any of them were potential kidnappers.'

Rice shook his head. 'There have been one or two, but the Guv's right. They were mostly just shirkers who were told to get on their bikes.'

'Anyone else he might have upset?'

'Quite a few, I expect. He's mellowed a bit lately, but when I first started working for him there were all sorts of rumours flying around.'

'What kind of rumours?'

'People said he'd got where he had in business because no one would stand in his way. They said that competitors in the same field just kind of melted away. I'm not saying it's true, but some people said he employed strong-arm men. One guy even described his outfit as "The Yorkshire Mafia". They said he moved down here to start afresh and get respectable. I wouldn't know.'

'How long ago was this?' Ben asked. They turned and walked slowly back through the aisle of the stable block, towards the centre of the complex.

'Oh, donkeys' years. Must be nearly twenty, I suppose. I've only been here about fifteen years but Trent used to work for the previous chap that trained here; then Eddie Truman came along, tore the whole lot down and rebuilt. It can't have been easy, at first, even though he had money – and to spare – because in the racing world you've got to have contacts and he didn't have any, other than as an owner. But he kept plugging away, and now the yard's one of the top ones in the country. Sixth in the rankings last year. Whatever you say about the Guvnor, he seems to have a genuine talent for the game. He can spot a good horse or jockey way before anyone else can see anything. And I guess he's not a bad boss, really. As long as you don't cross him,' he added.

Ben's ears pricked up. 'So who crossed him? Who were you thinking of?'

Rice began to look a little uncomfortable. 'Look, no offence, but this hasn't got anything to do with the Gold Cup, has it? I'm really not sure the Guv'd want me talking about all this.'

'Truman won't mind. Trust me. I'm not about to do anything to harm his reputation. I've got Mikey to consider.'

'Yes, I suppose so,' Rice said slowly. 'Well, I was just thinking of Lenny Salter, the last stable jockey we had before Rollo came. The Guv found out he was on the take – you know, pulling horses – and boy, did he come down on him! The thing was, it turned out he hadn't got anything on him that would stand up in court, and Lenny more or less thumbed his nose as he walked out the door. Eddie was furious. And then, a couple of weeks later, we heard . . .'

He tailed off, leaving Ben to prompt him.

'You heard . . . ?'

'Look, I think I've said enough.'

'Oh come on, you can't leave it there!' Ben protested. It occurred to him that this might be another of the matters that Truman would rather the police weren't reminded about.

Rice shook his head. 'No, I'm sorry. You'll have to ask someone else. The Guv's always treated me fair and I don't like talking behind his back.

181

After all, it was only talk; he may have had nothing to do with it. A chancer like Lenny probably had all kinds of scams going on.'

Ben sighed, trying to hide his frustration. They had come out into the brick-paved central area now, from which five more covered barn stables radiated. He looked around with interest.

'OK. Tell me about this place.'

Patently glad to be let off the hook, Rice gave Ben a top-notch tour of the facilities, showing him the forge, where the horses were shod; the veterinary building – where, it was hoped, a vet would one day be in full-time residence; the covered school with its indoor jumping lane; the deeply sanded barn, where the horses could go when they were hot and sticky, to enjoy a good roll and get some dust in their coats; and the horse walkers – three round, rotating metal cages with compartments in which the horses could be steadily exercised at various speeds. An equine swimming pool was under construction and Rice pointed to a site, across the acres of fields outside the wall, where a range of brick outbuildings stood on rising ground next to a copse. There, he said, Truman planned to build a stud to breed future champions.

'He's got big ideas,' Ben said, impressed.

'He wants to compete with the Arabs,' Rice said. 'But he hasn't got a hope. He's rich, but not that rich.'

As they returned to the main area of the yard, a steady trickle of lads was arriving for the second part of their working day. Some chatting and laughing together, some more solitary, they all headed for the tackroom and reappeared carrying grooming kits. Mikey passed with Caterpillar and Ben asked if they'd enjoyed their film; the response was an enthusiastic affirmative.

'Time to groom and skip out the boxes,' Rice said. 'Then it's tack cleaning and evening feeds and we're finished for the day. I'll have to do my two in a minute, but I'll just show you the feedstore and the tackroom area, if you like.'

The tackroom was huge and beautifully organised, with rows and rows of saddles and bridles on racks around the walls and banks of lockers; each, Ben learned, was allocated to an individual horse and contained rugs, blankets and any personal effects of the same. On the wall, a huge whiteboard listed all the horses, divided into the four lots for exercise, with a lad's name beside each; another gave details of runners in the upcoming race meetings, and which lorry was going where with what crew.

Beyond that, and with its own door into the yard, was a square room with a tiled floor and strip-lighting, with a profusion of framed photographs on its whitewashed walls, several cuttings books on tables, and various racing mementoes behind glass in three large display cabinets.

'Our "Hall of Fame",' Rice announced, as he held the door for Ben to peer in. 'Mostly for the benefit of visitors on our open days.'

The feedstore was as well organised as the tackroom, with another whiteboard keeping a note of exactly what each animal was to have in each of three feeds.

Rice explained that the horses were fed by

Truman or Finch at five-thirty a.m., one o'clock, and six p.m., with the exception of the first lot to be exercised, who had their first feed at eight-thirty when they returned from the gallops.

Stacks and stacks of numbered buckets, all scrubbed clean, stood against one wall, while on the other side, huge galvanised steel bins held the grain and performance mixes, and several huge plastic-wrapped bales containing chopped alfalfa waited to be opened.

'It's nutritious, gives them bulk and stops the greedy ones bolting their feeds,' Rice said, seeing Ben's interest.

Another corner was taken up with red string sacks full of carrots, and a cupboard contained drums, tubs and bottles of supplements.

'Must cost a fortune in feed bills,' he commented.

'It does.' Rice named an approximate monthly total that took Ben's breath away. 'Add to that bedding, shoes, vets' bills, insurance, tack repairs, and staff wages, and you can begin to see where the training fees go. It's not a hobby for the faint-hearted. And you have to remember that for every Cajun King and Pod Pea there are thousands of also-rans, some of whom never win anything much. They all cost the same to keep.' He looked at his watch. 'Look, I must go and do my two. Why don't you go and have a look at the Hall of Fame – it's quite interesting. Make yourself a coffee if you want, and when I've finished I'll show you the lorries.'

Ben thanked him and, as Rice went off to attend to his allotted two horses, made his way through to the public room to browse the photographs and newspaper cuttings.

The earliest photographs dated from around twenty years before; just one or two, recording modest wins at local racecourses by horses that were never destined to set the racing world alight. Then as now, Truman had had a mixed yard of flat horses and jumpers, and his success seemed to be split fairly equally between the two until suddenly – and apparently quite out of the blue – some four years after he started training, one of the Castle Ridge horses won the Derby.

Massingham.

Ben didn't remember the name, but then he'd have been, what . . . ? Sixteen? It was about the time he'd left home, still traumatised after the death of his brother less than two years before, and the subsequent break-up of his parents' marriage. No wonder, then, that he hadn't taken much notice of what was going on in the horse world. That had been a black time in his life and he shook his head now, as if to physically banish the memory.

For Eddie Truman, at least, it seemed that things had been coming up roses at that point in time.

Ben leafed back through the cuttings. Massingham appeared to have been virtually unraced before his big breakthrough. There was no mention of previous successes – actually, there were very few wins by any of the flat horses in the year leading up to the Derby. After the big race there were pictures galore: Massingham with Truman and the jockey in the winners enclosure;

the prize-giving; the homecoming; Massingham opening a fête in the village. Several pages were devoted to the celebrations. He turned a few more pages, reading with interest. It seemed that, a month or two after the Derby success, the number of horses in training at Castle Ridge had swelled to such a degree that Truman was able to justify having a retained jockey; one who was paid to ride for the stable, wherever and whenever he was required to. This was reported under a photo of one of the yard's winners, where Truman was described as 'an up-and-coming force to be reckoned with.'

Looking at the dates it appeared that the arrangement had been mutually advantageous; that particular jockey had ridden for Castle Ridge until his retirement six years later and the stable had had some notable successes. Over the next seven years the jockeys photographed on the yard's winners were many and varied, leading Ben to think that perhaps Truman hadn't had a retained jockey for that period. Then, for a couple of years, Lenny Salter had partnered many of the horses.

Lenny Salter, who, according to Rice, had left with a flea in his ear, and then . . . Then what? Ben felt strongly that he should find out.

'More research, Mr Copperfield?' Fliss had come in, soft-footed, whilst he was engrossed in the history of the yard, and now stood beside him, looking down at the open page. 'Oh, *Lovely Lenny Salter*!'

'*Lovely* Lenny?' Ben straightened up and found himself on a level with Truman's younger daughter, close enough to be aware of the youthful smoothness of her pale skin, tinged with pink now by the icy wind.

'I'm being sarcastic, of course,' Fliss said, looking down at the photo on the page. 'I never liked him. He was a rough sort – a rough diamond, Dad used to call him, which made him all the more furious when he found out he was just a lump of coal.' She smiled at her own joke, her green eyes twinkling.

'What did he do?'

'He was pulling horses. You know, losing to order.'

'So what did your father do?'

'Sacked him, of course. He hadn't enough proof to take him to the Jockey Club, but he saw to it that the word got around.'

'So Lenny doesn't ride any more?' Ben said, hoping she might expand on it.

'No. As a matter of fact, he was mugged just a few weeks later. Somebody kneecapped him with a cricket bat in his own garage. Did the world a favour, if you ask me.'

Ben thought she sounded fairly offhand about it. It clearly hadn't occurred to her that the attack was anything other than a happy coincidence. What wonderful things rose-coloured spectacles were, he mused, until you took them off. Well, he wasn't about to do it for her.

'I wanted to be a jockey when I was growing up,' Fliss went on. 'I was always begging Dad to let me take out a licence but he wouldn't. He kept saying, "When you're eighteen, we'll see," but by the time I was eighteen I was way too tall

187

to be a flat jockey, and I knew he'd never let me ride over the jumps. It's too dangerous. I think he knew I was going to be too tall,' she added ruefully. 'So now I shall just have to be a trainer, instead.'

'How old are you?'

'Twenty-two.' She answered freely; young enough not to be coy about her age. She turned round and parked her slim behind on the table, looking up at Ben from under her auburn fringe. 'Why?'

'So you could go and ride for someone else, if you wanted?' he suggested.

'Oh no, I'd never leave here! I wanted to ride for Dad. That was the whole point. Riding winners for *our* yard.'

'Or not.'

'Well, I hope I would have won sometimes. You're not a male chauvinist, I hope, Ben Copperfield. Like those commentators who say, "Well, she rode quite a good finish, but you can't expect a girl to ride as strongly as a man." That really makes my blood boil.'

'No, I'm not like that,' he assured her.

'Well . . . good.' She looked at him and a reluctant smile softened her face. 'Damn you! You made me get my soapbox out again, and I've been trying so hard not to do that. It's just – I would love to have been a jockey . . .'

'So now you're intending to put your father out of a job, instead?'

Fliss twinkled again. 'Well, maybe not yet awhile.'

Occupying pride of place in the centre of the

188

wall was an enlarged photograph of Cajun King winning a race in fine form. Ben stepped closer to read the caption.

'That's King winning the Champion Chase,' Fliss said proudly.

'He's nothing special to look at, really, is he?' Ben said, studying another photo. 'No, don't take offence! I just mean that he's fairly average-looking. If it wasn't for his short tail, I probably wouldn't be able to tell him apart from dozens of others.'

'Looks don't count for a lot on the racecourse. Look at Desert Orchid: even his most ardent fan couldn't claim that he's beautiful but he had that certain something about him that shouted Champion!'

'Are you saying King has that look, too?' Ben studied another picture but, with the best will in the world, couldn't see anything that even whispered Champion. He was just a pleasant-looking, well put-together thoroughbred, with a laughably short tail.

'Of course,' she stated loyally.

She stayed for another ten minutes or so, recounting various tales about the horses in the photos, though she was a little hazy on the earlier ones. 'I was only three when we first came here,' she said by way of an excuse, 'and seven when Massingham won the Derby.'

Ben agreed to let her off.

When she left, saying that she had a horse's foot to poultice, she added, 'You're welcome to come and watch, if you like.' But Ben declined. It wasn't that he wouldn't have been perfectly happy to spend some more time chatting with her – she was very pleasant company – it was just that he knew from experience the attendant perils of such a situation. Standing in stable doorways watching that kind of operation inevitably led to such requests as, 'Could you just move him over for me?' or, 'If you could just hold his leg up while I put this dressing on . . .' He knew that any of his ready stock of excuses would be recognised as just that by Miss Felicity Truman. There were clearly no flies on her.

With a sigh, he left the public room and wandered across to watch the work in progress on the building that was to house the swimming pool.

He was still there, deep in thought, some ten minutes later, when a voice hailed him and he turned to see Ray Finch approaching.

'You should be wearing a hard hat,' the assistant trainer told him, unsmiling.

As Ben was at least thirty feet from where the work was going on he ignored this. After a moment Finch spoke again.

'Saw Rice showing you round. Did you get what you needed for your article?'

'Some.' Ben gestured at the perimeter wall. 'Is that normal?'

'Some yards lock up at night, some don't,' Finch said, stopping beside him. A faint smell of alcohol pervaded the air. 'No point locking the gates if you can climb over the fence. Eddie's always been security conscious.'

'Your house is inside the wall,' Ben commented, having had the bungalow pointed out to him earlier. 'But apart from that, is there any other security? I mean a guard, or alarms.'

Finch nodded. 'Everything is wired up. Stables, tackroom, feedstore, the lot. And of course there are the boys.'

'The boys?' Ben raised an eyebrow and, for the first time, saw Finch smile.

'Come and see.'

He led the way across the complex to where a galvanised steel gate was let into the wall. This was at the furthest point from all the houses, and Finch described it as the tradesman's entrance. 'It's used for deliveries – feed, hay, bedding etc – and the diesel tank is here,' he explained.

On one side of the gate, and surrounded by a low, double-skinned breezeblock wall was a large, grey-painted fuel tank; on the other was a brick and timber building with an attached wire-netting run. As they approached, a black and tan face appeared enquiringly in the open doorway of the structure and uttered a short sharp bark. Instantly the face was joined by a second, identical one, and then two sleek Dobermans rushed out to stand at the front of the concrete-floored pen and give voice to a very effective warning.

'Meet the boys,' Finch announced proudly, raising his voice to make himself heard over their enthusiastic efforts. 'Kaiser and Rommel. They take care of security for us after lights out.'

'I can see how they might,' Ben replied, half shouting.

Finch laughed. 'Watch this.' He held up his right hand, making a circle with his index finger and thumb; then, as the dogs faltered a little in their furious barking, he said quietly, 'That'll do, boys.'

All at once there was silence and the two dogs sat down, but Ben noticed that they continued to keep him under close scrutiny.

'I guess that wouldn't work if I were to do it,' he hazarded.

'Nope. Only me and Helen's father,' Finch said, clearly revelling in the knowledge.

'Should have thought it might be awkward in an emergency.'

'Not really. They don't go out until after we've walked round the stables at nine o'clock, and if there's a problem with one of the horses and Trent has to go in and out, we just keep the dogs in. But all the people who deliver here know about the dogs, and the word gets around. They're the best deterrent.'

'What would they do if they got loose now? Would they attack me?' An unfortunate incident with a friend's Doberman when Ben was very young had led him to regard the breed with caution.

'They might if I let 'em. So you'd better stay on the right side of me,' Finch said with a sideways look. 'They take their job very seriously.'

As if to illustrate the point, the dogs began another frenzy of barking, this time directed towards the gate, and after a moment the two men heard the sound of an approaching vehicle. In due course, the bolt on the gate slid open; it swung inward and a rather unprepossessing character in dirty overalls peered cautiously inside, checking first on the dogs, before catching sight of Ben and Finch.

Ben got the impression that the man was rather dismayed to find them there, a fact that was borne out by his almost immediate withdrawal.

'Yes? What do you want?' Finch called loudly, starting towards the gate and silencing the dogs with a shrill whistle and the hand signal as he did so. They subsided with no more than a few stray barks. Ben was impressed.

The gate opened a few inches once more and the face reappeared.

'Sorry mate. Wrong turning.'

Looking distinctly annoyed, Finch went up to the man, spoke a few words and then, pointing this way and that, redirected him.

'There's a quarry half a mile up the road,' he said, rejoining Ben after the man had retreated. 'We're always getting people who've taken the wrong turning. It's a bloody nuisance.'

'Should have thought it'd be worth putting a sign at the end of the track, then,' Ben suggested. 'You know, "No Access to Quarry" or something like that.'

'Yeah, I know. I just never seem to get round to it.'

Finch sounded almost offhand and Ben didn't think the problem could be a very great one.

'I suppose you get through a lot of fuel with the lorries,' he remarked, gesturing towards the tank and adding apologetically, 'I overheard Eddie this morning, having a moan to you about it.'

'He's always having a gripe about something or other. But yeah, with the three lorries and a couple of Land Rovers, it's frightening how

193

much.' He looked at his watch. 'Well, I'd better be getting back to the yard. There'll be feeding to see to soon.'

'Rice said it's always either you or Eddie that does the feeds; doesn't your wife ever get involved with the horses?' Ben started to walk back towards the stables with Truman's son-in-law.

Finch shook his head. 'No. Helen's not really interested – especially not now she's got the baby. The only other person who's allowed to prepare the feeds is Trent, or Fliss. She knows as much about the business as any of us.'

'Yes, I was just talking to her. She's quite an ambitious young lady.'

'Takes after her father.' Finch didn't sound as though the fact filled him with joy.

'So, how long have you worked here? Were you here before you were married or did you marry into the job?'

Finch bristled. 'I'm fully qualified for the position. I worked for Belinda Kepple before I came here.'

From his response, Ben gathered that he had indeed married into the job.

'So, what's it like, working for the family firm?' he asked, probing for a reaction.

'It's crap!'

It seemed he'd touched a nerve because Finch's response came instantly, almost involuntarily, but was just as quickly retracted.

'No, I didn't mean that. If that gets into print I'll sue you,' he said, turning towards Ben and wagging a finger in his face.

Ben ignored the threat.

'Some people would say you'd got a cushy number: married to the boss's daughter; job security; house thrown in; but I guess it's not all a bed of roses . . .'

Finch back-pedalled, plainly regretting his improvident outburst.

'It has its moments but it's all right. It's a very good job.'

'But sometimes you'd like a little more freedom – that's natural.' Ben made it a statement, and there was no denial.

'So, have you got the hijacked lorry back now?'

Ben and Ian Rice were approaching the lorry park. It was almost dark, the sun having set into a glorious red sky, and the horses had all been groomed, fed and settled for the night.

'Yes, we got it back yesterday. It's the one on the end. The police have had their forensics people go through it with a fine-toothed comb. They even found a contact lens I lost a couple of weeks ago.'

'Now that is thorough,' Ben agreed.

'Do you want to see inside?'

Ben felt a cold sweat breaking out at the very thought. Could it really have been less than twenty-four hours since the drama with the Magyar horse? He wasn't sure he had the will-power to face his fear again so soon.

'No, I don't think so. Like you say, the police have been over it.'

Rice looked slightly puzzled. 'Yeah, but I meant, you know, for the article.'

Ben could have kicked himself. For a moment

he'd forgotten all about the supposed article. He blamed tiredness. He'd had less than three hours' sleep after the drama of the previous night.

'Thanks. It's great to have all the background stuff, but I think my editor really wanted me to concentrate on the horses themselves.'

'Come and see anyway,' Rice urged, his hand on the cab door.

Taking the emotional equivalent of a deep breath, Ben climbed up into the cab behind the travelling head lad and followed him through a narrow doorway to the area behind, where a small lounge-cum-dining space provided potential relaxation for those looking after the horses on a long day away. The shallow compartment above the cab, known as the luton, was shut off behind sliding wooden doors, and contained a thin mattress and a couple of pillows. This, then, was the place where Mikey had slept through most of the hijack. It wasn't hard to see how he'd remained undiscovered, staying as quiet as he obviously had.

Another narrow door led to the main body of the lorry, where the horses spent their journeys to and from the racecourses, hemmed in by padded dividers, standing on rubber matting and watched over via video links to the cab and seating compartment.

Rice held the door open so Ben could see into the back of the box. He leaned through to give it the obligatory admiring glance, feeling his chest begin to contract even then. In truth, although beautifully equipped, the Csikós' monster trans-porters cast the Castle Ridge lorries firmly into the shade; this was as one would expect, of course, for the Hungarians and their horses had to live in theirs for the best part of the summer.

As soon as he reasonably could, Ben made his way back into the cab and from there to the outside, greeting the bitter evening air with relief.

Rice locked the lorry and led the way back to the cottage, where they found Mikey and Bess in the kitchen. The others – Davy, Les and Caterpillar – had apparently gone with a group of lads 'down the chippy'.

'Coffee or tea, Ben?' Bess asked, her hand hovering over a selection of containers.

'Coffee would be wonderful. Strong and black.' He was dog-tired now, and the warmth of the Aga in the cottage kitchen was having a soporific effect.

'Did you see Rommel and Kaiser?' Mikey asked, almost childishly eager. He'd always loved dogs.

'I did.' With a guilty start Ben then remembered Mouse, confined to the Mitsubishi all afternoon. 'Would anyone object if I brought my dog over?'

Subsiding into a rather ropey armchair in the corner, Rice had taken one boot off and was massaging his foot. He shook his head. 'Shouldn't think so. As long as it's friendly.'

'Oh, Mouse is very friendly,' Mikey said.

'Well, actually she can be a bit stand-offish, but she doesn't bite or anything,' Ben amended.

'All animals are friendly with you,' Rice pointed out to Mikey. 'Did you know, Ben, your brother here has even made friends with the

197

guard dogs? I'm not sure the Guvnor would be too happy if he knew!'

'They weren't out again the other night,' Mikey said. 'I went out to watch the badgers in the copse and when I came back I whistled for the boys and they didn't come. They must have been shut in.'

'What time was that?' Rice asked.

''Bout ten-thirty.'

'Oh, I doubt it, then. Ray would have gone to bed by then, and you should have, too.'

'No. Ray was still up. He had his light on. Can I go and fetch Mouse for you, Ben?'

'With pleasure.' Ben took the keys from his pocket and held them out. 'It's locked but the alarm's disabled. It kept going off, so I disconnected it. Don't tell my insurance company!'

They sat companionably round the table and, in due course, Mikey returned with Mouse, whose melting brown eyes and air of gentle neglect made an instant hit with Bess. After another half-hour or so, Bess suggested sausage, fried mash and beans, and somehow Ben found himself staying for the meal.

Afterwards, the conversation rambled on but Ben took less and less part in it, until suddenly he found himself face down on the table with his head resting on his folded arms. He jerked upright and found Bess and Mikey laughing at him. They appeared to be playing chess – a game at which, oddly, Mikey excelled. Rice had retired to his saggy armchair and was out for the count.

'God, I'm sorry!' Ben said. 'Did I nod off?'

'Yeah. Two hours ago!' Mikey said. 'We thought

we were going to have to make you up a bed for the night.'

'We could probably squeeze you in, at a push,' Bess said seriously. 'But it might be the sofa.'

Ben shook his head. 'Thanks, but I'd better get back.'

It took a considerable effort to drag himself away from the peace and warmth of the little kitchen, but a look at his watch informed him that it was past ten, and he knew the cottage wouldn't be half as peaceful when the other lads returned. Mouse disagreed with his decision, and he had to take hold of her collar and forcibly remove her from the building. Casting him a reproachful look, she immediately began to shiver in the sharp, frosty air outside.

Unlike Mikey, Ben hadn't the propensity for catnapping and waking refreshed, and all his sleep had done for him was to leave him feeling even more heavy-eyed than he had before. The relatively short drive home was accomplished without driving into any hedges or running any red lights that he was aware of, but he was extremely glad that he hadn't got any motorway driving to do.

Turning thankfully on to the small rectangle of gravel he called his own, Ben was at first puzzled and then dismayed to find it already half-occupied by Lisa's Beetle.

'Oh, shit!' he said forcefully under his breath, recalling – way too late – her telephone message of that morning. She'd have every right to be mad at him now.

9

There was a light on in the hall and Lisa's full-length faux sheepskin coat hung on the old-fashioned hatstand behind the door. In the kitchen a single spotlight burned, illuminating the worktop where a note lay.

Have gone to bed. Dinner's in the oven. Love Lisa.

That was all. No accusations or reproaches. It was typically Lisa and Ben sighed with relief. He was still dog-tired and his head ached; just at the moment he couldn't have coped with a scene.

Tossing a Bonio into Mouse's basket, he took two paracetamol with a glass of water, switched the light off and made his way to the bedroom. The door was closed and on the handle hung a 'Please Do Not Disturb' sign, no doubt pilfered from some hotel, but Lisa had blacked out the word 'Not.'

Ben paused. Normally such an invitation would be welcome, but just now . . .

Oh God! he thought. A headache: the oldest excuse in the book! But he knew from experience that the painkillers would take ten to fifteen minutes to have any effect on a pounding ache such as this, if indeed they had any effect at all. Hoping that she was asleep and hadn't heard him come in, he retraced his steps and went instead to the lounge, leaving the light in the hall as the only illumination, and stretched out on the brown leather sofa with his eyes closed.

'Cup of tea for you. Shall I put it on the coffee table?'

Ben opened his eyes to bright morning light and Lisa standing beside the sofa in a white towelling robe.

'You look like an angel,' he mumbled, squinting up at her.

'You say the nicest things.' Her tone was placid, accepting his comment for the observation it was, rather than the compliment it might have been. 'I heard you come in. Why did you sleep out here?'

Ben sat up, groaning as his back protested. At some point Lisa had draped a blanket over him but he was still fully clothed.

'I had a really bad headache. I was going to come to bed when the tablets kicked in but I guess I fell asleep.' The truth sounded unconvincing, even to him. 'I'm sorry I was so late last night.'

Lisa sat on the sofa next to him, curling her feet up under her and cradling her own cup of tea.

'I expect you didn't get my text – I should have rung.'

Ben reached for his tea, tempted – but too honest – to take the easy way out she'd offered him.

'Actually, I did get your message, but I completely forgot. Last night – that is, the night before – I stayed over with the Csikós. You remember I told you about them? Yeah, well I was up practically all night because someone let some of the horses out. It was our friends, the animal rights group.' He took a sip of tea and gave her a brief description of the night's events. 'Then I spent the day at Castle Ridge researching an article on the Cheltenham Gold Cup. So, you see, I was completely knackered by yesterday evening and I actually fell asleep at Mikey's cottage. Nodded off at the dinner table, which was a bit embarrassing. I'm really sorry.' He scanned her face for disbelief and found none. She looked merely resigned.

'Well, what are you doing today?'

'I'm going racing this afternoon – Mikey's riding. You can come too, if you like?'

Lisa gave a little smile. 'Thanks, but I have to work later, and anyway, I think I might feel a bit like an afterthought.'

'Don't be daft. Come here.' Ben put an arm round her shoulders and pulled her close. 'What about this morning then? I don't think Mikey's riding till half-two. How about coffee and a big sticky cake somewhere?' He'd have to turn down Truman's offer of a lift to the course, but that didn't really matter.

'I'm on a diet!' Lisa protested.

'What on earth for?'

'Because I'm feeling old, fat and frumpy.'

'Ah. This wouldn't have anything to do with the looming, big three-oh, would it?'

'It might,' she said, wriggling a little in his grasp. 'But it's very ungallant of you to bring that up.'

'You forget, I've been there,' he told her. 'And if you think about it, in a few years' time you'll give anything to be thirty again, so just go with it. After all, it's only a number.'

'I know; but it's such a big number!' she said wistfully. 'OK. Coffee and cakes would be lovely, thanks. I'll start my diet tomorrow.'

Finishing the tea they went together to the bathroom and shared a luxurious shower that moved them both from contentment to passion, and presently, over breakfast, Ben found himself thinking that there must be a hell of a lot worse fates than waking up with a girl like Lisa for the rest of his life. Almost instantly, habitual caution caught up with his train of thought and he began to recoil. Why change anything when it was working so well?

Catching his eye, Lisa smiled and he winked at her, glad she couldn't read his mind.

She didn't need to.

'What are you thinking?' she asked.

Cornered by her question and his own honesty, Ben paused, but before his hesitation became noticeable he was rescued by the ringing of his telephone.

'Ben. When are you coming over? I'm planning to leave at twelve.' Truman, cutting to the chase as usual.

'Er, listen Eddie, I think I might make my own

way there. I've got one or two things I need to sort out this morning.'

'Can't they wait?' Truman demanded. 'What sort of things?'

'Private things,' Ben said without heat. 'My own business.'

'Well, it's a bloody nuisance. There's been a development, but I can't tell you over the phone.'

Ben hesitated. 'Look, I'm sorry,' he began, and then caught sight of Lisa shaking her head and mouthing, 'You go.'

'Hold on a minute,' he said into the receiver, then, covering the mouthpiece with his hand, 'What about our coffee?'

She wrinkled her nose and shook her head again. 'Doesn't matter, I've got stuff I should do, anyway.'

'You sure?'

She nodded, and he moved his hand. 'OK. I'll be with you around half-eleven.'

'Make it eleven. Ford's here,' Truman said, and put the phone down.

'I'm sorry,' Ben said, looking apologetically at Lisa. 'Technically, the guy's my boss at the moment, but it won't be for long; it's kind of a special case. Anyway, I'll make it up to you with double coffee and cakes next time.'

'Great! Then I really will get fat!' Lisa finished her toast and licked marmalade off her fingers. 'You've always said you'd never work for anyone again.'

'Like I said, it's a special case. I can't really tell you at the moment, but I will one day.'

'Ooh, a secret assignment!' she said dramatically.

'OK, I can wait. Oh, by the way, one of your editors – Taylor, would it be? – rang yesterday evening. Wanted you to get back to him, so I said I'd pass the message on. You seem to be in demand.'

Ben groaned. 'OK, thanks. That's the one I'm doing the Csikós article for. You really ought to come and see one of their performances. It's not like anything you've ever seen before.'

'Yeah, I'd like to. Look, I hate to sound like your mother or something, but if you're meeting this Eddie guy at eleven, you'd better get a wriggle on; it's half-ten already.'

Ben did hurry but he was still ten minutes late as he turned into the drive of Castle Ridge House. Thinking over the information he'd gleaned the day before, he was of the strong opinion that Lenny Salter's present whereabouts would bear looking into, and to that end he'd rung Logan once again. Unfortunately, Logan's mobile was either switched off or out of range, because the phone company's answering service cut in immediately, inviting him to leave a message – which he did. He'd also thought about ringing his editor before leaving the cottage, but that was as far as it got. In his experience calls from editors were rarely good news, and usually ran along the lines of: 'That piece you're doing for us . . . We'd like it twice as long as we agreed, and a week earlier. Oh, and by the way, the boss says sorry but there's no extra money in the kitty.'

Lisa saw him on his way with every appearance of equanimity, but he couldn't help feeling a little guilty and made a mental note to make it up to her one day soon. However loose the basis of their relationship, it was hardly fair to keep walking out on Lisa and to expect her to go on accepting it with such good grace. She would be away until Sunday now, she'd told him, and he was ashamed to admit, even if only to himself, that he was glad to be a completely free agent for at least the next couple of days. He was going to be busy and it would be easier if he didn't have the feeling at the back of his mind that he was neglecting her.

On the sweep of gravel in front of Truman's house stood an impressive array of vehicles. Glancing at the number-plates Ben could see that the Rolls and the Range Rover were Eddie Truman's, the Mercedes convertible was elder daughter Helen's, and the smaller, chunky four-wheel-drive belonged to Fliss. Parked beside these was a black Audi saloon with an everyday registration, which had presumably brought DI Ford.

Ben parked his own mud-splattered vehicle between the Rolls and the Merc with a secret smile, and headed for the house, hoping – without much optimism – that Ford hadn't been accompanied on this occasion by DS Hancock.

As he prepared to press the polished bronze bell, one half of the front door opened and Bess looked out.

'Hi Ben. They're in the study. Go on through. I'm just getting more coffee.'

'What, no butler?' Ben asked, stepping past her.

'It's his day off,' she replied, smiling.

'So, what's happened, d'you know?'

'Well we had another email, but I'd better let them tell you. Go on through.'

When Ben rapped on the door of Truman's study and let himself in he came face to face with Hancock, who was on his way out.

The DS greeted Ben with a sneer.

'Ah, here comes our intrepid crusading journalist. No need to worry now, then – Ben Copperfield's on the case.'

Over Hancock's shoulder Ben could see not only Ford and Eddie Truman, but also Truman's wife, two daughters and son-in-law.

'Give it a rest, Sergeant,' Ford said wearily, nodding a greeting at Ben, who sidestepped Hancock without a glance.

'Morning, Inspector.'

'Well, now you *are* here, come on in and sit down,' Truman said testily. As Ben went closer he could see the strain on the trainer's face; the fresh development was obviously not for the better.

He crossed to an empty chair and sat in it, acknowledging a muted greeting from Fliss as he did so and finding the leather already warm, probably from Hancock's recent occupancy. Sitting on a window seat, Truman's wife, Elizabeth, looked pale and anxious; opposite Ben, Helen and her husband shared the small leather settee. She was staring at the floor, her habitual sulky expression more pronounced even than usual, and only glanced up momentarily as Ben came in. Ray Finch nodded but seemed absorbed in circling one of the deep upholstery buttons with a forefinger. They might have been next to each other, but their body language put them miles apart.

On the other side of the room the door closed behind Hancock.

'Right, now we've got the pleasantries out of the way, can we return to the matter in hand?' Truman enquired. 'Tomorrow. I'm still not happy about trying to trick them, you know, Ford.'

'I thought you'd decided to pay up,' Ben said.

'Yes, yes, we have,' the trainer replied. 'But they've added another condition. They want Helen to drive the car to the drop-off point.'

'And I'm not bloody doing it!' his daughter stated.

'I'd do it, if it was me they wanted,' Fliss put in. A gleam of sunlight lit one side of her head, accentuating the rich copper of her hair. She wore very little make-up, as far as Ben could see, and her fresh-faced vitality was in sharp contrast to her older sister's air of jaded depression.

'Well, it's not you they want,' Helen pointed out. 'So you can't play the heroine, can you?'

'For God's sake, don't start bickering over it,' Truman cut in, forestalling Fliss's retort. 'Neither of you is going, so let that be an end to it.'

Ben frowned. 'Why do they want Helen to do it? Did they give a reason?'

Truman shook his head but it was Ford who answered. 'No. Maybe they think Mr Truman will be less likely to try anything if she's involved. What we'll do is use a WPC instead and hope that – if they watch the drop at all – they'll see a woman and not look any closer.'

'But do you think they'll really believe he hasn't involved your lot?'

'Some don't, you know,' Ford said. 'Some

208

people follow the kidnappers' instructions to the letter and we only find out about it afterwards, when it's all over, for better or worse, and they want us to catch the culprits. Makes our job ten times harder.'

'So what's the plan for tomorrow?'

Before Ford could answer Truman cut in with mingled frustration and annoyance.

'Dah! You're wasting your time. He won't tell you.'

'Not won't; can't,' the DI said evenly. 'We can make contingency plans but, until we see which way the wind's blowing, we can't really decide which will be our best bet.'

'What's to say they'll keep their side of the bargain?' Finch spoke up suddenly. 'What if they take the money, keep the horse and ask for more? What's to stop them doing that?'

'Well, theoretically, nothing,' Ford said. 'But, in practice, I would have thought very few people would pay again once the trust had been broken. And of course, as I've said before, picking up the ransom is the most dangerous part for the kidnappers, so why would they choose to do it twice? Why not just ask for more initially, if they think they can get it?'

The door opened and Bess came in.

During the momentary lull in the debate as coffee was handed round, Ford caught Ben's eye. 'My colleagues in Wincanton tell me you've been busy, Ben. Brawling outside a pub, wasn't it?' he commented, with the suspicion of a twinkle in his eye.

'Something like that. It got me the chance of

the inside angle on ALSA, though. I had a guided tour of their HQ.'

'Henry Allerton?'

'Yes, that's right. The lad I helped out turned out to be his nephew. I earned his undying gratitude. Well, it lasted a day or two, at any rate.'

'Best of a bad bunch, Henry,' Ford remarked. 'Find out anything interesting?'

'Not really. But one of them did let slip something about a project or campaign. They clearly didn't want to talk about it, so I, er . . . went back for another look round later, on my own.'

'And finding the door open you took a look inside?' Ford suggested.

'Well, in a manner of speaking,' Ben said with half a smile. 'Didn't find anything useful, though, and I nearly got caught by a couple of the group: Baz and Della. And then, as luck would have it, I ran into my friend Baz again a couple of nights ago. He was involved in a raid on a travelling horse circus I've been doing an article on, and what's more they caught him. Haven't heard any more.'

'I'll have a word with Sussex and see whether they're bringing charges,' Ford said. 'We've not seen or heard anything of ALSA that leads us to believe they have anything major on the go, and if they're still carrying out these kinds of nuisance raids, it seems unlikely they *do* have anything very important going on. As a matter of fact, the word is that the whole organisation is beginning to lose its way a little. Their number of supporters certainly seems to have dropped over the past few months.'

'I'm not surprised, with drop-outs like Baz and

Della involved. It's just the image that any bona fide organisation would strive to avoid. Those two look like your typical serial protesters. Roads; new housing; save the whales; you name it and I bet they're there.'

'Having established that ALSA haven't got my horse, can we return to the problem in hand?' Truman asked impatiently. 'What assurance have I got that these bastards won't just take my money and bugger off without giving King back?'

'None at all,' Ford told him. 'But I should think it's unlikely. After all, one would assume they wouldn't want to keep the horse, and letting it loose somewhere would be easier than trying to dispose of a creature that size.'

'And it couldn't tell us where it had been,' Ben added, earning a lowering glance from Truman.

'Oh, they've got to give him back! It would be so unfair!' Fliss said with a touch of desperation, as if it were only now hitting home that they could lose the horse for ever.

'Well, I'd better be getting back to the yard,' Finch said, draining his mug and standing up. 'Got runners to get ready for this afternoon.'

'Oh, Ben, I'm afraid you'll have to make your own way to Wincanton this afternoon,' Truman said. 'I've got a meeting with my bank manager. Wretched man's kicking up a fuss about my wanting to withdraw so much cash in a hurry. No one would think it was *my* money, the way he's carrying on. He needn't expect my custom in future, that's all I can say.'

Looking at him, Ben could see that it wasn't just an empty threat. He really would take his business elsewhere. Truman definitely wasn't a man to cross, even in a small way.

'Ben can come to Wincanton with me,' Fliss suggested. 'There's no point in taking more cars than we need to. Or you could probably hitch a ride in the lorry, if you'd rather – but you'll have to hurry, they'll be going any minute now.'

She couldn't know it, but there were very few things Ben would have liked less than going in the horsebox. On the other hand, he wasn't at all sure he should go with Fliss either, judging from the speculative frown on her father's face.

'Or I could drive you?' he offered, careful not to catch Truman's eye.

'You told me you weren't a chauvinist,' she said accusingly.

'And I'm not. But I like to think I'm a gentleman,' he countered. 'OK, thanks, I'm quite happy for you to drive.'

Fliss drove well if with a little too much aggression, possibly engendered by her feminist ideals. In an attempt to relax her, Ben asked about the stable routine on racing days and, her mind successfully diverted, she did indeed begin to drive more temperately.

'The travelling head lad – that's Ian Rice – is responsible for the horses once they've left the yard,' Fliss said. 'It's up to him to make sure they reach the racecourse safely and on time. Ideally that's three hours before the first one is due to run. Gives them time to settle, get over the journey, etc. He has to make sure each horse is accompanied by its passport and flu vac certificate, and get it signed into the stables. He also has to declare the runners at least three quarters of an hour before the race and take all the gear to the valet, you know – jockeys' silks, weights, saddle and suchlike.'

'Where do the valets come from?'

'All over the place. They follow the racing. You get about half a dozen valets at each race meeting. They basically look after the jockeys. We see them all regularly and know some of them quite well.

'Anyway, about an hour before the race we have to start to get our runners ready; twenty minutes before the off we take them to the saddling area and tack up. They're walked round the pre-parade ring and then when they're saddled they go through to the parade ring, which is where the jockeys get legged up, and then it's all down to them.'

'What do you do about feeding on race days?'

'The horses get an early feed and some hay, but nothing in the lorry and obviously not at the course. We remove their water buckets three to four hours before the race and just offer them a little drink in the stables, but not too much. As you know, a horse with a stomach full of water isn't going to run its best.'

'What about shoeing? They have special aluminium ones, don't they?'

'Yeah, they're called racing plates –' She broke off abruptly and leaned on the horn, earning an 'up yours!' gesture from the driver who had just skimmed across her bows. 'Moron!'

'He did have the right of way,' Ben pointed out mildly.

'Well, he should have indicated. What am I supposed to do, read his mind?'

'No. You're supposed to drive as if everyone else on the road is an idiot, because half of them are. Go on about the shoes.'

She cast him a look of annoyance but continued nonetheless. 'Plates. They're put on a day or two before a race, depending on when the farrier's at the yard. I remember we had one old horse that used to start getting excited as soon as his racing plates were put on. I swear he could tell the difference.'

'And how long do they stay on?'

'Well, if the horse is running again within the week we leave them on, but otherwise, next time the farrier comes he takes them off.'

'So what's the routine after the race?' Ben was genuinely interested, and he never knew when such information might come in useful on a future assignment.

'They're unsaddled – in the winners enclosure if we're lucky – then offered a drink, hosed down, scraped, covered with a cooler – you know, like a string vest – and walked for half to three quarters of an hour. They need to be cooled down and settled before the journey home. It's always at least an hour after our last runner before we set off. Then, of course, they all have to be fed and checked over when they get home. If it's one of the northern tracks or an evening meeting it can sometimes be nearly midnight by the time we finish for the day, and we've been up since half-four. Plus, Rice still has all the coolers and sheets and jockeys' silks to wash. It's bloody hard work.'

'But worth it when you get a winner.'

'Oh, yes,' Fliss said warmly. 'Always worth it, because of the horses.'

'Do the lads get a bonus when their horse wins?'

'Theoretically, but what we do is pool all the bonuses and split the money between all the lads at the end of the season. It's much fairer that way.'

'So has Mikey really got a chance today?' Ben asked, as they joined the end of a slowly moving queue of cars on the approach to the racecourse entrance.

'Yeah, he has, actually. As I said yesterday, Axesmith is a really strong contender. Rollo would have been riding him if he hadn't got himself suspended, but I don't see why Mikey shouldn't make as good a job of it. He seems to get on with the horse really well.'

Once they'd entered the racecourse itself, Fliss and Ben went their separate ways; Fliss to oversee the care of the Castle Ridge runners and Ben to wander with the crowds, place a token bet or two and enjoy the early spring sunshine.

As the first of the Castle Ridge horses was brought into the parade ring by its lad, Ben saw Fliss standing in the grassy centre area talking to the horse's owners. She'd changed before they set out. Gone were the trendy hipster jeans and branded sweatshirt that she'd worn at home, to be replaced by boots, a suede skirt and a sophisticated, tailored leather jacket worn over a cream jumper. The effect was perfect: she looked elegant, mature and far older than her twenty-two years. Judging by the look in the eyes of the middle-aged male owner to whom she was talking, he had no complaints about her father's replacement either.

Mikey came out presently, his expression serious and a little shy, but a few words and a smile from Fliss won an answering smile, and by the time he was legged up into the tiny saddle he was looking far more relaxed.

As the runners left the paddock to make their way down to the start, Ben took advantage of the trainer's pass Fliss had given him and climbed the stairs to the stands in order to get a better view. Axesmith wasn't due to run until later in the afternoon and, according to the bookies, Mikey's current mount wasn't expected to do a lot; but as he rode out on to the turf, settling the horse into an easy canter, Ben was intensely proud of his young half-brother. The long, dispiriting struggle of his school years was behind him. On the back of a horse he was anyone's equal.

By the time the starter got them settled and running, Fliss had joined Ben and was following Mikey's progress on the big screen, muttering to herself all the while. To Ben's eyes, Mikey's horse seemed to be jumping neatly and holding its own for speed, and as the field rounded the final bend and moved into the home straight, Mikey was sitting fourth or fifth, not more than two lengths off the leader.

'He's doing well,' he remarked to Fliss.

'He's doing *very* well,' she replied, transferring her gaze from the screen to the track, and there was a strong undercurrent of excitement in her voice.

The eight horses on the track began to string

out as the pace increased and, as they settled against the rail, Ben and Fliss saw that Mikey had pulled up to third place. Two more hurdles came and went and suddenly the second-placed horse was falling back and the Castle Ridge runner was neck and neck with the leader.

Ben could sense Fliss's growing excitement.

'Don't let him drift; don't let him drift. Keep him straight,' she urged the distant figure.

'He's going to do it!' Ben exclaimed. 'I think he's got him!'

'Come on, Mikey! Come on!' Fliss cried, jumping up and down as the two duelling thoroughbreds thundered down the last furlong. Her voice rose to a scream, 'Yes! He's done it! He's bloody done it!' She turned to Ben, half laughing and half crying, and threw her arms round his neck. 'He was brilliant! Dad's never going to believe this! That horse has been unplaced so many times we were thinking of renaming him Also Ran! Your brother's a magician.'

'So much for your brother-in-law's prediction,' Ben observed, as they drew apart.

Fliss began to straighten her jacket and hair. 'Ray's the kind of bloke who can't bear anyone else to get on. He didn't want Dad to take Mikey on in the first place. Listen, I must go down and walk him in. Are you coming?'

Visions of sidling, jostling thoroughbreds filled Ben's mind and he said with a smile, 'No, it's your moment. You go on. I'll see Mikey later.'

Fliss fairly skipped down the stairs and Ben watched her make her way through the crowd, acknowledging the congratulations of her many acquaintances. Suddenly, a familiar voice spoke close behind him.

'I wouldn't get any ideas in that direction, if I were you.'

He turned to find Belinda Kepple standing close by. Considering her hostility when they had first met, Ben was a little surprised that she should initiate a conversation now.

'Meaning?'

'Meaning that the last person who trifled with one of Eddie Truman's daughters without his approval found himself out of a job and out of the country.'

'Oh? Who was that?'

'Can't remember his name, it was some time ago. He was a jockey from Poland or Czechoslovakia or some such place. I believe Truman found him riding in South Africa and brought him over. He made a lot of noise about him; swore he'd be the next champion jockey. I think it was all a big publicity stunt. Though, as it turned out, he was good, exceptional even – but it didn't save his bacon when the crunch came. Got caught with his trousers down – literally, so I heard – and Eddie saw red. Threw him out the night before the Derby and made sure he never rode again.'

'You don't mean . . . he kneecapped him?'

Belinda raised her eyebrows. 'Oh, you've heard about that then? No, not this time. I meant he never rode *here* again. The word was that Eddie got him deported, somehow; sent him back to wherever he came from. I don't know if that's true, but nothing would surprise me about that man.'

'When was this?'

'Oh, Lord – I don't know! Years ago, when Helen was about fifteen or sixteen. He wasn't the man Eddie wanted for her; he had big plans. Though I can't help thinking she'd have been better off with her foreigner than she is with that miserable bastard she's got now!'

'I'd never realised there were so many foreigners in racing. Half the lads at Castle Ridge only speak pidgin English and the other half are Irish.'

Belinda nodded. 'It's the same everywhere.'

'Helen's jockey – the one that Eddie threw out – was that the year they won the Derby?'

'Yes, that's right. With Massingham. Everybody felt so sorry for the boy, he was a likeable lad. But listen, all I'm saying is, just be wary around Eddie. He's not the man to get on the wrong side of.'

Ben was puzzled.

'So why the warning? You don't pretend to like Eddie Truman and I didn't get the impression you were a particular fan of mine, either. What's it to you if he and I have a bust-up?'

Belinda pursed her lips.

'I don't know. Perhaps it's because Fliss is a nice girl, and I wouldn't want to see her hurt; or perhaps it's because every time I look at you I see your father, and he and I go back quite a way.'

Ben looked at the secret smile lurking behind her eyes and was hit by a certainty.

'You're lovers,' he said. 'Good God!'

'That's a long way from complimentary,' Belinda protested.

'No, I'm sorry. It's just – you know, parents and all that.'

'Life doesn't end at forty, you know,' she laughed.

'So, are you still together?'

'On and off. Your father doesn't like to be pinned down. I see him for a bit and then I don't. It's not what I'd choose but it's that or nothing. God, I don't know why I'm telling you this. It's absolutely none of your business.'

'Mm. Did I tell you I've been offered a job as gossip columnist for *Racing Life*?' he asked, tongue-in-cheek.

'Has anyone ever told you you're a obnoxious young man? Look, I've got horses to see to. Remember me to Johnnie, if you see him before I do.'

'Yeah, likewise.'

Belinda turned away and then turned back briefly. 'Oh, and by the way, tell that brother of yours if he ever wants a change of scenery, he can come and ride for me.'

'Thanks,' Ben said, surprised. 'I'll tell him.'

For a minute or two he stood leaning on the rail and watching the endlessly shifting crowds, his mind occupied with what he had just learned. Had she really thought there was something developing between Fliss and himself? Did Fliss think so? He hoped not; he'd certainly done nothing to convey that message. Attractive as she undoubtedly was, she was too young; besides, he was very happy with Lisa. Wasn't he?

He remembered the warm contentment of that morning.

Yes, he was happy.

Why, then, did he constantly shy away from

thoughts of permanency? Was it a hereditary thing? Belinda Kepple's description of her relationship with his father had struck an uncomfortable chord. But then his father had more excuse than Ben did. He had two broken marriages behind him; twice he'd been left. And the hell of it was, Ben firmly believed, that if it hadn't been for the accident that killed his brother, his parents would have stayed together to this day. Now, even after all these years, a shadow of guilt passed over him. One simple, stupid suggestion had started off the tragic chain of events on that morning nearly twenty years ago; one simple suggestion – and *he* had made it.

Giving himself a mental shaking, Ben moved away from the railings and descended the stairs to ground level. Suddenly the people and the noise grated on him, and he decided to walk up the course to the starting point for the next race, using the exercise and the cold wind to clear his mind. There was a stone building beside which he could shelter and watch them jump off.

There were fifteen runners in the next race, and they began to pass him when he was still some fifty or sixty yards from the start; tall leggy thoroughbreds, sleek coated and handsome, blowing ephemeral plumes of steam into the cold air, their jockeys not much more than dabs of colour on their backs.

Mikey was the last but one to go by, calmly cantering past on board a light-framed chestnut gelding. He didn't appear to notice Ben's trudging figure, and Ben did nothing to try and

221

attract his attention, aware that any undue movement might cause the highly-strung animal to shy.

Looking back down the course Ben could see a dark bay approaching, almost broadside on, tossing and diving its head in an effort to loosen its rider's grip. Even as he watched, the animal appeared to stumble and then, in one continuous movement, leapt into the air, twisting its body like a corkscrew.

The jockey had no chance. Hopelessly off-balance, his precarious hold was shaken loose as soon as the horse's feet hit the ground again and he pitched sideways in a flash of blue and yellow silks, the reins still clutched firmly in his hand.

At this point, the horse returned its attention to fulfilling its original ambition – that of reaching his companions as fast as he could – but the jockey had other ideas. Rolling over and coming swiftly to his feet, he tried to dig his heels into the turf and bring the horse to a standstill, but the bay was having none of it and, after a few stumbling steps, its rider tripped and measured his length on the grass.

'Let go of the reins,' Ben urged under his breath. 'Let go!'

Maybe the jockey was an apprentice, like Mikey, to whom every chance to race was precious, or maybe he was just naturally ten-acious; whatever the reason he hung on grimly, bumping and sliding across the ground as the horse, alarmed now, broke into a shambling trot, peering sideways at the horror beside it.

'Oh, let go, you stupid idiot!' Ben pleaded,

looking desperately up and down the course in the hope of seeing someone running to the jockey's aid.

The nearest possible hope was still some forty yards distant.

There was no one but Ben.

As if to force his hand the horse, still moving sideways, but faster now, was veering in Ben's direction; without conscious decision he ducked under the white plastic rail and walked calmly out on to the track.

In most cases, it would probably have been a vain attempt. The horse would have seen him coming, swerved around him and continued on its merry way, but this one was preoccupied with the trauma of having something dragging behind it, and didn't seem to notice Ben at all.

With a strange feeling of detachment, Ben reached out for the horse's offside rein. The moment his fingers closed round the leather the bay threw up its head and ran backwards but, with the combined weight of the two men, it wasn't going anywhere. It stopped, dropping gobs of white foam from its open mouth and staring down at Ben with white-rimmed eyes.

'Thanks, mate.' The jockey was on his feet in no time and moving towards the animal's head. 'Couldn't give me a leg up, could you?'

'Sure,' Ben heard himself say, as if it were the most natural thing in the world.

As the slight figure beside him took hold of the reins, the horse, baulked of the chance to go forward, or even sideways, reverted to running round them both in tight circles. Ben felt the beginnings of panic, and had there been anywhere for him to go, he would probably have gone – whatever the jockey might have thought of him – but the animal was effectively blocking all avenues of retreat at once.

'Just put me up,' the jockey said over his shoulder, bending his left leg at the knee.

It had been years since Ben had legged anyone into the saddle but the skill seemed to have stayed with him. The next moment the jockey dropped lightly into the tiny flat saddle and pushed his feet into the stirrups.

'OK?' Ben asked.

'OK.' The blue and yellow silk-covered head nodded. Ben released the reins and the horse was away, trotting on a tight rein to join its fellows at the start.

Ben ducked back under the rails and turned to lean on them, breathing deeply to settle his racing pulse; no longer anxious to reach the starting area and the company of people who might notice his perspiring skin and shaking hands.

As he stared down at the lush green turf beneath his feet, he remembered Jakob Varga's parting words. *Fear itself isn't weakness, you know. The weakness is not admitting it.*

Well, he wasn't going to deny it any more. What if that had been Mikey dragging behind that horse? This time he'd forced himself to act but it had been a close-run thing. Finally he was prepared to admit that if he couldn't conquer his fear, he should find himself another line of work.

10

Ben thought he was going to pass out.

Melles. Big-chested. Just at that moment the huge grey shire seemed to fill the stable.

Ben began seriously to doubt his own resolve. He'd come to the stables looking for Jakob, and had approached Melles' box on nothing more than a whim. He knew the heavy horse was possibly the most placid animal in the Csikós' string and, as the long head reached forward to greet him, ears pricked, he steeled himself to rub the soft muzzle with his hand. His pulse rate moved up a notch and his breath shortened, but he handled it, and when Melles lost interest and returned to his hay net, Ben screwed up his courage, unbolted the door and stepped inside. The horse turned his head and regarded him with mild curiosity, completely unaware of what it was costing Ben to remain within the stable.

If he'd stayed by the door, he would probably have been all right, but Ben was determined to test himself. Three or four smooth paces brought him to the horse's side and once more he reached out to stroke the animal, this time on the powerful crested neck, and once again – with slow deep breaths – he coped. A small swell of triumph rose within him.

And then Melles moved.

Suddenly a towering mountain of horseflesh blocked Ben's path to the door. He hadn't moved particularly fast but, somehow, by the time Ben realised his intent, it was already too late.

The loose box wasn't very big and with eighteen hands of shire blocking the light from the half-door, its dimensions shrank rapidly to claustrophobic. All the horror of the accident returned to stifle Ben. His vision started to break up and his chest contracted until he just couldn't seem to get his breath at all. Once again he felt the weight of the horse pressing him into the bodywork of the lorry and saw beside him the white, lifeless face of the person he held most dear: his twin brother, Alan.

Now, through his panic, Ben became aware of approaching footfalls; the quick, light tread that was characteristic of many of the troupe. Maybe that was why Melles had gone to the door. Pray God it wasn't Ferenc! In spite of – and also because of – his panic, Ben's pride recoiled from the idea of asking *him* for help.

A soft voice spoke to the horse in a tongue that could have been Hungarian, Romani, or a mixture of both, and Ben sent thanks winging upwards.

'Jakob?'

'Ben?' The answering voice sounded unsure.

The big grey moved back a step in response

to a hand on his nose, and Jakob's lined but infinitely welcome face peered in at Ben.

'Are you all right?'

'Yes, I'm OK.' Weak, nauseous and sweating from head to toe, but basically OK.

Jakob opened the door and came in, pushing Melles back another step or two. The big grey head dropped to nuzzle his hands for titbits.

'You shouldn't be in here. We have insurance, but not for this. Not for you on your own.'

Ben slipped past him and out into the yard. It was raining, a slow steady drizzle, which matched his mood.

Something of it must have shown in his face, for as Jakob shut the door and turned, he looked sharply at Ben.

'You *are* all right?'

Ben forced a smile and nodded. 'Yeah. Sorry about the insurance. You know I wouldn't have claimed, anyway.'

'I know. And Melles is not the horse to harm you. Unless, of course, he had stood on your foot. Tamás said you were looking for me?' The lift in his voice turned it into a question.

'Yes . . .' Ben hesitated, not sure if he could go through with it now.

'You want to ride again.'

'Yes. That is . . . I did. Now I'm not sure.'

'Deep down, you do. Or you wouldn't be here,' Jakob said simply. He put his arm round the younger man's shoulders. 'Come. First we will drink coffee and you will tell me from where comes this great fear.'

The canteen area was deserted when Jakob and

Ben reached it; the van closed and many of the chairs and tables stacked against the side.

'You're moving today,' Ben said, remembering.

'This afternoon. Come on in. I'll make us a drink.'

Jakob opened a door in the end of the catering wagon and they both went inside. Jakob immediately began to busy himself while Ben leaned against the worktop and watched, but the link between his eyes and his brain was only superficial; his thoughts were firmly elsewhere.

'If you want to beat this, you have to tell me everything,' Jakob said after a moment. 'You've kept it inside for too long. Fear thrives in dark, secret places. It grows bigger and bigger until you can't see the edges any more and you feel that if it escaped it would take control. But that's not true, Ben. You need to share it – to drag it into the open and face it, and then it will start to shrink. I promise you it is so.'

Jakob's phrasing was melodramatic but, nevertheless, Ben knew he was right.

Knowing it was one thing, but overcoming the habit of a lifetime was quite another. For the first fourteen years of his life he'd had Alan to confide in – who understood him as only a twin could. But after his death there had been no one; his parents had drawn inexorably and bitterly apart, and neither had much time for their remaining son except as a weapon with which to wound the other. Sharing his worries was a luxury he had learned to live without. Now, he wasn't even sure he could.

'Tell me the start of it,' Jakob suggested, placing

a mug of coffee on the worktop in front of Ben and pulling out a couple of tall stools to sit on.

Ben took a mouthful of strong, black coffee and burnt his tongue, but hardly noticed.

'Was it an accident? How old were you?'

'I was fourteen – *we* were fourteen; I had a twin.'

Jakob's prompting finally loosened Ben's tongue.

'There were always horses when I was growing up. My parents were dealers: they bought and sold show ponies and jumpers, and from the time we were big enough to sit in a saddle, my brother Alan and I would spend every weekend – and a good few weekdays – at horse shows. Mum and Dad would buy unbroken youngsters, back them and school them with us on board, and then we'd hit the shows to win prizes and bump up the resale value. It was a very successful operation, as far as I can remember. Dad, especially, had a great eye for raw talent, and Mum took charge of the breaking and schooling. Alan and I got to be very good at getting the best out of a variety of ponies – and then horses, of course, as we got older. We used to win all the time. I expect we were horribly conceited brats. Some of the other kids on the circuit really hated us, but it never mattered, of course, because we had each other.

'We missed a fair amount of school in our early years, but when we started GCSEs our parents got quite strict. We still did the weekend shows but on weekdays we had to go to school, unless it was a very important show. The horses we were riding were big enough by then for Mum to take over during the week.'

Ben paused, and when he continued his voice and expression were bleak.

'This one day, we should have been at school – our parents thought we were – but we'd bunked off. Played truant. It was the Bath and West, you see. One of our favourites, and we'd never missed it before. Dad had a heavyweight hunter he was pretty sure would take the championship and we wanted to be there. So we planned it in advance, got off the bus at the second stop and doubled back. We thought if we hid in the horsebox until we got there they'd be pretty angry, but it'd be too late for them to do anything about it.

'The thing is, we never got there. Halfway down the A303 some guy fell asleep at the wheel and jackknifed his articulated lorry right in front of us. Dad tried to avoid it, bounced off the crash barrier, ran up a bank and the horsebox went over on its side.'

He paused again, staring into his coffee cup.

'Dad's show hunter had pulled one of his leg protectors off earlier in the trip, and Alan and I were in the back, trying to put it back on. When the lorry went over, Trojan came over on top of us. With the lorry on its side he couldn't get up and we were trapped underneath him . . .' Ben swallowed hard, and the coffee in his cup rippled as his hand began to shake. 'I was near Trojan's head but Alan was under his belly. He couldn't breathe. I could just see his face. He cried out to me a couple of times and then went quiet. We were looking at one another and I watched him die.'

There was a long moment of silence in the catering van and Ben watched in surprise as a splash of moisture landed on the worktop. As he emerged from his memories, he found his vision swimming with unshed tears.

The discovery was shocking.

He'd never been able to cry for his brother before. At the time, shock had given way to a form of denial; a numbness that dulled all his senses for months to follow. By the time the numbness passed, suppression had become a habit.

Jakob was watching him, a wealth of sympathy in his hooded black eyes.

'Why are you blaming yourself, Ben? There was nothing you could have done.'

Ben put a hand to his eyes, shook his head and sniffed.

'But you see, it *was* my fault, because it was *my* idea. If I hadn't suggested it, Alan would still be alive.'

'I doubt it,' Jakob said. 'You were twins, Ben. I'm sure you only said what he was already thinking. If you hadn't suggested it, he would have done. You didn't force him to go along.'

Ben shook his head again. 'No. I didn't force him.'

'Then there is no blame.' Jakob made a small noise of disgust and spoke a few words in his own tongue before saying, 'Someone should have talked to you at the time. A child – and you were only a child – should never have been left to deal with such a thing, such a tragedy, on his own.'

Ben pulled a handkerchief from his pocket and made good use of it.

'My parents were too busy blaming each other,

and themselves,' he explained. 'They divorced less than a year after it happened. Everything was a mess.'

'And you? What happened to you?'

'Oh, I went to live with my father but he was determined to put it all behind him. He wouldn't speak of it. It was almost as if Alan had never existed. Pretty soon he got married again, and then he had a new life that I didn't really fit into. I packed up and left to go and live with my mother, but halfway there I changed my mind. I went to Dover, got on a cross-channel ferry and spent the next six months in France. I spent my sixteenth birthday working in a vineyard in the Dordogne.' Back on a more even keel, Ben took a sip from his cup. 'I travelled for a couple of years, then came back to catch up on my schooling and eventually went to university. That's basically it,' he finished, with an apologetic smile. 'I thought I'd put it behind me, but it just keeps coming back.'

'Every time you get close to horses, and yet, you choose to work around them. Are you punishing yourself for what happened, Ben? For the death of your twin and the break-up of your family? I think you are.'

Ben was taken aback. 'That's pretty deep, isn't it? Where did that come from?'

Smiling slightly, Jakob shook his head.

'You forget, I am Rom – Romani – or at least part of me is. We have the sight.' He read the burgeoning cynicism in Ben's eyes and threw up his hands to silence him. 'No, I'm not talking about tea-leaves or crystal balls, that's just for the Gadje – the tourists. I mean what we see in here.'

He tapped his temple with his index finger. 'Ah, I can see you don't believe – I don't need the sight to see that; it's in your face for the world to see.' He shook his head again. 'That's all right; I'm used to it. But I want to help you, Ben. We have to remove the fear so you can move on.'

'So, you think I must ride again.'

'Yes. You must ride again, and I will help you, if you will let me. Will you let me?'

Ben hesitated, feeling his heart begin to thud heavily.

'Yes. All right. But it must be now. We have to do it now.'

Jakob stood and picked up the cups. Putting them in the sink, he said, 'I am ready.'

'Duka?'

Ben had been waiting in the round pen behind the arena as Jakob had told him to. The same one where he'd watched, spellbound, as Ferenc put the Andalusian through his paces. Now Jakob appeared with the very same horse.

'You can ride. You told me you could. It is not something you forget. Duka will be perfect; he will do only what you tell him to. His training is of the very best.'

'I thought, perhaps, Melles,' Ben said weakly. 'I never thought . . .'

'Melles is placid but he can be – what's the word – arguing?'

'Awkward? Stubborn?'

'Yes, stubborn. He is stubborn and he is very wide. Duka will be perfect. Come.' Jakob pulled the stirrups down and tightened the girth.

Ben stepped forward, wishing he were practically anywhere else on earth. The proximity of the horse, its smell and the soft thud of its hooves in the sand all threatened to overturn his careful composure. At Jakob's bidding he swallowed hard, took the supple leather reins in his left hand, placed his right hand on the back of the saddle and bent his left leg at the knee.

Within moments he was in the saddle. His feet instinctively found the stirrups and his fingers felt for the reins. At Duka's shoulder, Jakob looked up at him and smiled.

'You see, I told you you would not forget. We will walk.'

Without waiting for a reply the Hungarian stepped forward, his hand on Duka's bridle, encouraging the horse to do the same. Ben's body immediately settled into the old familiar four-beat rhythm of the walking horse and, with a sense of wonderment, he felt his anxiety begin to melt away. Duka's neck arched proudly and Ben could see his forelegs flicking out sideways as he lifted them with the exaggerated action of his breed. The horse was light and obedient, balanced between rein and leg, and as his nerves evaporated, Ben began to glory in the forgotten joy of riding a fine horse.

'You are OK, Ben?'

Jakob's voice came from behind and to one side, and Ben saw with surprise that he had fallen back. He was alone with the horse and he was coping. More than that; it felt good.

'I'm fine.' Duka's white ears flopped to and fro as his head nodded, and the saddle creaked comfortingly. Ben squeezed with his heels and the Andalusian responded immediately, hindlegs powering him forward into a trot and then, after a circuit or two, into an armchair-comfortable rocking canter, his loosely plaited mane flopping against his neck and Ben's hands.

Back to the trot, across the middle of the circle to change the rein, and once more into a canter, Ben allowed his body to relax and go with the movement. When, after a few more circuits, he reluctantly reined the stallion in and turned to where Jakob stood at the edge of the ring, Ben couldn't prevent a grin from spreading across his face.

'I'd forgotten it could be like that,' he told the Hungarian.

'And Duka went well for you. You are good on a horse. A little stiff in your shoulders but that is to expect after – how many years?'

'Eighteen.' Ben slipped his feet out of the stirrups and dismounted, landing lightly at Duka's side. 'Christ, my legs are like jelly!' he exclaimed. 'I'll suffer for that.'

'Yes, I think you will. Just loosen his girth for me, would you?'

Jakob tossed the request casually at Ben, who went to step nearer to the Andalusian and then faltered. His eyes darted towards the older man and found that he was watching closely. The nightmare panic came back. After the heady success of riding Duka he'd thought his demons were effectively banished, but here, on the ground, it seemed nothing had changed, and instantly fear came flooding back.

'You can do it, Ben,' Jakob murmured softly. 'Look at his eyes – see how gentle he is.'

As if sensing Ben's hesitation, Duka turned his head and looked enquiringly at him, his big, dark eyes regarding him steadily, a little like a legal secretary peering over a pair of pince-nez.

'Look at his eyes, Ben.'

Ben looked, but the fear had nothing to do with conscious decision. He knew Duka had no wish to hurt him, but the knowledge didn't really help. The panic was rooted deep in his psyche, waiting there for a certain sound, smell or situation to trigger it to explode into his mind with disabling force. He bowed his head, wrestling with the urge to just turn and walk away – away from the horse, from the round pen, and from the troupe.

'If you go now, you'll never come back,' Jakob said quietly.

Damn you, I know that, Ben thought, not looking up. But suddenly he was moving again, close to Duka's side, lifting the saddle flap, feeling for the girth straps, loosening the buckles.

'OK, let's get him back to his stable,' Jakob said casually, stepping forward to take the horse's rein.

Ben moved back as Duka walked by, grateful to the man for his matter of fact manner. He felt drained and a little shaky; although he had survived the first encounter, he was under no illusion that the battle was won. The difference was that the joy of riding again had given him one important thing: the extra incentive that he needed to face up to his fear and conquer it.

*

236

As Ben left, the Csikós were busy with last-minute preparations for their move. He looked briefly for Nico, but no one seemed to know where he was so he asked Miklós, his brother, to pass on the message that he'd catch up with him at their next stop.

His journey back to Wiltshire was a thoughtful one, his mind see-sawing between the emotions of the morning and the ongoing puzzle of Cajun King's disappearance. If all had gone well that morning then presumably the horse would soon be returned, but that wouldn't necessarily be the end of his own investigation or that of the police. He couldn't see Truman being content to let the matter go. His towering ego wouldn't rest easy with the knowledge that someone had got the better of him, even if there hadn't been the little matter of half a million pounds to consider. If the kidnappers imagined that they were away and free, they should think again. With the horse safe, Ben knew Truman would spare no effort or cost to exact revenge and, remembering what he'd heard of the trainer's methods in the past, he very much doubted that his notion of settling the score would involve either the police or Her Majesty's justice system.

He thought back to his conversation with Belinda Kepple and what she'd told him about Helen and her unfortunate lover. Did that explain the apparent gaps in the pictorial history of the yard? Could Truman really have been so furious that he had destroyed all evidence that the boyfriend had ever existed? It would certainly explain the resentment Helen appeared to harbour for her father, although Ben didn't see why, if she'd felt *that* strongly, she hadn't followed her lover to Poland or wherever he originated from. Granted, she'd only been sixteen or so at the time but, after all, Ben had only been that age when he went to France. After a moment's reflection, he supposed it was different for girls.

Was it possible that this ex-Castle Ridge jockey could be behind the kidnapping? Could someone really carry a grudge for all that time? And why, for that matter, would someone wait that long? It was not as if Cajun King was the first Castle Ridge horse in fifteen years to be favourite for one of the big races. And apparently Eddie hadn't considered the deported jockey to be a threat, because he'd made no mention of him to Ben.

As his car rolled to a halt on the gravel in front of Truman's house, Ben wondered what the prevailing mood would be. He was slightly surprised that he hadn't heard from the trainer one way or another. Surely the ransom drop must have been made by now.

Unexpectedly, it was Helen who opened the front door; she didn't look exactly overjoyed to see him.

'Dad's up at the yard,' she said. 'He won't be long but you can go on up if you like.'

Squinting up at the moderately heavy drizzle that had started some twenty minutes before and showed no obvious signs of easing, Ben stayed where he was.

'I suppose I could sit in my car and wait,' he commented.

Helen regarded him with ill-concealed displeasure.

'Well, you can come in, but it'll have to be the kitchen because I'm feeding Lizzie.'

'Oh well, I'm not proud,' Ben declared obligingly.

Helen's look of dislike deepened as she stepped back to let him past and he wondered what, if anything, he'd done to merit this hostility, or whether it was just part of her general attitude.

'So how did everything go this morning?' he asked as she led the way through to the kitchen. 'Did they make the drop?'

'Yeah, but nothing happened.' Helen crossed to the high chair where her baby daughter sat, gurgling happily and pushing a plastic spoon round in a puddle of greenish puréed food. 'They're still waiting.'

'Really? You mean they picked up the money but you haven't heard anything?'

'No. I mean they haven't picked up the money. The police are watching the pick-up point but so far no one's come. We don't know what's going to happen now.' She picked up a bowl containing more of the purée and retrieved the spoon from the baby.

'So, where was the drop?' Ben asked, watching with fascination as Helen posted a brimming spoonful of mush into the child's open mouth and, in a continuation of the movement, fielded the overspill before it could go further than the little rounded chin. He remembered seeing his stepmother use precisely the same technique with Mikey when he was a baby, and wondered abstractedly whether it was something taught at ante-natal clinics or whether it came with the whole maternal-instincts package.

'Somewhere in the New Forest, I think. You'll have to ask Dad – I don't know all the details.' Helen's tone discouraged further questions and her body language plainly said that she was busy with more important things.

'She's a bonny baby,' said Ben, to whom all babies looked alike. 'How old is she?'

'Ten months. She'll be one on the first of May.'

'Oh, a May Day baby – but you didn't bow to pressure and call her May.'

'We named her after my mother, but May is her middle name,' Helen told him, relaxing and almost producing a smile as she aimed another spoonful unerringly into the small mouth. The baby's bright blue eyes opened very wide as she stared up at Ben.

'So tell me about your affair with the jockey,' Ben said, using underhand tactics and slipping the question in while Helen's guard was down.

It worked, too.

'Wh – what jockey?' she stammered, turning deathly pale. 'What do you mean?' Her concentration broken, the spoon stopped, suspended in mid-air halfway to the baby's mouth.

'I was told you had a – what shall I say – a liaison with one of the yard's jockeys when you were not much more than a kid, and that your father threw him out.'

'Daddy never told you that!' Helen had gone from ashen to decidedly pink, and the latest spoonful of mush landed with a plop on the plastic tray of the high chair while Lizzie looked on with an expression of comic surprise.

'No, it wasn't your father who told me,' Ben agreed. 'But someone who knows, nevertheless.'

'What else did they say?'

'What else do you think they might have said?'

'I don't want to talk about it. It's all way in the past,' Helen said, returning her attention to the infant, who was now happily dabbling her chubby fingers in the spilt food. 'Oh, Lizzie, what a messy girl you are! Look at your fingers – hmm? What a mess!'

Ben watched Helen use a damp flannel to wipe the tiny digits. She was going through the motions but he'd clearly rattled her.

He tried again.

'So where was it he came from? Poland? Czechoslovakia . . . ?'

'No. Look, I told you, I don't want to talk about it.'

'Was he a lot older than you?'

'Seven years, but it wasn't his fault; I told him I was eighteen.' Helen allowed herself to be drawn.

'He was due to ride in the Derby, wasn't he?'

'On the favourite. It won, too.'

'Did it, indeed? That must have made him pretty sick.'

'Oh, it was so unfair! He was absolutely brilliant – everyone said so. He would have been champion jockey one day if . . .'

'Helen!' Unseen by either of them, Elizabeth Truman had come in and was standing just inside the door. Neat and elegant, as usual, her face was as white as her daughter's had been just a few moments before. 'You know better than that.'

'I didn't tell him anything,' Helen protested, looking sulkier than ever.

'You shouldn't have said anything at all.'

'He kept asking . . .'

'About what? What's going on?' Suddenly Helen's father was there behind Elizabeth and you could have cut the atmosphere with a knife.

His wife and daughter exchanged tragic glances of theatrical proportions and then both looked at Ben; Elizabeth imploringly and Helen with a shot of pure venom.

'I've heard tell that you once fired a jockey for getting a little too friendly with Helen,' Ben stated calmly, taking the bull by the horns. 'I was just asking her about it.'

'Why don't you mind your own bloody business?' Truman demanded, explosively. 'That was years ago. Helen knows she was stupid and now she, and the rest of us, just want to be allowed to forget it.'

Ben's eyes narrowed. 'I may be working for you at the moment, but that doesn't give you the right to bawl me out. My business – if you remember – is asking questions. How the hell am I supposed to know what's taboo?'

In her high chair and temporarily forgotten, the baby began to cry. Out of the corner of his eye, Ben saw Elizabeth put out a hand towards him, as if to stop him saying anything further.

'No, Ben, please . . .' she pleaded.

'You shut up, woman!' her husband said

dismissively; then, in a quieter tone: 'Ben, I think we should go into the study.'

Ben inclined his head. 'OK.'

'Send Bess or Vicki through with coffee in a minute,' Truman said over his shoulder to his wife, who nodded, her face pink with humiliation.

Ben gave her a sympathetic smile before following the bulky figure of the trainer into the hall, feeling a little like a first-year student being summoned to the headmaster's office.

As the door of the study shut behind him, Ben braced himself for the expected tirade, but it didn't come. Truman lowered himself wearily into one leather armchair and waved him to another before saying, in a fairly matter of fact way, 'I thought we'd agreed that you would come to me first with anything you found out.'

'Yes, we did, but I haven't really found anything; that's why I was asking.'

'Well, you can stop asking. There's nothing in that sordid business that could possibly have anything to do with Cajun King's disappearance.'

'What about the jockey? Surely he was a man with a grievance.'

'He won't have come back,' Truman said with certainty.

'How can you be so sure?'

'Because he was an illegal immigrant. His papers weren't in order and I threatened to report him if he didn't go back to where he came from. I had him watched to make sure he got on his plane. That was, and is, the end of it. And look, I'd be grateful if you didn't discuss this with Ford. I've told him that much, but he doesn't need to

243

know about what happened with Helen. It's nobody's business but ours.'

Ben gave up.

'OK. So what happened this morning? I gather it didn't go exactly to plan.'

Truman rubbed his hand over his face, pinching the bridge of his nose between index finger and thumb. He looked tired and worried, and Ben partially forgave him his outburst.

'We don't know what happened – at least, we know what happened but we don't know what went wrong. Ford's WPC drove Helen's car – she was a fair double for Helen at a distance – and parked in Fordingbridge car park, as we'd been instructed. She had the money in a holdall and both Helen's mobile phone and mine, because we weren't sure which they would ring. Anyway, when she'd been there about ten minutes, they called on my mobile, and told her to take the money to Black Gutter car park, which is way out in the New Forest, halfway between Fordingbridge and the motorway junction at Cadnam. She had to leave it in the litter bin there – you know, it's one of those big square wooden ones. It was an odd choice because it's a long road across the moors with very few turnings and no cover, and although anyone following would have been spotted right away, so would anyone going to pick the money up. It would have been fairly easy to put someone on their tail.'

'Unless they came across the forest on horseback or a motorbike,' Ben suggested. 'But if you did catch them, surely you'd have to wave goodbye to any chance of getting King back.'

'Yes. I think Ford was hoping they'd lead us back to where they've got the horse,' Truman said.

'But Helen says no one came.'

'No. Hancock and a female officer in plain clothes followed Helen's car, stopped down the road to photograph the ponies, and then sat in their car for a while, but nobody came. They only stayed there for as long as it took Ford to organise long-distance surveillance from the trees on top of the far hill, then they drove on.'

'But still no one's come? Perhaps they'll wait until dark.'

'Mm. Maybe. We can only wait and see. Ford has got a couple of cars on hand to follow them, if they do.' He sighed. 'Do you know, just at the moment I'd gladly let them have the bloody money, if only they'd give King back.'

'You wouldn't feel like that for long, once you had him,' Ben observed.

'No, you're probably right.' There was a knock on the door and he called out, 'Come in.'

'Coffee?' It was a slim, blonde female whom Ben hadn't seen before. He assumed it must be the girl who helped Bess in the office.

'Ah, thanks, Vicki. Put it on the table, would you?' Truman said.

The girl gave Ben a bright smile and placed the tray on the leather-covered pedestal table beside her employer.

Almost but not quite out of Ben's line of sight, Truman brought his hand up and rested it on her hip, then squeezed her buttock lightly as she moved away.

Vicki gave no sign that she had even noticed, which Ben could only take to mean that such caresses were commonplace. His sympathy for Elizabeth deepened in direct proportion to his antipathy for Truman.

When the secretary had left the room, shutting the door behind her, the trainer handed Ben a mug, and sat back in his chair once more.

'Did you see the piece on the back page of the *Mail*, building the big race up? It was kind of a shock, reading about King as if nothing was wrong. When it's on your mind twenty-four hours a day, you forget that no one else knows. We've spread rumour that he's away for a few days, receiving treatment for an unspecified back problem, but the tipsters and journalists will start to watch the gallops soon, and how long will we be able to keep his disappearance a secret then? It's less than two weeks until the race.'

'Quite frankly, I'm surprised you've managed it this long,' Ben said. 'And who knows? – it might even be a good thing. With the general public on the lookout, it might spook the kidnappers into letting him go.'

'Or shooting him,' Truman said gloomily.

'There is that. Supposing you do get him back, will he be fit to race? After all, he's been away for nearly a week already.'

'Depends where he's been kept. If he's been cooped up somewhere, he probably won't, unless we get him back in the next day or two. But he's a horse that doesn't take much work. He's quite lazy at home and if you overdo it, he gets stale. If he's been well looked after and has had the run of a paddock, I don't see why he shouldn't be all right. I've had horses that have been resting injuries until a few days before they ran and have still won their races. A lot depends on character, and his is good.'

There didn't seem to be a lot more to say on the subject, so Ben commented, 'You must have been pleased with Mikey's performance yesterday . . .'

'What? Oh, yes, he did well; very well.'

'I think a few people are starting to sit up and take notice. Fliss said Axesmith went as well as he's ever done, and he gave that first horse a smashing ride.'

'You were something of a hero yourself, according to my daughter. Throwing yourself in the path of a runaway horse or something.'

'It was trotting and I caught its rein,' Ben said dryly.

'Oh well; *she* seemed impressed, at any rate. I think she had you down as one of life's spectators.' Truman looked up at Ben from under his gingery brows.

'Of course. That's what being a journalist is all about,' he responded evenly, choosing to ignore the taunt.

Truman looked as though he might pursue the point further but they were interrupted by a knock at the door.

'Yes?'

The door opened and Bess came in, looking pale and shaken. She held a sheet of A4 paper in her hand, which she hurried forward to give to her employer.

'This just came; I thought you'd better see it straight away.'

Truman took the sheet and scanned it rapidly.

'No! Damn it! They can't do that! We did everything they said. What more could we have done?' The hand holding the paper began to shake, but whether from fear or rage Ben couldn't tell.

'May I see it?'

Truman passed the sheet over and Ben began to read.

It was unmistakably an email print-out from a computer, and the printing occupied only a few lines at the top of the page. Addressed to EddieTruman@Castleridgeracing, and sent from a Hotmail address, it read:

Don't play tricks on me. I know you were watching. You have risked the life of your horse. Tomorrow the postman will bring you something to remember him by.

It was, predictably, unsigned.

'The fucking bastards!' Truman was in full flow now, on his feet and slamming his hand on his desk. 'When I find out who's behind this, I'll personally string them up by their balls and light a fire under them. If they touch that horse . . .'

'What do you think they'll do?' With her boss almost incoherent with frustrated fury, Bess turned instinctively to Ben, her brown eyes wide with anxiety. 'You don't think they'll . . . ?'

In all honesty, Ben couldn't reassure her.

'I really don't know, but they have said "risked"

rather than "forfeited", so maybe it's just another warning.'

'Give it here!' Truman said reaching for the email. He read it again, then jabbed his finger at the print. 'Yes, but they also say I'll have "something to remember him by"; so how does that fit in with your theory?'

Ben shrugged and shook his head.

'We can only wait and see. The wording is a little strange, don't you think? "You have risked the life of your horse" – it's a funny way of putting it.'

'Well, I'm glad you find it amusing. What the fuck does it matter if they can't put a sentence together? That's hardly the issue here, is it?'

Ben decided to keep his thoughts to himself. Truman was hardly in a mood to listen to half-formed ideas, and he couldn't even call them that. There was just something that struck an odd note.

'Shall I call DI Ford?' Bess asked, cutting through his thoughts.

'Bloody police!' Truman spat the words. 'They ballsed it up. Told me they wouldn't be seen. Should've kept them out of it, like I was supposed to. They've done nothing but waste my time from the start!'

'Yeah, I should call him, Bess,' Ben said quietly. 'He ought to be told.'

'And you've done no better!' The trainer turned his attention to Ben. 'Just where do you get off, giving orders to my staff, in my own home?'

Ben inclined his head.

'You want me to go – you just say the word. I've got better things to do than hang around here to be your whipping boy!'

He didn't raise his voice at all, but got through to Truman nonetheless.

The trainer stared hard at Ben for a long moment and then his hackles visibly began to come down.

'Yes, well maybe I shouldn't have spoken like that, but you know I've got a temper on me. It's my red hair. You'd best stick around for a bit.'

It was as close to an apology as he was likely to get and Ben saw Bess raise her eyebrows in exaggerated astonishment as she left the room.

'Well, it doesn't look as though anyone can do anything until the morning, so I'm for home and a hot bath,' Ben said, standing up and feeling his inner thigh muscles starting to complain. He had a notion they'd be creating hell by the morning but they were a physical memory of what he'd achieved, and that was more than adequate compensation.

'No Lisa tonight?'

Mike, Ben's Geordie landlord, was cleaning the gutters on the front of the cottage when he drove into the yard. In spite of the cold he was only wearing a checked cotton shirt, the sleeves of which were rolled up to expose his heavily tattooed, beefy forearms. Ben got out of his car and shut the driver's door behind him, hoping Mouse would keep her head down.

'No, she's working.'

'Cracking girl that,' Mike rumbled, coming down from the stepladder.

'Yeah, she is.' Ben swung his coat over his shoulder and made for the front door, trying to walk normally on legs that refused to co-operate.

Mike gathered the leaves and moss that he'd cleared from the gutter. Picking up the bucket and tools, he watched as Ben unlocked the door.

'Everything all right?' he asked. 'Need any more wood for the burner?'

'No, I'm OK at the moment, thanks.'

'OK, well, let me know.' Mike turned away then paused. 'Oh – and Ben . . .'

'Yeah?'

'You've left your dog in the car.' With that, Mike clicked his tongue, winked, and went on his way.

'Son of a bitch!' Ben said under his breath, and headed back to the Mitsubishi.

After soaking his aching muscles for half an hour in the hottest bath he could bear, Ben wrapped himself in a bathrobe, heated himself a ready-to-eat carbonara in the microwave, found a beer in the fridge and settled in front of the computer.

The strangeness of the wording in the latest email had been niggling at him all the way home, and even disturbed the longed-for, steamy stupor of his bath.

You have risked the life of your horse . . .

What does it matter if they can't put a sentence together? Truman had asked, but that was just it; there was nothing wrong with the sentence. In fact, it was put together almost too well – too carefully, as if by someone for whom English was a second language. Remembering what he'd learned about Helen's youthful fling, Ben found he wanted to know more about this jockey Truman had brought in from abroad. As it seemed that the Truman family were observing a pact of silence, he'd have to look elsewhere for his information.

Waking up the computer he went online, ignored his emails – most of which were certain to be unwanted – and called up his favourite search engine. For a moment, with the cursor winking patiently at him, he didn't know where to start. He tried Truman+Derby and the machine digested and came up with a bewildering number of results: anything from biographies of President Truman to tourist information on the city of Derby, taking in the Kentucky Derby, football and a couple of Derby and Truman family trees on the way. There was, naturally, a fair bit on the Epsom Derby too, but the problem was where to begin. Just at the moment he couldn't even remember the name of the Castle Ridge horse that had won the Derby. Biting his lip he tried again, putting in the stable's name this time instead of Truman.

That was more productive. This time it offered up the name Massingham, which Ben instantly remembered from the Castle Ridge Hall of Fame.

The first site he tried gave no more than a passing reference to the horse in a list of past Derby winners, but the second was a searchable newspaper archive and, after just a couple more clicks and the reluctant payment of a subscription fee, he found it: an account of Massingham's winning run in the Epsom Derby. At the top of the page was a photo of the horse and its radiant jockey returning triumphant to the winner's enclosure, with Eddie Truman, much younger but nevertheless unmistakable, striding proudly at his side. Underneath the picture the caption read:

Massingham takes a last minute jockey change in his stride, as he lifts racing's most coveted prize.

Ben scanned the accompanying text, looking for some further mention of the jockey change, which he found right at the very bottom of the page.

I imagine that there will be the mother of all parties at Eddie Truman's Wiltshire yard tonight, for not only is the businessman the trainer of this talented three-year-old, he is also the horse's owner. But while Truman's family, friends and staff will be in celebratory mood, spare a thought for Massingham's previous jockey. Jocked-off the night before the race for what Truman would only describe as unavoidable reasons, your heart has to go out to young Stefan Varga who missed the chance of a lifetime by just a whisker.

Ben stopped reading, and almost stopped breathing.

Stefan Varga.

'Oh God!' he muttered. 'Oh, dear God!'

11

The padded envelope delivered to Castle Ridge the next morning contained a photograph of Cajun King's head, a hank of equine mane or tail hair and a note, which read:

This time it's hair. Next time it will be an ear and then a hoof. Don't mess with me. Do as you are told.

This much Eddie Truman relayed to Ben over the phone. 'Ford sent one of his forensics chaps out to pick it up,' he added. 'We weren't allowed to open it in case we contaminated the evidence, and also in case it was booby-trapped. He took it all away with him and they'll apparently check that the hair actually comes from King, but I don't think there's any doubt – after all, they sent the photo.'

'Well, that proves that they had the horse at some point,' Ben said. 'But not that they have him now. Still, it looks like they're giving you another chance.'

'Well, I just wish they'd get on with it. I kept my part of the bargain. I tell you, if I ever get my hands on these bastards . . .'

'You told the police, though.'

'What?'

'You said you kept your part of the bargain, but you didn't – you told the police.'

'Well, I had to, you know that.' Truman sounded impatient.

'Yes, I'm not saying you were wrong; I'm just trying to see it from their point of view.'

'But how would they know, anyway?'

'I don't know for sure, but I suppose if it was someone who knew Helen well they might possibly have noticed the substitution, or . . . Well, I suppose you have to consider the possibility that they could have someone in your camp.'

'You're not trying to say it's an inside job – that's impossible!' Truman declared emphatically.

'I'm not trying to say anything; I'm just suggesting possibilities,' Ben replied soothingly. 'And at this stage I don't think you can afford to dismiss anything as impossible.'

'Well, what about you? Have you had any clever ideas? You seemed very interested in that email yesterday – have you thought any more about that?'

'Thought about it . . .' Ben admitted, but didn't enlarge. He would want to do a whole lot more thinking before he would be prepared to risk unleashing Truman's kind of trouble onto the Csikós. All he had at the moment was a name and a whole bundle of questions.

'I'm beginning to wonder what the bloody hell

I'm paying you for! I haven't had much to show for it yet, have I?'

'I never made you any promises,' Ben pointed out. 'It was all your idea, if you remember. I'd be quite happy to call it quits, if that's what you want.'

'No, it's not. Not at the moment. I may still have a use for you. Seeing as I'm the one who's paying, I think you should go back to Rackham. I'm still not convinced he isn't in this somewhere, and he's someone who'd recognise Helen, too.'

'Sure, if that's what you want me to do. But I think you're wasting your time.'

'Ah, but that's the beauty of delegation,' Truman observed. 'If I'm wasting anyone's time, it's yours. Let me know what you come up with. I'm racing this afternoon if the frost goes off, but I'll be in this evening.'

There was a crackle as the connection was severed without further ado, and as Ben put the phone down his vague sense of guilt was effectively wiped out by a wave of irritation at the man's high-handedness.

Yawning, he regarded a cooling cup of coffee and decided to make himself a replacement. He hadn't got much sleep the previous night, his mind too busy with the discovery he'd made.

Stefan Varga. There were probably dozens of Stefan Vargas in the world, but Stefan Vargas who were also jockeys? That surely narrowed the field a little. Ben wasn't generally a betting man but he'd have been prepared to put quite a substantial sum on the ex-Castle Ridge jockey being Jakob Varga's son. That being so, it would be naïve to suppose that the Csikós' presence in the country at the exact moment that Cajun King had gone missing was a coincidence.

Ben wasn't naïve.

On the other hand, there were still a couple of things that didn't add up, not least the fact that, if Jakob was to be believed, Stefan was dead. Putting aside his liking for the Hungarian, Ben was still inclined to believe him, because he had volunteered the information when he could have foreseen no reason to lie.

So where did that leave him?

Jakob?

Was he the kind of man who would nurse a grievance for sixteen years? Surely not. He was a passionate man, certainly, but he was such a steady character, so fair and non-confrontational. And yet, how well did Ben really know him?

Coming at it from another angle, though, there were other problems. The Csikós' tour would have been planned some way in advance; it wasn't the kind of thing you could do on impulse – there would be permissions to be obtained, venues and stabling to book and publicity to arrange. Surely the whole trip hadn't been arranged with this in mind?

Wandering into the living room, he stoked up the wood-burner and collapsed on to the sofa, cradling his hot mug of coffee and staring broodingly at the leaping flames.

The plain truth of it was that he didn't want it to be Jakob. But, trying to look at the matter from a completely dispassionate point of view, if it *were* Jakob, then who else was involved? Everyone? There had been at least three hijackers, according to Ricey. And if it weren't Jakob . . .

Ben considered the other members of the troupe. Nico? Jakob had certainly said that Nico had been very keen to come to England – but did one take such a risk in the memory of a cousin? And for something that had happened when you yourself would have been what – sixteen or seventeen? Ferenc then; Ben would have been happier to imagine that the surly Ferenc was behind it, if it hadn't been for the fact that he couldn't have done it on his own.

And where could the horse be hidden? The Csikós were on the move every four or five days. Had they got him at livery somewhere, or turned out in some farmer's field? In his mind's eye Ben went over all the horses travelling with the troupe, but to no avail. True, if one had the nerve one could conceivably have concealed the missing horse within the 'wild' bunch, except that among their unkempt number Cajun King, with his sleek coat and apology for a tail, would have stood out like a sore thumb.

Whatever the case, if there was even the possibility that the Stefan Varga connection between Eddie Truman and the visiting Hungarian horsemen was anything more than a coincidence, then he had no choice but to look into it.

Ben sighed, not relishing the thought.

If Ben wasn't looking forward to putting the Csikós under scrutiny, then at least he could take some small comfort from the fact that now he hadn't got to go so far to do it. After their move the previous afternoon, they were scheduled to be at Romsey, in Hampshire, and had been invited to park up in the grounds of a nearby stately home. Sure enough, when he'd navigated the narrow lanes around the estate, following the directions of a helpful groundkeeper, he turned into a field and there they were, the familiar transporters and attendant smaller vans, arranged in what Ben was beginning to recognise as their usual positions.

Bordering the field on one side were a cluster of large, tin-roofed breeze-block structures, arranged around a concreted area and reached by way of a wide metal gate. Beyond these, the arched roof of another, vast building showed white against the cloudless sky.

Seeing signs of activity in the yard, Ben drove towards the complex and parked.

Nico was the first person to notice his arrival and came over to greet him with every sign of pleasure, trailing Bajnok in his wake.

'Ben! Can't stay away, eh?' he cried. 'Have you come back for another riding lesson? Because Jakob is not here.'

'Oh? Where's he gone?' Ben tried to ignore the proximity of the big black horse.

'He's gone into the town with Gyorgy to buy food. We are nearly without hot dogs, think of that! The Csikós cannot perform without hot dogs – we would go to strike!'

'*On* strike,' Ben corrected, absent-mindedly. In his head he was remembering 'You have risked the life of your horse' and comparing the speech pattern of the Hungarian's words: '*He's gone into the town with Gyorgy . . .'* It was worryingly similar.

'*On* strike, then. But did you come to ride? They should be back soon.'

'Actually, I'm not sure I could even climb on board a horse today.'

Nico grinned broadly. 'You are a little stiff, yes?'

'Yes,' Ben agreed ruefully. 'Just a little.'

'I know just the thing,' the Hungarian declared.

'Not horse liniment?' he asked warily.

'No. Exercise. You can come and help me put in the posts for the round pen. It is a good site here but there is not so much, er . . . ?'

'Not so many facilities?'

Nico frowned, perhaps not sure of the word. 'Yes, I think. There is room for the horses but there is nothing more. Come, I'll show you.'

'So where will you do the show?' Ben asked, following Nico across the rough, wet grass and watching the toes of his shoes become saturated.

'Ah. There is a riding centre next door and they lend us their arena. It has seating for many people – more than last time – and it is already sold out for the first two performances. Soon everyone will have heard of the Csikós.'

'You're in the local papers,' Ben told him. 'I stopped for petrol and there you were. I bought a copy; hang on, I'll get it.'

Moments later, with a barely suppressed grin, he returned and handed the paper to Nico, then laughed out loud as he saw the Hungarian's eager anticipation turn to outrage. The front page carried a fairly creditable photograph of Nico and Duka doing their party piece, but carried the unfortunate headline, *The Cossacks are Coming!*

Nico stabbed the newsprint with his finger and said something in his own tongue which was chock full of indignation and, Ben guessed, a good few words that wouldn't be found in your average Hungarian-to-English phrasebook.

'I thought it was rather good,' he teased, feigning surprise.

'*Cossacks!* We are not Russian – we are Magyar; Csikós!'

'And I thought you were Rom . . .'

'You, my friend, are a troublemaker!' Nico declared with a glint in his eye.

Still smiling, Ben followed Nico and Bajnok into the nearest of the buildings, the cavernous concrete interior of which had been divided into a dozen or more pens, each bounded by four-foot-high breeze-block walls, topped with steel mesh. A central walkway gave access to the individual compartments and at the end were stacked fifteen or twenty huge bales of wood shavings. The stalls were occupied by the troupe's horses, who stood fetlock deep in crisp white shavings, pulling at haynets and looking, for the most part, supremely content. One or two of them had taken full advantage of their new bedding and rolled; they now stood looking like refugees from a winter storm, with pale flakes of wood clinging to their coats and trapped in their mane and tail hair.

'And that is exactly what Bajnok will do, as soon as I let him go,' Nico told Ben. 'I don't know why I just spent half of an hour brushing him.'

He took the big black to an empty stall and

led him in, sliding the metal door shut as he unclipped the lead rope and came out.

Sure enough, the Friesian stallion wasted no time. Barely had the door shut when he began to turn round, end to end, stamping his feet and swishing his luxuriant black tail. With a grunt he collapsed into the thick blanket of shavings and proceeded to whip up a blizzard as he enjoyed a prolonged and vigorous roll.

'Look at him, rubbing his mane in it,' Nico said disgustedly. 'I should have put plaits in. Why did I not think?'

When Bajnok finally got back on his feet, there wasn't an inch of his dark glossy coat that wasn't speckled with white. Nico rolled his eyes heavenwards before turning away.

'Come, we have work to do.'

Ben and Nico made a good team, marking out a twenty-metre circle with a crowbar, a length of rope and some sawdust, then taking it in turns to hold the posts and swing the mallet. After a short while they were joined by Nico's brothers, Miklós and András, who, armed with more wood and reels of wire, started to put up the rails – three between each pair of posts. The mood seemed generally light-hearted; Miklós and András even launched into an impromptu clowning routine for Ben's benefit. He wasn't normally a great fan of clowns, but he had to admire the pair's split second timing with the length of wood, and eventually found himself laughing out loud.

When he and Nico had erected the last of the posts they left the other two to finish fitting the rails and went in search of much-needed refreshment. Jakob and Gyorgy were still out and, although Ben had been intending to try and bring up the subject of Stefan with the older man, he began to see that Nico might, after all, be his best bet. Nico, in his present high spirits, was garrulous in the extreme and, with a little judicious steering, Ben felt that the conversation might easily include mention of Jakob's son.

In the event, it proved more straightforward than he could have hoped. Nico wanted to know about Ben's own family and, in telling him about Mikey, Ben was able to add quite casually, 'I gather Jakob's son was a jockey too.'

'Yes, he was. Who told you that?'

'Jakob did.'

'I'm surprised. He doesn't usually talk about him. What else did he say?' Nico had found the key to the catering wagon and was rustling up coffee and biscuits for them both.

'That he died in a car crash. Tell me about him; were you close?'

Nico shrugged. 'We are Rom – we have to be close. Gadje – outsiders – don't welcome our company. Stefan was my cousin, kind of. My Uncle Vesh – you've seen him around – is married to Jakob's sister. He was six years older than me, and when you're growing up, that seems quite a lot. I used to follow him around as a kid. I guess I looked up to him; he was my hero. Then he went to ride racehorses in South Africa, and when he was offered the job over here I wanted to come too.'

'He came to England, then? What happened?' Ben was careful not to sound too eager.

'He was a big success. Many people were asking for him to ride their horses, they said he had a gift.' For a moment, Nico almost glowed with pride. 'They said he had a big future ahead of him. He was only here for a few months – less than a year – but he made more money than the rest of us had ever dreamed of. Then he called and said he was coming home – to Hungary – you understand; there was something wrong with his papers and he couldn't stay.'

'Didn't he tell you any more?'

Nico shook his head sadly.

'His car crashed. It was old and they think the brakes failed. It turned over and over down a bank . . .' He illustrated the movement with his hands. '. . . And then there was fire. We never saw him again.'

'Poor Jakob.'

'He was . . .' Nico struggled to find the word.

'Devastated?'

'Yes, devastated. We were all so proud, and then – nothing.'

'Where did it happen?' Ben prompted gently. He'd already got more than he'd expected to.

'At home, near Szolnok, at night on a dark country road. But you won't write about this, will you Ben? It's private. Jakob wouldn't like it.'

'No, of course not. I'm sorry – I was just interested; because of Jakob. He's such a nice guy.'

'Everybody likes Jakob,' Nico stated matter-of-factly.

'Nico!' The shout came from outside and was followed by a rapid phrase that was incomprehensible to Ben but not, obviously, to Nico. He replied in kind, then, getting to his feet, translated for his visitor with a flash of his whiter-than-white teeth.

'Gyorgy says I should get off my fat arse and help him unload the van. I better do it. You stay here.'

'No, I'll come and help.' Ben drained his mug and stood up.

Jakob was outside with Gyorgy and, seeing them side by side, Ben was struck by how alike the brothers were. 'The Csikós' was a family business of a type rarely seen in England. Even Tamás, the vet, was married to Jakob's daughter, Dritta. They had welcomed Ben with generous hospitality, but he guessed that if he ever did anything that remotely threatened one of their number they would close ranks instantly and range against him. 'We are Rom – we have to be close,' Nico had said.

'There is something wrong, Ben?' Jakob paused in passing, his arms full of plastic-wrapped trays of tins.

'No.' Ben shook his head. 'Just thinking about families.'

'Ah, never work with them,' Jakob declared loudly. 'Look at this lot: a bunch of lazy good-for-nothings, and the shame of it is, I can't give them – what is that word you use? – the sack. I can't get rid of them.'

Nico rattled off something in his own tongue and ducked to avoid being cuffed by Gyorgy. He dodged away, laughing.

'The ingratitude of the young,' Jakob complained. 'He says they only keep us old people around out of pity! But you see he only says it when I have my hands filled with packets, eh?'

265

Ben laughed, but his enjoyment of the moment was tempered by the suspicions occupying his mind. If these people – any of them – were involved in the kidnapping of Eddie Truman's horse, not only would some of them undoubtedly be arrested, but the whole troupe would be discredited, their burgeoning reputation sullied beyond recall. 'The Csikós' would, almost certainly, be no more.

When the last of the supplies had been transferred from the van to the catering wagon, Gyorgy announced his intention of starting to prepare lunch, and Nico invited Ben to watch him schooling Duka.

'I teach him a new trick. Come, I'll show you.'

Ben went with him, hoping for a chance to have a look at the loose horses. The newly built round-pen was already in use, with Tamás standing at its centre, closely watching the Arab, Vadas, who was circling him at the trot.

'How is he?' Nico called.

With a step sideways and slightly towards it, the vet brought the free-running horse to a smooth but instant halt. He walked across and slipped a rope halter over the chestnut's head before answering Nico.

'He seems all right today. There's no heat in that foot. I think maybe we caught it in time.'

'That's good.' Nico turned to Ben. 'Vadas was a little sore yesterday and when Vesh took off the shoe he found the beginning of a – I don't know your word for it . . .'

'An abscess,' Tamás supplied, leading the horse out of the round-pen. 'It was lucky that we found it so soon. It was very small. Could have been a

266

piece of grit or even a grass seed under the shoe. It is open now. As long as it is kept clean there should be no more trouble.'

'Can he do the show tonight?' Nico ran his hands down the affected leg to the hoof.

'I think so. He's not lame. But no shoe until it has healed.'

'What happened with the horses that got out the other night? Have they all recovered?' Ben asked. 'And have you had any more trouble from the group that did it?'

'The horses are fine. Even the one with the gashed shoulder is healing well. We were lucky. There has been no more trouble but there were some people walking in the road with banners when we left the field yesterday; the police moved them on.' He laughed. 'When I was a boy, it was always *us* the police would be moving on, if they could.'

The vet moved away with the horse, fending off a sneaky nip from the Arab's ready teeth as he did so, and Ben and Nico followed behind, en route to the stable building and Duka.

After an enjoyable half-hour spent watching Nico teach the Andalusian to remove a broad-brimmed hat he'd donned for the purpose, Ben left him settling the horse back in his stall and wandered round the rest of the complex.

He was out of luck with the loose horse herd; they'd been turned out in a field behind the buildings and he couldn't get closer than fifty feet or more. Even at that distance, though, he could see enough to make him seriously doubt the feasibility of one of them being Cajun King. They were certainly all thoroughbreds but, of the ten, only half were of a similar colour and build, and none of these had either the same markings or the skimpy tail of the horse in the picture Ben carried in his wallet. It seemed he would have to think again but, if the Csikós did have the horse, where on earth could they have hidden it? Or where under the earth? His mind tagged the question on before he could stop it.

What he'd learned from Nico had given him a little more insight into the background of the ill-fated Stefan Varga but not a lot more. He still had no idea whether Jakob's state of mind was such that he'd consider putting the family's livelihood at risk to gain revenge. Also, if Jakob were indeed behind the kidnap, he couldn't have done it alone; but Nico hadn't given the impression of someone with anything to hide. There was only one thing that had really struck Ben as odd, and that was Nico's saying that the car that Stefan had crashed and died in was old. Surely, if he'd been as successful as it seemed, he would have bought or rented himself a newer car when he arrived home. It was almost always the first thing that any young man did when he came into some money, and he saw no reason why Stefan should have been any different.

'Have you come to ride again?'

Jakob had come up soft-footed and unseen, and Ben jumped, almost guiltily.

'No, not really. Actually, my editor wants to bring the article forward, and my other job is a bit quiet at the moment, so I thought I'd better come and ask a few more questions, check a few details, that sort of thing.' He was glad that it was at least the partial truth, because Jakob had a rather unsettling way of looking at one sometimes, which made him hesitate to try and bluff through.

'But now you are here . . . ?'

'Oh, I don't know, I'm still a bit sore from yesterday.'

'Nico tells me you have a saying, "hair of the dog" – have I said that right?'

'Yes, that's right. But I don't think it's scientifically proven,' Ben said, smiling. 'Both Nico and Tamás speak very good English; how does that come about?'

'Tamás spent a year in the USA when he was in study to be a vet, and Nico was in New Zealand, working. What were you thinking about?'

'Sorry?'

'Just now. You were standing watching the horses and I spoke to you twice before you answered.'

'I – I'm not sure. Lots of things.' All at once, Ben was conscious of an overwhelming urge to confide in Jakob. In his presence it seemed inconceivable that he could be a party to any kidnap plot, but he held his tongue, nevertheless; the risk was just too great.

Jakob shook his head. 'Forgive me, I should not have asked. Come; Gyorgy will be calling for us and it is a great wrong to keep food waiting.'

Ben left Romsey mid-afternoon, bound once more for Castle Ridge. After lunch at the catering wagon he'd gone with Jakob to watch Nico working

269

Bajnok, which had been a treat. He was riding him in a building similar to the one housing the horses but devoid of the inner partitioning walls. There was a thick covering of what looked like peat on the floor, and Jakob explained that they were using it to shelter the loose herd at night.

When they let themselves in through the huge sliding door Nico had warmed the Friesian up and was just starting to put him through his paces. Ben stood in awe as the big black horse and his rider performed. He'd seen countless numbers of riders in his time, and a fairly small percentage of those could – in his opinion – be called horsemen, but Nico went way beyond that. It was as if he and the stallion had some kind of telepathic link.

Music emanated from a battered ghetto-blaster in the corner by the door, and the horse was moving in time to the rhythm. Try as he might, Ben couldn't discern any physical form of instruction being passed between them; the horse just appeared to be dancing of his own volition, his neck arched and proud under the cascading black mane, his strong, feathered legs lifting high with perfect cadence as he turned this way and that. When the sound of the CD player died away and Bajnok sank into a graceful bow, Ben couldn't resist clapping.

Nico looked across and inclined his head with a slight smile.

'I used to think I was a fair rider but that was something else!' Ben told Jakob.

He nodded proudly. 'It was. I never tire of watching him. He has a true gift.'

'And your son; he was gifted too?'

'He was, but Stefan was still young when he died. Speed was his passion – he lived to race. Maybe if he'd lived longer he would have discovered the joy of what Nico has just shown us; but, even with the pride of a father, I can't honestly say he would have been as good. Nico is exceptional, but I wouldn't say it to his face.'

'What's that, old man?' Nico was riding over; Bajnok, on a loose rein, looking a completely different horse. He jumped off and started to run the stirrups up.

'I'll ignore that,' Jakob said, then, putting a hand on Nico's arm, 'May we borrow him for a few minutes?'

Nico turned his head with a slight frown, then, glancing at Ben, flashed his white teeth and said, 'Of course.'

Ben's initial protests were shot down and before he knew it he was aboard Bajnok and settling into Nico's deep, well-worn saddle. His leg muscles set up a token protest but, in all honesty, Ben had to admit it wasn't bad. The horse stood like a rock while Ben adjusted his stirrups and then moved off willingly to command. Having Nico watch him made Ben feel a little inadequate but, after a minute or two, when he'd begun to relax and enjoy the Friesian's super-comfortable paces, he glanced towards the door and saw him fiddling with the portable hi-fi, apparently disinterested.

Shortly after, Jakob called out to him to bring Bajnok back to a walk.

'Now, bring him shorter. Use your legs gently

and keep hold of his head. That's it, play with the bit . . . ever so gentle – good, you have nice hands.'

Bajnok's ears flicked back and forth as he tried to work out what his strange rider was asking of him and then, suddenly, Ben heard the music start up again. Instantly, the big black bunched his muscles and drew his head in until his chin was nearly touching his chest. With a sense of wonder Ben sat still as the horse began to dance, lifting his feet extravagantly high in diagonal pairs and holding each stride for a fraction of a second at its zenith, in a kind of partially suspended animation. Up, forward and down, as if he were treading on air. Ben knew the movement was known in dressage circles as 'passage' but he'd never experienced it before, and, although he was continuing to give the aids that Jakob had instructed, he was well aware that his part in the procedure was negligible.

Then, when he reached the other side of the building, Bajnok broke into a canter and the spell was broken. Nico turned the music down and, after a couple more circuits, Ben brought the horse to a halt beside them.

'Wow! That was incredible!' he said. 'Thank you. He's a wonderful horse.'

'Of course!' Nico declared. 'He's the best horse in the world. But you did well.'

'Riding by numbers,' someone muttered, and Ben saw that the door was open a foot or so. Ferenc had been watching too.

'Pay no attention to him. Nico's right; you did well,' Jakob said.

There was a derisive snort and the door closed as Ferenc withdrew.

It was a shame, Ben reflected as he slowed the Mitsubishi down on the approach to Salisbury, that he couldn't really pin the horse-knapping on Ferenc, but it had to be said, that if it were to be any of Ciskós, Ferenc and his sister Anna were the least likely suspects, being apparently unrelated to the main family.

Sampling the troupe's friendly hospitality once again had made him keener than ever to prove his suspicions right or wrong as soon as possible. In the face of Jakob's generous investment of time and trouble to help him overcome his fear, he felt little short of a traitor.

Thus, he was en route once more for Truman's stables, knowing that the man himself would be out and hoping that Finch might be too, leaving the way clear for a chance to speak to Helen again.

His luck was in.

When he called at the house the door was opened by Elizabeth Truman, whose look of mild enquiry hardened to something much less encouraging as she saw who was darkening her doorstep. Remembering the previous night, Ben quickly revised his plans and asked instead whether Bess was around.

Truman's wife looked at him in suspicious silence for a moment or two but apparently found nothing sinister in the query; she then volunteered the information that it was the secretary's afternoon off and suggested that he might try the cottage.

273

Ben thanked her, adding, 'I'm sorry about yesterday. I didn't mean to get anyone into trouble.'

At this, she unbent a little. 'Well, I suppose you couldn't have known,' she said. 'It wasn't a happy time, and we have tried very hard to put it behind us. Eddie doesn't like it spoken of.'

'But realistically, a teenage romance is no great scandal. Why is it still such a big deal?'

'Mr Copperfield, our family business is our affair and ours alone. Just leave it, will you? Please? For all our sakes.'

What started out as a snub, delivered with cold dignity, ended as a heartfelt plea, and Ben wished he could give her the assurance she craved. But the more he was warned off the subject, the more determined he became to get to the root of it.

Bess was indeed at the cottage. She invited Ben into the kitchen where a slim young man with wavy brown hair and a pleasant smile was lounging in the old armchair. Putting two and two together, Ben guessed that this must be Rollo Gallagher, the Castle Ridge stable jockey who, Truman had told him, was at present suspended from racing. No one else was around.

'Oh, have you met Rollo?' Bess asked.

'No, not yet,' Ben said. 'Hi.'

The jockey touched the brim of an imaginary cap and returned the greeting, not moving from his relaxed position.

'Sorry to disturb you. I was wondering if Helen's around this afternoon.'

'Yes, I think she's up at the bungalow. Why?'

'I just wanted to have a word with her,' Ben said casually.

Bess raised an eyebrow.

'You're living dangerously. I heard about last night,' she paused. 'Look, I don't want to interfere, but I'd be careful if I were you. Without being disloyal to the Guvnor, he's not a man you'd want to cross.'

'I've heard a couple of stories. Are you telling me they're true?'

'Well, I don't know what you've heard exactly. Look, I really shouldn't be talking like this – he *is* my boss . . .'

'The truth is,' Rollo cut in, 'the man's an egomaniac who'll bulldoze anyone who stands in his way.'

Ben glanced at him thoughtfully. He wasn't sure if the jockey was privy to the whole Cajun King business yet.

'Oh, I wouldn't go that far,' Bess protested. 'I know he can be a bit heavy-handed but he's not all bad.'

Rollo shook his head. 'You're OK as long as you're useful to him, but if you're not careful he'll pick you up, suck you dry and then spit you out.'

'But you're happy to work for him?' Ben quizzed.

'Work is work. His ambitions happen to fall in line with mine at the moment, but that doesn't mean I don't watch my back,' Rollo told him. 'And if you're set on rocking the boat, I'd advise you to do the same.'

'Thanks. Er – just one thing – is Ray Finch likely to be about?'

'No. He's gone with the Guvnor. You've got a clear field.'

The yard was a hive of activity when Ben passed through it. Looking at his watch he saw it was half past four, time for the afternoon shift: grooming, skipping out and feeding.

The Truman–Finch's bungalow was long, low and painted white. The strip of garden that ran along the front of it was planted with winter pansies and clumps of wallflowers; the path was weed-free and the door was glossily red. All in all, it seemed the epitome of domestic bliss, but Ben had a feeling that life behind its model façade might not be the proverbial bed of roses. Helen never looked particularly happy and, from what he'd seen, her husband had a surly, discontented streak. Together, they didn't give the appearance of a couple for whom each made the other complete.

Helen opened the door wearing a lilac velour tracksuit and regarded her uninvited visitor with a look of undisguised hostility.

'What do you want?'

'Just wanted to talk to you.'

'I've nothing more to say.'

'You mean you're not allowed to. Look, tell me what happened. I know his name was Stefan Varga; he came from Hungary, didn't he?'

Helen opened her mouth then shut it again, as if changing her mind.

'And I know your father had him thrown out of the country. Come on. Fill in the gaps, it could be important.'

'You think you know such a lot – you don't know anything! Just leave me alone.' She stepped back and tried to shut the door in Ben's face, but he swiftly put his foot against the bottom of it. 'Look, you'll get me into trouble.'

'And I wouldn't be the first, would I?'

Her face paled. 'What do you mean?'

'Your jockey friend . . . This air of tragedy – this family rift, it has to be over something more than a teenage crush. He got you pregnant, didn't he?'

She didn't answer, but the look on her face was reply enough.

'What happened to the baby? Was it adopted? Or did you have an abortion?'

Helen stared, her face a mirror for what was obviously a maelstrom of emotions. Eventually she seemed to decide on honesty.

'Yes. I had an abortion.'

'And no doubt you were told it was for the best?'

Helen's cheeks became suffused with a much healthier pink.

'My father only wanted what was best for me. I was just sixteen; too young to bring up a child.'

'Oh, he's taught you well,' Ben said, nodding. 'But I sense you've never quite accepted it, have you?'

'This is none of your fucking business! What are you going to do? Write a story on us? Dad'll crucify you if you do. Your career will be finished. Over. And you'll be lucky if that's all! If you don't take your foot out of the door, I'll tell Dad that you came here asking questions.'

'And I'll tell him you invited me to.'

'You wouldn't!'

'I would, too.'

'He wouldn't believe you,' she said, but with a measure of doubt.

'Shall we try him?'

'You're an interfering bastard!'

'And you're a bad-tempered bitch,' he countered, without heat.

That silenced her. She eyed him with loathing. 'Look, you've got what you wanted. Why don't you just go?'

'Yep. I think I will. And don't worry – I won't tell your father if you don't.' He started to turn away, then stopped. 'Tell me, did you ever hear from Stefan again?'

She shook her head. 'Dad used to check the post. If he did write, I never got the letters.'

Ben didn't think anything would be gained by telling her that Stefan had perished in a car crash, so he merely nodded. 'Thanks for your help, anyway.'

As he moved his foot the door was slammed shut, but not before Eddie Truman's elder daughter had spat at him like a brat from a city slum.

Ben shook his head as he moved away, thinking of the impeccable manners of Stefan's father. Eddie Truman had thought the couple ill-matched – how right he had been.

12

Ben left the bungalow in a pensive mood and almost walked right past Fliss without seeing her.

'Penny for 'em,' she joked. 'Though I guess, in this day and age, they're probably more like two pounds fifty! What did you want with my sweet sister?'

'There seems to be a distinct lack of familial affection amongst you Trumans,' Ben observed. 'Whatever happened to sisterly love?'

'She's nine years older than me. When we were young, all I ever was to her was a nuisance. We were never the right age to go out together, or talk about boys, or go shopping – you know, all the girly things that forge bonds. Quite apart from that she's been a miserable cow for as long as I can remember!'

'So you don't remember the family scandal?'

'Scandal?'

'Yeah, you know. Your sister and the jockey.'

'Oh, *that*,' she said dismissing it with scorn and a movement of her hand. 'Is that what you were talking to her about? I never understood what all the fuss was about. I was only seven, so no one told me anything, but I remember all the tears and long faces. Mum and Dad nearly split up over it. Mum took Helen away with her to her sister's for a while, and Dad was like a bear with a sore head. And for what? A stupid teenage crush.'

'And what happened after that?'

'I don't know really; not a lot. To be honest, I was just chuffed to bits to have Dad to myself. We did loads of stuff together – he spoiled me rotten. Then Mum and Helen came home and there were more tears and long faces. I used to think – when I was old enough to understand – that if it'd been *my* lover I'd have gone with him, but Helen's not like that. She'd rather moan about how life's treated her than get on and do something about it.'

She glanced at Ben. 'So that's the Truman family history. What about the Copperfields? What deep, dark secrets does your past hold?' Walking beside him she suddenly slipped her arm through his and leaned towards him.

'Oh, no dark secrets, really. We're quite a boring lot,' said Ben, wondering how soon he could remove his arm without appearing to snub her. He was uneasily aware of how many prying eyes might potentially be watching, and Belinda Kepple's warning was still fresh in his mind.

'Oh, come on, I don't believe that. Every family has at least one skeleton in their closet. And I wouldn't call you boring.'

'Are you flirting with me, Felicity Truman?' Ben asked, deciding that directness was his best policy. He took the opportunity of turning towards her and disengaging her hold.

'I might be,' she said, her clear green eyes twinkling roguishly. 'Would you mind?'

'I'd be flattered,' Ben replied, his mind racing. He mustn't make a big thing of this. 'But I'm not sure my girlfriend would be too pleased.'

'You've got a girlfriend?' Fliss sounded mildly disappointed. 'But then you would have, wouldn't you? Cute guys who are single are usually looking the other way, if you know what I mean.'

'And what about you? Don't you have a boyfriend?'

'Mm. Maybe. But don't tell Dad, or I'll get the ninth degree. I'm his little girl, you see.'

'Good God! You're twenty-two. How long does he expect you to stay Daddy's little girl?'

Fliss shrugged, linking her arm in his again. 'I don't know. I don't mind, really. He's just protective.'

Ben would have called it possessive, but he held his tongue.

'Anyway, it's nothing serious – my boyfriend, I mean. And as for your girl . . . Well, I won't tell her if you don't.'

'You're going to get yourself in a whole load of trouble with that attitude, you little minx,' Ben said severely. 'Not to mention me. Now tell me, do you have any idea where I can find Lenny Salter these days?'

'Um . . . He used to have a bungalow near Tisbury when he rode for us, but I've no idea whether he's still there. Why on earth would you want to find him?'

281

'Oh, I don't know, call it a whim. Could you give me directions, or an address?'

'I could take you there, if you like.'

'Thanks, but an address will do just fine.'

'All right, have it your own way, but I don't have it on me. You'll have to ask Bess.' She removed her arm from his, her manner cooling perceptibly. 'I've got better things to do, anyway.'

They parted; Fliss peeling off to go into the yard, and Ben heading down to the cottage with a shake of his head. Madam was rather too used to getting her own way.

Lenny Salter's bungalow was one in a road of identical properties, most of which stood, four-square, on perfectly manicured postage-stamp gardens with garages alternately to the right and left. Lenny Salter's was square and had its garage on the right, but there the similarity to its neighbours ended. The patch of ground it occupied was liberally scattered with rusting vehicle parts and other discarded junk through which grass, docks, bindweed and nettles had grown enthusiastically, probably for several years. Whereas the other bungalows had shiny front doors and neatly curtained windows, Lenny's sported peeling paintwork, and the torn and grubby remains of net curtains hung lifelessly behind filthy glass. The gate was rusting and hung crookedly on its hinges, causing the bolt to score an arc in the crumbling concrete, and the garage door was only two-thirds shut over the mountain of junk inside. The place didn't look lived in, but a bottle of milk on the step showed that someone must call it home.

Oh, I bet you're popular with the neighbours, Ben thought, and from the corner of his eye he saw next door's curtain twitch.

His feet crunched over broken glass as he approached the door, and after twice pressing a button that had probably long ceased to have any connection with its bell, Ben gave up and rapped on the woodwork. He had to repeat the exercise before he heard someone coming to the door but eventually it was opened by a shortish man who was supporting himself on elbow crutches. Ben knew from his conversations with Ricey and Fliss that Lenny Salter was only in his early twenties, but the man who stared out at him through puffy, bloodshot eyes, could have been anywhere up to his mid-forties. He looked at least three stone heavier than the Lenny Salter who had saluted the camera from the backs of a variety of winners in the Castle Ridge Hall of Fame and, even though he had never met the man before, Ben felt a degree of shock at seeing the sad figure that he'd become.

'What the fuck do you want?' Salter asked, pushing long, lank hair out of his eyes and leaning on the edge of the door to keep his balance. He wore a stained and dirty tracksuit bearing the Nike logo, and a pair of equally filthy trainers with their laces trailing.

'I'm a reporter doing an article called "Life After Racing",' Ben said, sticking to his rehearsed story, even though it was plainly laughable in the face of such wholesale deterioration. He flashed his press card. 'And I wondered if I could have a few words . . .'

'Are you havin' me on?' Salter was understandably incredulous. 'Is this someone's idea of a fuckin' joke?' He peered past Ben as if expecting to see the culprit lurking round the corner, laughing.

'No joke,' Ben assured him. 'Can I just ask a question or two? I needn't come in.'

'Too bloody right, you won't. And you don't need to ask no questions neither. You wanna know about life after racing – I'll tell you: it fuckin' stinks!'

Ben wasn't about to argue with that. He'd already taken a step backwards when the opening front door had allowed a waft of stale smoky air to escape, and now, as Salter spoke, he was assailed by alcohol fumes. Surreptitiously, he put his left hand in his jacket pocket.

'Yeah, it fuckin' stinks,' the ex-jockey repeated.

'You used to ride for Eddie Truman, didn't you? Do you ever see him these days?' Ben gave the embers a bit of a poke.

'No I bloody don't, and I don't want to neither, 'less it's over the barrel of a sawn-off shotgun! It's his fuckin' fault I'm like this. Him and his fuckin' stuck-up daughter.'

'Oh? Which one? Helen?'

'Nah, the skinny one. Caught me trying to kiss her, didn't he? She'd been leading me on, she had, playing hard to get. But she wanted me really.'

Remembering Fliss's reaction when Salter's name had come up, Ben doubted that, but he let it go.

'Even so,' he said, 'you must have known what Truman was like with his daughters.'

284

'Course I bloody did! But I'd had a bit too much to drink, you know? Just won the King George for him and he'd thrown this big party. Fuckin' bastard watches them girls like a hawk. He lays his hand on my shoulder and tells me to get out, all quiet like; didn't want no fuss. Didn't speak of it again, but a week later he accuses me of bloody cheatin'. Said I'd stopped a horse for money – but I never.'

'And then what? Did he report you?'

'Nah. He'd got no fuckin' proof, had he? But he made sure the word got round. Nobody'd bloody touch me.'

'So what happened?' Ben indicated the crutches.

'I was down the local one night – had one too many, you know – and, I dunno, I might have said some stuff. But anyway, the next day I was looking for somethin' in my garage and these two geezers come in, shut the door and did me over proper. Took out my bloody kneecaps with a monkey wrench and smashed up my car. Compliments of the Guvnor, they said.'

'And what did the police say?'

'I told 'em I'd been mugged,' Salter said. 'Told 'em it was druggies and they'd taken money from my wallet. Didn't want them bastards comin' back to finish the job.'

'Is that what they said they'd do?'

'They said they'd do my elbows, too. Then I'd be stuffed proper.' Salter's skin turned a shade paler at the very memory.

'Can't something be done about your knees? Surgery, I mean.'

'Dunno. They tried once but that did sod all. I'm on some waiting list or other.'

'So what now? Where do you go from here?'

'Down the fuckin' sewer, most like. I owe money all over the place and the police were round here the other day.'

Ford and Hancock? Ben wondered.

'So what did they want?'

'I didn't ask. Wasn't gonna be good news, was it? I kept my head down and they went away again.'

'Don't you have any family?'

'Brother. He's out in Spain. A builder.'

'Can't you sell this place; go out there?' In spite of Salter's uncouth manner and degenerate appearance, Ben felt a degree of sympathy for him. If he hadn't fallen foul of Truman, his life could have been very different.

''S not mine, is it? It's rented. Takes all my benefit, too.'

Apart from what you waste on booze and fags, Ben thought.

Belatedly, a thought occurred to Salter. 'Here, you're not gonna print this, are you? Truman would fuckin' kill me!'

'Hmm,' Ben made a show of considering the matter and Salter's expression turned to desperation.

'You can't do it. I'll deny everything.'

'You can try.' Ben brought his left hand out of his pocket to show the miniature cassette-recorder it held.

Salter stared at the device, his face drained of all vestiges of colour, and then lunged awkwardly to try and grab it, succeeding only in dropping one of his crutches and having to hang on to the doorpost to keep his balance.

'No, you bastard, you can't do that! He'll fuckin' kill me!' he said, almost sobbing.

'Did you really stop those horses?'

'No, I told you, I didn't! Why would I? I was on the up. I was doing well.'

'Do you have a passport?'

Salter nodded.

'OK. Tell you what,' Ben fished in an inside pocket for his chequebook. Clicking his pen on, he rested the book against the wall and wrote down a generous figure. 'I'll do you a deal. I'll give you this . . .' he showed Salter the cheque, '. . . and a week to get out of the country before I go to print. Go and find your brother. How's that?'

Salter peered at the piece of paper then transferred his gaze warily to Ben.

'What's the catch?'

'No catch. One condition. You have to speak clearly into this,' he indicated the cassette-recorder, 'giving your name, the date, and swearing that what you have said is true.'

'It is.'

'Well, it shouldn't be a problem then, should it?'

He held the recorder forward and flicked the switch on with his thumb, nodding to Salter as he did so. After a moment's hesitation, the ex-jockey complied.

Ben held out the cheque and Salter took it with alacrity, retreating into his hallway a little, as if afraid that Ben would suffer a change of heart and try to take it back.

'Good. Now remember, in a week's time I'm free to go to press if I want, regardless of whether you leave the country or not. But I'd strongly recommend you do. I should imagine things could get quite uncomfortable for you if you stay around here.'

'Are you gonna bring the bastard down?'

'I don't know,' Ben said. 'I hadn't thought about it. But I might . . . I just might.'

By the time Ben returned to Castle Ridge both lorries were back and the lights were on in the yard as the day's runners were settled for the night. After parking by the cottage he walked over to the main house, and was just about to ring the bell when one of the doors was flung open and Fliss stormed out, almost colliding with him.

He caught at her arm.

'Hey, what's up?'

'My bloody father!' she said, her eyes flashing in the porch light. 'And my bloody sister!'

'What's happened?'

'Helen must have been watching us – this afternoon, when we were talking – and she told Dad we were all over each other! Can you believe it? We only linked arms, for God's sake! Christ, she's a sad bitch!'

'And what did your dad say?' Ben didn't really need to ask.

'Oh, he was quite calm. Said I was too young to know my own mind – how patronising is that? Then he asked if you'd been bothering me! I said no, of course not; we're just mates. But that wasn't right either. He said you weren't the right sort of company for me, whatever that means. So then I got really mad and said if I want to go out with you I will, and he can't stop me.'

Ben closed his eyes momentarily and groaned, a mental picture of Lenny Salter and his crutches flashing across his mind's eye.

'That possibly wasn't the smartest thing to say,' he told her.

'Well, he just made me so angry!' she said. Then, on a curious note, 'Don't you want to go out with me?'

'No, I don't – no offence meant – and even if I did want to, I wouldn't. I value my kneecaps too much.'

Her brows drew down sharply.

'You're talking about Lenny Salter, aren't you? What's he been saying to you? Everybody knows he was mugged. That was nothing to do with my father.'

'No?'

'No. You can't say that! He wouldn't . . . Would he?'

'I'm very nearly sure of it,' Ben replied gravely.

She scanned his face, still frowning, then shook her head decisively.

'No, you're wrong. He's hot-tempered, but he wouldn't do anything like that. Lenny was a cheat and he probably cheated one person too many, but it wasn't my dad.'

'OK.' Ben shrugged. 'Let's hope not. Well, I suppose I'd better go in and face the music.'

'Do you want me to come back in?'

He raised an eyebrow. 'To protect me?'

'No, of course not,' she said crossly. 'It's just – well, I didn't mean to get you into trouble. I was just so mad, I didn't think.'

'Yeah. Well, thanks for the offer, but I daresay I'll be OK.'

As the front door was already open, Ben made his own way to Truman's study, where he found a fire crackling in the pseudo-Georgian grate and the trainer pacing the expensive crimson carpet with a cordless phone held to his ear. Relaxing in one of the armchairs with a whisky tumbler in her hand was Helen, looking particularly pleased with herself. Her look of satisfaction intensified as Ben walked in but, forewarned as he was, he merely glanced across indifferently and away. Out of the corner of his eye he saw her smug expression fade.

Truman saw Ben come in but seemed in no hurry to conclude his conversation, so Ben strolled over to one of the leather upholstered chairs, sat down and picked up a copy of *Country Life* that was lying on a nearby table. He turned the pages idly, wondering if Helen had taken a chance and told her father of his visit to her bungalow that afternoon. If so, he was in for a double dose of trouble. He wondered, also, where Truman's dogs went when the family were all indoors. He'd never seen them in the house. To him, owning a dog meant they shared the house as well.

Eventually, Truman finished his business and placed the handset on his desk.

'So, Ben. How's the article coming along?' he

asked, reminding Ben that Helen didn't know of his investigative sideline.

Ben tossed the magazine aside.

'Yeah, good,' he said. 'Been questioning your family and staff again; hope you don't mind . . .'

'Not if they don't,' Truman said with a dismissive shrug.

He clearly hadn't considered the possibility that Ben might have gone against his express wishes and re-opened the subject of Stefan Varga, and Helen evidently hadn't told him. That, then, was one less thing to worry about.

'You know, your brother put up a very good performance this afternoon,' the trainer said, taking a fat cigar from a beautifully polished walnut box. 'Very creditable indeed.'

'Oh, good,' Ben said, surprised.

'Yes. I think he could really go far, given the backing of a yard like this one. Of course, there are so many things that can influence a career. Unexpected things, one might say.'

Ben became very still, his eyes narrowing.

'Meaning?'

'Well, if word were to get around that he were – shall we say – less than honest, for instance . . .' Truman produced a gold lighter and lit his cigar, drawing in a lungful of smoke with obvious enjoyment.

Ben didn't need it spelt out for him. This was a warning: keep away from Fliss, or else. He took a deep breath to quell his rising anger and said, quietly, 'Are you threatening me? Because I wouldn't recommend it.'

This time it was Truman's eyes that narrowed.

He regarded Ben thoughtfully for a moment, then spoke over his shoulder to Helen.

'I need to speak to Ben on his own, my dear. Do you mind?'

Even with the query tacked on, there was no mistaking the words for anything other than an order. Looking even more petulant than normal, Helen put her drink down and got to her feet. The look she sent Ben in passing was brimful of loathing, but he had more pressing matters to worry about.

As the door clicked shut behind his eldest daughter, Truman turned his frown on Ben again.

'I want you to stay away from my daughter,' he stated with no further ado.

Ben raised an eyebrow.

'Which one in particular?'

'You know damn well which one!' Truman brandished a finger in Ben's face. 'Fliss. She says you asked her out.'

'Then she lied,' Ben replied quietly, his gaze never wavering.

'Nonsense. Why would she do that?'

'Perhaps because she resents being told who she can and can't see.'

Truman's finger was incorporated into a fist, which shook a couple of times under extreme tension, just inches from Ben's nose, and was then withdrawn. He turned away and leant on the desk, staring at the cigar in his hand, as if trying to find the answers in the thin curl of smoke that drifted up from its tip.

'She's too young. I'm only trying to protect her.'

Ben started to breathe again.

'She's twenty-two. Some women are married with two or three kids by then.'

'Yes, and divorced a couple of years later,' Truman pointed out.

'Sometimes we have to make our own mistakes; it's the only way to learn.'

'Oh, I know that, but it's different for Fliss. They'll be after her money – *my* money.'

'That's not very complimentary. She's a beautiful girl. She's got a lot more to offer than just wealth.'

'Bah! You're as naïve as she is!'

It was the first time Ben could ever remember having been called naïve, but he let it go. The man was completely blinkered where his daughters were concerned and there was no point in arguing with him.

Suddenly Truman's attention switched back to Ben.

'And you; you went to see Lenny Salter. What for? I never asked you to.'

'I thought he might be someone with a grudge, and I was right.' He supposed Fliss must have told her father and fervently wished that she hadn't.

Truman made a dismissive gesture.

'He's a gutless whinger. He wouldn't have the brain, the nerve or the contacts to do something like this, even if he wasn't a cripple.'

'I agree.'

Ben hoped that his succinct response would put Truman's mind at rest, but he still appeared uneasy. Blowing out a plume of aromatic smoke, he regarded Ben through the resultant haze.

'So, what did he do? Sell you some ridiculous sob story? He's a loser. You can't take him seriously.'

'He's certainly down on his luck,' Ben agreed, 'but he wasn't all that keen to talk.' Much as Truman deserved to worry about what his ex-jockey might have told him, he'd promised Salter a week's grace and he intended to honour that.

'He's usually all too ready to air his grievances,' Truman commented with a touch of suspicion.

Ben shrugged. 'He seemed jumpy; scared. I don't think he trusted me. He said the police had been sniffing round.'

'Hmm. And what about Rackham? Anything more there?'

Ben pursed his lips and shook his head.

'I begin to think I'm wasting my time and money with you, Mr Copperfield,' Truman remarked. 'Ford seemed impressed with you but you haven't shown me anything much, yet.'

'What money? I haven't had any! And the leads you've given me have been precious little use.'

'And if I *did* pay you what I owe you? Would you take the money and go?' Truman went round his desk and opened a drawer.

'I was promised an exclusive,' Ben reminded him.

'What would it take to buy you off?' He placed a chequebook on the leather desktop.

'It's not about a single pay-off – it's about reputation; my standing within the business. A scoop like this could set me up for life. And then there's the other side of it: can you really afford to cut me loose, with what I know about you and your family?'

Truman's gaze became intent.

'And just what do you think you know?' he asked quietly.

'I know enough to realise there's a lot more to the Stefan Varga story than you're letting on.'

'So, you've found out his name – I suppose that was to be expected. Who told you?'

'I got it off the internet.'

'And what else?'

'I know some of the press gave you a hard time over the business.'

'That was inevitable. They didn't know the full story. I wasn't about to tell them that my daughter had been violated by some illiterate Hungarian gypsy, was I? She'd have been ruined. We'd never have heard the last of it.'

'Was he illiterate?'

'Oh, I don't know,' Truman said impatiently. 'As good as, I expect, but that's not the point.'

'I wonder why he didn't go to the papers himself, to get his own back. He must have been gutted about the Derby, and I imagine they would have paid handsomely for a story like that.'

'I told you; his documents weren't in order. I gave him twenty-four hours to leave the country and he went.'

'So what exactly was wrong with them?'

'Well, for one thing, I'm pretty sure he lied about his age. From a couple of things he said, I'm pretty sure he was younger than he claimed.'

'How could that be? Didn't you meet him before he came over?'

295

'Not exactly. I saw him ride in South Africa a couple of times and knew of his reputation, so I contacted his agent and arranged it all through him. I just wanted him to ride my horses; I saw no reason to meet the man.'

'But he must have had a passport . . .'

'Of course he did, but he was bloody jumpy when I started to question him.'

'And you conveniently discovered all this at the same time as you discovered his affair with Helen? That's quite a coincidence.'

Truman began to look very uncomfortable.

'Yes, all right. I suspected something from the start, but he'd got here with no trouble, so who was I to rock the boat?'

'And if you'd reported him to the authorities yourself, you thought they might ask awkward questions about how long you'd known, is that it?'

'Look, where is this leading?' Truman asked. 'The man's gone. Nobody's heard anything of him since. Why drag it all up now, fifteen or twenty years later?'

'Just curious, that's all.' Ben couldn't tell him that Stefan was dead without explaining how he knew, which in turn would alert him to the fact that a sizeable part of the Hungarian's family were less than thirty miles away as they spoke, and he wasn't about to do that until he was a lot more certain of his facts.

The warmth and the mesmeric movement of the flames in the grate were beginning to have a soporific effect on Ben and he decided it was time he made a move. It was noticeable that he hadn't been offered a drink on this occasion.

'Well, if that's all, I'll be making tracks,' he suggested, getting to his feet. His muscles were still stiff from riding, but improving all the time.

'What are you going to do next? Are you still working for me?'

Ben shook his head wearily. 'There doesn't seem to be much point, when you block every lead I try to follow up. Or was that your intention? Did you think that if I was going to investigate anyway, you'd rather have me on your payroll so you could monitor my progress?' he asked, reading Truman's face. 'That's it, isn't it? What is it you're so afraid I'll find out?'

Truman gave a short laugh.

'Well, you might be a good journalist – I wouldn't know about that – but I'll say this for you: you're certainly an imaginative one! I've made no secret of anything. I admit, I wouldn't have thought of using you if you weren't already involved, but as you were . . . And as for being afraid – it'd take more than a nosy journalist to make *me* lose any sleep. I've got ways and means of protecting my interests.'

'Didn't do too well protecting King, though, did you?' Ben observed with debatable wisdom, irritated by the man's arrogance.

Truman's face darkened.

'Oh, somebody will answer for that, sooner or later, I can promise you! It's not over by a long way. By the time I've finished, someone's going to wish they'd never been born.'

Ben had had enough. Shaking his head again, he moved towards the door.

'Well, you've got my number if you want me. I'm going home.'

Emerging into the hall, he was just in time to hear the door on the opposite side click shut. Helen, he guessed, waiting to hear the result of her troublemaking. No doubt she would have been disappointed; her autocratic parent hadn't had it all his own way, by any means.

Ben was more than halfway home when he began to experience the first stirrings of unease about Lenny Salter. There was little enough about the guy to like, but it had to be said that he had done nothing to deserve such a wholesale fall from grace. From what he'd told Ben, apart from his misguided attempt to force his attentions on Fliss – which could probably be attributed to a combination of alcohol and euphoria after his win – his only mistake had been to air his grievances at the local pub. And now Salter had once again been brought to Truman's notice. Even though Ben had done his best to cover for him, there was no denying the fact that he was responsible for this.

If he'd had Salter's phone number – and always supposing his phone line hadn't been cut off long before – Ben would have considered making a quick call. But as it was, his sense of guilt deepened until, less than a mile from home, he found himself swinging the Mitsubishi into a convenient gateway and turning back to head for Tisbury.

As he turned into Salter's road, some twenty minutes later, he realised that he was already too late. The first thing he saw was a confusion of blue flashing lights up ahead and, much as he liked to think of himself as an optimist, it was patently unrealistic to hope that this was purely coincidental.

Sure enough, as he drew closer he could see that the activity was centred firmly on Salter's bungalow. An ambulance, a fire engine and two police cars were all stopped in haphazard fashion, completely blocking the residential road, while their fluorescent-jacketed crews bustled about busily in the ex-jockey's front garden.

Good thing it wasn't one of the other plots, Ben thought, parking at a discreet distance. Such an abundance of stout footwear trampling indiscriminately over the perfection of any of the neighbouring gardens would, no doubt, have resulted in acrimony and tears.

There was, predictably, a sizeable crowd gathered, into which Ben casually integrated himself. Peering through the gap between two other onlookers, he was just in time to see two paramedics load a stretcher into the back of the waiting ambulance. It was too far away for him to identify the blanketed figure, but then, he didn't really need to. Who else would it be but the unfortunate Lenny Salter?

The front of the ex-jockey's bungalow was illuminated by a couple of brilliant spotlights and on the patch of ground in the foreground two firefighters were in conversation with three policemen. As he watched, Ben saw another firefighter emerge from the open front door of the building with an armful of bedding. The glass in one of the windows was missing, the filthy net curtains mercifully a casualty of the flames, and a sooty stain swept upwards from the opening.

'What happened here, then?' he asked the nearest bystander; a stocky, bald-headed man who hadn't stopped to change out of his carpet slippers before coming to investigate.

'Dunno exactly. Sharon, who lives next door, reckons he fell asleep and left the chip pan on. He's handicapped, you know. The place is a mess. We knew something like this would happen, sooner or later. Stands to reason.'

Ben couldn't see that, but he nodded nonetheless.

'But he was lucky, though . . .' the man went on, '. . . because Tony – who lives two doors down on the other side – is a fireman. He just happened to be walking past with his dog and saw the smoke, so he broke the front door down and got him out. That's him, there, talking to the crew. Brave man, that.'

'Very brave,' Ben agreed, seeing a strongly built man of about fifty standing near the fire engine, in conversation with the station officer.

'Not that it was something any one of us wouldn't have done, in his position, but you have to give credit where credit's due, don't you?'

'Of course,' Ben said, backing away before the neighbour, who looked set to become tiresomely garrulous, could start up again.

Skirting the crowd of onlookers he made his way to the other side and edged amongst them again. Here, closer to the vehicles, the four sets of unsynchronised flashing blue lights produced an effect akin to a strobe light in a nightclub.

'What happened here?' he asked a middle-aged, tweed-skirted woman.

She turned and looked him up and down, then gave it as her opinion that the lazy, good-for-nothing occupant of the bungalow had finally got his just deserts.

'They're saying he left something draped over a gas fire. I expect he was drunk; he almost always is, as far as I can make out,' she added.

Ben thought that was a more likely explanation than the chip pan. Salter didn't strike him as the sort to do much cooking; he was more the send-out-for-a-pizza type. But that was always supposing it had been an accident at all.

'Is the guy all right?' he asked the tweed lady, as the ambulance started up and began to nose its way out along the congested street.

'I don't know. He looked pretty poorly,' she said. 'Mind you, he'd have been a lot worse if that chap from down the road hadn't been passing by. I believe he's an off-duty fireman.'

Feeling that he'd gleaned about as much information as he was going to from Salter's neighbours, Ben decided to beat a retreat before the police started making enquiries and someone remembered having seen his four-wheel-drive vehicle parked outside the bungalow earlier in the day. Although he had little doubt that the production of his press card would alleviate much of the suspicion, he still had no desire to spend the evening at the station answering questions about his interest in Salter, many of which might well lead uncomfortably close to forbidden territory.

Walking back down the road he felt bad about the whole business. He had foreseen the possibility of retribution on Truman's part, but he hadn't bargained on him finding out so soon, and he had greatly underestimated the speed with which the man would, or even could, take action. If Truman was indeed responsible for the fire, he must surely have arranged it as soon as Fliss had told him of Ben's visit, without waiting to find out what, if anything, his ex-jockey had said.

Backing into a convenient gateway and heading for home, Ben realised that maybe, in future, he should be more careful in his dealings with the trainer.

By the time he finally reached home Ben was dog-tired, and close inspection of his fridge revealed very little that looked even remotely appetising, so he sent out for a Chinese.

It had been his intention to relax for the rest of the evening but the events of the day kept replaying over and over in his mind, and even before his chicken chow mein had arrived, he'd booted up his computer and was searching the family history websites for a database of registered births, marriages and deaths.

What he found set his mind buzzing and caused him to sit back and rethink a large part of his investigation.

13

CHELTENHAM FAVOURITE IN DISAPPEARANCE MYSTERY

Ben stared at the headline with a sinking heart. Telephone receiver in hand, he'd padded barefoot along to the front door of the cottage to retrieve his Sunday paper, and he now stood on the sheepskin mat in the hall.

'Well?' Truman's voice barked down the phone.

'Yeah, I see it.'

'And I suppose you're proud of your handiwork?'

'Except that it's not mine,' Ben said, swiftly scanning the text underneath the title. Whoever had alerted Fleet Street hadn't given much away – or possibly didn't have much *to* give away. The article didn't name its informant, accrediting the information to 'sources close to Truman's Castle Ridge yard'.

'It's already in three of the papers and the others all want a piece. I've had reporters on my doorstep, all over the gallops, and tying up the phone lines all morning. I've had to get the police to move them on.'

'Well, I'm sorry but, like I said, it wasn't me. If it had been, I'd have wanted my name on it, I can tell you!'

'Well, if it wasn't you, then who the fuck was it?' Truman demanded.

'Could be any one of dozens,' Ben said. 'Your staff, or your family . . .'

'My family? Don't talk crap! They wouldn't do this. How dare you try and shift the blame!'

'There's no blame to shift as far as I'm concerned.' Ben went into his kitchen and tossed the paper on to the granite worktop. Wedging the handset between shoulder and ear he proceeded to fill the kettle, talking all the while. 'To be honest, I'm surprised this hasn't happened long before now. Any reporter with his eye on the gallops would have noticed that King hasn't been out for a few days, and it would be easy enough to get one of the lads chattering down at the pub. After all, it doesn't say anything specific, does it? Just that you're being secretive about his whereabouts. I'd say it was pure speculation; probing for a reaction on a quiet news day. With that frost yesterday quite a few fixtures were off, and they've got to find something to write about.'

There was silence for a moment, and Ben guessed that Truman was reluctantly seeing the truth of his argument. He sat on a stool to lift his feet off the cold flagstones for a moment and wished he'd taken the time to find a dressing gown and moccasins. Truman's call had caught him having a lie-in.

'Are you coming over today?'

Ben blinked.

'I thought I was a waste of time and money.'

'I was mad with you yesterday.'

'And you're not now?'

'Well, sometimes you make sense,' he conceded. 'Which is more than I can say for all these chattering women I've got round me all day.'

Ben frowned. To someone who had a great deal of respect and liking for the fairer sex, Truman's misogynistic undertones grated, to say the least. Though remembering the way his hands had wandered all over his part-time secretary, Ben supposed it was more accurate to say that the trainer held women in contempt rather than actual dislike.

Ben braved the cold floor again to get a mug from the drainer and reached for the coffee. Mouse came quietly in, glanced at him under her bushy brows and curled up, with a sigh, on her blanket under the table.

'I could come over later, for a little while. I was coming to see Mikey, anyway.'

'Make it lunchtime if you like,' Truman said. 'One-ish. Come to lunch. What on earth's that racket?'

'The kettle.'

'The kettle? Thanks a bloody million! Here am I dealing with a crisis, and you're making a cup of bloody tea!'

'Life goes on,' Ben observed. 'See you later.'

*

305

Ben was expecting Lisa back at some point that day, but his intention to spend what was left of the morning tidying up and cleaning the cottage was hampered by two further telephone calls: one from Taylor, his editor on the Csikós story, and the other from Logan.

Taylor, who – Ben thought a little sourly – must live in his office to be there first thing on a Sunday morning, was keen to wrap up the first part of the article on the Hungarians, not least because the troupe's performances were attracting so much attention that he was worried someone might pre-empt Ben's exposé. They would do a separate review of the preparation for and performance of the final, spectacular *son et lumière* at Brinkley Castle, Taylor said, warning that there would be hell to pay if someone else stole the magazine's thunder.

Logan's business was equally imperative.

'When are you going to tell me what the bloody hell you're up to?' he demanded without preamble.

'With regard to . . . ?' Ben asked cautiously.

'Well, try this for size: you ask me for information on ALSA, then our colleagues over at Midhurst pick a couple of them up after a midnight disturbance and who should be on hand but Ben Copperfield. You ask for info about one Leonard Salter, and guess what? A couple of days later he gets himself beaten up and almost fried to a crisp. And when we asked the neighbours if they saw anything strange in the last few days, they said yes – our Lenny had a visitor; a youngish man in a four-wheel-drive vehicle whose description was

306

you to a tee. Now, do you have anything you'd like to tell Uncle Mark?'

'He was beaten up? Again? Poor bastard! Will he be OK?'

'Well, he's off the danger list, apparently. But he's still hooked up to a machine and I'm told it'll be a while before he's up and about. It would appear that someone took a boot to him. I gather there was quite extensive internal bleeding.'

'They didn't – I mean, he told me he was terrified if they came back they'd break his elbows. They didn't, did they?'

'If who came back?'

'Whoever did his knees.'

'Well, not as far as I know. So, come on. What gives?'

'Nothing. Well, nothing new. I mean, you know what I'm working on. Ford and Truman have promised me an exclusive, and I'm just following up a few leads while I'm waiting.'

'And what's the connection with this horse circus thing?'

'No connection,' Ben heard himself say, lightly. 'That's another article I happen to be working on.' If only that could be true. He didn't like lying to Logan.

'So what did you find out from Salter?'

'Well, he's certainly not one of Eddie Truman's biggest fans, if that's anything. Quite apart from unfair dismissal and defamation of character, he seems to have no doubt that it was Truman who was behind the beating-up he suffered a few years ago.'

'Yet, when we interviewed him at the time, he

swore it was a couple of youngsters after dope money.'

'Well, do you blame him? When they'd just taken out his kneecaps with a monkey wrench and were threatening to come back and finish the job?'

'So, who was it this time, Sherlock?'

'What does he say? Haven't you spoken to him?'

'He hasn't said much at all yet; he's pretty drugged up. But, interestingly, your name has come up a couple of times. Why should that be, I wonder.'

Ben ignored him.

'Well, I don't know for sure who did it, but I do know that when Truman found out that I'd been to see Salter he wasn't a particularly happy bunny.'

'Well, we've got a man waiting to have a word, as soon as the doctor says he can. Until then I guess we'll have to hope forensics turn up something. And as for you, buddy, just remember there's a whole lot more to this thing than making the headlines in some newspaper, OK?'

'Yeah, I know,' Ben said. 'Believe me, I know.'

The atmosphere at the Truman dinner table was interesting, to say the least. It was Eddie Truman himself who opened the door to Ben and, aside from shooting a pithy dismissal towards the remaining couple of reporters lingering hopefully on his drive, he seemed perfectly genial. Somehow, rather than putting Ben's mind at rest, he found this a little unsettling. He was ushered into the huge, range-warmed kitchen where the rest of the family had gathered and was furnished with a glass of red wine. All the recessed spotlights were on and blinds were drawn over the two windows that overlooked the front drive, which Ben presumed was to guard against the possibility of prying eyes and camera lenses. Tactfully, he made no comment.

Fliss greeted Ben with a kiss on the cheek, glancing defiantly across at her father as she did so, and as the soup-and-sandwich lunch got underway it was obvious to Ben that she still hadn't forgiven either her father or her sister for the previous day's quarrel. Helen wore her habitually sullen expression, glaring at Ben whenever he looked her way, and her mother looked almost as if she'd been crying. Eyeing her, Ben wondered for the first time whether Truman's abuse of her ever went beyond the purely verbal.

As on the previous occasion, Finch seemed interested in his food and little else, so the conversation – such as it was – was confined almost entirely to Truman, Ben and Bess.

'Oh, I hate this false light!' Helen exclaimed suddenly, breaking in rudely on something Bess was saying. 'Can't we have the blinds up now?'

'You know why we can't,' her father said shortly.

'Because somebody blabbed to the papers. And we all know who that was, don't we?' Helen sent Ben a sneering glance, which he affected not to notice.

'It wasn't Ben,' Truman said.

'Oh, why? Because he says so? He can do no

wrong, can he? You let him talk his way out of everything. What is he, the son you never had?'

'Helen!' Elizabeth said sharply. She had put little food on her plate and eaten almost none of it.

'It wouldn't surprise me if it was *you* who spoke to the papers,' Fliss put in, looking at her sister.

'What? Don't be ridiculous! Why on earth would I do that?'

'Just to get Ben into trouble, probably. I wouldn't put it past you.'

Helen coloured, and it occurred to Ben that Fliss might well have hit the nail on the head.

'I did not, you vicious cow!'

'That's enough!' her father thundered.

Somewhere in the central part of the house a two-tone doorbell sounded, and Bess quickly offered to answer it.

'Why do you always take *her* side?' Helen complained bitterly, ignoring Bess's departure.

'It's not a case of taking sides, it's a case of behaving like civilised adults, which, quite frankly, neither of you are at the moment!'

'Well, it's not my fault she's got a crush on Ben!' Helen retorted.

This time it was Fliss whose face flamed.

'I have not! You made that up, you interfering bitch!'

'Oi!' Finch looked up over a spoonful of soup, finally moved to a nominal defence of his wife and, in the corner of the room, baby Lizzie hiccupped and started to cry.

Elizabeth rose to her feet to go and tend to the child but Helen pushed her chair back sharply

310

and jumped up, saying over her shoulder, 'Now look what you've done!'

Being opposite the door to the hall, Ben was the first to notice Bess come back and stand hesitantly on the threshold. He thought she looked flustered.

She cleared her throat. 'Er – Eddie . . .'

She had to say it again, a little louder, before he heard but then he too saw the look on her face and waved his hand impatiently at the others.

'Yes, Bess?'

'Er . . . There's a young man at the door. He says . . . He says he's . . .'

Suddenly, the young man in question was there, beside and just behind her.

'I *said*, I've come to find my mother,' he stated, in the squeaky-gruff voice of the adolescent male.

Somewhere in his teens, the newcomer was of medium height and slim build but with a breadth of shoulder he had yet to grow into. His hair was dark, as were his eyes and, even under a stress-induced pallor, his skin had a faintly olive tint. He looked terrified but Ben was impressed by the courage with which he faced the roomful of people, who were gazing back at him with a semi-comical array of expressions, none of them especially welcoming.

Into the stunned silence, Ben took it upon himself to speak.

'And you, I take it, are Stephen,' he said. Instantly everyone's attention was transferred to him.

'What the . . . ?' Truman seemed momentarily floored.

The boy's dark eyes had turned Ben's way, surprised and wary.

'How did you know? Who are you?'

'Call it an educated guess,' Ben said, smiling a little. 'I knew of your existence so it's not so very clever. My name's Ben Copperfield.'

'You're not . . . ? I mean . . .'

With a shock, Ben realised what the boy was trying to say.

'No, I'm not,' he said gently. 'You'll have to ask your mother about that.'

Stephen looked across to where Helen was standing, holding the baby tucked under one arm and her feeding bottle in the other hand. Her fingers had tightened and milk was dripping steadily from the rubber top but she didn't notice. Her eyes shot in panic from the visitor to her father and back again.

'You *are* my mother, aren't you? I guessed a while ago,' the boy said, advancing a step or two into the room. 'Why did you pretend you weren't?'

Helen seemed to have lost the ability to communicate. She stood, pale and visibly trembling, effectively confirming his statement by her very silence.

'Helen? What's he talking about?' Fliss was looking bewildered.

Her sister ignored her.

'This is utterly ridiculous!' Truman had found his voice again. He got to his feet and advanced around the table towards the youngster. 'I don't know who the bloody hell you are, but if you think you have some connection with this family, you're clearly deluded! I think it's time you left my house; you're not welcome here. Go back to wherever you came from.'

Colour came and went in Stephen's face as he turned to look at Truman.

'And who are you?' he asked with a touch of hauteur.

Truman nearly had a fit. He stopped in his tracks, his face turning beetroot red.

'Who am I?' he repeated. '*Who am I?* I'll tell you who I am – I'm the man who's going to call the police and get you arrested! I'm the one who's going to whip your bastard ass out of this house and halfway to the coast if you don't go by yourself! Do I need to be clearer than that?'

'Eddie don't, please,' Elizabeth pleaded, tears beginning to run down her ashen cheeks.

Her husband didn't spare her so much as a glance.

At the table, Finch watched intently, an unpleasant sneer twisting his heavy features, clearly having no intention of joining the fray. Ben wondered if he had known about the boy's existence, and decided he must have. He had shown little surprise.

'Well?' Truman demanded.

Galvanised, at last, by the violence of her father's tone, Helen stepped forward.

'Dad – please . . .'

'Shut up, girl!' Truman snapped, without taking his eyes off Stephen. 'Well? What are you waiting for?'

His courage wavering under this sustained attack, the boy took a step backwards, glancing in desperation at the other occupants of the room as if hoping for support. Ben took pity on him.

'Where have you come from?'

Wide, unhappy eyes turned his way. 'Bristol.'

'And how have you got here?'

'By train, and then I hitched. I can't go back – I've run out of money,' he added helplessly, suddenly looking very young.

'So what – you've come here for a hand-out?' Truman enquired.

'Where's Matilda? Does she know you're here?' This was Elizabeth, and her husband finally turned his attention to her.

'Oh, so that's the score is it? He's been living with your sister. How dare you cross me? All these years you've played the meek little wife whilst you've been lying to me – laughing at me, no doubt – with your slut of a daughter!'

Elizabeth quailed. 'No! No, it wasn't like that. But we couldn't just give the boy away. He's Helen's son; our grandson – our flesh and blood!'

'He's a bastard-born Gypsy brat and no kin of mine!' Truman stated through clenched teeth.

Clutched in her mother's arms, the baby started to bawl and Helen dissolved into tears.

Ben had had enough. Getting to his feet, he moved round the table and approached the lad who looked completely shell-shocked.

'I expect you're tired,' he said. 'Would you like a cup of tea?'

Stephen nodded gratefully, and Ben looked hopefully at Bess.

She came up trumps. Holding out a hand, as one would to a small child, she said, 'Come on.

I think we should give them a moment to clear the air. It's all been a bit of a shock.'

The boy hesitated, looking across at Helen, but, evidently deciding there was no support forthcoming from that department, he turned to go with Bess.

'Hey! Hold on!' Truman started forward and would have followed them had he not come face to face with Ben. 'Get out of my way!'

Ben held his ground.

'Eddie, you're not thinking! You've got reporters camped on your doorstep. If you throw this boy out, they'll have a field day. You can imagine the headlines – "Red Truman Disowns Daughter's Lovechild". My God, they'd think Christmas had come again!'

Truman paused, frowning at Ben.

'So what am I supposed to do? Welcome him into the family? Because I won't do it. I'm not having that Gypsy's brat under my roof!'

'I can't tell you what to do but, whatever you decide, you don't want the papers getting hold of it. They'd crucify you.'

Truman glared at him for a moment longer.

'And what about you? You're a journalist.'

'So I am,' Ben said blandly.

With barely stifled fury, the trainer brushed past him and walked to the doorway, but there he paused and seemed to reconsider, slamming his fist against the wall before turning back into the room. Temporarily deprived of his main prey, he vented his spleen on lesser targets.

'I can't believe you conspired with one another to go against my express wishes,' he said, looking

315

first at Helen and then his wife. 'Lying and scheming and cheating me. Your sister, was it? How did you persuade her to go along with it? She's even more of a wet blanket than you are!'

Elizabeth drew herself up.

'She couldn't bear to see Helen's child given away to a stranger. She wasn't happy about it but at least she had the human decency to give him a home, which is more than you did!'

'Good for you,' Ben muttered under his breath.

Helen was also clearly impressed by this show of spirit, looking open-mouthed at her mother, and for a moment Truman appeared much as one might if attacked by an earthworm.

'He was soon back on track. 'You had no business to even tell the nosy cow! I thought I made it clear no one was to know.'

'She's my sister. Besides, I had to do something,' Elizabeth protested. 'He's our grandchild, Eddie. And Helen was desperate. She was making herself ill.'

'She should have thought of that before she let that Gypsy screw her!' Truman said, his voice loaded with contempt.

Beyond crying harder, Helen didn't react. She'd obviously heard it all before.

'For God's sake! This is getting us nowhere,' Ben said. 'There's no point in squabbling about what happened fifteen or sixteen years ago. The boy's here, now. You have to deal with it, and just turning him out of the house won't answer.'

'Who asked you, anyway?' Finch demanded, finally roused. He wiped his mouth on the back of his hand and Ben noticed that he'd taken the time to finish his lunch; such was the level of his concern.

Truman faced Ben.

'All right, then – what do you suggest I do? You're always the one with the answers; sort this one out.'

Ben was a bit taken aback to find himself being regarded with varying degrees of expectancy by everyone in the room. Even Helen, not hitherto numbered among his greatest fans, had swallowed her sobs, mopped her swollen eyes with a corner of the baby's bib and was now watching him hopefully.

'Well?' Truman prompted, his chin jutting aggressively.

Ben took a deep breath.

'As far as I can see, it's not up to you,' he told the trainer. 'Surely this is Helen's business. Maybe you had the right to order her life when the boy was born – or maybe not, that's debatable – but I'm damned sure you haven't got that right now. She's a grown woman, for God's sake! Her relationship with her own son is nobody's business but hers.'

For a moment he thought Truman would hit him, and judging by the eager look in Finch's eyes, he thought so too, but after clenching his jaw a couple of times Eddie regained control.

'I'll not have him in my house or around my horses.'

'He hasn't asked you to,' Ben pointed out. 'All he seemed to want was to find out the truth about his family. You can't blame him for that.'

Truman's eyes blazed again.

'If I'd thought for just one moment he'd ever turn up here, I'd have made the little slut have an abortion!'

'I wouldn't have done it,' Helen stated, beginning to cry again. 'It's wicked! You couldn't force me – it was *my* baby.'

Sensing tempers rising once more, Ben cut through.

'Look, that's no longer the issue. The question is, what happens now? All I'm saying is, before you all start ripping up at one another again, wouldn't it be sensible to find out what the poor kid actually wants? If he's got any sense he'll want to get as far away from here as possible!'

His suggestion was greeted with a pause that he dared hope might signify at least some rational thought; then, before anyone formed a response, the front doorbell rang.

'If that's another bloody journalist, I swear I'll take his microphone and ram it down his bloody neck!' Truman exclaimed.

'I'll go,' Elizabeth offered, hurrying towards the door. Her husband made no move to stop her, and she escaped with obvious relief.

'What about you, Ray?' the trainer said suddenly, swinging round to address his assistant. 'You're keeping very quiet.'

'Nothing much for me to say. He's none of my blood, and he's sure as hell not getting anything from me!'

'But she's your wife. Aren't you supposed to stand by her?' Fliss, a spectator until now, entered the dispute, voicing the very thought that was in Ben's mind.

Finch shrugged. 'Just 'cos I married her, doesn't make me responsible for some bastard she produced when she was a kid,' he said, curling his lip unpleasantly. 'We've got our own to look after now.'

Fliss regarded him with disgust.

'You make me sick!'

'Good job I didn't marry you, then.'

What Fliss's response to this might have been they never found out because Bess reappeared.

'That was your wife's sister,' she told her employer. 'She's with Stephen now. He said he didn't want to see her but he hugged her anyway. He's really mixed up, poor kid!'

'I should go to him.' Helen put the baby back in her high chair and the bottle on the kitchen worktop.

'And how many times have you gone running off to see him before?' Truman wanted to know. 'All those shopping trips and the visits to your friend at Bristol University, I suppose. Do you even have a friend there?'

'Yes, of course I have. She used to come with me at first and we'd take Stephen to the park, then, when he was older, we'd go for days out. It was lovely.'

'What did you tell him?' Fliss asked. 'Who did he think you were?'

'To start with, we didn't tell him anything, but when he started asking questions, we told him I was a cousin. It wasn't till he was much older – just the last year or so – that he began to want details about his family. And what was I supposed to tell him? Aunt Mattie wanted me to tell him

319

the truth but I couldn't, so I thought it was easier if I stayed away, especially when Lizzie came along. He must have worked it out for himself.' The ready tears began to flow again, and she sniffed. 'He must hate me.'

'I don't blame him,' her sister commented.

'That's enough, Fliss!' Truman said impatiently. 'This is none of your business.'

'Speaking of which,' Ben put in. 'Having added my two cents' worth, I should be going.'

'Now?' Truman glanced sharply at him.

'Well, yes,' Ben was surprised, 'after I've had a quick word with Mikey. I can't imagine you want me here with all this going on.'

'Mikey. Of course. OK.' Truman seemed, understandably, a little distracted. 'Look back in before you leave, will you?'

Ben nodded. 'OK, will do.'

It being mid-afternoon, he found Mikey at the cottage. He was sat at the kitchen table, bent over a sketchpad, and looked up with flattering pleasure as Ben entered.

'Hi, Mikey. What're you drawing? Can I see?'

Mikey sat back to reveal his work, with no show of false modesty. It was a detailed pencil study of the yard, with several horses' heads looking out over the half-doors. As far as Ben could see, it was correct down to the last brick and door latch. The scale and perspective was spot on and it looked almost finished.

'Christ, Mikey! That's brilliant. It must have taken you ages. Did you sit out in the yard to do it?'

'No, I see it in here.' He pointed to his thatch of blond hair.

Ben shook his head in amazement. 'You must have a photographic memory. I didn't even know you could draw. Have you got anything else in there?'

He gestured at the sketchpad and Mikey pushed it towards him. With growing admiration, Ben turned the pages. There were many pictures of the horses, one or two of the dogs, some of the other lads – including Ricey, Caterpillar and others – and even one of himself.

'Who's this?' he asked, finding a portrait that was vaguely familiar.

Mikey looked across.

'Oh, some bloke that Mr Finch knows. Seen him up by the top gate a couple of times, when I've been up to see the badgers. Don't know who he is.'

'Just recently?' Ben remembered now where he'd seen him.

'Yeah, and once a few weeks ago.'

'And did Mr Finch seem pleased to see him?'

Mikey shrugged. 'I guess so. I think he knew he was coming 'cause the dogs were shut in.'

'Ah, that's interesting.'

Next door, in the living room, the television was broadcasting a sports programme to the accompaniment of occasional exclamations of enthusiasm or disgust.

'Who's in there?' Ben asked.

Mikey shrugged. 'Few of the boys: Les, Caterpillar, Davy, Paolo – I'm not sure who else.'

Davy. For what Ben had in mind, he would

much rather Truman's workplace spy wasn't within earshot, just in case.

'Tell you what. Why don't we take Mouse for a little walk? Have you got time?'

'Yeah.' Mikey was plainly delighted. 'I'll show you where the badgers are, if you like?'

'That'd be good.'

Taking a moment to stow his sketchpad out of sight of prying eyes, Mikey joined Ben outside and together they trudged off across the fields, skirting the yard and heading for the copse that was adjacent to the proposed stud site. The wind was whipping across the high ground next to the trees and, having duly inspected the badger set, an activity in which Mouse took great interest, Ben suggested they move down to the cluster of tumbledown brick buildings on the slope below.

Here, a range of mainly roofless outbuildings formed three sides of what had once been a size-able farmyard, with a large barn making up the fourth. It was into the shelter of this that they made their way, finding a thick carpet of rotting hay and straw underfoot, and various rusty implements standing about. Above them, a section of rusty tin roof flapped endlessly in the wind.

Ben took his miniature cassette-recorder from his inside pocket and showed his half-brother.

'There's something I want you to listen to – don't ask why, just listen.'

He switched the device on and waited, watching Mikey's face intently.

It didn't take long. As soon as Jakob's soft, lilting tones sounded in the frosty air, telling Ben about his homeland, the youngster's eyes narrowed. He listened obediently for another ten seconds or so, then looked up at Ben in puzzled enquiry.

He switched the recorder off.

'Well?'

'That's like the voice I heard when I was hiding in the horsebox the day they took King!'

'Are you sure?'

'Yes. Have you found them? Is King coming back?'

'Soon, I hope. I think I've found who took him, but I haven't found the horse yet. Listen, I can't say any more at the moment, and I've got to ask you not to either. No one must know about this, OK?'

'Not even the Guvnor?'

'Especially not the Guvnor! Not Ricey, not a soul, because you could get me in big trouble if anyone found out. D'you understand? This is really important.'

Mikey nodded earnestly.

'I won't tell anyone. I promise.'

Ben called in at the house before leaving, as Truman had asked, but whatever had prompted him to request this had apparently slipped his mind, for he didn't really have anything in particular to say to him.

The atmosphere in the house had lightened a little; Stephen had been temporarily removed by his great aunt to a nearby B&B, and Helen and her husband had withdrawn to their bungalow. This much Truman told Ben, but his anger was still visibly simmering, and Ben began to seriously worry for the boy's ongoing health.

This train of thought naturally led back to Lenny Salter, lying in his hospital bed, hooked up to drips and God knows what else. He'd have liked to mention it to Truman, just to note his reaction, but could see no way of doing so without betraying the fact that he'd returned to Salter's home the previous evening, so he held his tongue.

Not wanting to spend any longer listening to Truman's family problems and mindful of the fact that Lisa was expected sometime that afternoon or evening, Ben took his leave, driving fast and arriving back at Dairy Cottage, via the local mini-mart, just as the cold, frosty day was giving way to even colder dusk. Swinging into the small courtyard he saw with relief that Lisa's Beetle was not yet there. Now, at least, he would be able to tidy up and run the Dyson round before she came.

Laden with carrier bags full of shopping, Ben dropped his key and had to put half his load down to retrieve it, which at least meant he had a hand free to wave when he caught sight of his landlord passing the courtyard entrance.

He swore under his breath as two of the bags he'd deposited at his feet fell sideways, spilling their contents on his doorstep, and then decided to take the bags he still held through to the kitchen before returning to fetch the others. He'd have to come back out anyway, because Mouse was still curled up in the back of the four-wheel-drive. Light from the ornate, Victorian-style streetlamp outside lent the hall a soft glow, and Ben went straight through to the kitchen before turning a light on.

There he stopped short in shock.

The kitchen looked as if an earthquake had hit it. Every cupboard door was open and their erstwhile contents were strewn across the flagstones and granite worktops. All Ben's food containers had been emptied: flour decorated the window and sink where a bag had been thrown and split; sugar was sprinkled liberally across every surface and crunched underfoot, as did pasta, coffee granules and cornflakes. Crockery had been swept from shelves and smashed on the stone floor; all the drawers had been pulled out and upturned, and so had the table and chairs. There was, Ben realised despairingly, nothing that had been left untouched.

'Shit!' he breathed, rooted to the spot. It occurred to him to thank God that Lisa hadn't walked in on whoever had trashed the place, but before the thought had time to develop further, his world went suddenly and terrifyingly black.

14

For an instant, Ben froze.

Thick, rough material was pulled suffocatingly tight over his nose and mouth and his first panicky breath felt hot on his face. The hood didn't completely block the light – his own instinctive reaction of closing his eyes had done that, and as he opened them a hazy glow seeped through the fibres.

He found he was still holding the bags of shopping and had to consciously release his grasp, at the same time stamping backwards to where he hoped his assailant's feet might be.

They weren't.

His right elbow, applied vigorously behind him at rib-height, met with more success but his satisfaction was short-lived. Instead of loosening, the hood tightened and he was swung in a stumbling semicircle, which was only halted by the left side of his body and head impacting with something unforgivingly solid. His fingers touched smooth, cold stone: the kitchen wall.

Almost before he had time to properly register

the discomfort of the collision, his head snapped back as the hood was used to pull him away from the wall and pain exploded in his midriff as a fist hit him with wicked force, just below the ribs. He doubled forward, his hands clutching at the epicentre of the agony, and fell, gagging, to his knees.

He was still a long way from wanting to straighten out when once again his head was pulled back. This time as he tensed, waiting for the next blow, someone spoke in a semi-whisper, close to his left ear.

'We've been waiting for you, Mr Copperfield. Or may I call you Ben?'

With these words, any lingering hope that he had simply been unfortunate enough to walk in on a burglary in progress was banished. These men had business with him and, thinking of the fate of Lenny Salter – just twenty-four hours previously – it would be naïve to imagine there was no connection; equally naïve to suppose they didn't have something similar in mind. Ben thought of the ex-jockey's useless, shattered knees and was seized by a sudden wild panic that brought him surging to his feet, from where he drove his bodyweight backwards, carrying his first attacker with him until they both fetched up against one of the kitchen units.

This time the man behind took the brunt of the collision and, judging by the grunt and accompanying obscenity, he wasn't too happy about it. He didn't seem inclined to release his grip on the smothering hood though, so Ben tried a little extra persuasion in the form of a head-butt, throwing his head back hard into the man's face.

It just seemed to make him madder.

With the hood still firmly in place, Ben found himself dragged sideways and flung against the granite worktop, after which his head and upper body was forced down on to the work surface. Then, bent over the right angle of the units, Ben was slid sideways for six feet or so, carrying the mess of crockery, spilt food and empty canisters with him to crash to the floor at the end. Feeling like a rag doll in the hands of a spiteful child, Ben managed to get his hands beneath him before he hit the flagstones, but he hadn't even begun to get his act together when the breath was knocked out of him by what felt like a medium-sized elephant landing on the small of his back. Various unidentifiable objects were trapped beneath him and pressed, extremely uncomfortably, into his chest and stomach.

'You little shit!' the voice sounded close to his ear once more. 'You'll pay for that!'

Ben was under the impression that he already had, but even had he been able to make himself heard from under the stifling hood, he didn't think the comment would further his cause.

'Here, use this.' Another voice, presumably the owner of the powerful fist. From their accents, both men hailed from the Midlands.

Ben tensed, anticipating another blow, but instead his arms were wrenched awkwardly behind him and his wrists bound tightly together. He was unable to offer any shred of resistance; his body busy trying to cope on the minimal lung capacity the crushing weight allowed. Just as he felt he was losing the fight to stay conscious the pressure eased, the hood was repositioned, and he was again hauled to his feet, this time by his arms.

He spread his feet, hearing the crackle of debris under the soles of his shoes, and half hung in the grasp of the man behind him, trying to decide if their use of a hood was a good or a bad thing. If they were using it to protect their identities then it had to be a plus point, indicating that they intended to let him go. If, however, it was being used as an interrogation tool, to disorientate and frighten him – as he'd seen on TV documentaries about the Special Forces and terrorists – then it was definitely not good news. What was more – it was working.

'You're making this very hard on yourself,' the second voice remarked. 'We only wanted to ask you a question.'

Ben waited, his breath coming in shallow, painful gasps, as he concentrated on preventing his fear of constraint from sliding into panic.

'A little bird told us you had a certain tape,' the voice continued. 'But we've looked every-where and we can't find it, so we thought: let's wait for Ben, he can tell us where it is.'

'What tape?'

The question escaped almost involuntarily, and the next moment Ben's knees buckled as a fist slammed into his solar plexus for the second time. The hands gripping his arms stopped him from falling, pulling him upright whilst his muscles were still a cramping morass of agony. He groaned, tasting bile, and the voice close to his ear said softly, 'Wrong answer,' in a singsong tone, as if reciting a nursery rhyme to a child.

The hood tightened round his face once more, forcing his head back and making breathing even harder. He tried to think rationally. What tape were they talking about? The tape of Jakob talking, that he'd played to Mikey just that afternoon? How could they know about that? Or the tape he'd made the day before, when Lenny had told his tale? Whichever one it was, it didn't take a rocket scientist to guess who was behind the attack. Having heard so much about Truman's methods of exacting retribution, it seemed he was now experiencing them at first hand.

'Search him.'

Hands patted him down from chest to hips, pausing to remove his car keys, phone and spare cash, and toss them on to the floor. Questing fingers found his wallet inside his jacket and a fold of bank notes in the back pocket of his jeans.

'It's not there,' came the report.

'OK. I'll ask again. Where's the tape, Mr Copperfield?'

Ben shook his head dumbly.

His reward was an open-handed slap across the face, which, because of the hood, he didn't see coming. It rocked him, bringing tears to his eyes and a warm trickle of blood from his nose. He shook his head muzzily.

'I took the tape to the cops on my way home,' he tried to say, but the thick material distorted his efforts.

The hood loosened a fraction.

'Say again.'

'The cops have it. I took it on my way home. You're too late.'

330

There was a pause, during which Ben gratefully drank in the cooler air that had seeped in around his face. Then, with no warning, he was slapped again.

'We don't believe you.' The voice said conversationally. 'Try again.'

Ben shook his head.

'There's nothing else to say. It's the truth.'

There followed a murmured exchange between his captors, during which Ben waited, his head still spinning from the blows, not daring to hope he'd be believed.

His pessimism was borne out.

The third slap was harder and the voice that followed it was plainly losing patience.

'You're a reporter. If you uncovered a story you wouldn't run to the pigs, you'd take it to your editor. Now, if you don't start to co-operate, Mr Copperfield, we're going to have to get rough. You've met little Lenny Salter, I believe. We were talking to him ourselves, just last night. Ain't it a small world?'

From behind Ben there came a low chuckle.

'Ain't it just?'

Suddenly, strong fingers grasped Ben's face through the fabric.

'Tell us where the fucking tape is! We ain't going till we've got it, you know, and by the time we've taken out both your knees and started on your fingers, you'll sell your granny to save yourself, so why not be sensible and tell us now, huh? That way we're happy, the boss is happy, and you get to keep the use of your legs. Sounds like a good deal to me.'

It was starting to sound like a good deal to Ben, too, but it had also occurred to him that if he told the men where Salter's tape was, they'd almost certainly take the other tape, too. Once Truman had recognised Jakob's accent as identical to that of Stefan Varga, it wouldn't take any great powers of deduction to make the link between his ex-jockey and the Csikós, especially given the content of the recording. From there, surely, his thoughts would run along the same lines as Ben's had and, whatever crime they might have committed, he couldn't wish Truman's kind of trouble on Jakob and his troupe.

'Did Lenny say there was a tape?' he asked, when he was free to move his jaw again. The words came out slurred and, running his tongue round his mouth, he discovered that on one side his lip was cut and swollen.

'Oh yes. He said there was a tape and he said that you had it. When we got started on him little Lenny sang like a bird.' The speaker moved close to Ben's hooded face and said low and menacingly, 'We 'aven't got started on you yet.'

Ben tried to steady his breathing.

'Lenny would have said anything to get you off his back. I don't know what tape you're talking about.'

'Then why,' his tormentor enquired, 'did Lenny have a cheque with your name on it? What did he sell you, if it wasn't a story, huh? Tell me that, wise guy.'

Ben couldn't think of anything remotely convincing to account for the cheque. The muzziness in his head wasn't conducive to quick and creative thought.

'You can't, can you?'

As he braced himself for another blow to the head, a fist slammed into his stomach instead and the strength went out of his legs, leaving him hanging, gasping, in his captor's grasp.

Oh, Fliss, Fliss, what have you done? he thought, but the fault wasn't really hers – she couldn't have known.

As if from a distance he heard one of the voices say, 'We won't get shit out of him if you keep doing that.'

There was a pause.

'All right. Bring him through here.'

Ben was helpless to prevent himself being half-carried, half-dragged out of his kitchen and across the hall in the direction of his sitting room. The fact that a straightforward battering seemed, for the moment, to have been removed from the agenda might have been comforting had he been able to prevent his mind from wondering what might take its place.

Depressing thoughts as to the probable condition of his prized new leather suite flitted through his consciousness in the moments before he was dumped unceremoniously on the rug-scattered flagstones of the sitting room floor. For a moment the significance of the rattle and squeak of the wood-burner's door escaped him.

'Still hot, deep down,' one of the voices remarked. 'Wouldn't take much to get it going again. Be a shame to let Ben get cold, wouldn't it?'

A chuckle greeted this observation but, in spite

of the horror of the implication, suddenly Ben wasn't listening. Somewhere outside he'd heard the dull thunk of a car door closing.

Lisa. Oh, dear God, no!

If Ben had known terror before, now the level of fear was almost paralysing. She mustn't walk in on this. The thought of what his two visitors might do to her was unbearable. Of course, there was no question that he would give them the tapes immediately if there was any threat to her, but it was also desperately important that she shouldn't be exposed to even the hint of a risk because of him. The power of his need to protect her shook him to the core.

The way he'd fallen had left the rough hood gaping a little at his neck, allowing a sliver of light to find its way in. Wriggling his body downwards, caterpillar-like, he managed to rub the edge of the fabric on the rug beneath him and work it up a few more inches. The sound of hand-operated bellows covered any noise he might have made.

'Now we've got him scared. He don't fancy a hot poker up him,' one of the men observed coarsely, apparently catching sight of his movement. 'Or shall we take his eyes out with it? Wouldn't be much of a reporter if we burned his fucking eyes out. Couldn't see what was happening and couldn't see to write it down.' He laughed out loud.

Ben didn't share his amusement: He kept wriggling but, even as the edge of the fabric began to clear his eyeline, one of the men realised what he was doing.

'You idiot! He's getting the fuckin' hood off!'

A rush of footsteps and the rough material was

grasped and jerked back into place, wrapped tightly round his nose and mouth so that once again, breathing became an issue. Ben was flooded with furious frustration at the impotence of his position, and kicked out hard with both feet.

He was swiftly paid back in kind with a foot in the ribs.

'Stop a minute!' The command came from across the room.

'The bastard kicked me.'

'Just shut up! I heard something.'

They all paused to listen, Ben included, and heard the unmistakable sound of the front door shutting. Immediately after, soft footsteps moved away from the wood-burner and across towards the door as one of the men went to investigate.

Almost frantic with fear for Lisa, Ben drew in what breath he could through the fabric with the intention of shouting a warning. What actually made it past the stifling hood was little more than a muffled squeak, and even that was cut short by the firm application of his companion's hand. He also put a knee between Ben's shoulder-blades, pulled his head up and back, and hissed, 'Shut your fucking mouth!' close to his ear, regardless of the fact that he'd already done it for him.

Completely helpless and in some considerable discomfort, Ben could do nothing except wait, with a pounding heart, for the inevitable return of the second man with Lisa as a terrified hostage.

With the hood twisted tightly around his head, Ben's hearing capacity was severely depleted and, as the seconds ticked by with no apparent developments, the tension was unbearable.

It seemed his captor was getting a little twitchy too, for after a moment he muttered, 'Come on, come on . . . Where *are* you?'

The silence stretched on, with both Ben and the man who held him straining their ears for the slightest sound.

Nothing.

'Spence! Where are you?' the voice was threaded with a touch of panic now. 'What're you doing?'

No answer. They could have been alone in the house.

'What the fuck . . . ?'

Abruptly the pressure on Ben's back eased as his companion seemed to come to a decision. Grasped by his jacket, Ben was hauled to his feet and once more gagged by the hand across his mouth. His arms still securely tied behind him, he was just as helpless as he had been but several degrees more comfortable. He was no less mystified than his assailant as to what was going on, but the difference was that *he* could only view the apparent disappearance of the partner in crime as a good thing. Anything that unsettled either man was fine by Ben. Pushed ahead of his captor, he began to shuffle slowly towards the living room doorway.

'Come on, you bugger, where are you?' The words were muttered, almost inaudibly, next to Ben's ear.

Through the doorway and up the short corridor past the dining room, Ben sensed his position in the house, and with every step the tension mounted.

If that had been Lisa coming in, then where was she? Had she managed to shut herself in the bathroom and lock the door before the one called Spence had reached her? And if so, why hadn't they heard something? Or had the sound been that of the door shutting after she'd seen the chaos inside and gone for help? She was a level-headed girl who, he was prepared to bet, would choose a practical course of action. But if that was the case, where was Spence? If he thought she'd gone for help, wouldn't he have collected his colleague and beaten a retreat, with or without Ben? Surely he wouldn't just have left without saying anything to his partner. The worst scenario for Ben was that Spence had run after Lisa to stop her from raising the alarm, and that they were now struggling somewhere out there in the dark. She'd once told Ben that she'd done a self-defence course a couple of years ago, but there was no way that anything she'd learned there would have prepared her for the likes of Spence and his heavy-handed pal.

They moved on cautiously, and Ben judged that they must be approaching the hall and the kitchen doorway when a quiet voice just behind them said, 'Lookin' for someone, matey?' Ben's captor jumped as if he'd been shot.

Startled he might have been, but his reactions were impressive; Ben had to give him that, as an instant later he found himself being swung round to cannon into the owner of the voice with enough force to knock most people off their feet.

The newcomer obviously wasn't most people. He remained on his feet, catching and steadying Ben when he would have fallen, but even so, the velocity of the impact was enough to stop him in his tracks, and the curse it drew from him was followed shortly by the sound of rapidly retreating footsteps. There was an urgent exchange of words, and then the front door banged against the wall as it was flung wide open and Ben's attacker made his getaway.

'Bugger!' the voice said succinctly; then, 'Ben? Are you all right?' And all at once blessed light and air flooded round his face as the hood was lifted off and thrown aside.

Blinking as his eyes adjusted to the brightness, Ben found himself staring at the stud-fastening collar of a combat jacket and, looking up, identified his rescuer as his landlord, Mike.

Hard on the heels of this discovery, Ben found the walls tilting crazily and, the next thing he knew, his face was pressed into the canvas jacket-front and his nostrils were filled with the smell of leaf-mould and woodsmoke.

'I was afraid it was Lisa,' Ben told Mike a few minutes later, sitting on the sofa with half a tumbler of whisky in his hand. His head ached fiercely and there was hardly an inch of his body that wasn't bruised, but he felt a whole lot better than he had just a short while before.

Beside Ben was a length of electric flex, presumably ripped from one of the kitchen appliances, with which his wrists had been bound; next to that was the thick, tapestry-effect cushion cover that had done service as the hood. The luxurious leather sofa had been slashed at least once on each of its surfaces, as Ben had feared, and, looking across the shambles that was his living room, he could see that the second one had fared the same. His hi-fi was on the floor by the wall and looked as though someone had taken a sledge-hammer to it. All in all, it was deeply depressing.

Ben took a sip from the tumbler and winced as the spirit stung his cut lip.

'What made you come in?' he asked the big Geordie.

'Well, I saw you come back, and then, when I came back past a few minutes later, I saw your shopping was still outside the door and the door was open. It seemed odd, with it being so cold and all, so I came over to see if you'd forgotten and as soon as I looked inside, I saw the mess in your kitchen and guessed you were in trouble.'

'So what did you do with Spence?'

'The guy that came out first? Did you know them, then?'

'No. His pal called him that.'

'Oh, that was a mistake. Yeah, well, I slammed the front door and waited round the corner by the coat stand, and soon enough Matey came padding along, so I clobbered him. He seemed to be out for the count, and your pal was calling for him, so I slipped along to the dining room and waited in the doorway for him to come looking. The rest, as they say, is history. I just wish I'd taken the time to tie Matey up, because he managed to get up in time to leg it when your guy did.' He looked narrowly at Ben. 'How're you feeling now?'

'How do I look?'

'Hmm. Not good, I must say. They gave you a proper working over, didn't they? Am I allowed to ask why? I assume this wasn't burglary, looking at what they've done to your hi-fi and stuff.'

'They were looking for something. A tape – or rather, a micro-cassette.'

'Did you have it?'

'Mmm.'

'And that's what this was all about?' Mike indicated Ben's face. 'You wouldn't tell 'em.'

He sounded matter-of-fact, non-judgemental, for which Ben was grateful. He wasn't clear in his own mind whether holding out against Truman's men had been completely necessary – after all, Salter had already paid the price for talking to him, and if the worst came to the worst he could have warned the Csikós of the threat. He'd thought Salter's tape might be useful leverage, or, at the very least, a kind of insurance, but had it been worth getting beaten up for? He had a strong suspicion that for the most part his refusal to yield had been down to a mixture of pride and monumental stubbornness – and that really wasn't worth risking his life for.

Remembering the final threat, Ben shuddered involuntarily. Would he – or even *could* he – have kept quiet when his sight depended on it? On balance he thought probably not, but he wasn't at all sure whether his compliance, at that late stage, would have saved him. Spence and his pal seemed to enjoy their work a little too much.

'So what now? The police?' Mike asked.

Ben looked round the room bleakly, thinking of the consequences.

Sirens. Flashing blue lights. Half a dozen uniforms tramping in and out. Forensics. A statement. Photographs, both of the room and himself.

Doctors; maybe hospital; and questions – dozens and dozens of questions for days to come.

'Oh God!' he groaned. 'Must I? Do you want me to? I mean, it's your property.'

Mike shook his head.

"S all the same to me. They haven't damaged the building. If you don't want 'em, don't call 'em. But d'you think there's a chance these jokers will come back?'

'I don't know. Tell you what, there's a guy I know – a copper – who won't make a big fuss if I ask him not to. I guess I could call him, but I don't think I could cope with the other just now.'

Mike made the phone call, at his own suggestion, and Ben didn't know what he said to Logan, but the policeman arrived barely a quarter of an hour later, bringing with him a dour, middle-aged man in corduroys and a cardigan, who turned out to be a doctor.

After tutting over Ben's physical state and getting the basic facts about the attack with only a hint of 'I told you so,' Logan prowled off, presumably to inspect the rest of the damage.

'Certainly picks his times to call in favours,' the doctor grumbled, putting a leather holdall down on the remains of Ben's coffee table. 'I was just settling down with a sherry to wait for my dinner.'

Grunting in response to Ben's apology, he took a slim torch out of his bag and switched his attention to his patient, shining a beam of light into his eyes.

'Did you black out at all?'

Ben couldn't shake his head because his jaw

341

was being held firmly between the doctor's fingers and thumb.

'No, I don't think so.'

'Pain in the head?'

'It aches.'

'Double vision?'

'No.'

'How many fingers?'

'Three.'

The doctor switched the torch off.

'Don't think you're concussed. Now let's look at those cuts.'

In due course Logan reappeared with a compact digital camera in his hand. In his mid-thirties, lean and fit, with close-cropped fairish hair and blue eyes, he was no more than five-foot ten, but there was something about his quiet confidence that commanded respect. Ben could see that Mike was instantly aware of it.

The policeman asked no questions until the doctor had completed his examination of Ben and reluctantly admitted that he would probably survive without the benefit of hospital treatment.

'Painkillers and rest; arnica for the bruising, if you want. Can't see what internal damage they may have done, of course, so any sharp pains, bleeding from nose, ears or anywhere else, and you get yourself checked out properly, all right?'

Ben nodded obediently and thanked him. As Mike accompanied him to the door, the doctor could be heard saying, 'Well, I'll go and find my dinner then, though I expect it'll be cold by now. Good day to you.'

Ben glanced at Logan.

'Where did you find him?'

'Oh, he's an old family friend. He's always moaning but he doesn't mean anything by it. He's patched me up a time or two, and he'd be mortally offended if I went to anyone else. The thing is, he doesn't ask questions. Just does his job. He's a treasure. So . . .' he eyed Ben speculatively, 'Want to tell me what this was all about?'

'I think it may have had to do with my visit to Lenny Salter yesterday,' Ben said slowly. 'I don't have any proof, but I've a strong suspicion that my good friend Eddie Truman was behind it. You see, Lenny had quite an interesting story to tell, which I got on tape and persuaded him to put his name to.'

'How'd you get the bugger to do that? All I've ever got is the story about kids doing him over for drug money, and I presume that's not the story he gave you.'

'No, it wasn't. But he didn't know I was taping him. So then I offered him a large sum of money and the chance to get back at our mutual friend if he'd put his name to it. I just wish he'd got away before Truman cottoned on. I'm sure he thinks I double-crossed him.'

Logan shrugged. 'Looks like he dumped you in it, anyway. So they came here looking for the tape, is that it? And did they find it?'

Ben shook his head.

Logan looked round at the chaos.

'So where was it?'

'In my jacket. There's a mobile phone pocket, here – beside the zip. Just about the only place they didn't look. I was out all afternoon – Truman invited me over to lunch – so they had plenty of time to turn the place over.' He remembered the trainer asking him to call in before he left Castle Ridge, and suddenly it all made sense. 'I suppose they reported back that they hadn't found anything and Truman let them know when I was on my way.'

Logan strode over to the phone, pushed a couple of buttons, then shook his head. 'No. Nothing there. An 0845 number, eight-thirty-five last night.'

'The internet. Broadband hasn't made it to these parts yet.'

'So what's on the tape? Is it enough to make trouble for Truman? Is there anything we can work with?'

'No, not really. I'd be surprised if it would give any defence counsellor worth his salt any sleepless nights.'

'So why on earth get yourself beaten up over it? Why didn't you just hand it over?'

'Because Truman doesn't know that, does he?'

Logan looked at him long and hard, then shook his head slightly.

'I always thought you were a crazy bastard,' he said. 'Your landlord said they put something over your head, so I suppose it's no good asking for a description.'

'Yeah, this.' Ben showed him the cushion cover. 'One of them called the other one Spence, if that's any help, but Mike might have got a look at them.'

'I'll have a word. You know, we really ought to get CSI to go over this place. There might be something we can use.'

344

'Oh, God, no. They'll take for ever and, at the end of it – even if you nailed Spence and his pal – you can bet they're not going to lead you to Truman.'

'You're probably right.' Logan looked speculatively at him. 'So what are you going to do with the tape now?'

'Well, I was thinking maybe I'd ask you to take care of it.'

'OK. Can I listen to it?'

'I assumed you would anyway.'

Logan grinned.

'Probably, but I'd rather have your permission.'

'Yeah, go ahead.'

They heard the front door open and close and shortly after Mouse came trotting in, looking slightly apologetic, as she often did. Footsteps approached from the hall, and suddenly Lisa was there in the doorway, her eyes wide with shock.

'Ben? What's happened? Mike says – Oh, my God, Ben!'

Ben held out his hand.

'It's OK. I'm all right. It's all over now.'

Lisa came closer and stood looking down at him.

'You don't look all right.'

'She has a point,' Logan murmured.

They both ignored him.

'What happened? Were we burgled?'

Ben hesitated.

'No. Actually, it's a bit complicated.'

Sitting on the ruined sofa beside him, Lisa gave the impression of one who was prepared to wait.

'Try me,' she said.

Ben took one of her hands in his, looked into her clear blue eyes and had absolutely no idea what to say. Had it just been the two of them it would have been hard enough, but with Logan hovering, it was ten times more difficult.

His gaze dropped to their loosely clasped hands and he caressed her soft fingers with his thumb. When he looked up it was to see resignation spreading slowly over her face. She removed her hand from his.

'Lisa . . .'

She stood up. 'No it's all right. We said we wouldn't interfere with one another. I'm sure you have things to talk about with your friend. I'll go and make some tea – if I can find the tea bags.'

'Lisa . . .'

She left the room without looking back, and Logan raised his eyebrows.

'I know it's none of my business, but you'll lose that girl, you know.'

'You're right. It's none of your business,' Ben said sharply; then, as Logan raised his hands to signify withdrawal, 'Sorry, Mark. I'm not feeling my best. Don't pay any attention to me.'

When Logan and Mike left, some three quarters of an hour later, the worst of the debris had been swept up and deposited in three black bin bags which now sat at the entrance to the courtyard, awaiting collection the following morning.

Lisa had worked solidly to restore order to the kitchen and bedroom, whilst Mike had picked up the smashed remains of Ben's stereo system and CDs and attempted to seal the slashed sofa cushions temporarily with brown parcel tape.

The wood-burning stove had been stoked up and was billowing heat, which, in his aching, shaky condition, Ben found a great comfort. His token suggestion that he help clear up was given short shrift, for which he was immensely thankful, and so he spent the duration of the operation lying full-length on the ravaged leather, wishing he was the kind of journalist that covered village fêtes and hundredth birthday parties.

Logan had lent a hand with the clear-up but he never stopped trying to prise more information from Ben. Eventually, because it was on his mind, Ben asked him if he had any contacts in Hungary.

Logan had stopped, mid-sweep. 'Might have; why?'

Ben hesitated, already regretting the impulsive query.

'Er . . . I want to find out about a fatal car crash that happened nearly twenty years ago but I'm not sure where to start looking. I looked online but there's not a lot in English, and nothing at all going back that far.'

'And this is to do with . . . ?'

'I can't tell you at the moment. It's just a hunch and it could get someone in a whole lot of trouble.'

'Would this have anything to do with the horse circus you're spending so much time with at the moment?'

Ben glanced sharply at him and Logan raised an eyebrow.

'Does it?'

'Actually,' he said evasively, 'It has to do with

a jockey who used to ride for Castle Ridge. Can you help?'

'You know Ford will have looked into that already.'

'Mm. But nevertheless . . .'

Logan regarded him steadily for a little longer and Ben braced himself for further questions, but thankfully they didn't come. Logan merely made a note of the details, said he'd see what he could do, and then apparently lost interest.

Once they were alone Lisa ran Ben a hot bath, into which he creakily lowered himself, grimacing as the water touched the cuts and sore places. The bathroom mirror had, predictably, been a casualty of Spence and Co., only its antique frame remaining intact, but in his current state Ben felt that this was quite possibly a mercy.

Lisa found clean sheets for the bed, joined Ben in the bath, and then, afterwards, gathered together enough salvaged ingredients to make a passable shepherd's pie.

Ben ate slowly and without much appetite, his swollen lip making it awkward and his mind replaying the events of the day, over and over. He tried to concentrate his thoughts on the un-expected appearance of Truman's illegitimate grandson and how this might affect the overall picture, but his subconscious kept returning with uncomfortable clarity to the utter, terrifying powerlessness of his recent ordeal. Closing his eyes against waves of recurring panic, he took a couple of deep breaths and opened them again to find Lisa watching him through eyes that were swimming with tears.

'I can't do this any more, Ben,' she whispered and inevitably, the tears spilled over.

'Lisa . . .' he began, helplessly.

'This isn't what I want. Sharing your house and your bed when our paths happen to cross. I can't pretend that's enough any more.'

'But you said . . . I thought that was what you wanted – what we both wanted.'

'No, Ben! That was never what I wanted. I thought it was – at least, I thought it was better than nothing at all, but it's not. I can't do it any more. It's just too hard!'

'I didn't know.'

'No, how could you know? We never talk; not really *talk*, I mean, about things that matter. About how we feel. I have no idea how you feel. Is this enough for you, Ben, what we have? You're thirty-two. Are you happy with how things are? Don't you ever want more?'

'Lisa –'

'No, of course you don't – silly question – you're a guy, you'll always take the path of least resistance where relationships are concerned!' She was in full flow now, releasing emotions that had clearly been building up over a considerable length of time.

'Lisa, hold on a minute –'

'Well it's not enough for me. I need someone who I can share things with; not just everyday things but other stuff, emotional stuff, worries, you know . . .'

Ben rubbed his forehead. He'd had no idea this was all bubbling away under the surface, but he couldn't help thinking she could have timed it better.

'Lisa, I'm here for you, you know that. You can always talk to me, surely – I thought you knew that.'

'Oh Ben!' She slammed the tabletop with her hand in frustration, making him wince and the cutlery rattle. 'You don't get it do you? That's just the point: *I* can talk to *you*, but it should be a two-way street and you never talk to me! I never feel needed. I never get a chance to help you. Look at you now: you're hurting, I know you are, but you won't tell me about it. I never know what you're thinking, or even what you're doing, half the time. Who were those men today? What did they want? Why was Logan here? You see? I'm completely in the dark.'

Ben put a hand over one of hers. 'I'm sorry. I didn't realise you felt that way. I never meant you to.'

'Yes, well, I do,' she said unnecessarily, but she left her hand where it was. 'You're so bloody self-sufficient, it's like admitting you need someone is some kind of failure.'

'I suppose I thought I was protecting you. That if you didn't know, you wouldn't worry. I didn't want to load all my troubles on you.'

'But I want to be there for you! Not just when things are going well but all the time. It doesn't all have to be flowers and chocolates and candlelit meals, we're past that now. Don't get me wrong – it's nice to be spoilt once in a while – but what I'd really like is to feel like I'm a part of your life. All of it.'

Ben smiled crookedly. 'Not often you hear a girl asking to be taken for granted!'

'Oh, you know that's not what I mean!' she said.

His heart-rate stepping up a notch or two, Ben took a deep breath.

'You mean, for better or worse?'

To his surprise, Lisa snatched her hand out of his grasp and stood up, her stool scraping back over the flagstones.

'God, Ben, you've got lousy timing!' she exclaimed, taking his plate with its unfinished meal and stacking it on her own before removing them both to the sink.

Ben watched her in bemused silence. The proposal had been completely unpremeditated but genuine, nevertheless, and whether it was something to do with the battering he'd had or not, he couldn't really fathom why Lisa had reacted the way she had.

'I'm sorry . . .'

She shook her head without looking at him. 'No. Let's just forget it. My timing's pretty crap, too. You don't need this tonight. I'm going to bed, I'll do the dishwasher in the morning.'

Left alone and deep in thought, Ben stared at the open doorway until he found himself nodding off, at which point he levered himself to his feet by way of the tabletop. Switching off the lights he followed Lisa to the bedroom, his stomach muscles reminding him, with every step, of the abuse they'd suffered.

Between his physical discomfort and his mental state, it looked like being a long old night.

15

Lisa wandered into the living room at eight-thirty the next morning wearing an oversized 'Save the Rainforest' T-shirt and looking heavy-eyed.

'How long have you been up?' she asked, finding Ben there before her.

'Couple of hours. Couldn't sleep and I was afraid I'd wake you.'

'Not much chance of that,' she said, yawning. 'How d'you feel?'

'Marginally better than I look.'

'That's not saying a lot,' she commented, surveying him frankly.

'Well, I'm all right if I don't move, laugh, cough or breathe deeply. Sneezing is definitely out. Apart from that . . .'

'Coffee?'

'I've had one – but I'm sure I can manage another, thanks.' He held out his empty mug.

When she returned with the brew, Ben patted the sofa next to him and she sat close, folding her legs up and resting her head on his shoulder.

352

'About last night . . .' he began, but she interrupted him.

'No, please. I'm sorry, I shouldn't have said anything. I think it was just the shock of seeing you like that. Forget it.'

Ben shook his head. 'No. You were right. I haven't been fair. I guess it's got something to do with my family stuff – you know, my parents splitting up and what happened to Alan. I know that's not an excuse, but it's probably the reason. But anyway, I'm sorry, love. It's time I grew up.'

'So?'

'So, I'm in this relationship long-term, and I mean as a proper relationship, not a ships-passing-in-the-night affair. I can't promise that I'll get it right first time, but I promise I'll try.'

Lisa snuggled closer, the top of her bent head under his chin.

'You know you're a bastard with words? You've made me feel like a worm!'

'Oh, that's a shame, I think I ate the last one yesterday,' said Ben, apologetically.

With his recent pledge in mind Ben spent the best part of an hour, over and around breakfast, filling Lisa in on the Cajun King case and all its attendant twists.

'And you really think your Hungarians might have the horse?' she enquired, as he told her of the link between Truman and Jakob Varga. 'Where on earth could they hide him?'

'That's just it. If I'm right, they haven't hidden him. He's been on full view the whole time if anyone had thought to look.' He told her about the part the 'wild' horses played in the performance. 'They all look alike: all roughly the same size, no markings – just a bunch of brown and bay thoroughbreds milling around. You don't pay them much attention; it's all about the white horse that's controlling them.'

'You say Cajun King has white markings, but I suppose those could be dyed out.'

'Yeah, but the problem would be his mane and tail. All these horses have long manes and tails; his mane is trimmed short and his tail is quite frankly pathetic. Look.' He took the print Truman had given him from his wallet.

Lisa took it and studied it thoughtfully.

'I suppose – this is going to sound daft – but I suppose you can't do hair extensions on horses, can you?'

'I don't know. I hadn't thought of that. I don't see why not; it's hair isn't it? What's the difference?'

'Well, I don't know, but then I'm not a hairdresser.'

'No,' Ben said with rising excitement. 'But Jeta is! Nico's sister. And if he's involved there's no reason to think that she couldn't be. Lisa, you're a genius!'

'Well, thank you. I try,' she said, smiling. 'But if they have got the horse, it must be a million-to-one chance – I mean, you already doing an article on them and then Truman asking you to look into his disappearance.'

'You'd think so, wouldn't you?' Ben agreed. 'And, actually, I'd far rather I wasn't involved with the Csikós because the worst of it is, I like them a hell of a lot more than I like Red bloody Truman!'

'I'm not surprised. But if you're so sure he sent those men round here last night, can't you tell the police?'

'I did. I told Logan, but you see, I've got no proof.'

'But you've got the tape. The one they were sent to find.'

'Yeah, but I doubt it would hold up on its own, and I don't think we can rely on Lenny Salter standing up in court to tell his story, not that I blame him. Besides, even if he did, it would only be his word against Truman's; he's got no more proof of what he said than I have. Probably the most we'd achieve is a bit of bad publicity for Truman, and a whole load of trouble for ourselves.'

'So what happens next?'

Ben sighed.

'Next I have to find out for sure if my Hungarian friends really do have King and, if they do, try and persuade them to give him back.'

'Just like that.'

'Mmm. Well, something like that, anyway. It's the only way I can see that they've got a hope of getting out of it. They've been lucky so far but it can't last.'

'You won't go on your own?' Lisa frowned. 'Look what happened at that animal lib place.'

'I'll be all right. I can't see Jakob turning nasty.'

'But the others . . . You said yourself he couldn't have done it on his own.'

'No, he couldn't have. In fact, Ian Rice said

there were three of them when they pulled the lorry over. But Jakob is a kind of patriarch; they all respect him. It'll be OK.' As he spoke, Ben remembered something else. Ricey had reported that the hijackers had guns. He'd forgotten that, but, in spite of his promise of openness, he didn't think it was something Lisa needed to know. There was a limit to sharing, after all.

Lisa patently wasn't happy but she let it go, asking instead what he meant to do about Truman.

He shrugged. 'Not much I can do, really. But it'll be interesting to see his reaction when I turn up – all outraged innocence – with my tale of violent burglars.'

Lisa looked skywards. 'You know you're crazy, don't you?'

Logan rang just before midday.

'Ben? How're you doing?'

'Surprisingly, not too bad, thanks,' Ben replied. 'Just spent half an hour trying to get some sense out of my insurance company, but I guess we've all been there at some time or another. Apparently they're short-staffed just at the moment and it's unlikely that anyone will be able to come and assess the damage until Wednesday. The female I spoke to said it would be best if I didn't touch anything until then. Yeah, right!'

'I can print you off some copies of the photos I took,' Logan offered.

'Well, actually, I was going to ask you if you could,' Ben admitted. 'I told the girl I'd got pictures.'

'Yeah, no problem. Look, I got hold of a friend of a friend about this car crash in Hungary, and I've got some answers.'

'Already? Wow!'

'Well, there's no point in hanging around,' Logan said. 'Anyway, I don't know whether it's going to be any help to you, because we haven't really found what you were asking for.'

'Oh.' Ben was disappointed.

'Yeah, well, I don't know if you got the dates mixed up or something, but I got the guy to do a sweep of all recorded RTAs within a twenty-mile radius of Szolnok, and within a couple of years either side of the date you gave me. Stefan Varga's name didn't come up, but there were two in which the casualty was an unknown young man. One was a fair bit earlier – almost a year earlier, in fact – and the other was six months after your date.'

'Was he sure?'

'Yep.'

'Any other details?'

'In the first the vehicle was burnt out, and the second apparently drove into a wall at high speed. I think the verdict was suicide. Neither car was registered and there were no dental records, it seems. Whether that's because the Hungarians weren't hot on them in those days, or whether the deceased parties weren't registered with one, I'm not sure.'

'And did DI Ford find out anything more?'

Logan raised his eyebrows. 'That would be confidential police business.'

'But you did look, right?'

'He got more or less the same. I think he assumes that Varga was killed in the second incident.'

Which, Ben reflected, was the assumption *he* would have made, if Nico hadn't told him about the fire.

'So, are you going to tell me why you wanted to know?'

Ben hesitated. He didn't want to say too much at this stage; Logan was so damned sharp.

'Er, well, it's not common knowledge, but there could be a child involved. I just wondered whether there was any possibility that Varga was still alive.'

'The child is searching for him?'

'Not exactly. He's got no idea who his father was. At least, he hadn't when he turned up at Truman's yard, yesterday. I don't know what's happened since. I should imagine Ford must know by now.'

'And you think the boy might bear Truman a grudge?'

'Heavens, no! He's just a kid. A kid with a good deal of steel in him, but just a kid, nevertheless.'

'So what about the article in the paper about the horse? I take it that wasn't your doing.'

'No. My guess is Helen: Truman's eldest. I think she rather hoped I might get the blame.'

'Charming. By the way, I filled Ford in on the fun and games here last night and he's not happy, to put it mildly, that you didn't call in the troops. I got an ear-bashing and, unless I'm much mistaken, you're in line for one, too.'

358

Ben groaned.

'I suppose it was inevitable. Let's hope he doesn't bring Hancock with him, that's all. I swear I'm going to sock him one, one day.'

'Ah, DS Wanker,' Logan said on a note of recognition.

'You what?'

'Hancock. That's what one of my colleagues calls him: DS Wanker. He reckons the name Hancock derives from Handcock, but to be honest I think he made it up because he can't stand the bloke either. Listen: anything else I can do for you?'

'Um, I don't suppose you could find out what Cajun King's microchip identification is without letting Truman know you're asking? Ford would have it, wouldn't he?'

'Probably,' Logan said slowly. 'Ben, do you think you know where the horse is? Because, if you do . . .'

Ben hesitated.

'Let's just say, I want to be sure I know where he's not.'

'And just what the hell's that supposed to mean?'

'It means, I'm pretty sure the idea is crazy, but I'll sleep better if I check it out.'

In his car, rapidly approaching the Csikós' Romsey encampment, Ben remembered the soothing words he'd spoken to Lisa that morning, and doubted that he could imbue them with as much confidence now if she were there to hear them.

Zipped securely into his jacket pocket was a grey plastic device – roughly rectangular and some six inches by three by one – with a digital screen in the top quarter of one face. It was a microchip scanner, and Penny, the young, female vet at the RSPCA centre who'd handed it over to Ben at closing time that afternoon, had done so with no small measure of reluctance, making Ben promise faithfully that he'd return it first thing in the morning, as soon as the centre opened. He'd known Penny ever since collecting Mouse from the centre four years previously and had even dated her in the early days; he knew this was the only reason why she was going out on a limb for him now.

If getting the scanner had been a little tricky, finding the opportunity to put it to use was going to be even more so, and the mental picture of himself moving among the loose horses was one that Ben had to keep pushing away, lest his nerve fail before he started.

He had set out in good time but the route he took to Romsey was tortuous. He took in several narrow lanes – where he pulled into a couple of gateways to check for following vehicles – and once he did a complete circuit of a roundabout for the same reason. His fear was that Spence and his mate might be watching the cottage or the surrounding roads, with instructions to see where he went, and he really didn't want to turn up on the Csikós' doorstep with those two in close attendance.

If anyone was tailing him, they were obviously better at their job than he was, because he didn't spot them. He arrived at his destination as certain as he could be that he'd made the journey alone.

At his suggestion Lisa had left to stay with her mother, and phoned just before he set out, to say that she'd arrived safely, so that was one worry off his mind.

Logan had rung back midway through the afternoon with Cajun King's microchip ID number, but thankfully he'd asked no further questions about how Ben intended to use the information.

Looking at his watch as he climbed stiffly out of the car, Ben could see that there was less than half an hour to go before the show was due to start and the Csikós' camp was the usual hive of activity it was before a performance. The final touches were being put to the horses' grooming; tack waited, polished and shining, and the members of the troupe wore chaps and coats over their show costumes as they worked.

Not wanting to get in the way, but nevertheless loving the sense of controlled urgency that pervaded the stables at these times, Ben strolled through the building in search of either Nico or Jakob. He found the older man first, in the small barn helping Anna and Jeta brush out the long manes and tails of the string of loose horses. It was the first time Ben had seen any of the herd horses being handled and, in view of his mission, it was encouraging that they seemed content to submit to being tied up. Feeling the hard oblong of the scanner in his jacket pocket he wandered closer.

Jakob looked up with a welcoming smile.

'Ben! I didn't know you were coming tonight.'

'Last-minute decision.'

'Perhaps he's come to help,' Jeta suggested provocatively, glancing up from under her lashes.

'Why? Can't you manage?' Ben responded smoothly, turning the taunt back on to her.

'Of course I can!' Jeta flared immediately.

Jakob chuckled, straightening up and patting the rump of the horse he'd been brushing. Then he frowned. 'Have you been fighting, Ben? What happened to your face?'

Ben shrugged. 'Not all my assignments are as easy as this one,' he said. 'Sometimes people don't like me asking questions.'

'Your job?' Jakob shook his head. 'I never thought . . .'

'Well, it doesn't happen all that often. If it did, I'd find myself another career, I can tell you.'

Jakob looked as though he would have said something more but he was forestalled by a shrill whistle, which Ben knew was the signal to start making the final preparations: tacking up the ridden horses and peeling off the protective layers of clothing to reveal the costumes beneath.

The girls gave their two horses a final quick whisk over with the brush, undid them and set them free. As they passed Ben, Anna Kovac gave him a shy smile, whilst Jeta looked him full in the eye and reached up to run her hand lightly down his cheek as she went by. Ben couldn't prevent his gaze following her as she walked away, and she glanced back over her shoulder, confident that he'd be looking, and winked.

Shaking his head once more, Jakob muttered something in his native tongue.

'Don't worry, I'm not about to fall into that trap,' Ben assured him.

'I'm glad.' Jakob set his horse free to join the others and let himself out of the enclosed area, shutting the gate on a horse that would have followed him. 'Your girl? Everything is well?'

Ben nodded. 'Yes, everything's fine.'

'Good. Now I must find that brother of mine.' Jakob patted Ben's shoulder in passing, and disappeared in search of Gyorgy.

Ben watched him go then turned to look at the horses. They were all shifting restlessly, most with eyes and ears turned towards the bustle of the preparations. He supposed they had been with the troupe long enough to be anticipating the start of the show and their part in it, and he wondered what they made of their change of lifestyle. They certainly looked pretty eager.

There was no time now to attempt to catch and scan any of the herd before the performance began, but Ben used the time to take the photo of Cajun King from his pocket and try to single out the possible candidates. It was frustrating that they were all milling about; he couldn't be sure that he hadn't counted the same horse twice, though there were at least four that were entirely the wrong colour, and two more whose general appearance ruled them out. Ben found he kept coming back to two in particular and decided that when he got the chance, he would start with those. Even so, it was hard to equate the sleek, immaculately turned out thoroughbred of the picture with any of the horses in front of him.

'Ben! We start in two minutes.' Nico's voice sounded just behind him and such was the state of his nerves that he almost jumped out of his skin.

'Thanks.' Gathering his wits, Ben stuffed the picture into his jacket and turned, but Nico was already several feet away, striding off in the jaunty way that showed he was in showman mode, the silver trimmings on his costume gleaming. Before long he would be in the arena and the silver would sparkle under the blaze of lights as he wowed the audience with the seemingly casual brilliance of his horsemanship.

Ben sighed. How could Jakob put all this in jeopardy for the sake of revenge, however well-deserved? And how could he involve Nico, a young man with a glittering career ahead of him? It seemed so out of character, but then, when you considered how close they were as a family, perhaps it was inevitable. Indeed, maybe the idea had come from the younger members of the troupe; it was quite possible he would never know.

'Hell and damn!' Ben muttered. He looked again at the loose horses. It was still just possible that he was on the wrong track entirely, but he wasn't terribly optimistic on that front. The more he looked at the two strongest candidates, the more he felt drawn to the larger of the two. There was just something about him.

He took the photo from his pocket again and compared it with the horse in front of him. The one in the picture was considerably darker, having what was known as a blanket clip – which left the natural coat on the animal's back, quarters and legs – whereas the horses in the herd had all been clipped right out at some stage, presumably to remove previous clipping patterns such as King's. With the cold weather, though, their coats were already growing back.

'Still here, Ben?'

Jakob had returned with Gyorgy, each paying out a length of nylon rope that stretched off towards the arena; it was hooked up at strategic points to form a corridor down which the herd would pass on the way to their ten minutes or so in the limelight.

'You'd best get to your seat. This should be a good one.'

'I'm on my way.'

Ben was just in time to see the now familiar opening sequence, with the ten loose horses cantering into the arena and milling about aimlessly in the eerie greenish mist. Then, almost ethereal, came Duka, dashing round the herd and sending them down the arena in one tightly grouped bunch, with only the occasional glimpse of flattened ears or bared teeth as inducement. With his noble bearing and flowing, whiter-than-white mane and tail, he was the stuff of dreams and, looking into the audience, Ben could see wonder in the shining eyes of children and adults alike.

Unhappily aware of the job he shortly had to do, Ben couldn't enjoy the performance as he usually did. The scanner was digging into his hip,

365

as if to remind him, and he wondered, without joy, what mental state the horses would be in, having been rousted about the arena for ten or fifteen minutes by the Andalusian. His best opportunity would come, he felt, towards the end of the second half, when the entire troupe would be in the arena together, showing off the skills of the Magyar herdsmen. Then, with any luck, the area around the thoroughbreds' barn would be deserted. Resignedly, Ben settled down for a wait of ninety minutes or more.

The show was a huge success: the performance sold out and the crowd loud in its enthusiasm. In consequence the Csikós seemed to pull out extra stops. Each time Ben saw them, they seemed to have added something to their routine, and this time Nico even threw in Duka's trick with the hat – learned only two days before – which drew delighted laughter from the audience.

The interval, with its frenzy of ice-cream buying, came and went and the show continued. Suddenly the arena was full of whip-cracking Magyar plainsmen and Emilian was telling those watching about the girthless saddles. With a shock Ben realised that his moment had arrived – had almost passed, in fact. If he didn't get a move on, he wouldn't have time to catch his two suspects and scan them before the troupe left the arena again to prepare for the finale.

Slipping from his seat, Ben climbed the wooden steps between the tiered seating and descended to the door that led outside. A man he didn't know was guarding the entrance to the barn complex but he let Ben pass when he showed his 'crew' badge.

From the logo on his navy blue jumper, Ben knew the man was part of the security force the troupe's promoter had provided to steward their events.

His feet made no noise on the peat as he made his way through the shadowy nether regions of the warm-up area, finding it deserted except for Jakob and Gyorgy, who stood holding three horses apiece, blankets thrown over their saddles, patiently waiting for their next stint under the spotlights. Ben kept his eye on them, but they were facing the other way and he passed unseen into the walkway that led to the stable area.

Surprisingly, there were lights on in the barn.

Ben's steps faltered. He'd pictured himself moving quietly among the horses in the semi-dusk, able to duck down and merge with the shadows in the unlikely event that anyone came along. This put a different slant on things. He would have to try and locate the light switches because, lit as it was, he'd feel uncomfortably exposed. How could he, of all people, ever convincingly explain away his presence in a barn full of horses?

As it turned out, the question was irrelevant. He turned the last corner to see that Tamás was already there, his veterinary holdall open on the ground at his feet and a bowl of pinkish water beside him as he tended to a gash on the neck of one of the herd.

'What's happened?' Ben enquired as he approached.

Tamás looked round.

'Oh, they all tried to come through the gateway at the same time and that horse of Nico's kicked out. He's a troublemaker, that one.'

'I thought they were unshod,' Ben said,

observing a neat row of stitches in a shaven area on the animal's neck.

'I think he was pushed against the gatepost, where the metal sticks out,' Tamás said, indicating the catch.

'Shouldn't you be riding? Who's taken your place?'

'Jeta. She has plaited her hair and put it under the hat, so to look like a man.' The vet turned back to his stitching. 'She loves to show that she can do what the men do.'

'So, which horse is the troublemaker?'

Tamás didn't look round, but there was a sudden stillness about him.

'The big brown one,' he said, after a moment.

'It's a nice-looking horse.'

'Yes.'

'Why did you call it Nico's horse?'

Ben kept his tone casual and Tamás's reply was equally so.

'Oh, when we bought them he said it was the pick of the bunch, so whenever it makes trouble I say, "That's your horse again, Nico!" and he scowls so.'

He produced a fairly accurate, if exaggerated, impersonation of Nico in one of his more stormy moods and Ben laughed, allowing Tamás to believe he'd carried the moment.

Two more deft stitches and the vet straightened up. In the arena the music changed, heralding András and Miklós with their clowning routine which would be interrupted, as usual, by Nico's dramatic entrance, hanging precariously under Duka's neck.

'He'll be fine now,' Tamás said, patting his patient. 'And I must go. It is almost time for the finale.'

He turned the horse loose with the others and picked up his bag.

'I haven't time to put this back. Could you look after it for me, Ben?'

'Yeah, no problem.' He fell into step beside Tamás, taking the bag from him, glad to be able to postpone the examination of Nico's trouble-making horse.

The mood was high after the performance. The 'meet the cast' session seemed to go on for ever, and a cameraman sent by Ben's own editor begged a photocall with Nico and the others to get some promotional shots to flag up his article.

When the horses were all settled and the last members of the public seen off the premises, the troupe headed noisily towards Gyorgy's wagon for the usual post-performance gathering.

'Ben? Are you coming?' Nico called, seeing him fall behind.

'Yeah, be with you in a minute. Just got to speak to my editor.' Ben waved him on.

'All right, but don't be too long, my friend, or Emil will have drunk all the beer!'

He dodged as the portly Emilian aimed a lazy roundhouse at his head, and they were laughing as they made their way across the crisply frozen grass to where the canteen shone like a beacon in the darkness.

Moving swiftly, Ben retraced his steps to the stable complex and climbed stiffly over the locked steel gate that secured the area. He'd found out from Jakob that two security guards now patrolled the buildings at night, courtesy of the Csikós' promoter, who was obviously keen that nothing further should occur to deter them from returning to England. He'd been glad to learn that the men weren't accompanied by dogs and, from what he'd seen so far, they tended to do their rounds together, for the most part chatting and only occasionally shining their torches into darkened corners.

So it proved to be. Waiting until they had wandered down to the barns and back, Ben jogged down there himself, sliding the heavy door open a few inches and slipping through. Leaning back against the door he looked around him, breathing heavily and wishing his ribs didn't feel as though a herd of elephants had used him as a doormat.

The moon was three-quarters full and four sizeable polycarbonate roof panels let in a surprising amount of light, by which he could make out the shapes of the ten horses inside, all gathered around the two wall-mounted, galvanized steel hayracks. Their scent came to him, along with the usual sweet, dungy, dried-grassy smell of stables the world over. The atmosphere was calm, the air filled with the wonderfully contented sound of many sets of equine teeth munching on soft meadow hay, and the temperature was several degrees warmer than it had been outside. Every now and then, one of the horses would snort and blow as dust tickled its nostrils, but, although one or two looked up at

Ben's entrance, none of them seemed unduly worried by his presence.

So far, so good.

On the peaty floor, just inside the door and still outside the horses' enclosure, two or three bales of hay had been left, presumably ready for use the next morning. Ben dropped his car keys beside these, kicking some loose hay over them. This, he hoped, would provide him with a back-up story if, God forbid, he should need it.

This done, and having taken a quick look to check that the guards hadn't unexpectedly returned, there was nothing further to delay his foray with the scanner. Taking one or two deep breaths to try and bring his heart-rate down into the low hundreds, Ben lifted a rope halter from a nail by the door, threaded it over his arm to keep his hands free, and let himself through the gate into the horses' enclosure.

Several more heads turned his way this time, and one animal even started to amble in his direction, trailing a long wisp of hay from its chomping jaws.

'It's all right. There's nothing to get excited about. Go back to your hay,' Ben told it quietly, as much to reassure himself as the horse.

The horse stopped, ears forward, still chewing. Shame it wasn't the one Ben wanted to examine. He stepped round it and approached the group feeding from the nearest hayrack. Because of the low light and the fact that all the horses had their rumps turned towards him, it was impossible for Ben to see whether his main suspect was amongst the bunch. He was going to have to get closer.

It was nothing short of crazy to consider squeezing between them from behind, so that meant going round and ducking under their necks.

If Ben had allowed himself time to think, he would probably have bottled out there and then, but he didn't, and in a few moments he was beside the end horse, patting its neck and saying with a calm he was far from feeling, 'All right, lad. Just coming under, OK?'

The horse looked down his long nose at him with mild curiosity and pulled another mouthful of hay from the rack. A rather plain-headed creature, with longish ears; it was, quite patently, not Cajun King. Ben didn't waste any time on it. Pulse rate rocketing, and feeling at once both hot and cold, he ducked under its neck and came up in the gap between it and its neighbour, wincing as the action squeezed his bruised ribs.

This next horse tilted its head, slightly startled, as Ben appeared, but beyond taking half a step backwards, didn't react. Glancing quickly over it, Ben could see from the narrowness of its chest and forehead that this wasn't the horse from the photograph either.

'All right, lad. Gently.'

Once again, Ben doubled up and slipped under its chin, coming up in the centre of the group of five.

This time he was met with flattened ears and obvious annoyance.

'It's all right. I'm not going to bother you,' Ben said soothingly. 'You are a grump, aren't you?'

Thankfully the bad-tempered animal was also

a non-candidate, and before it had time to do more than glower, he'd ducked beneath its neck and moved on.

Here, though, things started to go wrong. The fourth horse in line had obviously been half-asleep and, as Ben materialised beside it, it jumped violently back and whirled away, forcing the next horse to go with it. Startled by each other rather than the man in their midst, two of the others also shied away, cannoning into one another in their haste; for a moment, chaos reigned.

Instinctively, Ben shrank back against the hayrack, holding his breath as the half-ton silhouettes scrambled, pushed and shoved around him in momentary panic. All ten horses were on the move now, and the airy barn was suddenly uncomfortably crowded. Hooves thudded in the peat, which in turn was flung up to shower the walls and Ben, and the strong, musky smell of horse filled the air as they tried to flee but couldn't.

Ben closed his eyes against the terror, counting steadily under his breath to try and keep control.

At ten, he opened his eyes.

The horses had stopped moving and were standing in a semicircle, watching him; one or two of them snorted softly as they stared, goggle-eyed, at the human who had caused their fright.

Ben swore softly. His plan to single out the suspect horse, scan it and follow the troupe to Gyorgy's wagon before he was missed had gone pear-shaped. How long was it going to be before the horses trusted him enough to return to their hay and let him continue his search? Were it not for the fact that he only had use of the scanner for this one night, he would have given up there and then.

He waited, murmuring soothing words in a shaky, breathy voice, his heart thudding painfully hard and sweat running down his face from his hairline. When this is over, he promised himself, I'll become a motoring journalist, test-driving and rating new cars.

One of the horses, finishing its mouthful of hay, lowered its head and regarded Ben thoughtfully. Then, apparently deciding that he was relatively harmless, it came forward to begin feeding once more, albeit at the other rack. One by one its companions followed, seven crowding in at one feeding station and just three nervously approaching Ben's.

He couldn't tell, after the confusion, whether any of the three were the ones he'd previously discounted, and to help matters along, the moon slipped behind a cloud, leaving the inside of the barn in almost complete darkness.

Cursing, Ben looked up, but with the distorting effect of the layered polycarbonate panels he couldn't tell how big the cloud was. Any moment now, Nico or one of the others might grow curious and come to find him. In the inside pocket of his jacket was a pencil-thin LED torch that emitted a surprisingly powerful beam, but with the horses in their current state of mind he hesitated to use it.

Just as he was beginning to think he'd have to risk the torch, the clouds cleared the moon once more and vision returned. Crooning softly, Ben pushed himself away from the wall and reached up to rub the neck of the nearest horse. For a fraction of a second it stopped munching, its ears flicking anxiously, but Ben continued his gentle caress and gradually it began to relax.

In view of the wasted time and the increasing likelihood of the return of the two security guards, Ben decided to throw method out of the window in favour of backing a hunch. The way he saw it, the horse Tamás had described as Nico's troublemaker was likely to be one of the leaders of the bunch and, that being so, it seemed likely that it was the one who'd led the others back to their fodder. With that in mind he turned his back on the three closest to him and transferred his attention to those feeding at the second hayrack.

For the first time that night it seemed something was going his way. As he drew closer, he realised that the animal he'd identified as the herd leader was in fact the one nearest to him. He could have cheered.

Unzipping his pocket, he took the scanner out and pressed the large central button to switch it on. With a soft beep, the screen lit up.

Ben knew the worst thing he could do was to let the horse see his fear, so he approached in a manner that he hoped conveyed calm confidence. The animal turned its head, still chewing, then pulled another mouthful of hay. In the gloom, it was difficult to say for sure that it was the horse in the picture but, on the other hand, there was nothing about it that ruled that possibility out.

Ben patted the sleek neck and, encouraged by its relative placidity, decided that the rope halter might not be necessary.

'Steady lad. Just want to see who you are,' he murmured and, keeping his thumb on the button, he swept the scanner smoothly over the horse's neck from just behind its ears to its withers.

The scanner stayed disappointingly silent.

Ben looked closely at it. The display said SEARCHING.

He covered the area again, this time more slowly and zigzagging across the search area, but with the same negative result.

What was he doing wrong? He tried to remember what Penny had told him.

'The official injection site for horses is on the left side of the neck, halfway between the poll and the withers, one inch below the midline of the mane, into the nuchal ligament.' She'd even showed him on a diagram in one of her veterinary manuals. 'The microchip has a synthetic membrane around it that adheres to muscle. It's about the size of a grain of rice, injected with a twelve gauge needle and, once in place, it rarely causes any problems at all, although it's not unknown for them to migrate – at least in cats and dogs; I don't know about horses. Anyway, the scanner then picks up the microchip's number, which can be fed into the universal database and used to identify the registered owner, wherever they are in the world.'

Ben scanned the horse a third time, passing the device over an even greater area.

Nothing.

The screen now displayed NO ID FOUND and, shortly afterwards, turned itself off, as if to finalise the matter.

The horse had no chip. It couldn't be Cajun King.

Ben wasn't sure whether to be glad or sorry.

Nico's troublemaker swung its head to look at Ben, clearly becoming a little irritated by his odd behaviour and, absent-mindedly, Ben scratched it gently behind the ear, allowing his hand to follow the line of its mane down to the halfway point where the chip should have been. There, just below its crest, his roving fingertips paused as they encountered a thin, scratch-like scab, maybe an inch and a half long. Just as the possible implications of this were seeping into his mind, the barn door rolled back and light flooded in.

16

For a moment, beyond letting his hand fall away from the horse's neck, Ben didn't move, his mind racing to find the most credible excuse for his presence.

Who had come? And how much had they seen?

He turned, almost casually, hoping beyond hope that he would see one of the security guards. But it was Nico who stood there, with Tamás at his shoulder.

The story about looking for his keys wouldn't explain his being amongst the horses, but even as Ben tried to formulate another Nico pulled the rug from beneath his feet.

'It's not there, my friend,' he said coolly.

'I'm sorry?' Ben had slipped the scanner back into his pocket as he turned.

'The chip. Tamás took it out. That was what you were looking for?' As Nico stepped forward, Miklós and András joined Tamás in the doorway. Gone was the easy camaraderie they had hitherto shared with him; they now appeared to Ben as a hard-eyed and implacable family unit, and he was very much the outsider.

'It was.' There was little point in denying it. 'How did you know I'd be here?'

'You were different tonight. I could tell something was not right. Then Tamás told me you'd been asking questions. He said he thought he might have given the game away. I didn't want to believe it, but when you didn't come . . . Was that what it was about all along, Ben? Did that bastard Truman send you? I thought you were our friend.'

'I *am* your friend,' Ben protested. 'That's why I came myself. Truman knows nothing about it. And you forget, I first came to you before any of this happened.'

One or two of the horses were moving towards the gate now, disturbed by the light and all the people, and perhaps hopeful of titbits. Ben kept ahead of them, reaching the gate just as Nico reached it from the other side. The horses crowded in on each side, jostling him, and Ben began to feel the familiar surging fear.

He put a hand out towards the catch but Nico's hand was there before it, holding the gate shut, and his dark eyes flashed with malice.

'All these questions, Ben – about Stefan, about the family. This article you pretended you were writing; all lies!'

'No! Not all lies! There is an article. But what I don't understand is why you agreed to me coming when you knew what you had planned? It was crazy!'

'No. Because no one should have known about the horse; it was between Truman and me.'

'And Jakob.'

A frown creased Nico's handsome face.

'Jakob?'

'Because of Stefan – I assumed . . .'

'Jakob knows nothing about it. This was my doing. Mine and my brothers.'

'And Tamás, and Jeta. Jeta disguised the horse, didn't she?' Ben prompted, trying to subdue the urge to forget pride and scramble out over the gate as three more horses came pushing forward and tempers flared amongst the herd.

'We are family,' Nico stated.

András stepped closer. 'The Gadjo has been fooling us all along, Nico, with this fear of the horses. He's been lying to us all.'

Nico looked closely at Ben through narrowed eyes and then shook his head.

'No, I think not about that.' He took his hand off the gate catch and stepped back and, with that simple act of humanity, unknowingly ensured that Ben would do everything in his power to extricate him from the trouble that was inevitably coming his way.

Closing the gate on the crowding horses, Ben turned to find that he was at the centre of a semi-circle formed by Tamás and the Bardu clan. Still wearing the studded black trousers and long boots that were remnants of their show costumes, they looked a bit like the cast of a spaghetti western. Worryingly, András still wore his whip coiled at his hip.

Ignoring the others, Ben looked straight at Nico.

'Thank you.'

Nico looked away and back again, frustration evident in every fibre of his being.

'Why would you work for a bastard like Truman, Ben? This is what I do not understand. Do you not know what he's like? Do you not know what he does to people?'

'I know now, but I didn't. My brother rides for him. He told me about the kidnap and Truman promised me the story if I'd help. I'm a journalist; there's no way I'd pass up a chance like that.'

'Well, if you care about your brother, tell him to get out before Truman ruins his life, as he did mine – ours, our family's. We Rom have a saying: *O zalzaro khal peski piri*: *Acid corrodes its own container*. Truman is like that with people, everyone around him gets burnt.'

'And it's corroded you, too,' Ben said. 'Look what you've done. You've put the whole troupe at risk, your family and your livelihood, for the sake of revenge. What Truman did to Stefan was unforgivable and he shouldn't have got away with it, but that doesn't change the fact that what you've done is against the law and if you get caught – no, *when* you get caught, he'll have won again. Come on, Nico! Loyalty is one thing, but is it really worth it? Do you think Stefan would have wanted you to put all this on the line just for the chance to get back at Truman? It was sixteen years ago, for God's sake! Look at what you have here.'

'I know it was sixteen years ago.' Nico's eyes sparkled dangerously. 'Did you think I would have forgotten? How could that be, when every day I am reminded of what he did?'

Ben regarded him thoughtfully and a suspicion began to crystallise into certainty.

'My God! It wasn't Stefan at all, was it? It was you. You came to England in his place! Truman said there were some discrepancies with the papers, and no wonder! All that stuff you told me about Stefan was lies!'

On the periphery of his vision, Ben saw András and Miklós tense, like dogs straining at the leash, but Nico held a hand up.

'No. I told you the truth. Stefan – my cousin – died in a car crash.'

'But before he was supposed to come to England, not after. Am I right?'

Nico nodded. 'He was on his way here and I was with him.'

'You were in the car when it crashed?'

'Yes. I was only seventeen and very . . . what is the word? Naïve? I was naïve and I thought if I came to England with Stefan I could be a jockey too; after all, I could ride just as well as he could. So I hid in the back of his car under some blankets. I would have been discovered sooner or later, I suppose, and I expect he would have refused to take me any further, but at the time I didn't think of that. I could only think of coming to England. But he never found out.' Nico's expression was sombre. 'I was sleeping when the car crashed. It was very old – I forget who it belonged to. It went off the road and rolled over and over down a hill. I hit my head and when I woke up I could see that Stefan was dead. I think maybe the blankets saved my life.'

'You told me there was a fire.'

'Yes. I was cold, shivering. I had to walk, so I put Stefan's jacket on, and in the pocket I found his papers. His passport and work permit, travel tickets and a letter from Truman. Stefan had been working in South Africa and the photograph on his passport was five years old. We were cousins but we could have passed for brothers. One Hungarian Romani looks much like another to the Gadje. It seemed the obvious thing to do.'

'You set fire to the car?'

Nico shrugged.

'He was dead. And it is, after all, the Romani way.'

'And Jakob knows about this?'

'Of course.'

András touched Nico's arm and spoke rapidly in either Hungarian or Romani, gesturing towards Ben. It wasn't necessary to understand the spoken words to know that he was becoming impatient.

Ben ignored him.

'And Truman didn't suspect?'

'I think, not at first. And then I started to win for him and people were patting his back. I think, then, he didn't care. He had what he wanted and so did I.'

'Well, you took one hell of a risk, and it paid off handsomely. And if you'd kept your hands off his daughter, you could have ridden the Derby winner.' Ben shook his head wonderingly. 'What on earth possessed you? Surely you knew how jealously he guards his daughters?'

'I thought I was in love,' Nico said ruefully. 'First love; I was thinking with my trousers.'

'You can say that again. Did you never try to contact Helen?'

'I sent letters, she never wrote back to me. But then, what could I offer her? She didn't even know who I really was.'

So Nico had known nothing of the baby. Ben had thought as much, but he had no intention of telling him; it wasn't his place to do so. The decision must be Stephen's, and the waters were muddy enough on both sides at the moment, without stirring them up even more.

'You didn't tell her your real name?'

'No. I kept that much sense, at least.'

'Well, considering the nature of the crime I think you got off amazingly lightly, by Truman's standards,' he observed.

Nico's face hardened in an instant.

'You think I got off lightly? What did Truman tell you?'

'That he threatened to turn you over to the authorities. He said he hounded you out of the country.'

'And did he tell you that he sent two men to put me on to the plane? Did he tell you what they did to me first?'

Ben shook his head and waited.

'My brothers aren't the only ones who have skill with the bullwhip. When I was a child we would all train together. I took my whip everywhere. I brought it to England with me. It was hanging on the back of my door when they came to my room.'

'Oh, God!' Ben murmured, with dawning horror. 'And you think Truman ordered it?'

'He was there. He watched,' Nico said tonelessly.

'But I don't understand. You went home afterwards? You let him get away with it?'

'Because he said I would go to prison if they ever found out I had stolen Stefan's papers, and I was young enough to believe him. And . . . I was ashamed.'

Ben sighed, finally understanding the depth of Nico's hatred.

'So now you steal his horse and hold it to ransom. But you didn't pick up the money. Why? Did you know the police were watching?'

'We never intended to take it; that was to mislead – to give us space to breathe. This isn't about money,' Nico stated. 'The plan was only ever to stop the horse running. I knew that would hurt Truman more than anything. He only cares about winning and that's the one thing his filthy money can't buy. He took the Derby away from me; now I will take the Cheltenham Gold Cup away from him. It is justice.'

'And then what? What did you plan to do with King after that?'

'Set him free – that was always the plan – and, one day, tell Truman who did this to him.'

Ben took a deep breath.

'And now?'

'And now?' Nico spread his hands. 'Now I don't know. Why did you have to come, Ben? You have spoiled everything. And what am I to do with you?'

His tone was soft – almost whimsical – but Ben wasn't fooled. The semicircle around him hadn't wavered. He glanced at them each in turn. Tamás appeared troubled but András and Miklós looked purposeful; it was hard to equate them with the bumbling clowns that were their alter egos.

He looked back at Nico.

'You have to let me go, you know.'

'To run to Truman with your tale?' he muttered bitterly. 'After all these years, to come so close. Nine days is all we need. If you go to Truman . . .' His eyes pleaded.

Ben's gaze was steady, though beneath the surface he felt far from it.

'You have to let me go,' he repeated, trying an experimental step forward.

Before he knew what was happening, András had stepped forward and shoved him backwards with enough force to send him crashing into the metal gate. It screeched and rattled, and the two or three horses that still waited in curiosity threw up their heads and shied away.

He spread his arms to regain his balance, temper rising, and found András waiting for him, his hand on the stock of his whip.

Ben took a deep, calming breath and nodded at the weapon with its lethal, twelve-foot lash.

'If you use that, tell me how that makes you any better than Eddie Truman?'

'András!' Nico's tone held a warning.

'Or perhaps you have a gun?' he said, remembering Rice's account of the hold-up.

'Those guns were for children – toys, bought at the market,' Nico said scornfully. 'We are not killers!'

'Then I can go?' Ben didn't take his eyes off András.

'Of course.' Suddenly Nico sounded weary and defeated. 'Let him pass.'

After a moment's hesitation his brother moved reluctantly back.

'He'll ruin us.'

'So, what do you want to do? We cannot keep him here.'

András made a muffled sound of sheer frustration and turned away, stubbing the toe of his boot into the peat and sending up a spray. Miklós and the vet looked on in gloomy silence.

Ben walked slowly between them, breathing a shaky sigh of relief as his way to the door was finally clear. Then, two or three paces on, he turned.

'I can help you, you know. If you'll let me,' he suggested tentatively.

Nico had been staring at the ground; now he raised his head but with little visible optimism.

'How? Will you keep our secret?'

Ben shook his head.

'No, and even if I did, it would do no good. One of the policemen is suspicious. It's only a matter of time before he guesses the truth. You must give the horse back.'

Miklós laughed harshly.

'And this will help? They will of course just stop looking? I think not.' He broke off and muttered disgustedly in his own language.

Nico nodded.

'My brother is right. It won't work. Truman will never give up.'

'I know this policeman, he's a friend. I'll talk to him. He's a maverick, a loner, and he knows what kind of man Truman is. It's worth a try.'

'And Truman wins.'

'He'll win anyway. This way, maybe you won't lose.' Ben scanned their faces but his words didn't seem to be making any impression.

'Nico, can't you see? You can't win. And if they catch you with the horse, you'll go down and in all probability, so will I. If you hand him over to me, I might just be able to carry it for you.'

'I say it's because of you this policeman suspects us – you have led him to us,' Miklós declared, jabbing an aggressive finger in Ben's direction.

'You may be right,' he admitted. 'But not intentionally. I wasn't sure myself, until tonight.'

Miklós muttered something in his own tongue and turned away.

'How would we do it without being caught?' Nico asked reluctantly.

Ben was careful to hide his relief.

'We'd have to work that out, but I thought maybe an anonymous tip-off to one of the papers, that sort of thing. If you said you'd only hand over to me, and specified no police.'

'And they'd do that?'

'You bet they would! What a scoop!'

'Oh, and of course you get the glory,' Miklós put in.

Ben looked at him.

'Someone will. It might as well be me.'

'You will trust him?' It was András this time, urgently pulling Nico to face him. 'Tell me why? Why should we trust him?'

Nico stared up at his brother and shook his head, the strain showing in his eyes.

'Because . . .'

Behind Ben, another voice spoke.

'Because he's here,' Jakob stated calmly. 'Because he could have sent the police but he came himself.'

Nico whipped round to look at his uncle, then became very still.

'You heard.'

Jakob nodded. 'Most of it. And I cannot be glad for what you have done, even though I understand why you did it. Your trouble is now trouble for all of us.'

'It is right that he should pay,' Nico said defiantly. 'What he did to me, he did to all of us.'

'And is it right that Ben should also pay?' Jakob asked gravely. 'What is his crime?' His frown wandered over each of them, coming to rest accusingly on Nico's brothers, who began to look very uncomfortable. 'This is not our way. Ben is our friend.'

'So why come in the dark to look at the horse?' Miklós wanted to know. 'Why does he not speak to us?'

'Because I came here hoping I'd got it all wrong,' Ben replied. 'I told myself even you wouldn't be so crazy as to steal a valuable racehorse and then parade it before the public, three or four nights a week.'

'And if we hadn't caught you, what then?' Miklós was still wary. 'The police?'

'I think I would have told Jakob. But now I know the whole story I want to help you, if I can; but you have to do it my way.'

Jakob nodded. 'We will listen.'

389

'OK. Well, if Truman gets the horse back in time for the race then maybe, just maybe, he'll concentrate on that for the next few days and not so much on the hunt for you; especially if there aren't any more leads. Er . . . no further clues – information,' he translated, seeing blank faces. 'As far as he's concerned, Stefan Varga – or the man who took his identity – died in a car crash in Hungary. You have what, two more shows here, and then you move on to Bath. There'll be no reason for him to make the connection and, with any luck, the police won't either. With Cajun King back where he belongs, I should imagine it would be difficult to prove he was ever here.'

He looked at Nico.

'You don't agree?'

'No. No, my friend, it's not that. I'm sorry. It's just . . .' Nico put both hands to his head and groaned. 'I hate that he should win.'

'Give me the horse, and I'll give you another way to hurt Truman,' he promised. 'We Gadje have a saying; *There's more than one way to skin a cat*. You have to trust me.'

Nico looked round at the others. Tamás and Miklós nodded their agreement and András shrugged but continued to look mulish.

His dark eyes found Ben again.

'We will trust you,' he said at last.

When Ben finally got back to his car it was almost two o'clock in the morning and the pace of the past couple of days had well and truly caught up with him. He hauled himself into the driver's seat

390

by way of the steering wheel and collapsed back against the upholstery with his eyes closed.

After a moment, with an encouraging word over his shoulder to Mouse, he started the engine, put it in gear and let the handbrake off; every action pulling on one sore muscle or another. Swinging the Mitsubishi round in a U-turn he headed for the field gate, the vehicle bouncing and rocking over the frosty grass.

The hand that landed none too gently on his shoulder nearly made him jump out of his skin. He slammed the brakes on and simultaneously reached round, grabbed the wrist of his attacker and pulled hard.

Logan grunted as his upper body jammed between the headrests and the roof of the vehicle.

'Good move!' he observed approvingly, through gritted teeth. 'What now?'

Relief flooded over Ben.

'I've absolutely no idea,' he admitted, releasing his grasp. 'What the bloody hell are you doing here?'

'Waiting for you,' the policeman said calmly, rubbing his upper arm. 'You don't take prisoners, do you?'

'Sorry, I've had a bad couple of days. But that was bloody stupid! We could have crashed.'

'Not in the middle of a field.'

'Well, you nearly gave me a heart attack, anyway. Exactly why were you waiting for me? And why here?'

'I followed you – yes, in spite of your praise-worthy efforts to lose me.'

'Not you, in particular. Anyone. I especially

didn't want to lead those two charmers from last night here.'

'You didn't. I'd have seen them.'

'D'you mean you've been waiting here all that time?'

'Well, not here precisely. I did have a wander round. Watched the show, as a matter of fact. And as for why I'm here? Well, I've been pondering your interest in the late Stefan Varga, who fell so foul of our friend Eddie Truman. And then I got to thinking about Hungarians in general. Not a race you stumble across all that often, you'd have to agree – so it's stretching co-incidence a little far to accept that these Hungarian horsemen of yours should just happen to be in the country right now, isn't it? And then, after a few judicious phone calls, I discovered that although the main performing family go – as advertised – by the name of Bardu, they are closely related to the Varga family. Furthermore, Jakob Varga – who appears to be part of the road crew – is none other than our own Stefan Varga's father! I'd say that blows coincidence right out of the water, wouldn't you?'

Ben's heart sank. Was his plan to save the troupe from retribution doomed to failure before he started?

'Have you discussed it with anyone?'

'No. I'm off-duty, and I wanted to see what you were up to first.'

Ben hesitated. He'd hoped to have a little more time to prepare before he tackled Logan. In the end he took a chance and jumped straight in at the deep end.

'What would you say if I said I've found the horse?'

'I'd say, congratulations. And then I'd wait for the rest. I have a feeling there's a big, fat juicy 'but' coming.'

'OK. The Csikós – the Hungarians – do have the horse, *but* I've persuaded them to give it back.'

'In return for which . . . ?'

'I don't say a word about their involvement. In short, one of my editors receives an anonymous tip-off as to his whereabouts, with the stipulation that I go collect him, which I do, with a cameraman at my elbow no doubt. So the paper gets a front page to die for, I get recognition and a big fat cheque, and Truman gets his Gold Cup horse back. Job done; everyone happy. But it would only work, of course, if you were to agree to be similarly mute.'

Logan frowned.

'That's a big ask.'

'I know it.'

'So give me one good reason why I should pass up on such a big pat on the back from my superiors?'

'Because you don't give a shit about that kind of thing?'

Logan chuckled.

'Actually I do. You can build up quite a bit of credit from the occasional big bust – you know, leeway in the future, when you step out of line.'

'You? Step out of line? I can't imagine that,' Ben mocked. 'But OK, look at it from another angle. If we point the finger at these guys, then Truman – who we're agreed is a bastard of the

393

first water, besides being the biggest criminal not behind bars – Truman gets to win on all counts. And I, for one, find that difficult to stomach. The Csikós, on the other hand, are, on the whole, a nice bunch,' he added, conveniently pushing the memory of András and his whip to the back of his mind.

'Some of the nicest blokes I know are criminals,' Logan remarked. 'And don't forget, these friends of yours, these paragons of virtue, held up a horsebox and four innocent crew with guns.'

'They were toy guns.'

'It's a crime, nevertheless. As is kidnapping and demanding money with threats.'

'They never intended picking up the money,' Ben persisted.

'Easy to say *now*,' Logan pointed out. 'Tell me, is the late Stefan Varga really the *late* Stefan Varga, or is that also a myth?'

'Yes, he is . . . Except he wasn't. It's a long story,' Ben ended helplessly.

'OK. Well, unless you're particularly wedded to this spot, shall we head back to my pad and you can tell me over a beer or two?'

It was nine o'clock the following morning before Ben made it back to Dairy Cottage.

Instead of beer, Logan had produced a bottle of home-made wine given to him by a neighbour, which had turned out to be rather good. Recounting the tale of Nico and Stefan had taken quite some time and the further down the bottle they got, the longer it seemed to be taking. In the end, Logan rummaged in his freezer and came up with a pizza which, after twenty minutes in the oven, became a welcome accompaniment to the wine. When, at nearly four in the morning, they were all talked out, it seemed much the best thing for Ben to spend the night in a sleeping bag in the spare room.

The upshot of it all was that Logan agreed, if the Csikós handed Cajun King over to Ben within the next two days, to say nothing of what he'd learned.

'But you owe me, big time!' he warned, when Ben had tried to thank him.

Dairy Cottage sat quietly in the winter sunshine, and Ben got stiffly out of his car to find that Mike had been watching for his return.

'Everything OK?'

'Yeah, thanks Mike. Our visitors haven't been back?'

'Nope. Not a soul.'

Despite having breakfasted at Logan's, Ben made himself toast and coffee, lit the wood-burner, and settled down to spend the day working on the Csikós article.

By the time he got up to switch the lights on at dusk, Ben was beginning to feel a little twitchy. It was just too quiet. Why hadn't Nico called? He'd given him two days but what was the point in delaying? They'd thrashed out the details before he left their camp. All that remained was for Nico to implement them. He prayed the Hungarian hadn't changed his mind.

At half past six in the evening, when the winter sun was but a memory and the moon was lifting into a sky full of stars, Ben's phone rang and he picked up the receiver to find one of his London editors on the other end of the line, sounding cautiously euphoric. He told Ben what he'd learned.

'So I thought I'd give you a ring first, before I did anything else, just to see if you thought there was any chance it might be kosher, he finished.

'There's every chance,' Ben replied, putting excitement in his own voice.

'So the bugger got it right! The horse is missing?' he said, alluding to his rival on the paper that had carried the story. 'So tell me why they're asking for you to collect the animal and not any one of a hundred other more likely people.'

Ben had been prepared for this question.

'Maybe because I'm already involved. My brother, Mikey, works for Truman, and he was there when the horse was taken.'

'And you didn't think to share this titbit of news with an old chum?'

'Sworn to silence, I'm afraid. Police business. But you were first on my list for the exclusive.'

'I should sincerely hope so!' He took a deep breath. 'Right; action. First things first: do you know where this Turf Hill place is?'

'I think so. If you send the photographer here he can follow me.'

'He's already on his way. He was in Southampton anyway so he should be with you in twenty. They say the horse will be there at seven. How long will it take you to get there?'

'All of that,' Ben said. 'Better give me your guy's mobile number and I'll give him directions.'

'OK, and meanwhile I'll call Truman to get his first reaction.'

'Er – look, could you hold that thought for ten minutes or so? We don't want him getting to the rendezvous first, do we? You can take it from me he's a bit of a sod to deal with, and you don't want him buggering up your big moment, do you? Ten minutes'd just give us a bit of a head start.'

'Just at the moment, Benjamin, I'd give you just about anything,' his editor declared.

'Ah, good. I was just coming to that,' Ben said with alacrity. 'Have you got your chequebook handy?'

The return of Cajun King to his rightful owner went more smoothly than Ben could have dared hope.

The photographer followed his instructions to the letter, arriving at the New Forest car park at Turf Hill just seconds after Ben. Together they set off along the gravel track beyond the barrier, with Mouse trotting at their heels.

Ben had jogged the half-mile or so across the open, moonlit moorland, cursed every step of the way by his overweight colleague, who complained that he'd got his equipment to carry as well. But Ben kept going, anxious that no late dog-walker should discover the horse before they did and report it to someone official or, worse still, take it home. It was the one possible flaw in the plan, but it didn't happen.

Just as the anonymous email had promised, Cajun King – with the dye removed from his white star, and his tail returned to its usual meagre proportions – was waiting in the stout wooden corral into which the New Forest ponies were herded come round-up, or drifting, time.

With the photographer snapping frantically, Ben steeled himself to enter the pen and catch the horse. Happily, in the event, this proved remarkably easy with the benefit of a tip Nico had given him about King's penchant for Polo mints. Even so, without his recent sessions under Jakob's calm and patient eye, Ben wasn't sure he could have pulled it off.

The horse had behaved like a star, doing no more than jiggling beside Ben as they approached the car park once more to find it ablaze with vehicle lights and noise. When they were still fifty yards distant, Truman, Fliss, Rice and Ray Finch hurried out to meet them and the photographer got pictures to build a career on.

In the midst of all the excitement, as the horse was led away to the luxury of the Castle Ridge horsebox, Ben turned and caught Helen's husband watching him.

The look in his eyes would have curdled milk.

17

If Ben had expected the pace of life to be calmer after Cajun King's celebrated return to the Castle Ridge fold, he would have been sadly mistaken. Almost before the ink had dried on the first, sensational front-page story he was hot property, and reporters, racing journalists, TV and radio companies and local newspapers all wanted to hear his side of what looked set to be the greatest racing story of the year.

As 'The Man Who Brought Cajun King In From The Cold' Ben was the hero of the hour, and the media seemed reluctant to accept his stated opinion that he'd been chosen for the task purely on the basis of his connection with Castle Ridge through his brother and the article he'd been researching.

'A lot of people are speculating that it was you who brought about Cajun King's release; are you saying it wasn't?'

'It's a claim I'd love to be able to make but, unfortunately, I can't,' Ben told them regretfully.

'But as the man who famously beat the Jockey Club to the line over the Goodwood betting scam, you surely don't expect us to believe that you weren't taken into Truman's confidence over the disappearance of his top horse?'

'No, of course not. I was aware of the kidnap, and naturally I did what I could – as did the police – so maybe our investigations frightened the kidnappers into giving the horse up, who knows?'

'Have you any idea where Cajun King might have been hidden over the past eleven days?'

Ben shrugged. 'He could have been anywhere, really. That's what made it so hard. One horse in a field looks much like another from a distance, especially with a rug on. All I can say is that he looks to have been well looked after.'

'Why do you think the kidnappers chose to return the horse in such a public way?'

'If I ever meet them I'll ask them,' Ben promised.

There was laughter and the questions went on, and by returning non-specific answers, he was able to get through without selling his soul to the devil.

DI Ford was not so easily satisfied.

'Well, it looks like you've done it again,' he observed, settling himself into one of Truman's red leather chairs and regarding Ben with a thoughtful eye. 'The Goodwood Scandal and now this. It would seem that CID has missed out on a star recruit in you.'

From his position, leaning on the mantelpiece, Hancock smirked.

It was the second day after King's return, and Truman himself was out on the gallops, no doubt watched by dozens of hacks and tipsters eager for a sighting of the equine celebrity of the moment. Ben was alone in the trainer's study with the two officers.

'I'm afraid I can't take the credit for this one, Inspector,' he said, ignoring Hancock. 'I think I came up against the same dead ends as you did.'

'I daresay you did, but it's not the dead ends I'm interested in, Mr Copperfield. It's whatever you found out that precipitated this sudden change of heart from the kidnappers that I'd like to hear about.'

'You don't think they just got cold feet, then?'

'It's possible, but I have an enquiring mind, Ben – I like to think it's what got me where I am today – and I find I'm always exploring other possibilities. I find I'm always saying to myself, *what if?*'

Ben began to feel a little uneasy. The DI was an extremely clever man; Logan had warned him of that.

'Go on . . .'

'Well, in this instance, I find myself thinking *what if* Mr Truman – who I secretly suspect of having quite a, shall we say, colourful history – *what if* he put you on to a lead that he didn't feel able, for whatever reason, to mention to myself or Hancock here?'

Ben waited.

'And then, *what if* this person, or persons, were persuaded – by whatever means – that it would be in their best interests to give the horse up in

401

such a fashion that the motives of all parties could be left discreetly out of the public eye?'

'That,' Ben said admiringly, 'was quite a sentence!'

Ford's lips twitched.

'Wasn't it just?'

'So, if that was what happened, what would you say the chances were of you ever getting to the bottom of it?'

'Not good, maybe,' Ford admitted. 'But it wouldn't stop us trying. It wouldn't be unprecedented for someone to have their collar felt, way down the line, for something they thought they'd got away with.'

Ben was relieved that the DI's suspicions seemed to be leading him in a direction that would almost certainly not trouble the Csikós but, even so, he wasn't entirely comfortable with the tone of the conversation.

He shook his head, affecting mild puzzlement.

'If you're after some kind of confession, Inspector, I'm afraid you're going to be disappointed. I've certainly had no hand in anything Truman might have engineered. Is it really likely after this?' He raised a hand to touch his face, which still bore the marks left by Spence and his pal. 'OK. I'll admit he did ask me to check out a couple of things for him; a couple of people he felt might hold grievances, but the arrangement wasn't a success. We have fundamental differences, Mr Truman and I, and I discovered that the more I came to know him the less I liked him. Apparently the feeling was mutual.'

Ford scratched his head for a moment, looking

preoccupied, then said, 'What do you make of this business with the long-lost grandson?'

Ben's palms started to feel a little sweaty. What was Ford fishing for?

'In what way?'

'In any way.' The DI evidently wasn't going to help. 'What do you know?'

'Much the same as you, I expect.' He gave Ford a potted version of the sorry tale of Stefan and Helen. 'Then, when Stephen turned sixteen, he decided to try and track down his dad.'

Ford nodded. 'That's about how I have it, though Truman didn't mention the child when I first spoke to him about Stefan.'

'Yeah, well, believe it or not, he didn't know Helen and Elizabeth had conspired against him to stay in contact with the boy. As you can imagine, he wasn't a happy bunny.'

'Did you try and track down the jockey?'

'Yeah, but I didn't have much luck. Lost the trail after he left the country,' Ben said casually.

'That doesn't surprise me. From what Truman told me, I've a strong suspicion that the young man was here on someone else's passport and, as his description probably fits half the Romany population of Europe, I think the kid's going to stay fatherless.'

'He'd have done better to stay grandfatherless, too. Though I guess you can't blame him for wanting to find his family, whatever it's like. He seems a nice enough lad.'

'Mm.' Ford appeared to be absorbed in squeezing a splinter from the tip of one of his fingers. He spoke without raising his eyes.

'What do you think of Finch?'

'I try not to, unless I have to. Why?'

'He has the look of someone with a secret. Never quite meets the eyes, does Mr Finch.'

'Well, I'm pretty sure he's selling the odd tankful of diesel behind pa-in-law's back, if that's anything,' Ben said.

'Is he now? Well, well. You are a mine of information. Have you mentioned this to Truman?'

'No, not yet. I thought life was complicated enough.'

Over Ford's shoulder, Ben could see Hancock scowling.

'Look, Inspector, is there anything in particular you wanted to ask me? Because, if not, I've got a deadline to meet, and I promised Lisa I'd take her to the theatre tonight.'

'Anything nice?' Ford switched effortlessly to social matters.

'Haven't the foggiest, but she assures me I'll enjoy it, so who am I to argue?'

'Well, in that case, I wish you a comfortable seat and a large ice cream in the interval,' the DI said with a smile. 'I'll no doubt see you around, Mr Copperfield. I should imagine you've been invited to witness the big race?'

'Oh, yes – through clenched teeth.'

'Let's hope the bloody thing wins!' Ford said as they shook hands.

It looked as though the day of the Cheltenham Gold Cup was going to be just one more wet and windy day in a wet and windy week, but by mid-morning the heavy grey blanket of cloud had separated in places to allow the March sunshine through. By noon the sky was clear and very blue.

As the weather lifted, so did the spirits of the racegoers, and it was a large and noisy crowd that gathered to witness one of the most important day's racing in the National Hunt calendar. Smart casuals made of corduroy or tweed were topped off with an assortment of hats, ranging from the stylish to the purely functional and, at ground level, the occasional pair of high heels slipped and slithered through the mud next to the more sensible stout shoes and wellies.

As the start of the big race drew close, long queues formed at the Tote windows and around the bookies on the rails. In view of the heavy going, money was spread fairly evenly amongst three or four of the more fancied runners and favouritism chopped and changed every few minutes.

Truman had hired a large, glass-fronted box alongside the finishing straight and filled it to bursting with family, friends, and owners, very few of whom Ben knew at all. DI Ford was there, apparently at ease and accompanied by a well-rounded, fortyish lady he introduced as his wife. Hancock had either not merited an invitation or had been too busy to take it up. Ben rather suspected the former.

Fliss and Helen were there to act as joint hostesses during their father's frequent absences; Helen sipped premature champagne, clearly enjoying the occasion, whilst her younger sister just as clearly railed against her enforced role. Ben knew she would far rather be down among the mud and horses.

One person Ben couldn't see was Elizabeth. When he got the chance he quizzed Fliss over it.

'Ah,' she said significantly. 'Actually she's packed her bag and gone off for a fortnight's holiday with Aunty Tilda and Stephen.'

'I bet that didn't go down well.'

'No, you can say that again, but she went anyway. I was never so surprised, and Dad was gobsmacked! I think it must be the first time she's stood up to him in thirty-five years of marriage. God knows what'll happen when she gets back.'

If she gets back, Ben thought, but kept it to himself.

Rollo Gallagher put in a mud-splattered appearance between the first couple of races, shaking hands with the owners whose horses he was due to ride and listening solemnly to a series of instructions from Truman, who was splitting his time between paddock, parade ring and box.

Rollo said 'hi' to Ben as he passed on his way out.

'Got your instructions, then?' Ben observed, low-voiced.

'Mmm.'

'And do you follow them?'

'If it suits me,' the jockey said. 'Usually I just listen and nod, and then go out and follow my instincts. If I win, he pats himself on the back, and if I don't, I get bawled out for not doing as I'm told. We both know it's rubbish, but we play the game anyway.'

'Isn't Bess here?' Ben asked.

Rollo jerked his head.

'Over in Tattersalls with the riff-raff,' he said with a grin. 'But she prefers it there, anyway.'

When he'd gone, Ben took a handful of canapés from the heavily laden table at the side of the room and left the overwarm room to follow him down the stairs and out into the fresh, breezy sunshine.

Here, one of the first people he bumped into was Belinda Kepple, who was warming her hands round a large paper cupful of cappuccino, as was her companion: a tall, lean, man with short, iron-grey hair and tanned good-looks.

'Hi, Belinda.' He nodded to the man. 'Dad.'

John Copperfield turned with eyebrows raised.

'Ben. Well, well. Was that horse I sent along suitable for what your friends wanted?'

'Yeah, fine. Thanks for that.' He turned to the trainer. 'So how's Rackham's horse – Tuppenny Tim, isn't it? I see he's quite well up in the betting.'

Belinda bent towards him, conspiratorially.

'Don't tell anyone, but I'm quietly confident,' she told him, and the excitement was there in her voice. 'He's got the heart of a lion and he's a complete mudlark! He'll run on anything, but on this kind of going he'll stay forever, when all those around him are floundering. You should put a fiver on him. I think he's got a real chance.'

'OK. I might just do that. Er . . . What you said that time – about Mikey – were you serious?'

'Absolutely,' she said. 'Why? Is he looking to leave Truman?'

'I think he might be, soon. Even if he doesn't know it yet. Thanks. I'll be in touch.'

He moved on, stopping to take advantage of

the mid-race lull in business at the Tote and put twenty pounds on Rackham's horse to win the Gold Cup, and ten pounds each way on Cajun King. Then, lured by the smell, he bought a large cappuccino, adding another for Fliss, who appeared unexpectedly by his side.

'I couldn't stand it a moment longer,' she explained, seeing his surprise. She took the coffee, gratefully. 'All those people who've got no real interest in horses waffling away as if they know it all. I'd much rather be down here, and when I saw you escape . . .' She linked her free arm through his. 'Did I see you talking to the opposition a while back?'

'Mmm. The guy with her is my dad.'

'Oh, I see. Funny, I've never thought of you having a dad.'

Ben laughed.

'Why ever not? Did you think I'd beamed down from some distant planet one dark night, thirty-odd years ago?'

'Is that how old you are? Thirty?'

'Thirty-two, actually. Lisa – my fiancée – is thirty,' he added significantly.

He felt her immediate, miniscule withdrawal.

'I didn't know she was your fiancée.'

Neither does she, Ben reflected, but kept it to himself.

'So, where is she then?'

'Working.'

'Oh. Nice outfit, by the way.'

'Thanks. You too.'

'Did you know you left your leather jacket at the house the other day?'

'Yeah. I've been meaning to come and fetch it.'

'I could bring it over if you gave me your address.'

'You could, couldn't you? I'm sure Lisa would love to meet you.'

Fliss leaned round in front to look at him.

'Are you really as straight as you make out?'

'Yep. Boring, isn't it?'

There was silence for a moment, then Fliss said with determined cheerfulness, 'Well, I suppose we'd better get a wriggle on if we want to see King do his stuff.'

Ben allowed himself to be steered through 180 degrees and marched back the way he'd come, feeling like a traitor with the two betting slips in his pocket.

In the event, the race was a close-run thing.

As the horses rounded the last corner Cajun King was sitting pretty on the shoulder of the leader and looking full of running. Apart from one peck on landing early on – forgivable in the heavy going – he had jumped superbly and given Rollo a wonderful ride; but Ben, with his inside knowledge, couldn't help letting his eyes drift back to fourth place. There, running fairly wide, Rackham's big grey horse was going equally well; his long, honest head bobbing steadily with each ground-covering stride.

Indeed, comparing the two, it had to be said that Tuppenny Tim's rounded action was a lot better suited to the mud than King's flatter, reaching stride.

Then, as they rose to the second last, the other horses fell away and suddenly there were only two of them left in it. Looking over his shoulder, Rollo urged King to greater speed, perhaps recognising the danger and trying to put enough ground between them to take the heart out of his rival.

For a moment it looked as though his tactics had succeeded. As the clamour within Truman's box rose to deafening levels King took the last some four lengths clear but, for the second time in the race, he stumbled on landing. Even though both horse and jockey swiftly recovered their balance, it was clear to all but the most determined optimist that the mistake had knocked the stuffing out of the horse and he was now tiring fast.

If the room had been noisy before, it was now complete bedlam as, stride by stride, Rackham's big-boned grey steadily cut down Cajun King's lead. For a few heart-stopping seconds it looked as though the finishing post would come just in time to save the Castle Ridge horse but, to the accompaniment of a howl of anguish from Truman's box, Tuppenny Tim finally overhauled the exhausted horse two strides before they crossed the line.

All at once there didn't seem to be anything much to say. After one huge gasp of disappointment, Truman's guests, aware of the level of expectation there had been in the Castle Ridge camp, fell quiet, looking at one another and their host with little rueful shrugs. The trainer himself stared at the horses in stunned silence as they

410

slowed rapidly and turned to come back to the paddock, King executing the sort of low-headed shambling trot that indicated extreme fatigue.

Truman scowled as he saw Rollo give the winning jockey a congratulatory pat on the back. He then turned to look at the television in the corner of the room, as if hoping that the action replay would show a different outcome. Fliss stood beside her father, her green eyes glistening with rising tears, and Ben saw Helen down her champagne and refill her glass, perhaps unwilling to miss out now that celebrations were off the cards.

Across the room, Ford caught Ben's eye and grimaced before putting his glass on a convenient table, collecting his wife and quietly withdrawing.

The replay over, the television screen displayed the official result, putting the seal on the shattered hopes of many of those watching; it wasn't even close enough to merit a photograph.

Ben could imagine the jubilation in the Kepple camp. His own feelings were ambiguous. A tenuous loyalty to the horse itself and genuine sympathy for Fliss's distress battled against the pleasure he felt on Belinda Kepple's behalf and a secret joy that Truman's rampant ambition had suffered a blow. Whichever emotion proved stronger, he felt it probably wasn't the time to jump up and down waving his Tote ticket for twenty pounds to win on Tuppenny Tim.

Gradually the voices around him rose to a steady hum once more, and Ben saw Fliss take her father's arm and rub it consolingly.

Truman wasn't in a mood to be consoled, however. He was still watching the TV, which showed the runners filing wearily back, caked in mud from head to hoof; the jockeys, goggles now discarded, looked out from pink-circled eyes. Rice, dressed smartly for the occasion, led the Castle Ridge horse in with an expression of resigned disappointment, in sharp contrast to the exultation that surrounded the big grey just in front. As the wave of applause followed the winner, Rollo leaned forward to pat King's steaming neck and gave a brief smile and a nod, no doubt in response to words of sympathy from one of the many who hurried alongside.

At this point, Truman broke his silence.

'I'll give him something to fucking smile about!' he exclaimed, his Yorkshire accent very noticeable. 'If he'd rode the horse the way he was told to, we'd have won that bloody race hands down. Always thinks he knows better, fucking little upstart!'

Slamming his glass down on the table he stormed out of the box, pushing through his guests with scant ceremony and almost colliding with a waiter who was on his way in with extra champagne and glasses.

'We don't need that now, you imbecile!' he growled, before disappearing from view.

Glancing self-consciously round at the half-embarrassed, half-amused faces left in the box, Fliss put down her champagne glass and followed her father, apologising to the startled waiter on the way.

The repercussions from Cajun King's inability to come up with the goods were felt for several days.

The very public dressing down that Truman gave his jockey in the unsaddling area resulted in Rollo's icy calm but immediate resignation, which in turn left the Castle Ridge trainer with no rider for his runner in the last.

After some frantic enquiries, he passed over Mikey in favour of a more experienced jockey whose horse had been withdrawn; even so, the animal came in a poor fourth, which didn't help the general mood.

In the following days Truman told anybody who cared to listen that his horse's failure had been brought about by a combination of the jockey's poor judgement and the after-effects of its being absent during a crucial stage of its training. Neither of these excuses held much water with anyone in the know, because Rollo's growing reputation spoke for itself and the trainer had, several times in the past, been heard to boast that King was a horse who showed little at home and thrived on minimal preparation. In fact, Truman would have done much better to be content with the general opinion that King and several other hopefuls had, on the day, been beaten by the heavy going and an improving horse.

The only person who benefited from Rollo's departure – in the short term at least – was Mikey, who picked up a good few rides that would never ordinarily have come his way. He made excellent use of them, too, clocking up a number of winners and attracting no little attention, with owners warming to his shy good manners and obvious love of the job.

Beyond checking up on his brother a couple of times, Ben had no reason or wish to visit Castle Ridge in the days after the Cheltenham Festival. Since the return of his horse Truman had been civil but unwelcoming, and Ben was fairly certain the trainer suspected him of knowing more than he was telling about the whole business. Nothing was ever said on either side regarding the visit of Spence and his sidekick, nor was the subject of Lenny Salter brought up again. In fact, had it not been for the existence of Stephen, Ben would have been quite ready to wash his hands of the whole Truman clan.

Stephen, who went by his great aunt's maiden name of Garvey, was still away and, although Ben had been back to see the Csikós a couple of times, he hadn't yet mentioned the boy's existence to Nico. The main reason for this was that he wanted first to get some idea of how Stephen felt about the matter. For himself, if he'd been in that position, he couldn't imagine not wanting to meet his father whatever his race or creed. But there was still that possibility, and he didn't feel it was in any way right to make the decision for him.

There would be time enough, if the boy was keen, to sound Nico out on the prospect, although Ben was pretty sure what his response would be; family was everything to the Csikós.

Another loose end, in Ben's mind, was Lenny Salter, who remained in hospital but was making a good recovery. When he eventually paid him a visit, he almost walked past his bed by mistake. The ex-jockey had had his hair washed and trimmed and his eyes, though dark-circled, were no longer puffy and bloodshot. Clean-shaven, he looked much nearer his real age, and he appeared to be sharing a joke with a slightly older, dark-haired man with a golden tan.

The sight of Ben had put paid to the laughter, until Lenny had been reassured that his visitor bore him no ill-will for passing his name on to Truman's two thugs.

The tanned man was introduced as Richie Salter, who'd been alerted to his brother's predicament by an anonymous phone call. He was presently making arrangements for Lenny to return to Spain with him when he was discharged from hospital.

'The phone call. It wasn't you, was it?' Lenny asked, almost shyly.

Ben shook his head. No, it wasn't, but he was happy for him. Privately, he suspected Logan might be behind it.

It turned out to be a day for renewing old acquaintances. On his way home he'd stopped off at his local village shop to pick up dog biscuits for Mouse, and he found himself queuing at the counter behind a familiar shock of pink, frizzed hair.

Della, studded with even more metal than Ben remembered, seemed to be in conversation with the shop owner about the possibility of putting up a poster. Tilting his head to see, Ben was surprised to find that, rather than the expected ALSA campaign propaganda, it advertised an exhibition of paintings.

'Hello Ben!' Henry Allerton appeared from the other aisle, carrying a loaf of bread and two tins

415

of baked beans. 'I'm glad I bumped into you. I have an apology to make.'

'You do?'

'Yes.' Allerton deposited his shopping on the counter beside Della's poster. 'Della told me what really happened that night the hut got trashed, and I'm sorry I jumped to conclusions.'

'How is Baz these days?' Ben enquired dryly.

'He's got a court case coming up. That business with the travelling show was nothing to do with me, Ben. I admit we were going to picket them, but I never intended them any harm, as such. Baz was a loose cannon, recruiting troublemakers and making decisions on his own. He was getting out of hand.' Allerton sighed. 'I've disbanded ALSA for the time being – maybe for good, though I still believe in what it stood for. Della and I have other things on our minds at the moment. She's moved in with me and turned my attic into a studio; I'm going to manage her career, among other things,' he added, putting his arm round her waist.

The pink frizz tipped sideways to rest on his shoulder momentarily before its owner turned to look at Ben.

So they were a couple. A decidedly odd pairing, but that was entirely their business.

Della and he exchanged greetings, Ben reflecting with amusement that the last time he'd met her, he'd thrown her into the nearest hedge. Life was strange.

It was a relief to get home.

Dairy Cottage waited, warm and welcoming, with a wisp of smoke rising from the chimney.

Mike had been gardening in the courtyard and was just packing away his tools in the fading light.

'All right, Mike?' Ben knew his landlord kept a fairly close eye on the cottage these days, especially when Ben was out.

'Yeah. Everything's quiet.' He stood up, stretching his back. 'That's not a dog in the back of your car, is it?'

Ben looked and shook his head. 'Nah.'

'Oh, that's all right, then,' Mike said as he turned away.

Inside, with the wood-burner stoked, the kettle on and Mouse fed, Ben was happily contemplating an evening spent with Lisa and a movie on DVD when the telephone rang.

He stretched out along his new sofa to pick the receiver off the coffee table, hoping it wouldn't be Lisa saying she had to work.

'Yeah, hello?'

'Ben?' Female, but not Lisa.

'Speaking.'

'It's Helen.'

'Hi. What can I do for you?' This was unexpected.

'I want to see Stefan. Can you take me? Please.'

The shock temporarily robbed Ben of speech. His mind raced.

'Ben?'

'Yeah, I'm here. What d'you mean?'

'I saw your article – on the Csikós.' She pronounced it wrong. 'And as soon as I saw that man, Nico, I recognised him. It's Stefan. *My* Stefan – Stephen's father – and I have to see him. You know him. Will you take me?'

417

'Whoa, hang on. I'd have to ask him first.'

'Can you do that?'

'Yeah, I guess so, if you're sure?'

'Now?'

'Well, OK. I suppose so. Give me a minute.'

'Ben, could we go tonight? Everyone's going to the party, so nobody'll ask questions. I'll say I've got a headache and stay behind.'

Ben remembered Mikey saying something about a party at the local pub to celebrate Ricey's birthday. He hadn't sounded too keen.

'Surely you're not all going. What about the yard?'

'Oh, Ray'll be here, but I can handle him, and Vicky's babysitting Lizzie at Dad's. So *please*.'

Ben sighed. It was the last thing he felt like doing but, from the sound of her, Helen might try to do it on her own if he didn't agree to help.

'OK. I'll try and get hold of him, then ring you back.'

He rang off and sat looking at the handset, then a thought sent him hurrying towards the kitchen and a pile of unopened mail that sat on the dresser, awaiting his attention.

There were two or three magazines amongst it but it didn't take him long to find the right one – it had a lovely cover picture of Nico and Duka, with the words Hungarian Magic printed underneath. Inside it carried the first of two four-page features on the Csikós, plainly credited to Ben Copperfield.

'Oh, bugger!' he said out loud, then reluctantly called Nico's mobile number. This wasn't at all how he'd hoped to arrange things.

'Hello?'

'Nico. Hi. Er . . . I'm not quite sure how to ask you this . . .'

Five minutes later, Ben was back on the phone to Helen.

'OK, he'll meet us, but they've got an early evening performance tonight and then they're moving on, so he'll be really busy until then. But he says when the others go, he'll wait behind and catch them up later. They've been camped just outside Bath – that's where he'll be.'

'After the show? OK. What shall I do? Come over to you?'

'No. I'd better come and pick you up. You'll never find this place in the dark. I'll see you in a couple of hours' time. About half-seven. And Helen; your father hasn't seen the magazine, has he?'

'No. He's out at the moment but he'll be back for the party.'

'Good. Look, it's important that he doesn't see it, OK? I'll see you later.'

It was twenty-five past seven when Ben drove into the parking space opposite Mikey's cottage, activating the security light over the gate to the stable yard. The usual cars were there but, as the pub was within walking distance and a fair amount of alcohol would no doubt be consumed, this wasn't surprising. The cottage itself was in darkness, save for a lamp over the door.

Thinking that it wouldn't have hurt Helen to walk down from the bungalow to wait for him, Ben got out of the four-wheel-drive and let himself into the fenced-off stable complex. It wasn't locked, so presumably Finch knew he was coming. He wondered what Helen had told her husband.

As he passed the lorry park a security light came on, almost blinding him, and when he moved out of its range, walking along the cinder path between the first two stable blocks, his night-sight was absolutely nil.

His hearing was unaffected though, and what he clearly heard as he approached the open centre of the yard itself was a rattling, indrawn breath and a long, low, throaty growl.

18

The Dobermans!

Ben froze.

Oh, yes, Finch had been expecting him all right. He'd been told that the dogs weren't normally let out until nine but an exception had clearly been made, especially for him.

The snarl had definitely come from somewhere in front of him and, from the sound of it, not very far in front. Ben judged he was about twenty feet from the central yard, and maybe eighty feet of cinder path lay behind him.

No point in running, then. He reckoned he'd make all of ten feet before the dog caught him. He looked sideways at the brick walls that flanked the path.

Smooth, seven or eight feet to the eaves, with windows every fifteen feet or so. Barred windows. No help there.

The Doberman drew in another ragged breath and growled again.

'All right, lad,' Ben said. 'Good lad.'

What had Finch said they were called? He pummelled his brain and came up with one name.

'All right, Kaiser. That'll do, boy.' For good measure, and assuming that the dog's night-sight was way better than his own, Ben tried the hand signal he'd seen Finch use.

The Dobe wasn't impressed. The growling continued unabated.

If only he could see. There was a torch in his glove compartment – why the hell hadn't he brought it with him? If nothing else, he could maybe have shoved it in the dog's jaws instead of his arm or whatever the dog had in mind. There would be a little more light in the open yard, and several doors that might or might not be locked. More possibilities than he had now. And if the alarms were set and he tripped one – well, that would do nicely. He decided to risk moving, very, very, slowly.

Almost sliding his feet along the cinders, Ben began to edge forward.

The pitch of the growl intensified.

He took another tiny step and, just when he was beginning to think that it was merely waiting for him to come within biting range, the dog gave way and shuffled back.

Ben rejoiced silently. Now the precedent had been set he was reasonably confident that the animal would back up again, and so it did.

Moving like partners in some deadly, slow-motion dance they covered the distance to the central yard, never once taking their eyes off each other. Ben's shirt was stuck to his back with sweat under his thick jumper and fleece-lined jacket, and beads of perspiration rolled down his face.

Now that the dog was in the open Ben could just make out the lithe, deep-chested shape of him, and what little light there was in the sky gleamed on a particularly fine set of bared teeth. The sight shook his resolve.

'Oh, shit!' he muttered, his step faltering. Perhaps being able to see was a mixed blessing.

What now?

Where now?

In spite of his earlier optimism the nearest doorway was a good fifteen feet away to one side. It led into one of the blocks of barn stabling; could he perhaps get himself inside and leave the Dobe on the outside? It was worth a try. Better not to consider the possibility that it might be locked.

One cautious step sideways, however, wasn't promising. The dog seemed to regard lateral movement as evidence of fear and it advanced, snarling with renewed vigour, until Ben could swear he felt its hot breath on his leg.

Unnerved, he stopped again.

He considered shouting for help, but discounted the thought. Everybody was at the party. Who was there that could help, except Finch? And *he* wasn't likely to, even if he heard; the bungalow was at least 120 feet away and double-glazed.

He considered shouting at the dog, but he didn't think it would scare easily. In fact, shouting might well make it even more aggressive, if that were possible.

It seemed they had reached an impasse. Maybe if he just stood still the animal would eventually lose interest. Ben wasn't hopeful, but with the brick wall behind him and the slavering dog in front, he didn't have much choice.

He wondered how long Finch was going to let him sweat. If he was correct in assuming that Helen's husband had let the dogs out on purpose, knowing that Ben was coming, surely he would come to find him sooner or later, even if only to crow and send him back to his car. After a moment or two, it occurred to him that Finch might well be waiting somewhere near, listening.

Raising his voice over the dog's continuous growl, Ben swallowed his pride and said, 'All right, Ray. You've had your bit of fun, mate. Come and get the bloody dog!'

No answer, but there was a movement in the shadows on the other side of the yard, and Ben took his eye off his tormentor just long enough to glance across. It wasn't Ray Finch; it was the second dog.

This was obviously the decisive one of the pair.

No sooner had it spotted its pal with quarry at bay than it accelerated across the open space, skirting the central fountain, and tore at Ben, barking.

Raw instinct took over. He took one look and fled.

Either he or the charging dog activated the sensor and suddenly the area was flooded with light from two halogen bulbs, one on each side of the yard. Expecting to feel teeth closing on some part of his anatomy at any moment, Ben ran for the nearest sliding door, yanked it open and practically fell inside.

Unfortunately the metal door was both heavy

and well-oiled and, having applied such force to get it moving, it was quite another matter to halt the door's progress and send it back the other way. Before he could do so, one Doberman had forced its shoulders through the gap and was immediately joined by its mate, both of them scrabbling and yelping in their eagerness to get at him.

Ben kept up the pressure, self-preservation winning out over animal welfare, but the second dog was evidently a fraction slimmer and it began to slither through, climbing over the trapped one.

The time had come to move again.

Hitting the light switch on the wall beside the door, Ben glanced down the length of the barn and saw that all the horses were staring over their half-doors, alerted by the pandemonium at the end. Just at that moment, the horses didn't interest him. What did were the various items of horse-clothing, headcollars and buckets that were piled neatly against the wall outside each stable. These, quite possibly, represented salvation.

Abandoning his position at the door, Ben raced down the central aisle to the first bundle of equipment. Even as he turned, the Dobes were close behind him, one slightly ahead of the other. He couldn't be sure which was which by now; the latecomer's enthusiasm was catching.

The first thing his fingers closed on was a cooler – the string vest of the horse world, used to prevent a sweaty horse getting a chill while it dried off. Ben pulled it from the pile, opened it out and threw it at the approaching pair like a fisherman of old casting his net. It fell neatly over the first dog, tangling in its running paws and bringing it down, but the second yelped in fright and dodged, slipping out from under the edge and coming on once more.

Ben scrabbled for something else, but even as his hand found the nylon straps of a headcollar, the dog was upon him.

Forty-odd kilos of Doberman hurtling at top speed is enough to knock most men flying, and Ben was certainly no exception. As the dog hit him he crashed sideways into the wall and went down with all the snapping, snarling fury on top of him.

Instinct told him to curl up, to hide his face and protect his belly and throat. This he did, the movement temporarily dislodging the animal, but it was soon back, fastening its teeth to Ben's upper arm and pulling. Ben tried rolling to loosen its hold.

It worked, but in the process he left his face unprotected. The Doberman lunged at his throat and only by thrusting his forearm between its jaws did Ben save himself.

Out of the corner of his eye he saw the other dog fight free of the enveloping cooler and he braced himself for a second impact, but for the time being it seemed well occupied in venting its wrath on the cotton netting.

The thickness of Ben's jumper and fleece afforded a certain amount of protection from the Dobe's formidable teeth and the dog, seemingly aware of this, pulled back, tearing a hole in the fibres. It spat fabric and lunged again, but this time Ben managed to get his knees up and, straightening his legs sharply, he threw the animal back several feet.

This only gained him a few precious moments' grace, and it did nothing whatever to improve the beast's temper. Ben got halfway to his feet, reaching for something – anything – with which to defend himself, but was promptly flattened by both dogs landing on him simultaneously.

There seemed to be teeth and paws everywhere. Sleek black and tan coats covered incredibly hard, muscled frames; they felt almost slippery, impossible to hold.

Although there was no time for conscious thought, it occurred to him that their frenzy seemed excessive, even for trained guard dogs. Kaiser and his partner weren't going to be content with pinning him down and standing over him. They wanted him dead.

Ben's ambition narrowed down to trying to keep his face and groin protected. Lashing out was difficult with a large dog hanging on your arm and, perforce, left tender underparts exposed to attack. These dogs were trained, but one thing he was sure they hadn't needed to be taught was which parts of prey were vulnerable. The knowledge was innate, handed down from their pack-hunting ancestors on the plains of Africa.

In that moment, Ben could sympathise with the zebra and wildebeest he'd watched on TV documentaries; pulled down by wild dogs who began their feast whilst the poor creatures were still breathing.

As the Dobermans continued their onslaught, it was all about damage limitation for Ben. He'd got into a position curled, foetus-like, against the wall, face down, resting on his knees and elbows

427

and concentrating his efforts on resisting the dogs' attempts to get their long snouts through his defences. He had no idea how long he could hold them off but he had to try. The alternative held no attraction at all.

His left side was protected by the wall but he suffered repeated buffetings as Kaiser and his partner pushed one another aside to get at him; every now and then one of them sank its teeth into his shoulder or lower rib area and pulled at his fleece jacket. The powerful jaws easily penetrated the layers of clothing but, strangely, he felt little actual pain.

Endorphins. The word materialised in his brain. Nature's morphine, produced in moments of extreme physical stress. Was that a good or a bad thing? If he couldn't feel the pain, was he in fact more seriously injured than he knew?

Suddenly it occurred to him that the dogs' activity was waning. Unless he was much mistaken, only one of them was actually worrying at him now. A sustained bout of pawing followed, the dog using both front paws in rapid succession to scratch away at his arms and shoulders where they were curled around his head and face, then even that stopped. Ben could feel the animal's hot, panting breath ruffling his hair. After a moment it whined in frustration and he heard its claws on the concrete floor as it padded away and back again.

The situation was a whole lot better but not satisfactory, not by any means. Ben wasn't fooled. He was fairly certain that any attempt to move would be rewarded by an enthusiastic return to hostilities. It was effectively checkmate but, if the worst came to the worst, he was prepared to stay where he was for as long as it took for rescue to arrive.

Now that the dogs were quiet, he could hear the horses. Spooked by the ferocity of the dogs, they were moving restlessly round their boxes, some banging their doors, one or two whinnying and snorting their alarm.

Not long ago, the proximity of so many horses would have brought him out in a cold sweat; now their presence was somehow comforting.

'Is anyone there?'

The voice cut through his reflections unexpectedly, coming from the open doorway at the top of the barn.

Mikey's voice!

Fear ballooned again.

'Mikey, be careful! The dogs are here!' As he spoke, one of the dogs issued a low rumble.

'Ben?'

'Mikey, stay back! Go and get help.'

He was too late.

As he cautiously raised his head, one of the dogs was already moving away from him and towards Mikey. Ben opened his mouth to yell at the boy to get out and shut the door. Then, incredibly, he noticed that the Doberman's six inches or so of docked tail was wagging furiously.

The other dog hesitated, took one more long look at Ben, and then followed its mate.

'Hello Kaiser, hello Rommel,' Mikey said, putting his hand down to them. Now, both tails were wagging as they fawned over him.

Ben sat up, breathing hard.

'Mikey, can you catch them? Put a couple of lead ropes on them or something. For some reason, they *really* don't like me.'

'They shouldn't be out, yet,' Mikey commented as he carried out Ben's instructions. 'I heard them barking, and then I heard the door open and the horses started making a racket, so I came to find out what was going on.'

'Well, it probably wasn't the most sensible thing to do but I'm bloody glad you did. Why aren't you at the party?'

Mikey made a face.

'I went down to start with but I don't really like parties, so I thought I'd come back and watch the badgers. There, I've got them.'

'You make me very happy, little brother,' Ben told him, thinking that it was probably time he stood up, but his body was reacting to its sudden deliverance from danger with a violent bout of shaking, and his legs didn't feel as though they belonged to him.

When Ben finally made it to his feet with the help of the wall the dogs growled a warning, their heads and hackles up.

'Hey! Quiet boys,' Mikey said.

'How about you take them outside and I'll follow?' Ben suggested, moving stiffly forward. Another downside to the ebbing adrenalin was that he was beginning to feel the damage the Dobes had done.

'Are you all right, Ben?' Mikey was regarding him doubtfully as he came out into the light.

A sarcastic retort was on the tip of his tongue but it wouldn't have been fair on Mikey.

430

'I will be, don't worry,' he said. 'Look, I need you to do something.'

'Yeah?'

'I want you to go and put the dogs away, then go back to the cottage and throw some pyjamas and stuff in an overnight bag as quick as you can and then wait for me in the car.'

'Yes, but –'

'No questions, Mikey, please,' Ben cut in. 'I'll explain later.'

'OK.' He moved away, the dogs trotting happily beside him on their makeshift leads, their stumpy tails still wagging.

Ben shook his head briefly in wonder, then turned his steps towards the bungalow. A look at his watch showed him with a shock that barely ten minutes had passed since he'd arrived at Castle Ridge. Lights were on in practically all the rooms of the bungalow as Ben approached, but there was still no sign of Helen. Was it possible she'd known what her husband intended and was keeping a low profile?

He leaned on the doorbell beside the red front door, feeling decidedly rough, and after a moment or two he heard the Yale lock operate and the door opened to reveal Helen, looking harassed.

'Ben. I'm sorry, I was going to come down but I can't find my keys.' Her eyes widened. 'God! What happened to you?'

'The dogs happened,' he stated dryly.

'The dogs?' Her blank astonishment seemed genuine. 'But they shouldn't be out until later – much later.'

'I quite agree, but they were. Can I come in? I think some Elastoplast might be needed . . .'

She stared at him for a moment then stepped back.

'Of course. But we'll still go?'

'Yes, we'll still go. Tell me, where's Ray?'

'I don't know. We had a blazing row and he went out.' She led the way into the sitting room, which was shades of dusky pink, even down to the squashy leather suite. As she turned he could see she'd been crying. 'Ben, Dad's seen the magazine.'

'Oh, for God's sake! What did I tell you?' The stress of the last few minutes had taken its toll on Ben's temper.

'It wasn't my fault! Ray overheard me talking to you, and he told him,' she said. 'I didn't know till Dad came storming in.'

'You didn't tell him where we're going?'

'Ray must have told him.'

'And when was this?'

'About half an hour ago. I tried to ring you but your girlfriend said you'd already left. God, Ben! Your jacket's a mess.' She began to take it off him, and exclaimed, 'It's ripped to shreds!'

Ben shrugged the jacket off, impatiently.

'Tell me exactly what happened. What does your father know?'

'Ben, you need a doctor.'

'Not now, woman! Tell me what your father said.'

'Don't shout at me! You need seeing to. Come into the kitchen.' She turned and walked away, forcing him to follow so he could hear as she went on talking.

'When I got off the phone to you, Ray asked me who I'd been talking to. I just said it was a friend. So he said "It was Ben, wasn't it? Why's he picking you up? Where are you going?" And I told him to mind his own business. Anyway – sit down – I think he must've seen the magazine; I had it on my knee when I was talking to you.' She paused. 'I've got some cotton wool somewhere.'

'So he told your father?' Ben sat obediently on a stool at the breakfast bar, glancing around him at the white-painted kitchen units, chrome appliances and black and white floor tiles.

'Yes. I think he must have rung him, because as soon as Dad got back he came straight over here.' She found cotton wool, antiseptic lotion and plasters in a cupboard, then half-filled a bowl with water and poured a generous capful of the lotion in, which turned the water cloudy. Ben eyed it with disfavour. In his experience, such liquids were liable to sting.

'And what did he say?'

'First of all he asked me what was going on. I wasn't going to tell him but then Ray showed him the magazine and, of course, I could see by his face he recognised the picture straight away, the same as I did. So then he tried to tell me it wasn't Stefan, and said I should leave well enough alone. Oh sorry! Did I hurt you?'

Ben shook his head. 'No, that's all right, go on.'

'Well, I told him it *was* Stefan, and that you'd spoken to him, and he was furious! He wanted to know what you'd got to do with it. He pointed to the magazine and said, "Is this where you think

433

you're going tonight?" and I said yes, we were, and that you knew Stefan – Nico – because you'd written the article. And then, it was weird . . .'

'Yes?' Ben flinched again. 'What was?'

'Well, he went really quiet, and he just said, "*Did* he now?" It was worse really than when he was shouting.'

Ben groaned inwardly.

'And then what?'

'God, Ben. This looks awful! I never thought the dogs would go this far.'

Ben glanced at what he could see of his right shoulder and arm. It wasn't pretty, that was for sure; bruised, lacerated and oozing.

'I'll get it looked at tomorrow,' he promised. 'Just slap a bit of lint on it and stick it down. I don't want to keep Nico waiting too long. Where's your father now?'

'Well, I don't know, exactly. He said to Ray, "I suppose I can rely on you to take care of things here," and when Ray asked him what he was going to do, he just said, "I've got to see a man about a horse." It was odd, really. Didn't seem to make much sense after everything else.'

'Oh, I'm afraid it does,' Ben said grimly. 'Look, we have to go. This'll have to wait.'

'Just let me stick this on, then,' Helen said, placing a wad of lint over his shoulder and sticking the edges down with tape.

Ben thanked her through gritted teeth and stood up, swaying slightly. The combination of white kitchen, bright fluorescent lighting and Helen's ministrations was making him feel unpleasantly muzzy.

'Well, you can't put this on again,' she observed, holding up the fleece jacket, which now sported vast ragged holes in the shoulder, back and sleeve.

'What the hell's going on here?'

They hadn't heard Finch come in, but now he stood in the kitchen doorway, his brow thunderous.

'I think you know exactly what's been going on,' Ben stated, turning a little unsteadily to face him. 'Because it was you who let the dogs out, wasn't it?'

'Nonsense. You can't prove that. I've just been out to check on them and they're exactly where they should be.'

'Yeah, thanks to Mikey.'

'I'm just getting Ben something to wear, and then we're going,' Helen told her husband, her face pink with defiance. She pushed past him and disappeared.

'He's not having any of my fucking clothes!' Ray shouted after her then turned back to Ben. 'Not much point in you going – you'll be too late. Eddie's gonna fuckin' cream your Hungarian buddy.'

'Oh, I don't think so. He's not been gone long and he won't know where he's going. We'll probably get there first.'

'He's got the magazine, hasn't he? Gives all the venues. And I can tell you, he won't go alone.'

Ben thought of Spence and his mate, and of Nico waiting, unknowing and alone, on the deserted camping ground.

His mobile was in the car. He swore and Finch chuckled.

435

Helen returned, pulling on a coat and holding out a jumper and leather jacket to Ben.

'Here. I think the jacket might be yours, actually. You left it at Dad's. I don't know what it's doing up here.'

Ben took it and turned it over in his hands, frowning. The hemline and lower part of the sleeves were scratched and dirty and, in several places, bore small puncture marks. The light dawned.

Glancing up quickly he was just in time to catch Finch smirking, and something snapped inside.

'You vicious bastard!' he exclaimed and, taking a short step forward, aimed his fist slap-bang in the middle of the smirk.

Finch staggered back, crashing into the kitchen door, which swung freely, depositing him with a crash amongst a pile of crockery on the drainer.

'Ben! What're you doing?' Helen stood with a hand to her mouth, shocked.

'Ask your bastard of a husband! Ask him why the dogs were half-mad to get at me, and then look at my jacket.'

'Ray?' Helen's tone pleaded for some reasonable explanation.

Finch ignored her. He straightened up, heedless of the plates that slid into the sink and on to the floor as he did so. His nose was bleeding freely, and he wiped it with the back of his hand. He looked at the resulting smear and sniffed.

'I hoped they'd fucking kill you!' he spat. 'Comin' in here; suckin' up to the Guvnor; telling everybody what to do – who d'you think you bloody are? Well, he's wise to you now, I can tell you!' He wiped his face and sniffed again. 'If you've broken my nose, I'll sue you!'

Ben gave him a withering look and pulled the jumper on over his head, making sure his vision wasn't impeded for more than a second. He didn't rate Finch's courage very highly but just at the moment he wouldn't want to turn his back on him. The jacket sat a little tightly over the wadding on his shoulder but he was feeling better all the time, and the satisfaction of delivering Finch's comeuppance had given him a real high.

'Come on, Missus. We need to hurry,' he told Helen, who was still looking at her husband as if he'd grown two horns and a tail. 'I want to try and get Nico on the phone to warn him.'

'You can use ours.'

'Except that I don't know his number. It's in my mobile's memory, and that's in the car.' He started for the door. 'Oh, and if you still want your keys, I should ask your husband. I think you'll find he's got them. A little delaying tactic to stop you coming down to meet me, unless I'm much mistaken.'

They reached the car to find Mikey waiting in the back with a holdall on the seat beside him. He was bubbling over with questions but Ben cut through them.

'Not now, Mikey. I've got a call to make.'

Retrieving his phone from the glove compartment, he keyed in Nico's number. It didn't even ring. A message from the network provider informed Ben that the person he'd called was not available and invited him to leave a message.

'Damn! We'll have to try again in a minute.'

Ben handed the phone to Helen and gunned the engine.

'Do you know exactly where we're going?' she asked as he backed up and then accelerated down the drive.

'Yeah, I was there the day before last.'

'But . . . haven't you finished the article, now?'

'Yes, I have, but we've become friends.'

There was silence for a moment as Ben negotiated the junction with the road. He pulled away, pushing each gear to its limit and wishing it were a sports saloon instead of a four-wheel-drive.

'Have you told him about Stephen?'

'Not yet. I wanted to ask the boy first. But it's up to you, of course.' He threw a glance at Helen, who looked pensive.

'Yes, I suppose so,' she said. 'I'm not sure what I'll do.'

'Well, for now,' Ben said, overtaking a slow-moving truck, 'I suggest you try and get Nico again. If your father gets to him first you may have to visit him in hospital.'

'No, Daddy's not like that!' she protested. 'He loses his temper and shouts sometimes, but he wouldn't actually hurt anyone.'

'He doesn't need to. He's got men to do that for him.'

Concentrating on the road, Ben nevertheless sensed her staring at him. There had never been much affection between them but he had an idea he was rapidly exhausting any there might have been.

'Look, just ring, will you?'

She pushed buttons and waited.

'Answerphone again,' she reported after a moment, with a touch of childish triumph.

'OK; press the phonebook button, scroll through and find Mark Logan. See if you have any better luck with that. If you do, I'll speak to him.'

'Who's he?'

'A friend of mine – he's a policeman.'

'But what about Dad?'

'If he's as blameless as you say he's got nothing to worry about, has he?' Ben observed reasonably.

As it turned out, Logan was unreachable too and, although they kept trying both numbers at regular intervals, Ben had a horrible feeling that he was all the cavalry Nico was going to get. That wasn't good. Driving the Mitsubishi close to its limits, his attention divided between checking his rear-view mirror for police patrol cars and scanning the road ahead for speed cameras, he was really beginning to feel the effects of Kaiser and Rommel's attentions.

He made the journey, without undue incident, in well under an hour; nearly twenty minutes less than it usually took. Though he wasn't one hundred per cent sure he wouldn't be getting a speeding ticket through the door at Dairy Cottage in the next week or two.

Helen had finally managed to get Logan about a quarter of an hour earlier and passed the phone to Ben.

'Mark? I've got a problem. Truman's found out about Nico and I'm pretty sure he's on his way to confront him.'

'Look, Ben, I'm not sure I can help you. I'm on duty this evening and I've been seconded to Swindon.'

'Swindon?'

'Yeah, but I'm out near Chippenham at the moment.'

Ben's spirits soared.

'Excellent! Nico's been camped near Bath. You're only ten minutes away.'

'I've got company,' Logan warned.

'In this case, the more the merrier,' Ben assured him. 'So has Truman.'

'OK, give me details. We'll be finished here in five and get there a.s.a.p.'

Now, as Ben drove through the gateway on to what had been the Csikós camping ground and caught a distant glimpse of at least three vehicles in the headlights, he felt Logan couldn't come any too soon.

Finally meeting the kind of ground it was designed for, the Mitsubishi tore across the sloping field effortlessly, though the ride was by no means smooth. With the seat bumping against one side of Ben's shoulder and the seat belt pressing on the other, it was an experience he could have done without but, judging by the low-voiced 'Wow!' from the rear seat, Mikey, at least, was enjoying it.

There was obviously no possible element of surprise, so Ben opted for the bull-in-a-china-shop approach. As they drew closer, his head-lights showed Gyorgy's catering wagon pulled up against the hedge, effectively boxed in, with Truman's Range Rover parked across its nose and a big saloon car at the back. The scene was partially lit by the lights on the side of the wagon, and there were at least five people present, in two groups – one person sitting or lying on the ground – but Ben couldn't make out who was who until he was almost upon them.

Gritting his teeth, he drove between the two sets of people, maintaining his speed until the last moment and then jamming the brakes on hard. The vehicle skidded a little on the frosty grass, coming to a halt only inches from the nearest figure which, fittingly enough, turned out to be Truman himself. Yelling to Helen and Mikey to stay put, Ben leaped out and ran towards the trainer.

A few yards away a heavily built man was using a mattock to batter Gyorgy's wagon. The tyres, windscreen, and serving window had already fallen victim, and he'd started on the bodywork with devastating effect. Inside the van, Ben caught sight of another man at work.

Recovering from the fright of his near miss, Truman sneered.

'Come to watch?' he enquired, raising his voice to be heard above the noise of the demolition.

Furious, Ben grabbed the front of Truman's jacket with one hand and pointed with the other.

'What are they doing?' he yelled in his face. 'That's not Nico's van!'

'And you think I care?' Truman said.

Ben looked past the trainer and away to one side where yet another man, armed with a base-ball bat, stood guard over two men, one of whom was sitting on the grass, cradling his left arm. Letting go of Truman, he hurried across.

'Nico! What happened?'

Nico straightened up from attending to the injured man, who Ben now saw was Gyorgy, but before he could reply the man with the bat cut in.

'Oi! Stay back!'

Bald, with a pierced ear and eyebrow, he must have been at least six-foot three, and Ben did as he was told.

'I wait for you and then these come.' Nico was clearly smouldering with suppressed anger. 'They start hitting at Gyorgy's wagon and, when we try to stop them, they hit Gyorgy. His arm is broken. There is nothing I can do to stop them, then I see Truman and I understand. But he says you told him where to find me . . .'

'No. That's not true. He saw your picture in the magazine.'

Ben took a step closer, desperate that Nico should believe him, and the big man waved the baseball bat in his direction.

'Oi, you! Get over here with your friends, where I can see you.'

Ben could see his problem. With Nico on one side and him on the other the guy was outflanked, and the bat obviously wasn't any use as a long-range weapon. To commit to using it against one of them would lay him open to attack from the other.

'Or what?' he asked, stepping sideways to compromise the man's position further.

Baldy took a step back and appealed to Truman.

'Boss?'

The trainer had other things on his mind.

Contrary to Ben's order, Helen had got out of the car and was approaching her father, her expression one of complete bewilderment.

'Dad? Stop them! You can't do this! It's wrong!' she cried, grabbing his sleeve.

Welcome to the real world, Ben thought sourly. A glance reassured him that Mikey, at least, was doing as he was told.

The two wreckers seemed absorbed in their task.

'Come any closer and I'll bash your fuckin' head in!' Baldy had now apparently realised he was, at least temporarily, on his own.

'You can only take one of us at a time.' Nico had seen what Ben was doing.

Baldy swung towards him, looking back nervously over his shoulder at Ben.

'That's right, I'd keep an eye on me if I were you,' Ben said approvingly. 'I've got a score to settle, for the other night.'

It was a guess, but it appeared to have been a good one; Baldy swung round to face him, slapping the bat into the palm of his free hand.

From behind him, Nico stepped swiftly forward, looking worryingly like David to his Goliath but, like David, he had a hidden arsenal.

As Baldy glanced round, he may have been just in time to see the foot that floored him, but personally, Ben doubted it. After launching the Ninja-style attack, Nico slipped on the frosty ground and almost fell, but within moments he was poised and ready for action once more.

However, as far as Baldy was concerned, action was no longer necessary. He'd relinquished his hold on the baseball bat and was lying on the ground at Ben's feet, looking decidedly groggy. Ben kicked the bat further away and looked across admiringly at Nico.

'Any more where that came from?'

'Plenty,' Nico assured him. He gestured towards the discarded bat. 'You don't use that?'

'No, I don't think so. The police are on their way.'

'Then let's hope they come soon,' Nico said, nodding significantly to something behind Ben. He turned to see that the thug with the mattock, under direction from Truman, had paused in his assault on Gyorgy's wagon and was heading purposefully in their direction.

'Oh, shit!' Ben said. He had no doubt that the man inside the van would soon be recalled to join the fray.

Shocked and tearful, Helen was pulling at her father's arm, pleading with him to call the men off.

In spite of their past differences, Ben felt a moment's sympathy for her. Everything she thought she knew and could rely on was being turned upside down in the course of a few short hours.

A moment was all he could spare, however. He and Nico had much more pressing matters to attend to. A quick, desperate look towards the gate revealed no comforting, blue flashing lights, and he wondered whether the baseball bat might perhaps have been a good idea after all.

'Go on, lad. Teach them a lesson,' Truman urged as the man with the mattock passed him. Helen's pleas were interspersed with sobs now, and her father was holding her firmly by the wrist, away and to one side of him. For the time being, she was clearly no more to him than an inconvenience.

The mattock man was almost as big as his mate had been, and any lack of inches was more than made up for by the ugliness of the weapon he held. Behind him the third man was descending the steps of the wagon, and Ben's heart sank as he saw the wood axe in his hands. Nico's martial arts skills were undoubtedly impressive, but against such as these . . .

He shot a swift look at Nico, finding him tense but not noticeably dismayed.

'The axe will make him slow,' the Hungarian said, not taking his eyes off the oncoming men.

'Oh, good!' Ben doubted it would make him nearly slow enough.

'Which one do you want?' Nico asked.

'Neither!' Ben said with feeling. Was he kidding? If only Gyorgy were fit and able. Jakob's brother was at least half as heavy again as either of them.

Nico moved up to stand a foot or two to Ben's left, and the man with the mattock waited, about six feet away, for his mate to catch him up.

'Do you have a plan?' Ben asked, under his breath.

'I think we should get closer to Truman,' came the response. 'Go, now!'

On the words Nico pushed Ben away from him and started running so that, within seconds, they had flanked the two advancing men, causing them to turn on their heel to keep their quarry within view.

As Ben turned in, level with Truman, he saw

that the move had thrown the axe-man off balance. Carrying the cumbersome weapon in his right hand and turning to his right, he was in no position to use it.

Nico was quick to take advantage. A trained and super-fit stuntman, he was almost never off-balance and now he stopped, bouncing on his toes to absorb the change of direction and, quick as lightning, attacked the bigger man with a spinning kick that impacted somewhere in the region of his right ear.

It was a testament to the axe-man's strength that he didn't drop in his tracks, but he staggered back, the axe dragging in the grass as he struggled to keep upright, and finally stumbled heavily into the man with the mattock.

Taking the only chance that was likely to be offered, Ben darted forward and jumped at his man, using his forearm and elbow to hit him as hard as he could across the side of his neck and jaw.

It wasn't hard enough.

The mattock man obviously had the strength of an ox, for although Ben's forearm punch drew a grunt from his target, it didn't floor him. With a twisting movement he managed to shake Ben off and send him sprawling on to the frosty turf, where he immediately began rolling to avoid the very real prospect of being disembowelled.

Was Truman mad? Did he really think he could get away with murder?

Something landed heavily on the ground, not six inches from Ben's head, as he stopped rolling. He blinked and brought it into focus.

The axe!

Bloody hell!

He scrambled away and came to his feet in one panic-stricken movement; only then did it register that the weapon had fallen with the blade flat to the turf. It had been dropped, not wielded, and its owner was lying prone on the grass, his eyes peacefully closed, presumably a victim of another of Nico's deadly kicks.

The man Ben had attacked was looking a deal less confident than he had just a few seconds before, but even as he was beginning to believe that – against all the odds – he and Nico might actually come off best from the encounter, the balance of advantage changed once again as Baldy returned to the fray. He loomed out of the darkness, minus the baseball bat and not, it had to be said, looking his best, but six-foot three of muscle is pretty menacing, whatever state it's in, and he had one big ace in the hole: his beefy forearm was locked tightly around Gyorgy's throat. The Hungarian appeared dazed and helpless.

'Ben!'

Nico shouted and pointed, drawing his attention to the fact that Truman was also on the move. Almost flinging Helen away from him he strode forward, pulling something from his pocket which, a fraction of a second later, extended with a snap into a two-foot long baton.

'All very heroic!' Truman raised his voice so everyone could hear. 'But I'm in control now. You . . .' He pointed the baton at Nico. 'I let you off last time with a flogging but you foreigners just don't learn, do you?'

'You'll never beat me again!'

In the light from Gyorgy's wagon, Nico's eyes burned with hatred and he took a couple of rapid steps forward.

Truman took an equally quick step back.

'Decker!' he barked. 'Break the old man's neck.'

'No!' Sick with fear for Gyorgy, it was Ben who moved forward this time, but he didn't duck quite fast enough as Truman's baton cracked across his neck and shoulder in a stinging blow.

Helen screamed something but her voice was lost as the Mitsubishi's engine roared into life and it swung round with its headlights on full beam, simultaneously blinding nearly all the players in the drama.

Mikey? It had to be.

The vehicle accelerated and Ben threw up an arm to shield his eyes. He saw Truman glance fearfully behind him and leap aside to avoid being run down, but Mattock Man wasn't quite quick enough and took a glancing blow which bowled him over and sent him rolling away into the gloom.

Mikey braked hard to avoid hitting anyone else and the car's engine stalled, but in the silence that followed Ben heard the eminently welcome sound of police sirens approaching.

Unsurprisingly, the sound provoked an entirely different set of emotions in Truman and his hired muscle, and by the time the blue lights were in view Baldy and Mattock Man had collected their semi-conscious companion and were making good speed towards the saloon car.

Truman stood, irresolutely, looking from the oncoming police car to his Range Rover, and then across to where his daughter stood, still sobbing into her hand.

'Don't bother, Eddie,' Ben called out. 'There's nowhere to go.'

Perhaps realising the truth of this, Truman let the baton fall to the ground and walked slowly across to put his arm round his daughter.

Gyorgy, abandoned unceremoniously, was rocking on his feet and Ben saw Nico hurry to his side. In the other direction the saloon car reversed at top speed, spun in a ragged hand-brake turn and started off across the field, bottoming out as it hit uneven ground.

Rubbing his sore neck, Ben watched as the first police car turned to pursue it, then saw with relief that another had followed it in, and a third was even now pulling up across the gateway. Logan had come up trumps.

'Ben? Are you all right?'

Mikey had got out of the car.

'I'm fine, thanks to you. You were brilliant! I didn't even know you could drive.'

Mikey grinned apologetically.

'I've been taking lessons. It was going to be a surprise.'

'Oh, it was,' Ben assured him. 'One of the best I've ever had!'

Moments later, the first of the police cars pulled up beside them, blue lights flashing but siren off. The doors opened to reveal a petite female officer who efficiently took charge of Truman, and Logan, who came straight over to Ben.

'All right, mate?'

'I'll live. Nico's uncle isn't so good.'

'There's an ambulance on the way; should be here any minute.' He patted Ben cheerfully on his bad shoulder and went to see how Gyorgy was doing.

'Pity they smashed up the wagon. I could just do with a cuppa,' Ben remarked whimsically; but when Mikey set off to investigate: 'No, Mikey! There could be gas.'

Feeling less than chipper, Ben leaned against the Mitsubishi and awaited developments, the first of which was the advent of the ambulance and the paramedics.

Much happier now that Gyorgy was being attended to, Ben turned his attention to the area by the gate where Truman's hired help had been apprehended and safely gathered in.

'What will happen to the Guvnor, now?' Mikey asked, frowning. Ben remembered that, to his brother, the events of the evening must have seemed totally incomprehensible, making it all the more amazing that he'd done what he had.

'I very much hope he'll go to prison for a very long time,' he replied. 'I'll explain it all to you later, if I've got the energy. Meantime, remind me to buy you the biggest ice cream sundae that money can buy!'

Mikey shook his head.

'Not this week. I'm riding at Fontwell on Saturday.'

'Yeah, well I hope so.'

Just feet away, the WPC was loading Truman into the back of the police car, a guiding hand on his head. Helen hovered, her face haggard with shock.

For the trainer, that would be the final indignity, Ben reflected. Being arrested by a woman. It was a satisfying thought.

Logan came back.

'Looks like you've had fun and games,' he commented.

'Yeah, it was some reunion.'

'Well, I'm afraid this is going to take a while to sort out. Are you all right?' He shone his torch over Ben from head to toes and back again.

'Yeah. I should go and see Gyorgy. Poor bloke; this is nothing to do with him.'

'You should go and see the paramedics,' Logan suggested.

Ben raised his eyebrows.

'You would appear to be leaking.'

The policeman shone his torch at Ben's right arm, and he lifted it to find blood running down the back of his hand.

'Oh, bugger. That was the dogs, earlier.'

It was Logan's turn to raise his eyebrows.

'Not that hairy mongrel of yours, surely!'

'No. Truman's guard dogs.'

Logan shook his head and sighed.

'I think, when you've got yourself patched up, that you and I are going to have to have a very long talk,' he said.

Epilogue

The Csikós' last performance of their first short tour of England was a sell-out long before they arrived at Brinkley Castle in Hertfordshire. They had, in fact, sold out three performances on three consecutive nights.

Work to prepare the grounds of the stately home for both the show and the influx of people it was expected to generate, took nearly a week. Ben knew, from past conversations with Jakob, that the full road crew that normally accompanied the troupe in Europe had been shipped over beforehand to set up the complicated technical equipment needed to stage the French-style *son et lumière* show.

As the Mitsubishi joined the back of the slow-moving queue for Brinkley Castle, Ben smiled at Lisa, then looked in his rear-view mirror, where he could see Stephen and Mikey engaged in a good-natured debate which apparently revolved around something or someone they had seen in a passing car. The two boys, only a year apart in age, had, over the last few days, formed what looked like becoming a lasting friendship. Stephen already had a maturity that Ben's brother would probably never achieve, but Mikey's growing reputation as an amateur jockey had seen his confidence blossom and, somehow, with their shared love of horses, they functioned as equals. Normally quiet and introspective, Stephen seemed relaxed in Mikey's company.

After the disaster of Truman's interference, the idea of a reunion between Helen and Nico seemed to die a death, with no real inclination on either side. For each, it seemed, the present reality of the other was so far removed from their gilt-edged memories that they might as well have been strangers. So even now, seventeen years on, Truman had managed to come between them. They had exchanged a few words on that wretched night near Bath, but it seemed that Helen had taken Ben's advice on board, and nothing had been said about Stephen.

Nico knew now, of course, and had received the news from Ben with a mixture of wonder and incredulity.

'Does he know? Will he see me?' he'd asked after a moment. Then, more sombrely, 'Do you think he should, my friend?'

Ben had repeated his conviction that the boy should decide.

While her father was absent, awaiting trial, Fliss had taken over the reins at Castle Ridge, and so far there had been few complaints from any quarter. The horses had continued to show good form and Mikey, who was aware of Belinda

Kepple's offer, had nevertheless elected to stay with the bigger stable for the time being, especially since Finch had been shown the door by Helen.

Stephen had come back from his holiday with knowledge of the events surrounding his birth, but still in ignorance of his father's true identity, and Ben had braced himself to bring the subject up.

In the end it had been unnecessary. Mikey had provided the information when Ben went with him to Wincanton one day.

'Stephen says he's going to Hungary in the summer,' Mikey told Ben as they walked through the crowds to the weighing-room. 'He wants to look for his father.'

'You didn't tell him about Nico?'

'No. You said not to.'

'Good. Thanks for that.'

The Csikós' show, entitled 'Kings of the Wind', was a masterly blend of special effects and quite staggering horsemanship. The action took place on a natural, grassy stage in front of Brinkley Castle and just across the river from the audience; it was also relayed via a big screen to one side.

Even Ben, who had grown accustomed to the beauty and skill of their performances, was captivated. The *son et lumière* element turned the whole experience into a thing of wonder and, when he could drag his eyes from the spectacle, he was rewarded by the utter fascination of Lisa and the boys.

When the final bows had been taken and the

floodlights came on to assist with the dispersal of the crowd, Ben instructed his party to stick close to him. He fought his way to the river's edge, from where he led them to a narrow bridge, and from there to the field where the Csikós' transporters were drawn up in the familiar pattern.

The first person they encountered in the backstage bustle was Jakob, leading four of the Magyar horses, two lead reins in each hand.

'Ben! How did you like the show? It was good, yes?'

'Very good,' Ben said warmly. 'Absolutely brilliant!'

He introduced Lisa and the two youngsters, and Jakob greeted them all with his usual charm, his eyes lingering thoughtfully on Stephen.

'And how is Gyorgy?'

'Yes, he is well,' Jakob said. 'His arm is on the mending.'

'On the mend,' Ben corrected, with a smile. 'I'll find him in a minute and thank him again. And I want to thank you, too. Nico says it was you who persuaded him not to wait for us alone.'

Jakob frowned. 'I had a bad feeling. In here,' he said, tapping his chest.

'Well, I'm sorry for what happened to your brother, but I think it might just have saved Nico from much worse.'

'My father was Hungarian,' Stephen put in suddenly. 'He was a jockey.'

Jakob nodded, his eyes suspiciously bright. 'I thought as much,' he said, adding to Ben, 'He's seeing to Bajnok, I think.'

Following Jakob's directions, they caught up with Nico as he led the black horse back to his stable. Still wearing his black and gold braided jacket, his dark face flushed with the high of performing, he presented a picture such as any fatherless boy might conjure up in his fantasies.

The Hungarian greeted them with a flash of his brilliant smile and then faltered, as the significance of the dark-haired, dark-eyed youngster at Ben's side clearly hit home.

Stephen looked faintly puzzled by Nico's reaction and glanced up at Ben enquiringly.

'Mikey told me you wanted to know,' Ben said gently. 'But we don't have to do this. We can turn back right now and never mention it again. It's up to you.'

Stephen's eyes narrowed and he looked back at Nico.

'You . . . ?' he asked.

Nico nodded, slowly.

It was Mikey who broke the tension, with a characteristic, low-voiced, 'Wow! I wish he was my dad!'

Nico smiled, but his eyes quickly returned to Stephen.

'I have to see to my horse,' he announced, patting Bajnok's sleek black neck. 'You can come, if you like.'

He turned and walked away, and for a moment it looked as though Stephen would let him go, but then, with a fleeting glance at the others, he followed.